SONG
OF
DARK
TIDES

Also by Beka Westrup

Beneath the Bloody Aurora

Blood in the Tea Leaves

The Seldom Wings

Song of Dark Tides

BEKA WESTRUP

Lake Country Press
Publishing & Reviews

Copyright © 2023 by Beka Westrup

All rights reserved.

No part of this book may be reproduced in any form or by any electronic or mechanical means, including information storage and retrieval systems, without written permission from the author, except for the use of brief quotations in a book review.

This is a work of fiction. Any resemblance to actual persons, living or dead or actual events is purely coincidental. Although real-life locations or public figures may appear throughout the story, these situations, incidents, and dialogue concerning them are fictional and are not intended to depict actual events nor change the fictional nature of this world.

First published in the United States of America November 2023 by Lake Country Press & Reviews

Cataloging-in-Publication Data is on file with the Library of Congress.

ISBN: 979-8-9877391-9-8 (paperback), 979-8-9889859-0-7 (e-book)

Editor: Borbala Branch

Cover: Fay Lane (Book Cover Witch)

Internal Art: Bryan Camargo (@falloutbryan)

Author website:

https://www.bekawestrup.com

Publisher website:

https://www.lakecountrypress.com

AUTHOR'S NOTE

Hello lovelies. Song of Dark Tides is a dark fantasy romance, and while it is a work of fiction, it does address some heavier themes that may be sensitive to some readers. Below is a list of potentially triggering content and I encourage you to look over them before proceeding.

Please take care.

Attempted Assault
Threat of Rape
Themes of Sexism and Patriarchy
Anti-Religious Rhetoric
Graphic Violence
Death
Cannibalism
Torture
Graphic Sexual Content
Dubious Consent
Knife Play
Bondage
Blood/Gore
Alcohol Use
Suicidal Thoughts
Mention of Childhood Abuse
Mention of Childhood Sexual Abuse (not graphic - chapters 4 & 30)

PLAYLIST

1. Siren - Kailee Morgue
2. Villains Aren't Born (They're Made) - PEGGY
3. Dark Horse (feat. Juicy J) - Katy Perry
4. I'm Gonna Show You Crazy - Bebe Rexha
5. Nightmares - Ellise
6. Would've, Could've, Should've - Taylor Swift
7. Chains - Nick Jonas
8. Drop Dead - Holly Humberstone
9. I Did Something Bad - Taylor Swift
10. Hate Me - Ellie Goulding & Juice WRLD
11. like that - Bea Miller
12. You'd Never Know - BLÜ EYES
13. mad woman - Taylor Swift
14. Take - Echos
15. Atlantis - Seafret
16. In the Water - GAWVI
17. Blue Blood - LAUREL
18. Sacrifice (feat. Jessie Reyez) - Black Atlass
19. Atlas Hands - Benjamin Francis Leftwich
20. Ultraviolet - Freya Ridings
21. Wave - Meghan Trainor
22. Sirens - Fleurie
23. Cosmic Love - Florence + the Machine
24. Belong - Cary Brothers
25. Remind Me to Forget - Kygo & Miguel
26. New Soul - Yael Naim

for everyone out there who grew up a little too soon

PROLOGUE

The blood shows all. Future and past; life and death and every whisper lost to the ocean. They are made known to him—the *King*. There are no secrets capable of being hidden when he communes with the spirits tied to this crucible under the surface.

He sacrificed hundreds of witches to harness this power, *this sight*, and it was well worth it, because of all the dangers in the deep he could watch through this swirling pool of blood, he chose *her*. From the first moment he saw her, he claimed her. He won't take his eyes off her now, even if she does pretend to be his enemy.

What a wonderful liar she's become.

His hands grip the edge of the basin as he leans in closer. He absorbs every soft curve of her face. Her wide eyes and thick white lashes. That delectable pout she makes when she thinks no one is watching. If he leans in close enough, he can pretend he's really there, watching her lean up against a brick wall Above. How foolish she is to spend her time up there, where she does not belong.

His thumb hastens its movements, worrying a thin braid wrapped around his right hand. The hair is frayed and darker than it once was, aged into a deep mulberry wine—it doesn't matter, it's still hers.

It's the last piece of her he took before sending her away.

Quite a long-suffering lesson this has turned out to be, much to his surprise and discontent. She should have crawled back to him by now, low to the glowing floor of his palace, laments rolling off her tongue straight onto his cock... but she's damn determined to have her way. So stubborn.

He has no choice but to wait here, holding onto this lock of her hair. Admiring her face at a distance. Pretending her centuries' worth of dismissal hasn't been slowly driving him mad. It only makes him want her more.

That stubborn witchling loves to torture him.

A chill surrounds him, prickling the back of his neck, warning him that he's no longer alone in the divination room. He spins quickly enough to catch a glimpse of the shadow in one corner, as it shifts and thins, shying from his attention.

It's been happening more and more—wandering spirits stumbling upon him and this sacred room, drawn to the crucible and its power. Drawn to *him*. This time, though, he isn't so sure it's a wandering spirit. There's something familiar about it. The shadow shifts again, and he recognizes the curves of it, the significance.

He feels *her*, grazing his arm with invisible icy fingers.

His stomach turns. His blood bubbles. He feels his power being tugged on, pulled out. *She* wants to reap him. Without hesitation, he flings a net of lightning into the water around him, effectively scattering the spirit. The water brightens and the invisible weight disappears from his veins. She leaves him be, for now.

With a low snarl of warning, he returns to the basin.

The witchling's visage flickers in the center of the bloody whirlpool, as irresistible as ever. She will come back to him, and when she does, he'll be more than happy to teach her all the wonders of his love, all the delicious pain and pleasure that comes when she finally submits to him. She'll realize what she's been missing and regret this insolence.

But until then, he waits... and grows wary of the deity that would try to undo him.

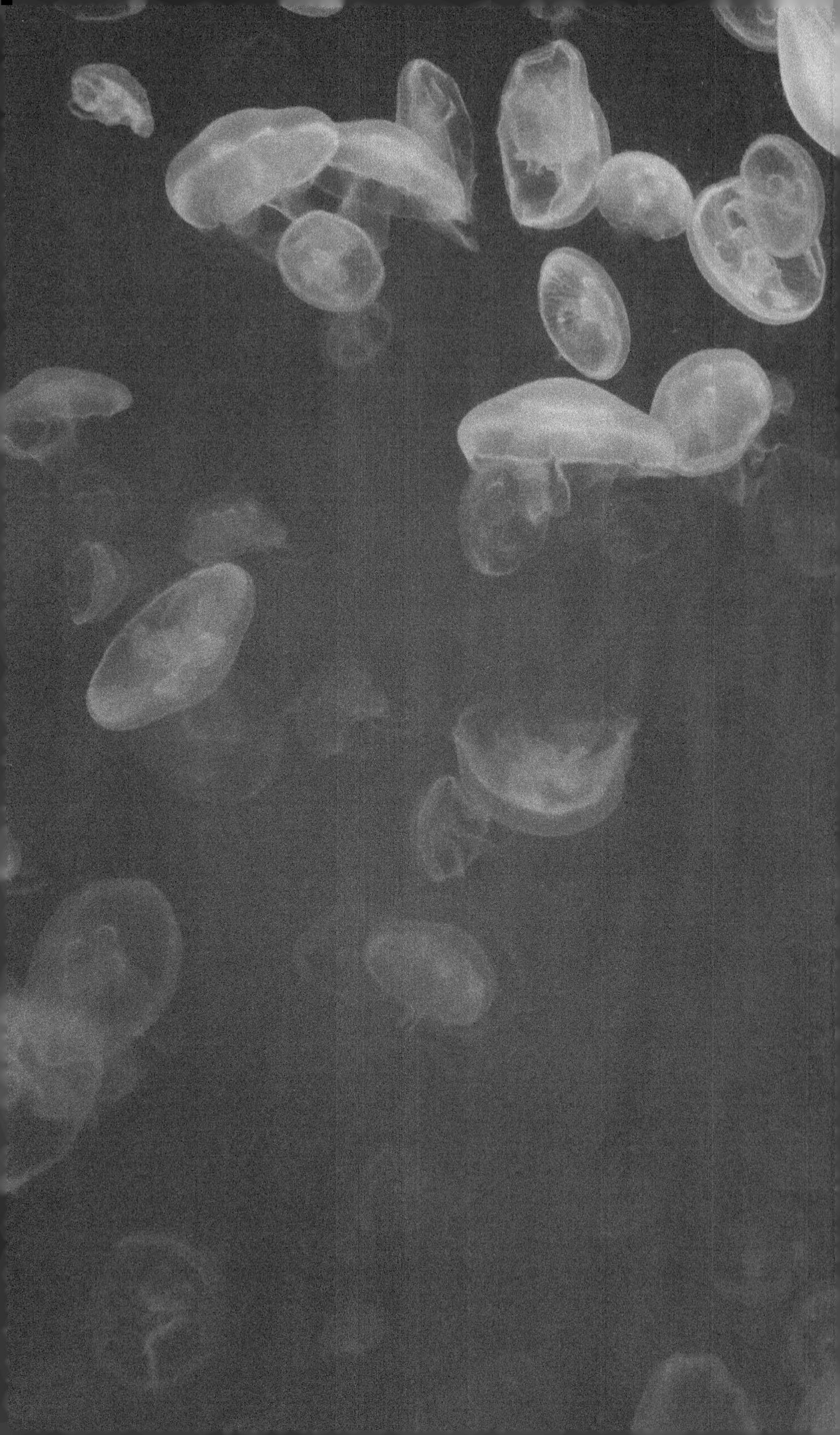

CHAPTER 1
VIOLA

Hunting a soul on land is twice as thrilling as doing so underwater.

My three hearts hammer in tandem as I lean around the brick corner, my lips pressing together as I spot my target. The male ambles down the cobblestone alley with a woman on his arm, his eyes alight with malevolent humor. She attempts to tug her gloved hand out of his, clutching her skirts in an anxious motion. It's getting late, and he's leading her farther from home. I'm out of my element right now, surrounded by air and flower boxes filled with acidic earth.

The fragrance of sourdough drifts across canals and gleaming mosaic squares to saturate every alley in the city, and I have to force my eyes not to drift closed at the scent. If I had more time, I might have sought some for myself. Fresh bread and garlic oil; the temptation is as loud as music to my senses.

Saliva pools under my tongue.

If there's one thing I envy humans for, it's their food.

What we eat Beneath doesn't compare; ocean dwellers have no need for taste buds.

It's unfortunate they can't change form like I can.

Already, the ocean calls to me, demanding my return, but I endure the soreness in my hearts a little while longer. I've come to retrieve what belongs to me.

I don't remember his name, didn't care to memorize it.

What I do remember is his reputation Beneath. I've been waiting months for him to submit to his true nature. His horrible, predatory instincts. I smile as the memory of our first meeting returns to me—when he scrambled for the surface after I first gave him legs, his eyes bulging in fear, his body vulnerable and foreign to him for the first time in his life. I knew there would be no lasting change for him. Men like him never change. I can shift his tail to legs, his scales to skin, but there's no power in the world that can fix someone's heart.

I've already tried, and failed, to fix my own.

Bad men deserve to know what it's like. Life, whether Above or Beneath the tides, isn't fair to womankind... so I've dedicated my life to balancing the scales and I *do*, even if I can only help one person at a time.

My patron goddess, Mora, encroaches on my shoulder, peering around the corner with me. She's my eternal, vengeful companion. The Star of the Sea.

I feel her reflect my delight and anticipation for what's to come.

The only part of hunting I don't enjoy is the waiting. Waiting for the moment of fear the women must feel, the moment that will allow me to collect what's due. I sensed when *this* male made the conscious decision earlier—to hurt his newest human fascination. I won't let the woman get hurt, of course. That's why I'm here, on two legs—but I know that fear is the worst part. The unknown. The temporary but seemingly unending terror.

If I had it my way, no woman would ever feel the need to imagine the worst.

The male pulls his unwilling companion closer, his eyes raking over her waist. He yanks her toward the alley wall, his hands grasping at her bodice, ignoring her protests. They're all the same. Always greedy for what they can't have, always eager to take what they want as if it's a game.

He has an opponent now.

I slip out from behind the corner. My bare feet don't make so much as a whisper against the cobblestone as I close in, as he shoves the woman into the wall and her shoulders make an audible clap against the brick.

Her face twists with pain. And that's enough.

You mustn't hurt any woman above the surface, I told him.

I made him swear it upon his soul.

It was a deal I knew he'd lose, despite any and all efforts, despite his most selfish intentions. It didn't matter to me how he did it. If he had stumbled into a woman at the market and she fell and skinned her knee, I would have come. The fact that he broke the deal like *this* makes my retribution that much more exquisite.

Little does he realize, there's unfinished business waiting for him Beneath.

He leans in to steal a kiss from her, but I'm already lifting my hand. Ice spurs in my hearts, the cold of a lightless ocean, of the voids leading to the center of our world. I've heard humans say they believe the core is hot, roiling magma... but as someone who's sunk farther Beneath than most, I know it's the opposite.

The enchanted wound on my chest, the one torn through bone and sinew to peer in at my clustered hearts, alights with a soft glow. The glow is muted by the slip I borrowed from a clothesline, but the golden rays still seep through enough to snake around him.

They take possession of his soul.

He shrinks and folds, twisting with the metaphysical current, until his body finally molds to my desire: a worm at the woman's feet.

I pluck him from the ground, smiling savagely as he wriggles between my fingers. My eyes flick up to the woman, and I incline my head in the slightest of bows. She's not a member of the nobility, judging by her modest dress and worn lace gloves, so I think my respect unsettles her even more than the magic had.

Her dark eyes are wide and shining. She grips the beads around her neck and whispers prayers to a god in the sky.

Ridiculous. I'm the only one listening.

The city knows me. I've heard them talk. I'm the spirit that walks along their canals, seducing poor men who wander too close. That's what they *say*. If only they knew the truth. This woman can be frightened of me if that is what her heart tells her she must do, she can believe the worst. It doesn't matter. She's safe the way I wish I could have been. She will go home to the people she loves and I will relish in even more suffering.

I return down the alley without a word, following the quiet cobblestone streets, crossing bridges until I reach the stairs to the fisher's bay.

Waves slap the beach and wooden boats sway in the harbor. It's utterly serene. Once I've left behind every trace of the sleepy city and white sand spreads out under my feet, I let my hearts flare with golden light again. My fingernails sharpen into talons, and I pinch the worm in half before tossing it onto the shore.

Another twitch of my fingers, and the quiet is shattered by blood-curdling screams. The merman's body is in its natural form again, though it's severed through the stomach.

"*Viola.*" He screams my name as if it means something, as if it'll somehow make me stop. But it's just a name. I'm so many things to so many people. A witch. A hellish spirit. Someone who must be crushed and feared and manipulated. It's all lies and seaweed, barriers to wade through but harmless to those built for it. Harmless to me.

The two halves of the mer's body reach for each other with stringy flying flesh. His legs meld together with burnt orange scales and iridescent fins. He screams louder as his torso reassembles, my abilities saving his life, but bringing him indescribable agony as I allow sand to sift against his organs and settle under his skin.

My magic can't affect just *anyone*. There's rules, as all power exists within one confine or another. This mer belongs to me. His soul has been tied to mine. It's an extension of my heart now, similar to that of a limb to a body, and so I can do whatever I wish to his form.

How unfortunate for him.

I step forward, allowing my own shape to adjust. The familiar weight of my tentacles sprout around my hips. I keep my human legs to help me travel across the sand easier, but my white tentacles brace the beach and wrap around his neck and shoulders as I descend on him. My lilac-rimmed suctions attach to his skin, sucking to the point of drawing blood. As I kneel, I drive a knee into the scaled pocket concealing his cock, earning me a high-pitched wail.

Goddess Mora's approval rakes like nails down my back. *Yes, child. Good.*

An unrestrained smile breaks across my face, my elongated canines pressing into my lower lip as I lower my face toward his. Digging my claws into his face, I force his cheeks to hollow out. I pry his mouth open and draw on his energy, drinking it in.

My hearts illuminates as I drain him, washing his bloodshot eyes in golden light. I pull and pull on his life force, swallowing it into my belly until he eventually slumps against the sand.

I pause before finishing him off.

I don't want to kill him, and I also don't want to consume his life essence and risk inheriting any gift he might carry. No reminders. I just need him weak enough to drag back home without a struggle.

Peeling away, I ignore the throb in my core and the lust in my body urging me to continue.

More, more, it screams. *Take it all.*

It's not enough. I could feed on a hundred men or mer, and it wouldn't fill my emptiness. The more I take, the less satisfied I feel. That's what Triton wanted. The King of the Ocean cursed me with this hunger, this longing for power. This desire to take what does not belong to me. He told me I deserved it, *earned* it by spurning his advances. He took and took, and when I fought back, he took the rest of me. All the parts he thought I loved the most. He fettered my magic and bound me to the sea because that was the only way to bind me to him. Then he isolated me.

I stopped mourning decades ago. I put myself back together and proved to myself over and over that I don't need him. That I don't need anyone. I wouldn't ever apologize for my cruelty, because this cruel world has never apologized to me.

With measured steps, I drag my new soul-bound into the ocean, my tentacle a solid chain around his neck.

He doesn't fight it.

I'm tired of dealing with these mer, even if I do get to exercise my wrath upon them. I miss the good I once found in the ocean, when I roamed this sea with my coven. I remember my coven mother, seldom warm but always kind, who took me in off the slums under Atlantis and gave me a future. I remember the happiness I had with them, however briefly.

This is all I have left: memories of a witch with better intentions; stolen breaths of clean air; relief so brief that if I blink, I miss it.

The memory of their burnt flesh returns to me in that moment too, turning my stomach. I remember, and my life is ripped away all over again.

As the tide reaches my waist, I shift my human legs away and rip the dress from my body with my claws.

Before I can slip the rest of the way under, I hear a song on the wind.

A chasmic, dissonant voice rolls across the ocean. It echoes from nearby, not from the city behind me, but from the intermittent rock lying at the base of the cliff-sides just south of here. The same direction of the human palace.

That voice isn't human, and yet it holds all the painful urgency of one.

It would be foolish to trust a voice from the sea. The foulest of souls carry the loveliest of lures—a predator can't hunt without them, after all—but I find myself paralyzed by the depth I hear in this voice. Mortals are superior in the way of feeling. It's agonizing to watch them, as they live and love and die. Rarely, I come across a mer who is like them, who longs for humanity, who *needs* that fragility to feel complete and alive. When I meet a mer like that, my hearts demand that I step in, because I wish there was someone out there who could do the same thing for me.

Curiosity rears up inside me, as vicious and unyielding as my hunger.

It's been a long time since I helped someone who truly deserved it. Decades. It makes me feel better, makes me feel like I'm more than the product of my circumstances, more than the starvation. So despite the whisper in my head encouraging me to return to the deep, I dive under and swim toward the beckoning call of a siren.

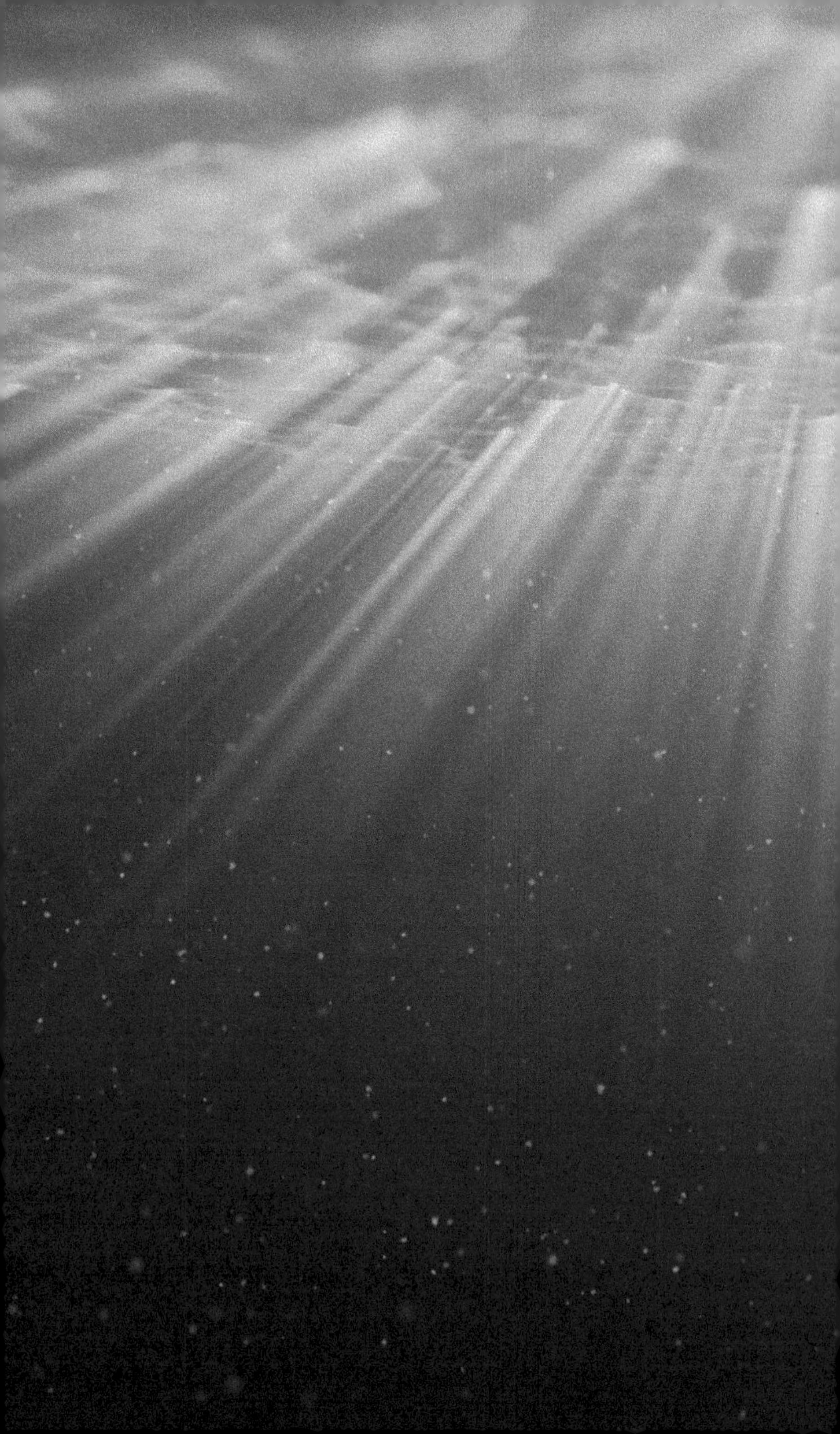

CHAPTER 2
ARIC

My gills sting in the open air. Rock digs into my palms as I lean back and gaze up at the palace. A few feet of crag rises over my head and gives way to the scaffolding of the tower. A familiar balcony hangs over the cliff, lights and shadows dancing together on it from the room beyond.

Any minute now, she'll come to me, and I can forget everything else for a little while.

I run a hand through my hair to push it out of my eyes, the red tendrils nearly brown in the dark. My algae-green scales glint in the moonlight as I bounce my tail beneath me. I'm more impatient than usual, but it's been too long since our last visit, and today has been a *nightmare*.

A delivery intended for my gallery got intercepted by whales, and half the haul was swallowed. We lost a client because of it.

I'm the one who insisted on immediate recovery despite my business partner's warnings. She told me the whales were migrating, and I ignored her. We both paid the price.

And if that alone wasn't enough to soil my entire day, Father finally came to the decision to mate me off.

My right ear rings, soft laughter echoing into it, and I irritably tug on the gossamer tissues rippling off the tip of my helix. Every inch of my skin tightens at the reminder.

I think again of my father's callous expression this morning when he told me of his plan. *Me*, mating for life? Playing right into his artful hands is more like it. He said I would have a choice, but in the end, I know he'll be the one to choose. He'll lump me with the most unbearable noble maid he can find—one that won't challenge my decisions or his *guidance*—and then he'll expect us to spit out a few tadpoles before he hands me the scepter of power and his prickish personality to perpetuate for generations to come.

My cock shrivels up just thinking about it.

Better me than the others, I suppose. I drop my gaze to the shark tooth strapped to my chest. Removing it from the sheath, I watch moonlight gleam across its hills and valleys. I scrape the tooth over the surface of the boulder beneath me, relishing in the harsh sound it makes, then I settle the blade into a cleft and begin sharpening a dull edge. Not too much. As my only shark blade, I have to be careful. If I wear the ivory down too much or chip the edge somehow, I'll be forced to replace it. And I really don't want to do that.

My mind drifts to my family and what will happen to us once I'm crowned.

Instead of being pitted against my siblings, I'll be forced to pit my children against theirs and my children against each other, as Father did to us. As his father did before him, and his grandfather, and on the cycle goes. My brothers will avoid me more than they already do, and there's no way I'll be able to work at the gallery anymore. I'll be totally fucking miserable. *Anchored.*

A creak on the balcony pulls me out of my worries, and my entire being narrows in on the light footsteps approaching the railing.

"Aric, are you out there?" Her soprano coats my body like a second skin.

A silhouette appears peeking over the edge, the side of her brown face illuminated by a lantern's flame. She can't see me—not even the light from a full moon can cut through the darkness surrounding me; there are too many towering rocks. That doesn't stop her from seeking me out. Sometimes I come to the palace just to hear her call for me, with no intention of answering.

When I first saw her pacing her balcony several months ago, looking out at the ocean as though she wanted to dive in and explore the darkest tides, I knew she'd be susceptible to my song. My charm works best on humans with a fascination for the sea.

The female sirens, of which there are plenty, never have cause to complain, but it grew monotonous for me to prey on the *men* who sail from shore to shore. Human women have more fight than their male counterparts. They're prettier too.

When I set my gaze on the princess, I wanted to become everything to her simply to prove that I could. And sure, she resisted my song for a while, cowered from the visions I projected into her mind, but she always returned to her little balcony after a time, searching for excitement on that distant horizon. If she truly wanted to be rid of me, she only needed to stop sitting on her balcony at night. She only needed to stop listening. I would have let her. But she didn't.

I took her continued presence as permission. Or at least, permission enough.

Her shyness was only a mask, a product of her human upbringing. She loved the back and forth, the pursuit and retreat. She loved being seduced by me. And for me, she's been the perfect distraction.

I smirk even though she can't see it. "I'm here, Angel Face."

She melts against the stone railing, resting a cheek on her folded arms as she gazes into the dark. She loves when I call her that. It has to do with that pesky religious devotion she has; to her, it's a sweet comparison. When she initially explained the idea of unseen winged humanoids serving a god in the sky, I laughed. If *I* could fly anywhere in the world, the last thing I would do is serve someone hiding in the stars.

If she knew I called her Angel Face with a secretive sneer, she probably wouldn't think it so sweet.

"Where have you been?" she asks with a pout, her dark hair falling in frizzy curls around her face. "I've missed you."

"I'm here now," I reply tightly.

She doesn't care where I've been, only that I haven't been *here*. She doesn't want to hear about my life or my troubles. That won't get her off.

A slow, partially-restrained smile twists her lips. "Are you here to sing for me?"

"That depends." My voice is dark and distorted, threaded with temptation. "What will you give me if I do?"

Her smile widens as she unclasps a bracelet on her wrist, dangling it like bait on a hook. A thrill rolls up my spine. The gems twinkle in the lantern's glow, the faint refractions as red and lavish as her nightgown. Jewelry. She must be damn desperate tonight.

I'm not ashamed of whoring out my gift for profit.

There's no one else around to witness it or report back to my father, and these past few months with her have single-handedly carried all the costs of excavation for the gallery—

so how could I feel anything but pride? There are worse ways to gain power and respect.

"And the other," I demand, my tone leaving no room for argument. I know a mermaid or two who'd pay me handsomely for the set.

Her expression falls a fraction, but she unclasps the matching bracelet from her wrist and places them both close to the edge of the railing. She braces her forearms on either side of them and waits.

She can't look into my eyes right now, but that's of no consequence.

There are two ways to influence my victims: either through direct eye contact or by touching their senses with my voice. In the dark, this far from her, it has to be my voice, so I start to chant. I don't know what I'm singing, but it doesn't matter—the spirits of the ocean always lend me the melody I need. They pass through me, creating the perfect song, one spirit after another after another. I am their vessel, wielding them against the target of my choice.

Purple mist rolls off my tongue as I sing, billowing over the water like mist on a cool morning. It crawls up the rock face, over the salt-washed bricks and through the hewn pillars of the railing. The tendrils slide over her arms, and she gasps in pleasure. I linger there a moment, waiting, caressing her skin with my power and drawing out her need until she lowers her face toward my magic. *Permission enough.* Her eyes flutter as the mist suddenly turns and careens into her irises, coating her vision in a violet haze.

In her head, I'm no longer singing to her from down below.

I'm on the balcony.

Her emotions assault me as they pass through her mind.

Lust and desperation. Sour, earthy selfishness. I wish I could ignore the reach of her emotions the way I can in reality. Here, they're inescapable. I'm inside her, and so I must feel everything.

She turns to the corner I've settled myself in.

The lantern silhouettes her figure, the red material sheer enough to see every curve. I'm one with the shadows. Anything is possible in this little slice of the world I've created for us. She can't see my face or any other distinguishing feature as I peel away from the corner and walk across the terrace.

Walk, because I'd be lying if I said these visions weren't a little of my own wildest fantasy.

I keep myself covered in shadows as I sing to her, revealing just enough of myself to play into the scene and nothing more. She trembles as I circle her. She sways to the rhythm of my song. We've been here, done this, many times. I'm an expert in the art of seducing her. I finally close the distance between us. Dragging her hair away from her neck, I bend to lick her skin, and she shudders.

There's no taste or smell here because my gift can only manipulate sensation and sight, but that's plenty.

I take a step back, my hands grasping the collar of her nightgown. The material rips under my hand, and she flinches. I smile, slowing down as I slide the material off her shoulders, drawing gentle lines across her skin with my nails. What I really want to do is shove her against the banister and take her apart like a demon from the depths of her human hell—fuck, I've let her prattle on about her beliefs so many times that the lore is etched into my brain—but even after months of leading her into my corruption, I know she's still too delicate for it. She wants to be *loved*.

The reward will be so much sweeter if I give her what she wants… so I pretend to be someone, *something*, else.

I lick my way down the column of her neck, across her collar to the swell of her breasts, suckling on one hardened peak. I've always had a fascination for the female body, for this particular place of womanly softness. Humans need to get their priorities in order. I'd sooner worship breasts than some invisible god. Breasts are hidden behind priceless shells and other decorative items in Atlantis. No mermaid has ever let me touch hers like this, allowed me to lick and nuzzle and nip like this human princess does. Perhaps that was part of my initial satisfaction in this whole endeavor—she isn't like the maids I spent my time chasing and bedding underwater.

I push aside the thoughts of home, the useless comparisons. I came here to escape them.

As Angel Face's gown falls around her ankles, I crouch to grip the back of her thighs and lift her into my arms. She's gyrating against my belly. My cock is hard and ready beneath her.

I pause, choking on my song, giving her time to break free of the vision if she wishes to, and the vision wavers around us. She would only need to look away. Everything would fall apart. She'd be alone on the balcony, and I'd be too far to touch her. But no, her eyes continue looking deeply into mine. She knows what she wants. She's willing to pay for it.

I force her down onto my length with a firm grip on her hips. "That's a good girl, Angel Face." And all right, maybe I let the shadows part enough to reveal my mouth and the sneer screwing it.

Her breath catches.

I taste her emotions surging through the vision into me, catching them like a net to rest bitterly on my tongue. Conflict and unease. She shuts her eyes, as though what she saw in my shadows scared her. Her muscles clench around me. She's close.

My hand flies up and wraps around her neck.

"Give me your eyes," I hiss through gritted teeth, squeezing my fingers until her eyes flash open. "Your pleasure belongs to *me*." I siphon every ounce of feeling from her through our connection, soaking it up as she burns and twists and frays under my ministrations. A film of fear edges her ecstasy, and I have to bite back a groan. *Fucking delicious.*

Oily regret threatens the edges of my mind. I don't know why. I don't understand how I can be so conflicted about something that is so vital to my nature.

Scaring her? That's the least of what I should be capable of.

I've always been too sensitive, too reticent to kill, ever since I was a child. I'm a siren, but a broken one. These visions give me the opportunity to explore the ideals of my gift, and over time, I've desensitized myself to the violence. The killings. All the expectations. In here, I can visualize my better self—the Aric I should be. It's like putting on a second skin, an armor, and in the fantasy, I'm not afraid of anything. Because in other people's heads, it isn't real.

But somehow, it still feels... *wrong.*

It's the same way I felt during my first hunt, when I killed a great white for my first blade. What has always been a long honored tradition for the young mermen of Atlantis—what *should* have given me some sense of fulfillment and pride—caused a sick twirl in my gut.

Anger replaces my confusion. Anger with myself and all that is broken inside me.

Other sirens wouldn't hesitate the way I have, the way I still do. Their visions are iron-clad. Unbreakable. They wouldn't wait for permission, and they certainly wouldn't give their victims even the semblance of choice.

As I thrust into Angel Face harder, quickening my pace, I realize she isn't satisfying me. I used to glean so much satisfaction from her pleasure, but my heart no longer races from being inside of her. Her face does not thrill me. I imagine a thousand other eyes as I look into hers; her features swim and stutter, torn in a hundred different directions as I search for something that will reach across the cavity in my soul and touch me. Change me. Make me *right*.

My chest vibrates with vicious unrest, and I feel as if I could burst.

The warring voices to either side of me don't help.

When I was a younger mer, I withdrew the conscience from my body and split it into two halves, two starfish that a witch in a far off sea embedded in the skin of my earlobes. I thought myself so clever at the time. Running behind my father's back, going against his orders to avoid witches, assuring myself that this was the best way to view circumstances in a just, detached manner. Without emotion, his *lessons* didn't hurt so badly. I could feel nothing, if I wished it. I thought it would make me a better king than my father, someday.

As it turns out, the voices prefer to bicker rather than offer me any real guidance.

On one side, I carry that part of my conscience most like my father. His anger, his need to control and manipulate and possess. That part of me which *wants* to please him in everything he asks, despite the brutality it requires.

But there's another piece of me, as strong and enduring as the ocean floor. That part like my mother. And even though she's gone, I still feel her here. Her quiet wisdom and gentleness. Sometimes, I wonder if she's one of the spirits that linger nearby and sings through me. That's how it works. Our ancestors become one with the ocean when they die, joining with the eternal spirits that give life to this water and to our magic.

I can't trust either voice completely. Now, feeling nothing is a habit I can't seem to break.

It would be all too easy to take that last step and toss Angel Face over the railing. She'd die outside the vision too, would toss *herself* over the edge and tumble down to me. That's what a siren would do. My father made it clear what's expected of me—to be the best, to be a king worthy of admiration, I have to be without weakness. And isn't weakness what I display by allowing this woman to live through my visits, by giving her pleasure and choice instead of pain?

If Father finds out about her, I'll be punished. Or worse, *annihilated*.

I have six younger siblings, five brothers and a sister, and they're all trained to take the throne should I fail. I should do this. I should kill this human that has started to bore me and prove to myself and Father that I have what it takes to be his son.

But the other half of me isn't so sure.

Angel Face whimpers, pleasure overcoming her body, her fear becoming a distant memory as she comes. My hand on her hip slides around to her back, holding her, and I can't decide if I'm holding on to keep her safe or to destroy her.

Before I can find out, a shout shatters the vision, and I ricochet back to reality.

My mouth clamps shut, the purple wisps between me and the balcony dissipating to nothing. I'm lying back on the boulder. Angel Face gasps as she returns to herself, ripping her hand out from beneath her hitched nightgown and spinning away from the railing as someone emerges onto the balcony behind her. A male speaks to her, in a voice too low for me to hear individual words.

"Yes, Papa. Of course." She turns back to the railing and reaches for her lantern, her cheeks red and eyes wide.

I hear something scrape against stone and realize in the next moment that she pushed the bracelets over the ledge. They plop into the water a few feet in front of me, and I dive for them before they're lost to the pebbly ocean floor. By the time I resurface with the gems in hand, Angel Face is gone.

That's it—the last time I'll ever see her, because I'm not coming back.

I might have gotten caught up in that vision, might have let my father's words and lessons hold me captive for a moment or two, but deep down, I know I don't want to hurt her. I don't want to kill her. She doesn't deserve to drown, and I don't know when *deserving* began to mean anything at all to me... but it does.

It's stupid of me to play with a human. To distract myself and pretend my responsibilities don't exist.

My cock aches, but I've lost the desire to take any pleasure from these meetings. I simply can't get off on something that's not real. I can't remember the last time I got off *at all*. As I slip under the waves, I open the satchel on my hip and deposit the bracelets inside, the water around me brightening I withdraw my glow stone.

It's too late into the evening to see much beyond black rock and sparse seaweed.

Brushed my hair out of my face, I dart into deeper waters. By the time I reach the edge of the rocky maze, I notice vibrations surrounding me, bouncing off the stone, echoing into every current. I halt, slowly twisting in place as *laughter* registers. Cold and feminine, threatening.

A creature emerges from the maze of rock behind me, and it is not a stranger. It's an enemy. *The* enemy. The Violent Sea looks me up and down, smiles without emotion, and croons, "Well, well. What do we have here?"

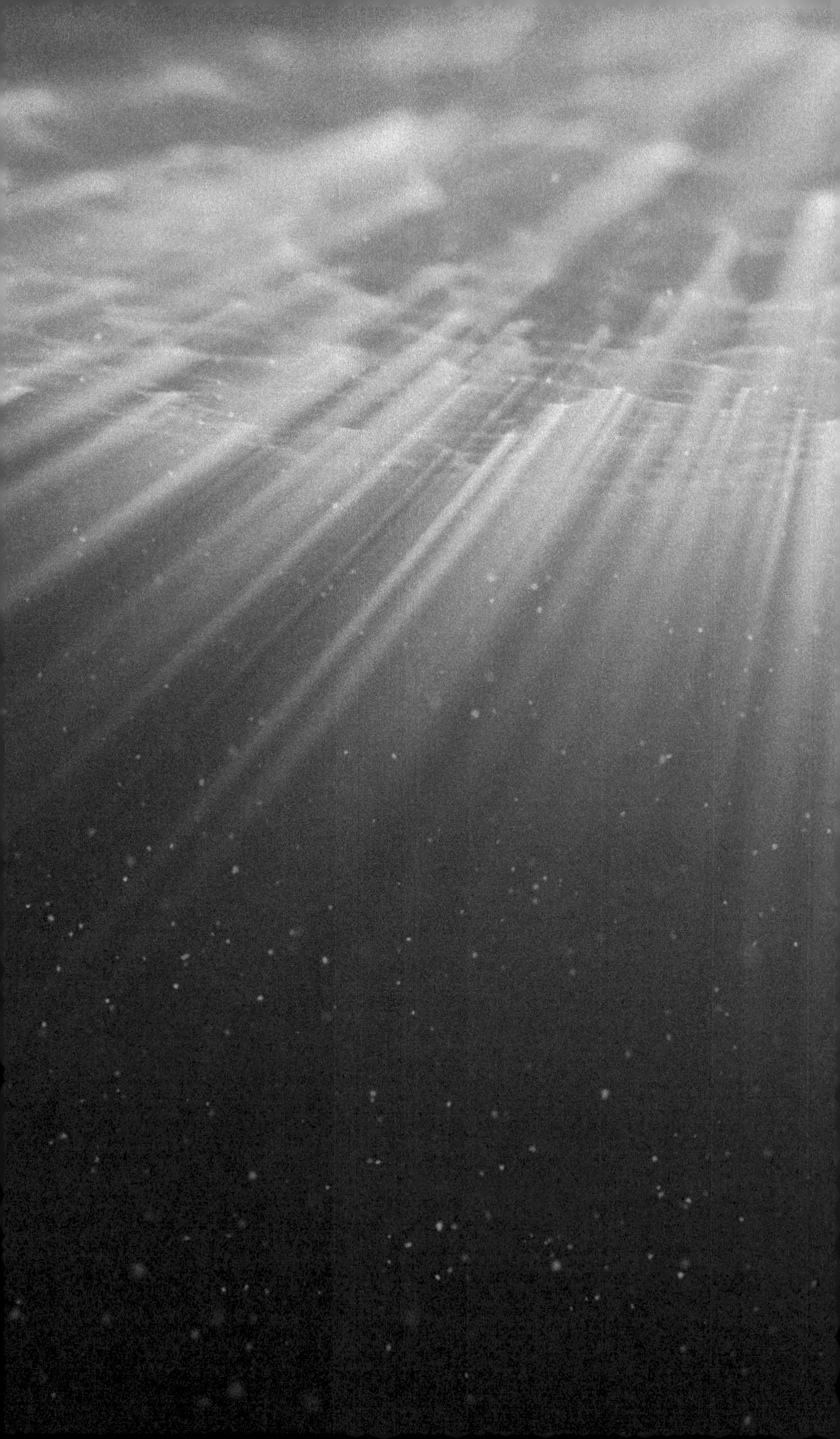

CHAPTER 3
ARIC

Body drifting with the ocean's dance, I search for what to say, what to do. My temperature rises degree by degree as anger rushes through me, the cold water biting after my time Above.

My fingers twitch toward the shark tooth strapped to my chest, but I don't draw it.

The Violent Sea is arguably the most dangerous creature on this side of the ocean, aside from my father. Not because of her inheritance—the white and amethyst tentacles twirling under her torso don't make her particularly special—but because she has a personal vendetta against the throne. Against Father. And certainly against *me*, if she knows who I am.

I haven't met her in any official capacity, so I might be safe. Well, as safe as anyone could be in her presence. I only recognize her thanks to the theater. Every year since I was a young mer, I've been acquainted with her likeness in the drowned amphitheater back home.

It didn't do her justice.

Her face isn't what I imagined. There is no hint of malice or age. It's heart-shaped, with the faintest tickle of dimples in the center of each cheek, *two* dimples in each cheek actually, which makes her look alarmingly innocent.

I bite my cheek at the unwelcome thought.

She's not innocent.

She murdered my mother.

My mother, adored in Atlantis by all who had the privilege of meeting her, had been a prominent active siren before her death. She was beautiful and passionate, with a fondness for the underdwellings and the theatre despite Father's aversion to both. She made the city a more welcoming place.

The Violent Sea took advantage of that.

The Violent Sea used up my mother's magic, then her body, and there wasn't even anything left to mourn over when she was finished.

Still, my eyes catch on the sea witch's chest. I can't help it. Her skin is the most luminous alabaster, like the rare statues my patrons demand of me so frequently. Blame it on the lingering desire in my body, my fascination over her survival of Father's wrath, or the murderous fantasies flying through my mind one after another, but I struggle to look away. My gaze skips and catches higher, on the hole carved into the flesh over her heart.

I have to restrain myself from smiling, then.

Father's mark. Her skin is torn in the shape of a shark eye shell, the swirl peeking in at her hearts. They don't look as black and decayed as the plays suggest. In fact, they glow a warm dusky yellow, illuminating the water between us better than even my glow stone.

The Violent Sea clears her throat, and my eyes flick up to meet hers. "Quite the show you put on, siren." She smirks with a false sort of amusement. "The princess looked half-ready to toss herself over the edge of the balcony, though. I hope that wasn't your intention."

She tilts her head as she leaves the rocks behind, and I see she's dragging a merman along behind her. One of her tentacles is wrapped around his neck, her white flesh modified to hold him like a shackle.

His eyes are half-mast, his body boneless.

A part of me wants to intervene, but I know better. If he's in her clutches, he gave himself over willingly, and I can't get involved unless I want to be at The Violent Sea's mercy as well. It's the way of the ocean, the way of magic. Possession and permission. I lift my chin and cross my arms, pretending her presence doesn't make my scales stand on end.

"Is spying a habit of yours, witch? Or am I simply unfortunate enough to be stumbled upon in your nightly terror of this sea?"

Her lips twitch. "Both are true. But how would I find souls that need my help if I didn't stay vigilantly aware of my surroundings? You were the one singing, *loudly*."

The merman in her grasp glances up, and alarm sparks in his body when his eyes land on me. He turns to The Violent Sea, fighting to loosen her hold around his neck enough to speak. "Viola, he's—"

I flinch as the sea witch's hand snaps up.

Her chest flares, lighting up her face and the air in front of her prisoner. As the golden rays fade, I see that his mouth is gone. No lips. No tongue. No more words. She didn't even need to look at him to do it.

My head spins.

I can't believe he said her name. *Viola*.

Back home, she's only ever referred to as The Violent Sea. Seeking out her name is forbidden. Everyone knows the act of speaking it will draw her to you, like glass makes its way to the shore or the moon pulls forth new tides. It's inevitable. But I suppose there's no point in *not* saying it when she's right fucking here.

"Souls that need your help?" I reply through a scoff. "Souls that crave your magic, you mean."

She halts a few feet away, pursing her lips. "Is there a difference?"

Her voice is so sweet, it makes me want to vomit, and her eyes remind me of a painting I acquired for the gallery a few months ago. *Field of Mallow Flowers*.

I can't think of a better description as I look into her light purple eyes. Her hair is the same shade, undulating in the ocean's currents above her like liquid coral. My body seems to move on its own, or maybe it's the ocean current pushing us closer together. I've never met a predator quite as pretty as her. And that makes her even more dangerous. I now understand how someone might foolishly trust her long enough to give their soul away.

"I don't think anyone has wanted a hag like you in ages," I snarl. I don't know who I'm trying to convince more of my disinterest, her or myself.

Her eyes darken and my hackles raise, the fins on my spine vibrating in warning. Admittedly, I'm not much younger than her. Considering how long our lifespans are and how many human lifetimes we've already racked up, we're at a comparative age now. I was only eight when she tried to seduce Father out of his throne though. And only the foulest sort of monster would kill a *mother*, would leave children worse off than orphans, helpless in a violent king's hands.

She has no idea what she's done to me, has no idea what I wish I could do to her in return.

"Watch the way you speak to me," she murmurs with

mock severity. "I could help you, you know, if you at least *pretend* to be friendly."

A harsh chuckle drags its way up my throat. "Is that right?"

She drifts an inch closer, her eyelids lowering in a slow blink. "Oh yes. It's what I live for. Helping good oceanfolk find happiness is my specialty, and my deals are more than fair." Her body changes course, and suddenly, she's skirting around me, her tentacles spreading wide—stretching much longer than they should.

She's cutting me off from open waters.

I twist to follow her revolution and nod at her occupied tentacle. "Is that what you did for him?"

"Well, he wasn't very good at all." A half-smile plays on her lips. "And a female's got to eat." The humor in her voice is thick and warm.

I should try to dart around her, to do *something* to get out from under her attention, but she tilts her head again—a predator's consideration—and I get a sinking feeling low in my gut. I wouldn't succeed if I tried.

I look into her eyes, searching for something to hold onto instead, and her emotions reach for me immediately. Curiosity steeped in a golden hue. I can't remember the last time someone offered their emotions up so quickly, so openly. I usually take my readings by force or coax it with promises of pleasure if I want them. And I don't want them often. They're more of a defense to me than a predatory skill.

It's as if The Violent Sea doesn't *care* what I see or what I learn about her. She's unafraid.

And fuck, if that isn't a surprise.

I'm not exactly harmless. Both those Above *and* Beneath fear sirens for a reason. Getting familiar with someone's emotions, what they feel like, what they *taste* like, makes getting into their head a thousand times easier.

She's so... *blue.*

It's not a flavor, like most emotions are. That happens to me sometimes, when I sense something so *other* that I see a color or an item in my mind. She's like the blue of the underwater diamond caves, when the tide recedes enough for moonlight to peek through and refract silver into the sea. Deaths are honored there. It's a place as unsettling as it is beautiful, and it's not somewhere to visit unless one has a reason to, lest they wake the lost souls that haunt it.

I've only been there once. *Because* of her.

I shake my head, rejecting our brief connection. What the fuck is wrong with me?

When I meet her gaze again, every trace of her previous vulnerability is gone, and so is mine. "I'm not interested in you feasting on my heart anytime soon," I hiss. "But thanks for the offer."

She pouts and I sway backwards, trying to get some space to see her more clearly.

I can tell something isn't right. I'm missing something beyond her obvious beauty. My eyes scour her form again, then the water around her. And—*Ah.* I see it now.

Pheromones twirl through the currents, so faint to my eye that at first, I overlooked them. They glitter like crushed translucent scales in the water.

"You're on your cycle," I snarl.

"I am." She confirms with a shrug, her tentacles spinning faster and faster beneath her. The pheromones vibrate. Her body is calling to mine. "Does that tempt you?"

Absolutely.

I know as well as anyone why the witches were banished from Atlantis. *Their sacred cycles.* It's a gift from their patron goddess, and a curse to everyone that falls prey to them. When a witch's cycle begins, they give off the strongest pheromones known to the ocean to attract a mating, and whoever answers the call is destined to die.

I dug into the lore once when I was a much younger mer, out of a morbid sort of curiosity.

The goddess that gifted them their cycles was unbelievably beautiful. So beautiful, it was said, that every male in the ocean wanted her, was driven mad for her. And her love was *magic*. Whoever she slept with was blessed by her, their powers amplified and their lifetimes extended, and that blessing was passed down to their children. It was a blessing many sought, but few ever received.

Then there came a king.

He begged for her favor, over and over, and she faithfully turned him away. Eventually, he grew desperate enough that he threw a celebration in her honor, drugged her, and simply took what he'd wanted. The king was unworthy of the blessing he had stolen and yet he possessed it like someone would possess a trinket, tossed it into a corner of his home, never to be admired again. When the goddess woke, the entire ocean felt her rage. She gathered her children and loyal subjects, and she began plotting her revenge. The witches became a vital part of that. Her hands. Now every male they kill, every victim to their lustful bloodshed, is only a balancing of the scales to the goddess they serve.

I can't say I begrudge them for it.

But considering that, am I truly tempted by The Violent Sea beyond my body's instincts?

"Not even a little bit," I growl.

The sea witch eyes twinkle. "Hmm. What was your name, again?"

"I didn't tell you my name, and I have no intention to."

She opens her mouth as if to explain why I should, but my eyes drill into hers, snaring her.

With a thunderous roar, a kraken surges out of the ocean floor. Its beaklike maw swallows the witch whole, the length of the monster's body gleaming like ink in front of my face as it shoots up and up and up. I listen to the forceful swallows, the gurgle of its stomach, straining to hear The Violent Sea's scream. I hum to myself to keep the vision going, now that her eyes are out of view. If I was smart, I would leave—but I can't stop myself from hanging back a moment longer. I want to witness her fear, *taste* it.

But I don't hear a scream.

I hear... laughter.

I blink, returning to myself, and the vision falls away. Her laughter fills my ears, her sparkling eyes absorbing my thoughts as she presses a hand against her chest.

I don't need to sing with my tongue if I'm close enough to my victims. A shared glance lets me make full use of my powers. I shouldn't have done it, but she put herself in my way, cornered me, so she had it coming.

"A risky decision, Silver-Pipes," she says after catching her breath. My upper lip curls at the pet name. "But amusing. Lucky for you, I have my hands full tonight or I might have shown you what a kraken *really* looks like."

She can do that, *become* that? I swallow hard.

Her smile slides into a flawless smirk as she pulls her tentacles in and backs away, giving me enough space to swim past. "Now swim along before I change my mind and give you the show of your life."

I don't trust her.

She should be ripping my organs out of my ribcage, not letting me go. Every inch of her expression mocks my hesitation. It's a silent challenge, and one I refuse to back down from. Slowly, I swim toward her. As I pass, one of her arms raises in front of me, flirting with the water and keeping me beside her.

This day is really, truly fucked.

Instead of attacking like I expect, she simply says, "It's your loss, I suppose, to never experience life alongside the hot-blooded ones. To never walk with them or talk with them. To never feel the fleeting, warm embrace of a woman." She pauses. It feels as though the entire ocean stills around us as I meet her demanding stare. Something flickers in her eyes, something *real*. "The ocean can feel so very cold sometimes, don't you think?"

I lean in, just close enough to see the tiny air bubbles clinging to her cheeks. I'm not the only one that breached the surface tonight.

She frowns at my proximity, but doesn't pull away.

"I think," I whisper, "you're *starving*, witch."

Her eyes widen slightly, the reaction controlled enough that I wonder how I've managed to see so many of her smiles today. I wonder why she gave them away so freely.

Before I can hear any more of her lies, I dart into the nearest current and disappear.

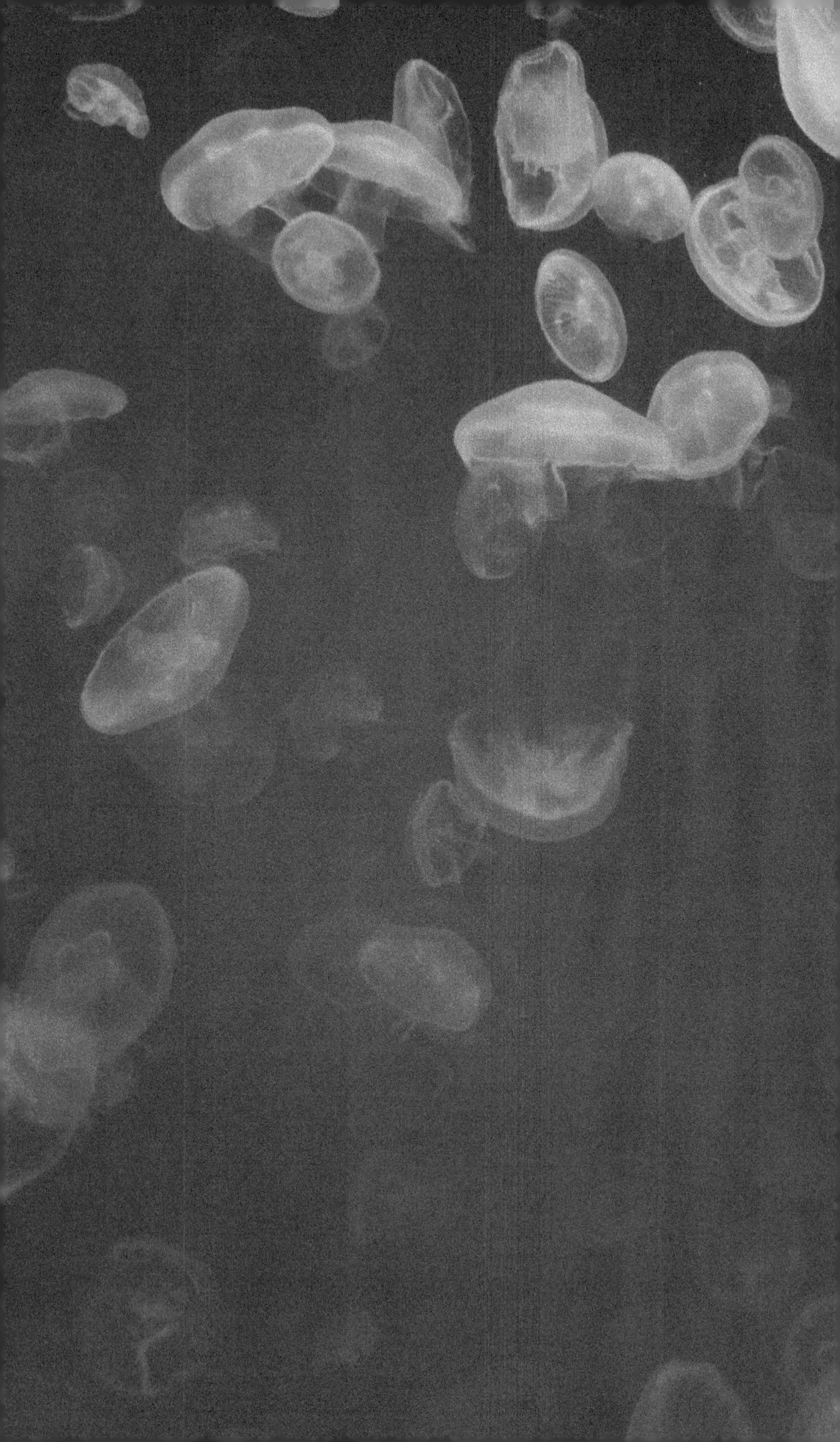

CHAPTER 4
VIOLA

*chapter content warning: there is (non-graphic) reference to childhood sexual abuse in this chapter (page 50)

Home is as lively as ever.

The room swirls with jellyfish, the luminescence spilling out of them in shades of blue and pink and purple. Their tendrils brush through my hair and over my shoulders, kissing me with comforting little zaps. They paint the torture unfolding before me in unparalleled beauty.

The merman I brought back from Above is paying for his evil, tied to the broken floorboards of the captain's quarters. *My* quarters.

It's a new wreckage, but the walls have already been emptied of the useless human items and replaced by my spell bottles, crystals and divination tools, the preserved body parts of my previous conquests. An eyeball stares at me from a cloudy green container, its tail of vessels floating in a long curl beneath it.

The mermaids who live here with me were delighted by my newest retrieval, Perla more so than the rest. This might be the very first time I've seen the black skin around her mouth crease with a smile. Perla is how I first learned of him. She's the reason for the target on his heart. She returns every moment he made her suffer and more, and I'm fine sitting here on my coral-crusted throne, watching her do so. Perla's laughter as she tears into him, the look of relief on her face, is reward enough.

My home is open to any mermaid cast aside by Triton's sparkling city, those scorned and forgotten in the same manner I was.

No one remembers who I was before I became the enemy, but all pain is seen and acknowledged here. With me, it's *avenged*. So many come, and sometimes they stay. I hope Perla is one who decides to stay. I like her a lot. If I was brave enough to admit it, I might even say that I love her.

As much as I allow myself to love anyone.

My fingers dangle over the edge of my seat, playing with an anemone growing on a sharp rock that juts into the wreckage. The rouge tendrils caress me back.

Little blue fish dart in and out, daring the habitat to try to capture them, and I smile at their fearlessness.

It reminds me of the mer I ran into last night.

My whole body tingles at the thought of him, my core throbbing to the border of pain. My mating cycle is intensifying, its peak imminent, but I know my lingering desire is a little bit because of him too—his piercing stare and snide attitude, his sun-kissed body and the way he made no advance toward me despite my state. It's a test of will for males to resist the Goddess's pheromones. I nearly succumbed to the cycle myself last night. I would have taken him if he allowed me to, condemning him to die buried inside of me... but then he'd wielded that vision against me, and I laughed for what felt like the first time in years.

I decided then to happily let him go. I just wish I'd gotten his name first.

A whoosh and rumble sounds behind me.

I turn to observe a hammerhead shark outside the shoddy lattice windows of the ship. The gray creature twists and bucks, obviously irritated, and my smile slips when I recognize the figure attached to its back, the rusty hooks it has buried in the shark's skin. The merman shoves away from the shark and flips over backward, aiming for the hole leading into the captain's quarters, between the reef and the remnants of the ship's deck.

He slips inside with a raucous laugh, his gray scales shimmering and his fingers stained with rust.

This male is another permanent guest here, but *his* soul is also bound to mine, his life attached to one of my three hearts and bent to my mercy until he dies or I grow tired of him.

Gorging on a soul suffices only for a day, but if I keep life forces on tap like this one, I can better control the hunger.

I always keep two mer in my service at all times. If I drain one too much, I can turn to the second until the first regenerates. And that's what Maggot is: my *spare*.

The hammerhead tries to follow my soul-bound in, but its head gets caught on the opening. I glare at Maggot as the room shakes around us, but he only drifts forward with a wily grin and settles against the floor next to my chair. He reaches for one of my tentacles. I grit my teeth and curl away, a pointed refusal.

After another few moments of ramming at the hole, the shark finally gives up and bolts away.

I don't honor Maggot by speaking to him. I return my gaze to the red-tinted water billowing on the other side of the room and the swarm of tiny carnivorous fish that surge above to feast on the cloud.

Maggot mutters a greeting to my other soul-bound, Fluke, who floats in the corner.

Fluke was the first merman to ever seek *me* out, thinking he might outsmart me with a cleverly worded deal. It didn't work, clearly. But I let him think it would for a couple months before I reaped him.

He hates my guts.

I call him Fluke because he's no better than a parasite, tirelessly searching and latching onto anything he can suck dry of love or wealth. He had a mate when he came to me, and *several* children. He'd chewed through her money and decided to move on in the only way he knew he'd be completely free—abandoning the ocean altogether. He couldn't be loyal to one woman, even when his life depended on it. That's how I caught him. How fitting that his soul now belongs to me for the rest of time.

Maggot is named so because, well, he has an obsession with dead bodies.

His handsome, joyous smiles are a veneer to hide the monster. He stalked and murdered at least twenty-five Atlantian females before I caught up with him, and the last obsession he ever had was the reason he made a deal with me—he asked for a new face and body to entice her. She was already happily mated, and the moment she rejected him, he was mine. At least he's nice to look at now... tall and dark and his body exquisitely honed. Not that I look much.

Warmth spreads over my hip. "You look beautiful today."

I look down to find Maggot leaning against my chair, his chin propped on the seat and his dark swathe of hair close enough to brush my skin. I snarl at him, carefully angling my body to keep us from touching. "Leave me alone."

"You don't want that."

I lean against the opposite armrest with a sigh, the green wood groaning.

Fluke emits a low noise of disgust. "Tentacle-licker," he says under his breath.

I bite down on my smile. Strangely, I like it when Fluke is mean to me. His insults keep my heart glowing, even if it is out of anger.

"Better to lick them than be fucked by them, Fluke," Maggot says brightly.

Fluke mutters something else.

I don't have to hear the words to know it's vile.

"Careful, Fluke," I warn quietly. "Or I'll remind you what these *tentacles* are capable of."

Maggot's brow creases. He leans close to me and whispers, "What about me?" His gaze turns black. "I wouldn't mind—"

"No," I growl and wave a hand in his face to dismiss him.

I was kidding, for tides' sake.

"Oh, come on." He flicks one of my suctions. My skin tightens in response to his affection, and not in a good way. My body is still humming with desire from my run-in with that mystery mer. It's like Maggot can smell it. "Don't pretend you already forgot about our night together. This hard-to-fuck shit stopped being fun once I felt your cunt squeeze around my fingers—now I'm just frustrated."

It was one night, after what felt like an eternity of loneliness. It was the very start of this cycle, before I even realized it had begun, before I could brace myself against it. I brought

Maggot with me on a patrol of the canals, and it led us to walking along the shore together, which led to touching and needing and forgetting all the evil in him.

It was a mistake, one I don't plan on making again.

My gut churns every time I think of what I let him do, every place I let him touch. I should put him in his place. Fluke certainly heard what was said just now, and he'll watch to see how I react. But Maggot is touching my tentacle again, his skin hot and his smile possessive. His pupils dilating. And even though I'm on a throne of my own, having dragged myself up to the top of the food chain in a place far enough from the open ocean to feel a modicum of safety, the wooden walls on either side of me close in. The ocean freezes against my skin.

It's not just Maggot. This is my body's reaction anytime *anyone* tries to touch me when I'm not expecting it, when I don't initiate contact first.

It's always the same. I return to this moment, this feeling of helplessness. I'm trapped again, electric bars separating me from my life as Triton's eyes stare down at me. The memory of his touch is an itch under my skin. He smiles, and I know it's over.

I press a hand against my diaphragm, desperately needing the pressure. If I lose one more inch of control, I'll be shaking... and no one in their right mind would fear me then.

I shoot out of my chair and away from Maggot's unwanted fingers. I need to gather my senses. Then I'll come back and discipline him. Although, lately he doesn't seem to mind the brutality. He's taken to begging for it. Maybe this thing between us has been escalating for a long while, and I simply turned a blind eye to it.

Maggot follows me.

He's never hesitated to bathe in my shadow, and tonight is no different.

I throw one of my tentacles behind me, knocking him in the chest to force his body away. "Don't. Stay there."

His eyes flash, handsome features screwing into a snarl. "Fuck, Viola, would you wake up and breathe the oxygen? He's *gone*. It's time to move on from that piece-of-shit nobody."

I halt in the doorway to the rest of the ship, my hand seizing either side of the frame as his statement drops weightily into my stomach. Slowly, I look over my shoulder.

The mermaids cease their torture.

Perla gives Maggot a dark stare, then her eyes flick to mine with a questioning slant to her brow. As I drift back into the room, Perla waves at the other females, and they all scatter in a flurry of multicolored scales.

"*What did you just say to me?*"

He recognizes the look on my face, the death in my eyes. For the first time in years, he seems frightened. But nothing will save him now. He shakes his head, as if seeing that too, and gestures between us with his hands. "He couldn't protect you, Viola. He was weak, and not all the shapeshifting in the world could've pulled him out of his bottom-feeder instincts. He wasn't strong like me. If I had been there, I never would have let Triton do what he did to you."

I'd been wrong. His last obsession wasn't that mated mermaid. It's *me*.

I swim forward, my tentacles stretching beneath me. They graze the floor, then rise through the water on the other side of Maggot. He retreats right into my clutches. My tentacles wrap around his arms, pulling them behind his back so his chest is exposed and pointed toward the ceiling. I drag him forward. The closer he gets, the more my body wraps around him.

Maggot doesn't care for me. Not really. He's done the same thing to other women that was once done to me, so I can see right through him. His valiant words are only an act.

Males like him will say anything to keep their true selves secret. Liars use words because they can never prove themselves with action. Sometimes, those lies even extend to themselves. Bad men delude themselves into thinking they're good while they do something evil, and good women are told that it's always their fault.

"He didn't *let* Triton do anything," I say softly. "Triton murdered him, and then he murdered everyone else I ever dared to love—friends, family, acquaintances. All of them." A cold laugh bubbled out of the back of my throat. "I don't love you. If you had been there back then, I still wouldn't have wanted any piece of you."

Maggot's eyes narrow, and I know he wants to lash out, to kill me the way he did the rest of his obsessions. He's never been able to handle rejection. It's too bad the soul bond and my hold on his limbs keeps him from doing anything about it.

I lean in to whisper in his ear, "You have not burrowed your way into my heart, Maggot, because I have no heart left to be won. But if you so badly want to give me yours, I'll take it."

Without another word, I thrust my hand into his stomach. The skin splits in an avalanche of blood, his organs squelching and clinging to my fingers as I turn my hand and drive it upward. His heart fits perfectly in my hand, the muscles clenching as his pulse radiates into my palm. I squeeze slightly, and it looks as though his eyes might pop right out of his skull.

"Go ahead. Say his name, Maggot," I taunt. "*Francis.*"

His eyes shutter, the veins bulging on his forehead as I squeeze his heart even harder. For a moment, I think he might actually defy me in this. But then the name seethes through his teeth. "Fran—"

I rip his heart out.

Then I raise his heart to my mouth and bite into it, and my entire existence whittles down to the lust in my stomach. His blood and power flows down my throat. I devour *everything*. My hunger twirls, reminding me of those human women in the city who dance in the rain every spring. I watch them from the canals. Jealous. Aching. My love for rain and storms disappeared the instant Triton cursed me, the instant he used his powers against me. I miss that love almost as much as I miss my freedom.

Maggot's life force settles in my gut and a veil shrouds my mind, slipping across my vision, sharpening my senses and thoughts.

I'm suddenly aware of every bubble of air in the room. Every body part bobbing in the glass bottles on the shelves illuminate with a cool blue outline. I look down, and see that my own form is outlined in bright white.

Am I seeing... *body heat*?

I didn't think Maggot had a gift, but in death, I see I was wrong. His obsessions, his propensity to stalk and track. It went beyond desire and selfishness. Maggot was a *hunter*.

My adoption of his gifts won't last long. Only a day or two, long enough for my gut to digest him. If I had known, though, I would have killed him the old-fashioned way—with one of the shark teeth on my altar. I don't want the reminder of him.

No. Reminders.

I look up from my meal and catch Fluke smirking in the

corner. His outline undulates bright green, pulsing in his chest as though he were trying to contain laughter. *That* unsettles me. I can't shake the feeling that I've just made some kind of mistake. I release what's left of Maggot's mutilated flesh, and the bloodthirsty fish dart in, nipping at the exposed arterial chambers. Still, Fluke stares at me, his smirk slowly fading.

I turn away before he senses my discomfort.

My newest soul-bound watches me from his place on the floor, flinching as I glide to him and cut through his restraints. Like Fluke, his body pulses with a vibrant green line. His hands grapple with the jagged floorboards, fighting against the current to keep as far from me as possible.

"It looks like I need you. So let's get expectations out of the way, shall we?" I smile, and he recoils from my searching tentacles. "I *own* you. If you're tolerable, I might keep you around for a century or two, but you will never touch another woman, with ill intentions or otherwise. You serve the mermaids in this ship as totally as you serve me. If they tell you to hunt their dinner, you do it. If they tell you to bow and worship at their fins, you will."

His gills flare, but he doesn't respond. He still doesn't have a mouth to speak with.

"You will not return to the glittering city or fraternize with Triton's royalists without my explicit order to do so—trust me, I'll know if you try." I grab his shoulder and add, "And I suggest you prove your worth to me before I replace you the same way I did him." I nod to Maggot's body floating against the ceiling.

He still hasn't let go of the floorboard. It's as though he's trying to anchor himself.

What a useless pursuit in a world like this.

Waving a hand in front of his face, light skitters over his

features. His mouth returns. He expels a rough breath as I push my magic into the rest of his body, relieving him of the most life-threatening injuries but leaving the rest. Almost anything can be regenerated, except for the heart.

By the time I return to my throne, Fluke has thoroughly composed himself, his gaze focused on coral growing in the corner of the room.

I recline in my chair, my hands clutching tightly to the armrests. Now that my fury is ebbing, my body feels closer to breaking than ever, and I try not to show it. I lean over the side of my chair and occupy myself with the cluster of anemones again.

The silence is thick enough to choke on.

"Dispose of the body, Fluke," I command in a bored voice.

I want to dismiss them both and take some dearly desired time on my own. Maybe cower in one of the cupboards for a little while. But then Fluke would know—know how close I am to losing it. So I ignore them both as Fluke gathers up Maggot's body and darts through the opening in the roof.

"Viola." My new servant's voice is weak, raspy from the damage his contained screams did to his throat. "There's something you should know."

I mildly raise a brow in his direction.

"The man we ran into earlier tonight—that was Prince Aric. Triton's firstborn son."

The words burst like ripe berries beneath my skin.

That mer had charmed me... with his quick mouth and sharp humor. I sat here, thinking of him, hoping I would see him again so I might show him who I am beyond the lies that weigh on my name.

But he must already know the truth, as Triton's son.

I had let him go because I thought he was afraid of me. I

don't blame anyone from Atlantis for fearing me, because I've done nothing to ease the rumors. Now I wonder if his actions went beyond self-preservation. It would make sense for Triton's son to follow in his footsteps, to deal me the same suffering for his father's namesake. His sons will teach their sons, generation after generation, and this prison of mine will never end.

Triton knew how to charm me too.

'Look at you, such a sweet little witchling.'

I'd been out of the underdwellings less than a week when my coven mother brought me along on her home visits, showing me what my future held. Tonics and fortunes. Necromancy on the entire city's behalf.

We were summoned to the palace, and I was left alone with him. I don't remember how. I was still a mer at that point, a girl, not yet gifted with tentacles or additional hearts. He looked down his nose at me from his throne of pearls and coral, and grinned with all his teeth. At *me*, the dirty orphan girl.

When he offered to let me sit with him on his throne...

It was so beautiful, I couldn't resist. Even though his smile had scared me a little .

I wish I could tell that little girl what I know now. That I was right to be scared. That the fear was *instinct*, an awareness that weighed on every woman from the moment we were born until the day we died. That no man, despite title and reputation, is above evil. I wish I could have warned her away from the king who tricked her into trusting him with false kindness.

I trusted him with too much, as children do. Even the spirits of the ocean did not see it coming, could not stop it.

Goddess Mora found me afterward.

I shake my head sharply, burying the memory.

Goddess Mora is here with me now, stroking my back with invisible fingers, cooing in my ear. My voice is shaking slightly as I ask, "What would the Prince of the Ocean be doing in these waters? What purpose is there in singing to human princesses?"

He shakes his head, wincing at a slice Perla made in his gills. "Aric could be up to anything. He's not known in the city to be particularly obedient to the court. He's wild. I doubt Triton has even half a clue of what his son does behind his back."

Oh. So there's more to find out about Silver-Pipes?

Maybe the spirits have a little luck to spare for me, after all. Goddess Mora laughs.

The hunter instincts flare inside of me, imagining a thousand different paths, a thousand ways to claim Aric for myself. It's going to happen.

I tug the invisible string in my chest that attaches to my new soul-bound and he groans, pulling himself toward me across the floor. When he comes within reach of my tentacles, I drag him to my throne and grip his chin between my sharp fingernails. "Tell me everything you know."

If I can't destroy Triton, I'll destroy everything that matters to him instead. Starting with that siren prince.

CHAPTER 5
ARIC

I barely make it back onto palace grounds when I see my brothers waiting for me.

Luca and Warley are in the yard directly outside my room, brooding, brittle concern etched into their eyes. They are two of the siblings closest to my age, third and fourth in line to the throne. Something must have happened after I left Atlantis yesterday. I hoped to get some sleep before dawn, but I guess the ocean tides are still swelling against me.

Warley pushes off the castle where he was dozing, the side of his face glowing with residue from the wall.

In the distance, several servants are already rolling on more jellyfish pulp to keep the stones gleaming, the shade slightly more yellow than green today.

The circles under Warley's eyes are nearly as dark as his auburn hair, a match to mine. His blue fins twitch as he waits for me to close the distance between us. When I'm absent from the castle, he's the one pestered with any problems that arise, and he doesn't cope with it well. Not because he's bad at dealing with issues, exactly, but because he simply cares too much. Everything seems to weigh heavier on him.

"What happened?" I demand.

"Benji," he begins, and my entire body coils tight. Our youngest sibling. Our little sister. "She invited one of the noble's daughters over today and tested out a new blade on her."

All semblance of warmth drains from my body.

Benji earned her first blade mere weeks ago, by killing her first shark and ripping it from the creature's maw herself. She was a tad young for the rite. Father barely even let her participate, seeing as it's a harsh process and she's his only daughter, but she's never been one to favor feminine pursuits. I convinced Father to let her participate because I figured it would make her happy. Maybe that had been a mistake.

I knew she was obsessing over her prize, the way we all do for a time, but—*fuck*.

There's no holding back my rage. "She's *fourteen*," I growl. "What are you doing leaving her alone with guests?"

It hits me only after the words are out that I'm not angry with them. I'm angry with *myself*. For not being here.

Warley grimaces. "I didn't know Benji brought her in, Aric. No one did—not even the guards, that masterful little sneak. The girl told us afterwards that Benji promised her a tour of the dungeons if she played along. She didn't realize Benji really intended to cut her up."

I turn away and tug on my earlobes, urging the voices to speak up and offer even a sliver of guidance. I hear nothing. It figures they would be silent now, when I need them. That's how it always is.

Luca floats behind Warley, his arms crossed. A pillar of silent support. His long silver hair curls around his shoulders. The piercings lining his brow pinch together as he frowns at us.

He doesn't talk much, especially to me.

Warley, Simon, and I are the only ones who share the same mother. The rest of my siblings are half. They have stronger ties with one another and Warley. I think their mother, my father's current wife, has warned them away from me.

I'm too powerful, too much of a *threat*, to be seen as a brother.

It should technically be the sibling closest to my age, Simon, taking on these responsibilities when I'm gone, but he can be as cruel and difficult as Father and we all know it. We all avoid them both when we can.

I return my attention to Warley and ask, "Is the girl still here? What needs to be done?"

Warley exchanges a look with Luca.

The earring on my right finally pipes up, whispering that they might be scheming against me. I have to remind myself that they can't possibly despise me as much as I think they do. We're family. And family means something, doesn't it? Even if they dislike me, even if they hate me. Even if they only see me as a destructive force to be used when the circumstances require it.

I protect them, and they continue to need me.

Warley finally says, "We've taken care of the girl. It's Benji we're at a loss about. Someone still needs to talk to her."

"And you want *me* to do it?" I huff an empty laugh. "Where's her mother?"

"Passed out cold," Luca interjects, the chains strapped across his chest and pierced through his nipples glinting as he uncrosses his arms. "She didn't even get around to weighing herself down before the urchin kicked in."

Warley nods. "Besides, we think she needs a little more... discipline than the queen is capable of."

"You want me to scare her." It's not a question.

They don't respond, but their stares are admission enough.

Right. Because nothing bad could come out of scaring an already frightened kid who is clearly lashing out. I know Benji. As my littlest sibling, she got more time with me than the others. I comforted her when she was a babe, while her mother was distracted with the court. I entertained her with games around the palace while our other brothers were busy enjoying their adolescence. These violent outbursts are new and strange, and I'm going to get to the bottom of it.

I dismiss my brothers with a wave of my hand and enter the castle in search of Benji. It's not a long search.

I find her in her bedroom.

The walls are dark—apparently she doesn't allow the painters into her private room. But then, neither do I. She's lying on a flat rock in the center of the room, a glow stone illuminating her hands as she fiddles with a lump of metal. As I draw closer, I realize she's carefully binding a silver blade with whale skin.

The sight draws me up short.

Pure silver is lethal to mer. One accidental touch is enough to burn our skin clean off. Extended exposure eats away at our muscles and bones, and can even force our organs to fail.

"What the fuck are you doing?"

Benji startles and drops the blade, and it falls to the surface of her work space. Her eyes are wide as they land on me. Surprise and fear register before her juvenile sensibilities kick in, and she quickly hides the emotion behind a mask of indifference.

She shrugs. "What does it look like?"

"It looks like you're playing with death metal. Do you understand how many of Father's laws you're breaking by having this here?"

"It's my room," she retorts haughtily. "I should be able to do what I like in it."

I narrow my eyes at her. "That's not how he would see it. You'd be punished *severely*, Benji, and that's granting you don't accidentally kill yourself with the silver first."

Fear flickers across Benji's face. "Are you going to tell him?" she whispers.

Slowly, she crosses her arms in front of her tightly wrapped chest, and a glimpse of the little girl she used to be makes a brief reappearance. She ducks her head, looking down at the bereft blade, her dark hair drifting forward to shield her.

She's been subjected to Father's anger since the last time we spoke. I can tell. I suspected as much, figured that was why she's been dealing out pain to those around her.

There are ways to spare my siblings. I learned that after my mother died. Once she was gone, I understood the depths of Father's volatility. I understood the ways she protected me, and Simon, and Warley. By the time Warley was old enough to be targeted, I started steering Father's attention elsewhere or absorbing the wrath myself if I was close enough to intervene.

I didn't work up the courage in time to spare Simon from his own suffering.

I also don't suppose he had the same memories of mother to hold onto that I did. I think that's why he's so cruel, why he turned out more like Father than I did. I sometimes wonder if he has any recollection of nurturing touches at all.

The rest of my siblings, though—I still try to protect them.

"No," I eventually admit. "I have no intention of telling him what you do alone in your room. But I'm very concerned. Why do you even feel the need to own a silver blade?"

"Can we just get this over with? I know why you're really here—Warley and Luca told you what happened. Give me my punishment and go."

My stomach churns at the helplessness I hear in her voice. I know addressing the real issue at hand won't get us anywhere, so I change tactics. "That's an impressive bruise on your cheek."

Benji's hand raises to touch the purpling, and then rolls her eyes to mask a wince. "Yeah. When the little bitch got free of her restraints, she hit me."

Her disrespectful tone... the choice of words. I don't expect them. It drags back to my childhood, to one particular night when my father caught Mother and I coming home from an event at the theater, and she sent me up to my room. I disobeyed her and stayed, hiding high up in the scaffolding of the throne room as Father called her that name. *'You little bitch. Where have you been—'*

My mom didn't deserve how my father treated her. She didn't deserve her life or her death.

Violence roars to life in my ear, goading me into giving Benji a matching bruise on her other cheek for such a reminder, and I quickly tuck the urge away.

Instead I say, "Good."

"You think that's good?" she squeaks. "I'm a princess, *her* princess. Hitting me is practically treason—I can't believe Warley let her get away with it."

"I would have let her get away with it too. In fact, I probably would have let her get in a couple more punches," I confess, my tone sharp. "You hurt her, *abused* her. You betrayed our city's trust. If she were to tell someone what happened here and it got out—"

"It won't," she interrupts. "We already took care of it."

Just like that. As though the abuse meant nothing, as if that *girl* meant nothing.

This is the real issue with this place: no one fucking *cares* about each other. They need to. Otherwise the cruelty and dishonor will ruin us all. There is no throne without trust. No throne worth fighting for, at least.

"Why did you do it?" I demand.

Benji falls silent and thoughtful, clearly weighing the idea of telling me the truth or a lie. A smile flits over her mouth as she turns to me and admits, "Simon thinks I could be a great secret-master. He suggested I practice."

I scramble to organize my thoughts beneath the voices now swirling in my ears.

The violent side of my conscience wants me to track Simon down, to punish him for planting these dreams in Benji's head. The quieter side begs me to stow this information away, another stone to pile on top of the others. Weight to be used against him later.

But, the truth... my littlest sibling needs to hear the truth right now.

"Simon wants to use you, Benji." I pick up the silver knife, holding the wrapped area of the hilt between two fingers. I admire the honing of the blade, the quality of the skin, then hold the weapon up to her. "He wishes to wield you like this blade. But you are not a weapon. He did not conquer you, and he does not own you. You are entirely your own. You are strong enough to carve a life for yourself away from this family if that is what you desire, but you are still too young to realize it."

Benji's smile fades. Her eyebrows stitch together. "I don't understand."

"Let me show you." I hold out a hand.

Eventually, she accepts it.

My brothers expect me to scare her into obedience, but any threat I make wouldn't be real. That's not how her brokenness will be fixed. I can't strike her fissures and expect them to heal.

So I show her the distant shores I've seen instead, and the ones I've only dreamed about. The lands I've seen depicted in wood and canvas and pigment. I share the warm breezes, wicked rainstorms, and the small pockets of bliss that I've discovered in the seven seas and beyond. Life scattered to all four corners of the earth.

"There are so many different worlds out there for you," I whisper through the vision. "A million opportunities, with a million futures. The darkness you feel is heavy, but it *will* pass... because you can get out of this place. You can see those worlds, experience new things, and the old will be forgotten in time. Time is all you need. You aren't anchored here, and if you thought about what's waiting for you outside this city, I think you'd realize you don't want to be."

She rips her hand out of mine, and the vision ends.

Benji studies me. "How do I know you aren't just trying to get rid of me?" she says tightly. "Maybe you simply fear my alliance with Simon."

"Why should I fear Simon?" I raise one brow, daring her to tell more of the truth. The truth I already know. "Do you happen to know of other plans he has for me?"

She quickly looks away. "Of course not."

"Benji, it would be naive of me to expect anything less from Simon, but I'm not worried about him in the slightest. And do you want to know why?"

She peers up at me, her curiosity a small spark twinkling in her eyes.

I smile and smoothly transfer another vision before she can blink. The ground falls away from under us and a great blackness replaces it. It's all around us, above us, it swallows us whole.

Benji gasps.

Vulnerable children always fear the dark, even when they grow up in it, should be used to it. Children fear the dark even when it's all in their head.

I laugh, and the scene dissipates.

Benji glares in my general direction, but wisely avoids my eyes. That's good. She's learning.

"I'm too clever for Simon," I declare. "When you face off with an opponent who blurs the line of fantasy and reality, the only way you win is by keeping your wits about you. He's too proud and wounded to guard his fears. He still acts like a child. But he also knows that he will never be free of this place—he is favored in court and with our father. He wants to keep you here, suffering with him."

I set Benji's knife back down, and her eyes follow it.

As I drift backwards, I say, "Do not let him, or anyone else, stop you from escaping this place."

I turn to leave, but she says my name.

When I glance back, she asks, "You really think I could get out?"

I'd be lying if I said I wasn't jealous of Benji, for having a chance to leave this ocean behind. But I'm even more excited for her, and hopeful for her. I give a shallow dip of my chin.

"When you are older, I'll pay for your escape myself. If you decide that's what you want."

I can't be sure in the dark, but I swear I see her smile as I turn away.

As I go through the motions of tethering myself down to sleep in my room, I think of the times my father chained me here, bleeding and dreaming and wishing for a mother that was stolen from me. I think of the past until it feels like my future. And in moments like this, floating in the quiet of my room, knowing sleep will never come, I am vulnerable enough to long for my own new world. For freedom. For a chance to hear my own voice so I might recognize it in the silence.

Tonight, I think of The Violent Sea's offer, and what it might have been like to become human in something more than a fantasy.

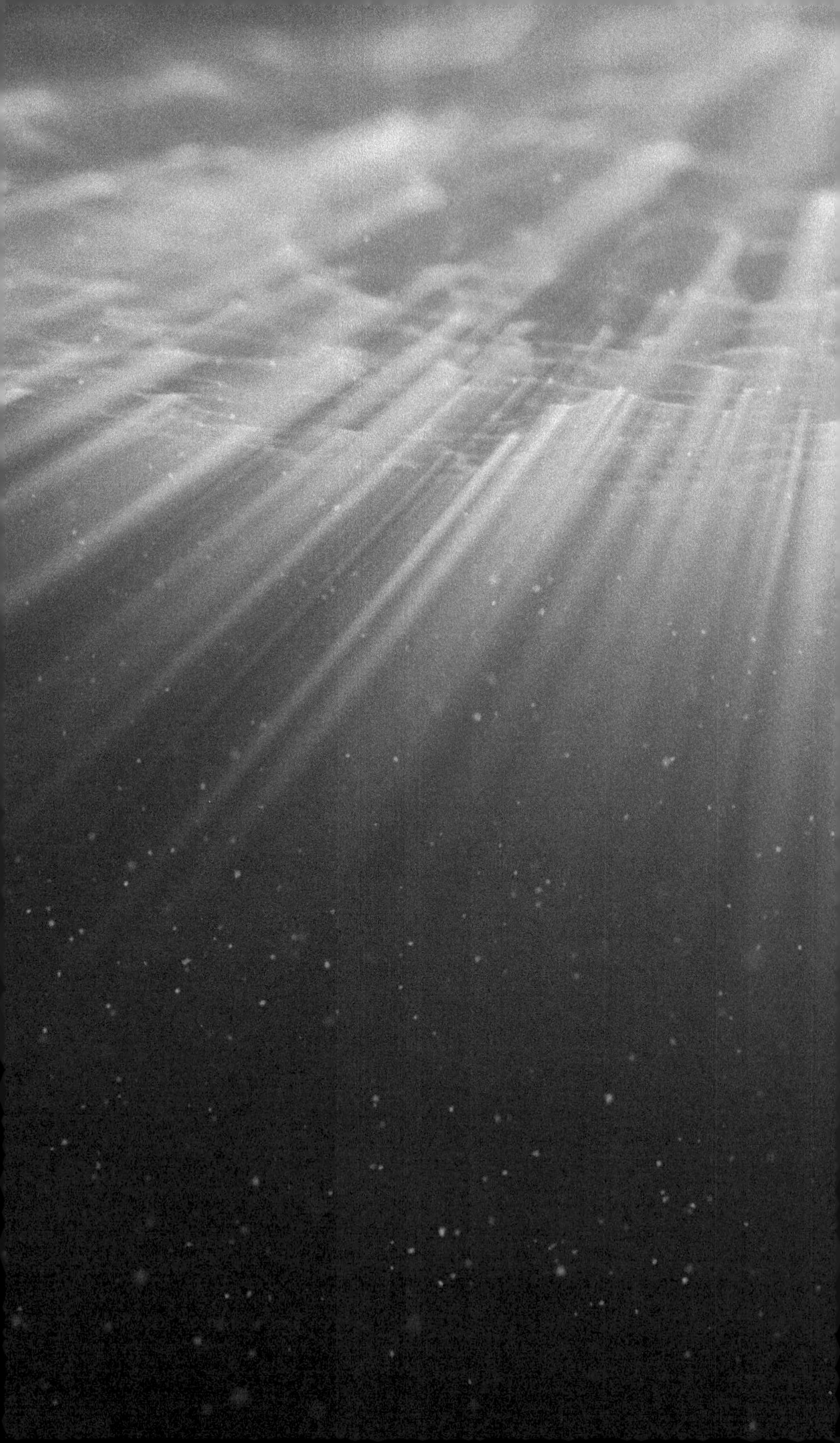

CHAPTER 6
ARIC

The gallery is silent as I part the seaweed over its entrance and swim in. I'm instantly surrounded by a blue glow thanks to the lanterns placed around the cavern. Each holds several luminous seahorses drifting lethargically in their containers.

A sigh ripples from me as the familiarity of this place invades my senses.

This cavern is deep enough underwater that nearly everything is perfectly preserved. Canvases stare at me from the walls, their paint glimmering through the water. Gems wink on rickety tables. What's left of the intercepted delivery lies against an adjacent wall, ready to be sifted through for the next showing. There's work to be done. I get to it.

At least here, I can rest in a sense of belonging away from the demands of my title. Here, I'm only Aric.

I rearrange old novelties to make room for new, setting aside a few treasures I know have been lusted after by our regulars. By the time the entrance lightens in color—a sign of mid-day and sunny weather above the surface—I've focused my attention on the centerpiece of the next show: the twin ruby bracelets.

I'm anchoring them to a column of dead coral when my partner glides in.

Andrine's pink scales appear almost red in this light. Her dirty blonde hair is tied back in a tail, forcing her features to stand out in fierce angles. I don't spare her a second glance before returning to the bracelets.

She comes to a stop beside me, fluttering her fins as she waits for me to finish the task.

"Good tides," she says as I finally turn to her, the corner of her fin flicking out to graze mine in greeting.

I grimace. "Calm waters, my friend."

"That's a dazzling set of cuffs you've found." She leans in to admire the bracelets.

"Earned," I amend under my breath, then add in a louder voice, "They're the best we've ever had. I'm going to have patrons bid on it at the show tonight." I offer her a smile.

Andrine nods thoughtfully. "Whatever you think will reap the greatest reward."

The pearls we deal in for the gallery are the rarest form of trade. Better even than the gold that sometimes manages to find its way down here. They aren't common pearls, though those are still a fair currency. The ones *we* collect are magical.

Oceanfolk can extract the happiness attached to the best memories of our lives and infuse it into pearls. They can extract sadness too. Any emotion may become a possession. Joy simply sells better. Imbued pearls are highly sought after because they serve as a cure for melancholia. Or, well, a *temporary* cure. That happiness fades eventually, the way all happiness does, like waves receding from the shore once their magic has run its course. Some folk think the pearls we deal in are foolish, perhaps worse for us than the sadness we felt in the first place... but I know better than that, because in the darkest moments, even a glimmer of light looks like the sun.

I share most of what I make with the underdwellings, dropping the pearls in the streets where children play, throughout the burrows under the city, to all those who need small happinesses the most. I know it's a weakness to feel compassion, but I can't stop. I know that's how my mother was targeted by The Violent Sea. I remember the way my father tried to cut and scold the instinct out of me, and how I quickly learned to bury it. But it's still here.

I think it always will be.

Andrine sighs and glances around at the arrangements. "Well, I came to assist, but I see you've got everything beautifully handled."

"I do." I fight a prideful smile, but it evaporates as I remember what happened yesterday with Benji, and I sigh. "Listen. After this next show, I believe it might be time for me to take a step back from the gallery. You can keep the money we make off these bracelets and use it to fund the next excavation."

Andrine doesn't react. She only tilts her head, studying me closely. "Why?"

Atlantis will demand more and more of me until there's nothing left to spare. She has to know this, but curiosity often gets the better of her. Andrine ran this gallery alone before I came along. It took her a long time to trust me with any part of it. She's always been a little wary of me, because she doesn't understand why I do this. It's not as if I need the pearls. It's not as if I have time to waste.

I shrug. "I don't think I should be spending so much time here when Atlantis needs me."

Andrine nods, but I can sense her thoughts turning. She

folds her arms over her chest and asks, "What in your life will make you happy if you leave the gallery? What will serve *you*, instead of the other way around?"

Her question stuns me.

She's always so quiet, but I should have known that simply meant she was listening. Observing. Absorbing. Now she thinks she *understands* me.

I shake my head. "You should go home to your family, Andrine."

"Yes, the sooner the better," a familiar voice interjects.

Andrine and I startle, turning to face the creature who spoke.

The Violent Sea hovers several feet away, her tentacles filling out the entrance. Both a warning and a barrier. She stares at Andrine, but there is no hint of malice in those purple eyes. "Swim along, now. I would hate to drag an innocent into our private matters."

Andrine pales. Her hands shake as they reach toward me, unwilling to look away from the sea witch. She knows as well as I do that a predator strikes the instant you forget to fear it. "What have you gotten yourself into this time, Aric?"

The Violent Sea frowns, her tentacles twirling faster—a sign of her impatience, I think. She wants me alone.

"Go," I growl at Andrine, swatting her hands away. "Don't make your mate mourn you."

She wouldn't. Despite the friendship we've shared, I know she loves her mate and children. And no one loves me.

"May the deep spare you," she mutters before spearing toward the exit. To my surprise, the sea witch moves out of her way.

"I do love how they scurry. Like little crabs." The Violent Sea muses, laughter choking the words. Then she looks at me and practically purrs, "Hello, Silver-Pipes."

Her smile is monstrous, her hair a dark sapphire in the lanterns' glow. A piranha hunting blood trails. Heaviness settles low in my stomach.

"What are you doing here? What do you want?"

"You didn't think I'd let you get away with that stunt you pulled, did you?" Her eyes are lit with mischief. Those ivory tentacles thump against the cave floor in an erratic rhythm, throwing vibrations into the water around me. "I'm here to balance things between us."

"Nothing could ever make us even."

If she hears the buried meaning in that statement, she doesn't show it. "Probably not, but you're so fun to play with."

My face pinches. "So I'm a toy to you?"

"No." That smile again. I hate that fucking smile. "You're a funny prince who prefers dark caves over his sparkling city. I think you're longing for a different life than the one you have now, and I want to help."

I forcefully unhinge my jaw. "I don't need your help."

The Violent Sea glances around the room, her smile fading as her eyes lock on the closest lantern. She reaches out to graze a finger over the glass. One of the seahorses tries to nudge her back, hitting his snout on the glass and recoiling with a flash of brighter blue.

"These are barbaric," she growls. "You really couldn't think of a better light source than imprisoning bottom feeders? You have to use their bodies?"

Heat spreads through my torso, the fins on my spine beginning to vibrate. I can't stop myself from biting back, "And you couldn't think of a better source of food than imprisoned mermen?"

Her eyebrows raise.

I think I've pissed her off, but I can't be sure.

In a ripple of movement, all eight of her tentacles lash out, extending with the support of her magic to crash into the lanterns around the room. The glass crumbles and all the seahorses dart out. They bolt into the small crevices of the cavern, escaping into the ocean currents, but there are a few who seem disoriented by their release. They linger near the broken lanterns, turning in circles.

Alright, so maybe some of them were suffering... and maybe it doesn't feel good to know that. But *damn*. It'll take months to recollect the ones that were lost, and there's a show tonight.

The Violent Sea drifts forward. Her heartslight radiates into the cavern and paints her face with golden fire. Looking at her is like looking through miles of stormy water. She appears to have no shadows, but I know that can't be true. "Do you love this ridiculous gallery, Silver-Pipes?" Her fingers trace the length of a table as she swims closer. "Does it give you joy and comfort and a sense of individuality under your father's thumb?"

"Fuck off back to your sea, witch."

She runs her tongue over her sharp teeth. "There's no need to be rude when I'm trying to commiserate with you." Inclining her head to one side, her lips quirk. "I want to be your *friend*."

"Not a chance," I spit.

She shrugs. "It's okay, I won't hold a grudge. You'll treasure my offer of friendship soon enough."

"How do you figure that?"

The Violent Sea draws so near to me that her heartslight caresses my skin in something close to a physical touch. It drives away *every* shadow in this cavern, even mine. Her gaze scours every inch of my face, unforgiving in its captivity, brutal in its strength.

She lifts an arm, her claws stretching toward my chest.

I catch her wrist. I don't squeeze or rip, not wanting any more of her touching me than I need to push her away. Before I can drop her hand, she sweeps even closer, until her chest brushes mine.

"Because, *funny Prince*," a force of levity weaves into her voice, "Triton has received an anonymous letter by now, informing him of his son's illicit activities in this cavern."

My body tenses. I don't comprehend it for a moment, but, yes... she really just said that.

"You didn't." My words are breathless.

The Violent Sea tears her wrist away and glides backward. Her grin remains, but only barely. It's not the smile of someone who is proud of what they've done. It's a sad smile. A forced smile. It is so unlike the grins she gave me when we met. "I only did what's expected of a loyal servant. Aren't we all subject to the King?" She says that, but her magenta eyes scream something else.

The cavern begins to rumble, and my heart drops.

All my organs quiver at the hint of my father's power saturating the water around us, trembling from the furious vibration. He's coming. *He's coming for me.*

"Uh oh, sounds like daddy's angry. Nothing will be able to save you from his wrath now—well, nothing except for me, of course." Her expression grows mockingly solemn. "I wonder what he'll do with you." Her seriousness dissipates in the next instant as she croons, "If you want a way out, you know where I'll be."

And then, she fucking *winks*.

My vision darkens around the edges. She's all I see, all I can think of as I lurch forward to grab her. I'll make her pay for what she's started, for what's shattering inside of me with every shudder of the cavern. She dodges my hands with a distorted laugh. I'm blinded by a flash of light, and then she's gone.

As my eyes adjust, I see she's only shifted.

A seahorse rises through the water with surprising alacrity, the figure purple and undulating with magic. She dives through a pore in the rock wall before I can catch her. I scream as my palms hit the wall to either side of her escape, and I swear I hear her laugh again, the sound echoing in my ears.

The cavern begins to shake so hard that items are being dislodged from the walls. Father's close.

I have to get out of here. As long as I'm not caught, I can deny guilt. If I tell Father of what I'm dealing with—The Violent Sea and her recent obsession with me—surely he'll write the letter off as a lie. He'll believe me. *He has to.*

I race to the entrance, but the curtain parts before I get there, revealing a broad silhouette.

With the lanterns broken and seahorses scattered, only the barest details are illuminated. Midnight blue scales. Silver hair. Not Father, but not much better than him either.

It's my brother, Simon.

As the two eldest brothers, my father did his best to keep us at odds. Simon's desire to overshadow me evaporated any chance of a relationship between us, and I let the pieces fall where they needed to. I never thought I'd regret letting us drift apart, until now.

He braces his hands on my chest to push me back. His blue eyes are wide, blazing. "Father is nearly here, Aric," he says. "I tried to talk sense into him, to delay him, but he's furious. You need to get out."

"That's what I'm trying to do." I aim for the entrance again, and the water falls eerily still around us. *Not* a good sign.

Simon catches my arm. "He'll see you if you go that way. He's too close. There's got to be a back exit to this place, right? Let's go that way instead."

I hesitate, trying to sense his emotions, but he refuses to look me in the eye.

"Hurry the fuck up," he insists, tugging on my arm, pulling us farther into the cavern. "If he sees me helping you, it's my skin at risk too."

I don't have time to guess his motives, to think of anything but evading Father's storm. I'm in the eye of it, and my window of action is rapidly closing.

Leading us back through the gallery to the rear wall, we close in on an area of the cavern coated in fossilized coral, the cavity disguised by a curve in the passage. Anyone looking at it from the inside would assume it's a dead end. As I reach for the opening, white lightning streaks across my vision, erupting through the water in a torrent of bubbles and cutting off my advance.

Electricity tickles my mouth as I recoil. The bolts of light split off and bar the passage in a grate. It's Simon's magic, the alignment with storms that he inherited from Father.

He laughs. "Thanks for making my part easier, brother."

I slowly turn to face him.

"What are you doing?" I growl. But I know. Deep down, I know exactly what he's doing. My heart hammers hard enough that I'm vibrating with the force of it, or maybe that's just the cavern trembling again.

Simon's sharp teeth flash. "Father's orders. He couldn't have you running off before your punishment, could he? You know, I'm thinking I've just obtained a front-row seat to your demise and my ascension. It's about time Father came to his senses."

Backstabbing bottom-feeder.

I tear toward him, my hands outstretched to pull him into a violent embrace. One look, and I can overpower him in his mind. But he slithers out of my way at the last second; ducking under my arm, he sends a bolt of lightning across my abdomen. The pain doubles me over. He didn't cut me open, but he came damn close.

Simon seizes me in a headlock. Lightning coats his arm, a silent but pointed threat against further struggle.

My neck prickles from the charge. He's holding himself back, but that could change in a split second. I let him drag me back into the belly of the gallery because there's nothing else I can do.

Father's arrival is felt before it's seen. A low rumble possesses the cave. My throat constricts, and it has nothing to do with Simon's arm around my neck. Blue light crawls into the room, twirling on a current like disturbed sea urchins, blindly preceding his presence.

And then the King glides into the cavern.

His long hair is tied at the nape of his neck, the tendrils of moonlit white curling forward around his arms. His aura pulses blue. If there was any chance of making it out of here unscathed, it's gone now.

Violence razes my thoughts—the violence I know he's capable of.

He looks the two of us over, then nods sharply. "Good, Simon."

Simon smiles against my cheek, his lightning flaring around my neck, biting slightly. I swallow a wince. His delight in Father's praise is palpable enough to taste. It's red like blood.

Father gestures around the cave, blue bolts sparking off his fingers. "You are going to learn your place, Aric, and you will learn what the consequence is for stepping outside of it.

You are not a human who weeps over art. You are a prince. First, I'm going to take care of this shitty under-dwelling, and then I'll take care of you." He points at me, blue light rolling forward and collapsing in the water between us.

The meaning is clear. His punishment isn't going to kill me, but it will hurt. *Significantly*.

When I was younger, Father dealt me punishments all the time, when I swam too close to the surface or ventured too far into the under-dwellings. He would cut me between my scales, where no one could see, but I felt it with every movement of my tail afterward. I couldn't swim for days. I was anchored in the city, in court, *learning my place*.

Father turns, stretching his arms, and light spears into every crevice of the gallery, rending canvas and dispersing particles of glass into the water. The shards graze my skin and scales. But it's nothing compared to the pain of losing the gallery, of knowing that Andrine will return to this place and mourn the summation of her life's work.

The Violent Sea did this to her. *I* did this to her.

I look away from Father's destruction, which is difficult considering it permeates every inch of the room. My eyes land on a tarnished mirror. It's angled in such a way that I can see myself trapped in Simon's electric grasp. A pitiful excuse for a prince, the both of us.

Father is right. I don't know my place. I have never felt equipped for my title. Once he drags me back home, he'll slice the truth into me, and I don't know if I can bear it. Not again.

I hum low in my throat.

Purple wisps spring to life, sparking off my skin. I squint, willing every scrap of my power into that mirror, willing the wisps to caress my brother's ears. I will Simon to pay attention. As I struggle, his electricity pricks my skin. He makes me bleed, but I keep moving, keep fighting. I elbow him in the stomach. He turns his head to hiss in my ear and his eyes catch in the blackened, amber glass.

I smile.

The scene shifts so subtly, I know he doesn't notice. In his head, I'm not smiling. I'm not struggling. Father's bolts fly wide, the glance-offs coming closer and closer to our corner of the room. Simon retreats, but the threat follows us. Father's face lights with an icy glow, reflecting the craze of his anger. He's lost to the storm.

A stray bolt ricochets off a wall of the cavern and hurtles into us.

Reality comes back into focus as Simon lets me go and dives out of the way. I'm free. The ricocheting bolt was never real, but Simon is disoriented long enough for me to grab the chain of an old bell beside us and wrap it around his neck. I twist the iron links together and hold on tight through his writhing, through the lightning he blindly throws behind him, until he finally goes limp. Then I drop him and charge through the back passage without looking in Father's direction. My focus is on getting as far as possible from here before he discovers what I've done.

I'm barely clear of the cave when Father's roar radiates into the ocean.

I keep swimming until it becomes a faint rumble, until I'm surrounded on all sides by kelp and my body is shaking so hard that I have to collapse between two arching boulders. I lean my head against the cool stone and sink to the ocean floor.

I try to salvage my body, my breath, my sense.

The Violent Sea got what she wanted. I can't remain in the ocean now—Father will find me, no matter where I swim to. His pride would never allow him to let me go unpunished. I have to seek sanctuary from *her*.

But if she thinks she's going to win this war she started, she's wrong. I'll play her game. I've spent my whole life acting as a puppet for my father. I'll let her believe she can control me too. Then I'll find a way to rid the ocean of her. If she came after me, she'll come after the rest of my siblings eventually, I'm sure of it.

This is the only way I can protect my family from her. This is the only way I will be able to regain Father's favor and return home.

By becoming human.

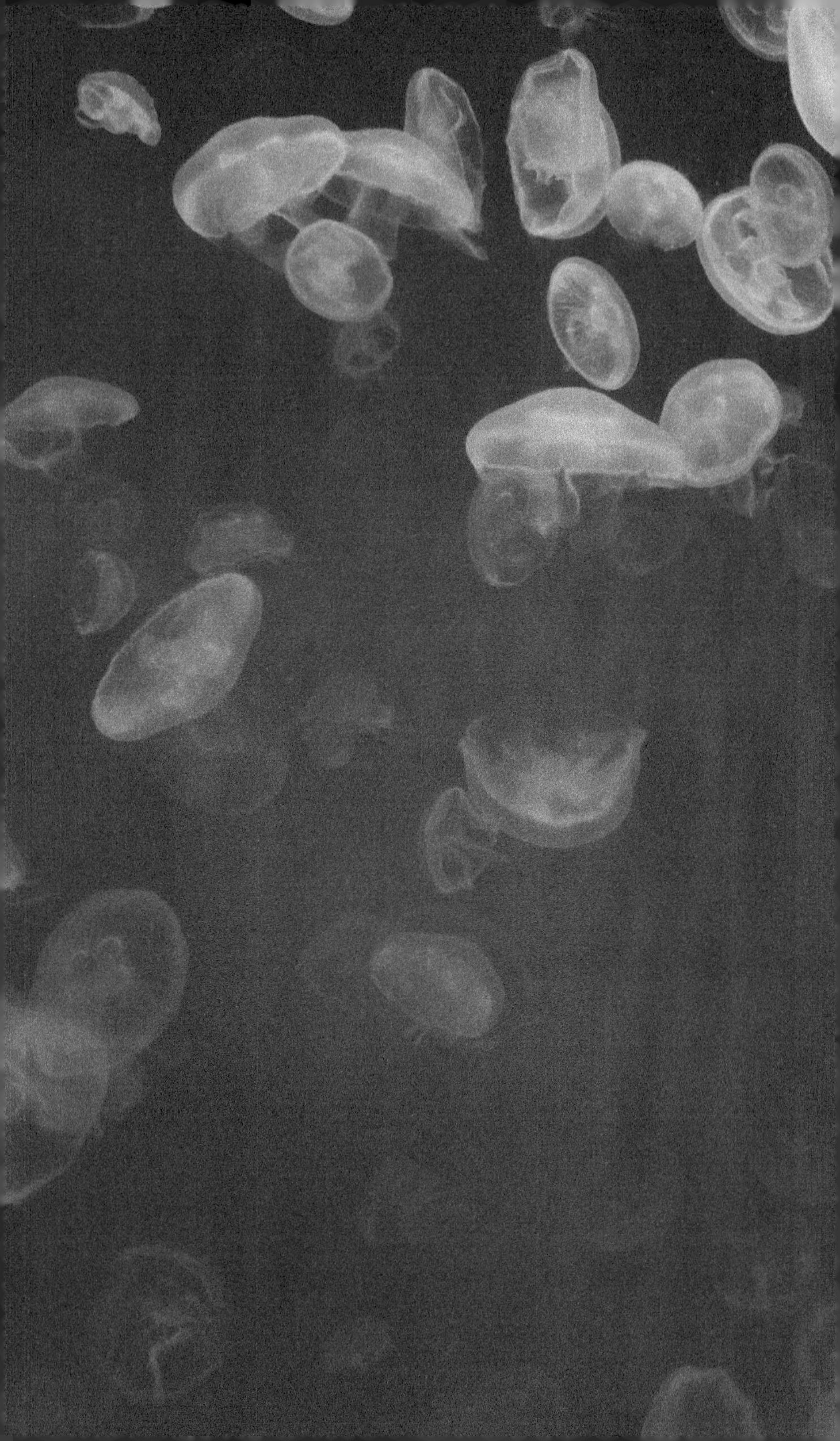

CHAPTER 7
VIOLA

"Look at what the tide pulled in," I muse, all eight of my tentacles draped over the sides of my throne. My hand clutches the divination bones I've been reading for the last hour as I consider the prince hovering in my doorway.

Every inch of his body is rigid, every breath controlled.

I address my soul-bound in the corner. "Who could have guessed the crown prince of Atlantis would seek help from a sea hag like me. It's almost embarrassing, isn't it, Fluke?"

"An utter humiliation," he replies without inflection.

I chuckle.

Aric's mouth tightens. His dark eyes sear into mine, the shade deepened by the glow of jellyfish coasting around his body. The muscles of his chest twitch as galvanic strings brush his skin. His red hair sticks straight up.

He looks nothing like Triton. I can't find a resemblance, even searching for it.

"You have me right where you want me, witch." The

prince's voice is soft, but not weak. "Now what are you going to do about it?"

"So many options," I reflect aloud. "Should I save us both the trouble and kill you now?" I drop the bones into the shallow, velveteen box in my lap. With the ivory coated in several layers of gold to make them sink in the water, they quickly fall into place, landing side by side by side. A clear *no* from Goddess Mora.

She stands at a distance, watching.

I know better anyway. His death would serve no purpose.

"I suppose I shouldn't." I drag myself upright, vaulting off the armrests to glide into the center of the room. "Tell me, Aric. What do you want more than anything else in the world?"

He doesn't respond, just holds himself there over the threshold, so still, he could be a corpse. So beautiful, he could be a challenge.

My tentacles spread beneath me, the muscles taut and expectant. I want to wrap myself around him. I want to drag him into the deep dark. I beckon him closer instead and give him room to do so.

Aric enters, but remains at a distance.

I don't need to be swept into one of his visions to know what he desires. "You want to hurt me, don't you?" As I circle him, Aric pivots. He returns my stare without blinking, cataloging every motion. I open my arms in invitation. "Take your best shot. I'll even look into your eyes to make it easier for you."

Again, he doesn't react.

I want him to explode, to spiral with rage like his father does. That's the kind of man I can anticipate, can outsmart and trick and punish. This silence isn't familiar. It isn't safe. I click my tongue. "Cowardly Prince."

Finally, that triggers something. His brown eyes flash, his hands fisting as he leans forward to hiss, "If you're going to give me legs, get on with it."

"I'm not going to *give* you anything," I snap. "I make dreams come true, but at a price."

"You destroyed my life by leading Triton to the gallery. Isn't that enough?"

I scoff. "I got rid of the chains keeping you here. I did you a favor."

"Is that how you justify it?" Aric's upper lip curls. "You ruined Andrine's life too. She has children and a mate that rely on that gallery's income. And now they have *nothing*."

I didn't know there was someone else involved when I showed up at the gallery, when I sent that letter and sealed Aric's fate. But what's done is done. Admission of any guilt I feel won't fix it. It won't soothe my hearts.

I avert my eyes. "I told you, it's not my desire to involve innocents in these matters…"

"Whatever helps you drift at night," he replies bitterly.

Nothing helps me drift. With the curse weighing on my body, I sink more often than not. My nerve endings stir and tingle, driving me closer to Aric without my conscious awareness of it.

I feel his heat reaching towards me as if in reply.

He lifts his chin in defiance.

"We need to discuss the terms," I tell him. "What you want, what I can provide, and what the limits are. In the end, you aren't just making a deal with your words. You surrender to me, body and soul. I am a fair witch. I will give you a chance at real freedom. A chance to remain above the waves until you die a human death, as long as you follow my rules."

He considers that. "What rules?"

"You need to accept the risk. You need to understand that the instant you break our agreement, you will be *mine*."

Aric rolls his shoulders. "I understand."

He hasn't accepted the risk yet, but he will. That was one thing the bones were sure about. He'll belong to me.

I withdraw from his body heat, my purple hair swirling in front of my face as I return to my chair. I perch on the edge of it, my hind tentacles bracing the wood behind me. One of them wraps around a silk bag resting beside my throne and draws it up beneath me.

"Do you remember the human princess?" I ask. Aric blinks a few times, confusion written across his features. I continue in a musing tone, "You must. You seemed so smitten when I caught you singing to her, when you were so lost together that she nearly tumbled over the edge into your arms. So I was thinking... by becoming human, you have an opportunity."

Aric shakes his head, but it's too late. I've already decided.

When I ran into him near the human palace, before I knew who he was, I did want to help. No siren I know has ever left a human victim alive, on shore or in the ocean. So at first, I didn't consider him the way I do predators. I wanted to know why he was singing to her, if he truly loved her despite the world between them.

The world can seem so small in the shadow of love. Land and beast and sea can mean little. It's true.

When I met Francis, my entire perspective of the ocean changed. He was an eel. I was a witch. It never should have been considered, much less attempted, but I had cared for him. Even when he was mute and weak and his body was too different to couple with, I cared for him. He was my most loyal companion, my closest friend. The spirits took pity on me and helped me change him, despite the fact that it was an act of supreme selfishness to do so.

Sea witches don't bind their hearts with selfish intent, not without consequences. I lost my entire coven when I chose Francis, and I imagine even sirens are not immune to that kind of irresistible love.

As Triton's son, though, Aric's love is sure to destroy. So here I am, taking care of it myself.

I rise from the chair. "The terms are thus: make the princess fall in love with you before sunset three days from now. That is, she has to agree to marry you. If you run, I will track you down." I halt within a handbreadth of him. "There is no place on earth that my heart will not feel you if the deal is broken."

The tanned skin around his eyes tightens. "And if I say no?"

My chin juts out as my tentacles twist beneath me. "Triton will come to retrieve you and drag you home." One meaningful look at my newest soul-bound, and he slips behind Aric to bar exit through the doorway.

Fluke inches in front of the hole in the ceiling.

Aric watches them move and piques one eyebrow. "You think you can keep me here?"

"I can and I will." I smile, and my mouth shifts. Three sets of shark teeth peek out from my gums, there and gone in the next heartbeat.

His eyes flicker. "And if I agree, what happens here? Right now?"

"You'll pay me for my trouble, then rise to the surface."

He frowns. "I have nothing to compensate you with."

I tilt my head one way, then the other, lifting my hands over his shoulders. Not touching, not claiming. *Not yet.* "Dear siren, that's the best part. It won't cost you too much.

Just," my fingertips graze his throat, and he flinches, "your voice."

"What?" he breathes.

Slivers of blue mark his topaz irises, aligned like two arrows pointing toward the surface. A sign, if I indulge the watery spirits and my Goddess—as always, I find them difficult to ignore. Maybe he was always meant to be here. Maybe I was always meant to have him, to ruin him.

"What's wrong with that?" I muse. "A mute tongue is nothing in the face of true love. In fact, I bet the human princess will fall easier without the obstacle. Men can ruin just about anything by opening their mouths."

"Why do you want my voice?" His body drifts back in a current. He's seemingly unaware of it, so I grasp his shoulder to keep him close.

"Because it means something to you," I explain quietly. Then I tell him a little more of the truth. "And it's as close to your power as I can get without ripping your heart out first."

He scans the room around us. He's looking for a way out, as they all do, but I pinch his chin to align his face with mine.

Aric's eyes latch onto the soul-bound behind me.

"Don't bother looking for help from them," I warn. "They can't hurt me. Our merged souls won't allow it."

His gaze darkens. "Does that mean that before you reap me, I can defend myself? *I* can still hurt you, if I wish to?"

"You could certainly try, but I don't recommend it."

He smirks. "I don't imagine you would."

"Just say the word, Prince, and we can take a whirl with another of your fantasies. I beg of you to do better this time. The kraken was unimaginative."

A scowl screws his features. Poor, sensitive siren, no longer coddled and pampered in his enormous castle. It must hurt.

"One request, before I accept," he grinds out.

"Anything." I shouldn't have said that. It was too great an admission.

I'm desperate for him. The cycle is humming through my body, making me want him in more ways than one, more ways than are acceptable. It aches in my lower abdomen and back. The kind of ache that makes my hips swivel, an ache that burns through my core and has me twirling my tentacles in an attempt to ease even a fraction of the tension. I won't give in to it. *I won't.*

Aric doesn't hesitate, doesn't realize how true my *'anything'* was. "I need to send a message to one of my siblings. I assume you have a way to do that without my father finding out about it."

Narrowing my eyes, I say, "I do, but they won't be able to save you."

"I don't want to be saved." It sounds like the truth.

"All right, then."

I swim to the shelves and dig through my jars, pulling out three from the very back. I carry them to the opposite corner of the room and drag the covered cauldron to the center of the room. Then I rip the dark, weighted sheet away.

An orb of air sits in the cauldron—there's only so many spells I can cast with soggy ingredients. There's only so many spells that can be created with items solely from the sea. I snap my fingers and light erupts in the center of the orb, a blazing white flame. Thrusting my hands into the center, the light flickers to gold as I methodically uncork the vials. The flames crackle with every addition. Star anise and rosemary and basil. As they burn, I long to smell the symphony of herbs coalescing. But they're soon gone, surrendered to the spell, and I'm turning to face Aric again.

He watches the cauldron with uncertainty, the amber

light shedding from it coloring his eyes black and his hair dark brown.

I offer him an enchanted scroll. "Will what you wish to be written into the parchment, then toss it into the fire while thinking of where you want it to appear. It will listen to you."

"How do I know it will work?"

What he's asking is whether I'm lying to him, cheating him.

"You won't." I smile dryly. "You'll just have to trust me."

His lips press into a flat line. He surveys the scroll in my hand, then the cauldron again, and slowly draws closer. Without meeting my gaze, he takes the scroll from me.

The scroll begins pulsing with golden light as he stares at it. Moments pass, and the light flares brighter and brighter as the parchment is etched with his silent thoughts, until he looks up into the flame and the scroll dulls to a faint glow. His brown eyes burn a luminous red as he pushes the scroll into the orb of light. The flames consume his message, licking to the very edges of the orb. Amber fades to gold, then fades to white.

I snap my fingers again, and the room goes dark.

He doesn't look away from me. "All right," he breathes. "Let's get this over with."

I draw the silk bag up from beneath my tentacles and tug it open. I extend it toward him. "Pull a stone."

"Why?" He eyes the runes with trepidation.

"Because my Goddess likes to play as much as I do," I purr.

She and the spirits of the ocean play a vital role in my deals. I can share my shifting abilities with another only by their grace and assistance. Soul strings, after all, are a matter of spirit; they move on a plane beyond the physical. Triton's curse or not, I answer to the ocean, and I know they'll tell me exactly how much Aric needs to suffer.

"The rune you draw will determine how badly this hurts," I explain.

His head bobs back. "That's a cruel game."

"I never said I wasn't cruel," I retort. "Only that I'm fair. If you're frightened, then it's only because you have good reason to be, and so the game is just."

His face tightens, his jaw clenching as he stuffs his hand into the bag and rips out the first rune he touches. He throws it at my chest. I snatch the crystal out of the water with a barely-contained chuckle.

When the rune settles face-up in my palm, my heart skips a beat. I grimace at the marking.

"What is it?" Aric's voice wavers.

"You drew The Gift." The spirits don't want his transformation to hurt. If I was a younger, less damaged witch, I might even interpret it as a demand for pleasure. Like with every other divination ritual I've performed today, I come away confused. "My Goddess seems to like you."

"I don't care," he grumbles.

I glare up at him. "*You should.* She's granting you more mercy than you deserve."

He tries to pull away, but I still have his shoulder in my grasp. At this point, I don't plan on letting go. He's *mine*. His head inclines, a sharpness surfacing in his eyes as he whispers, "I think you should judge your own reflection before you judge me, witch."

Heat as complete as the sun blazes in my belly.

One of my arms shifts into a sharp whip and lashes his chest before he can react. One direction and then the opposite, carving an 'X' into the skin over his heart. Blood immediately starts pissing from the cut. I tighten my hold on his shoulder as he tries to recoil, and my heart flares with light, washing his pained expression in gold.

He reaches for the point of impact, but I bind his wrists with two tentacles.

"I thought I drew a merciful rune," he growls.

"You did, but all hearts must first bleed." I tug him forward and align the opening of my chest with his.

Flutters of sensation skip beneath my skin. Bewilderment fills his eyes, his body stiffens, but I turn my attention downward, watching as a brilliant worm of light crawls out of my chest cavity and burrows into his exposed muscle. The string for my third and final heart.

He gasps at the first touch.

I don't let this string rip and rend like the others have, the way I've ripped into Fluke and Maggot and my newest soul-bound. I *guide* this one. My breast vibrates against his, the heartstring sensing every curve and wind of the veins leading to his heart. No pain, no suffering. I haven't formed a connection without them in several decades, but I won't disobey my Goddess, even if I don't fully understand why she's asked this of me. She's never led me astray before.

Aric's eyes lift from the wound and meet mine.

Without the pain to latch onto, our binding takes on an edge of warmth. That ache threads into me. It throbs in my head and my chest and my core, driving all thought into the darkest abyss. The grip I have on his shoulder intensifies, my nails digging into him and causing a second bleed. His essence wraps around me. The sea moves. Trapping us in a whirl of copper and light. Before I can stop myself, my tentacles wrap around his tail. I cling to him, pulling him so close that I can't remember a day when we weren't connected.

I sense the brokenness in him, the splintering of a thousand shipwrecks.

His body softens, leaning into me rather than away, and my lips brush his as a consequence of our proximity. Still, he stays. Our eyes are open gates, every emotion passing back and forth as our hearts finish stitching together. The heart itself is only a gateway to the soul beneath.

I feel his being surrender to mine, the inside softer than expected. *Giving.*

The gift.

I blink, my mind sobering a fraction. I refuse to believe it means *anything*. The light dims—a sign that the binding is complete, but I don't withdraw my string from his chest yet. I still need payment.

His gaze sharpens, the effects of our binding fading for him too. "Finish it," he growls.

"I have a request first, dear Prince," I mutter, cupping the back of his neck. He raises an eyebrow, as if to ask what more I could possibly want. He doesn't realize that I want *everything*. "I want you to address me by my name. Enough of this *witch* nonsense. I know perfectly well what I am."

His teeth bare in a silent threat. "If you insist, *Viola*."

I cradle his jaw in my other hand. "Good," I murmur. "Now *sing*."

I feel the vibrations of his vocal cords first, thrumming against my skin. The heartstring hums along with it. I absorb his voice like a shattered bottle of wine in shallow water, letting it spread into me, temporarily staining me as it erupts from his mouth into mine. His voice is a power all its own.

I swallow it.

Consuming just enough of his soul to memorize it, I lock the familiarity away in case I ever need to use it to track him down. I realize as it settles in my center that his voice, his being, the sliver of him that I can feel but cannot possess, is *almost* enough to satisfy me.

It's the closest to whole I've felt in a long, long time.

Aric is Triton's flesh and blood, an inheritor of the throne and certainly a match to his wretched soul. Heart bonds are gateways to the soul. And children... don't children carry bits and pieces of their parents?

All these years under Triton's curse, I've been forced to accept that I will never be free, that the only way out was to wait for him to grow tired of me and free me from this torment, to wait until I could take his life myself, take his power and use it to fill the empty hollows of my heart. It was an impossible solution.

What if Aric's soul is enough to dissolve the curse?

I wish I could test the theory. I wish I could swallow the rest of him and attempt to make myself whole, but now we have this agreement between us. This heartstring. Goddess Mora and the spirits of the ocean will ruin me if I break it.

It's a trivial annoyance.

He'll fail on his own soon enough.

Hope swells through me like a tide, so strong that I have to forcefully wrench myself off Aric as his new body settles into place. His green tail splits into two long legs, and they begin to kick beneath him as he realizes he can no longer breathe. His eyes bulge, and he slices his arms through the water, struggling toward the hole in the ceiling.

We're in a shallow area of the sea, close enough to shore that I'm not concerned with his ability to make it there alive.

Still, my chest constricts, my heartslight flickering as I watch him strain for the surface. He's my last hope. I won't let him die before I can reap him.

I wave a hand to capture Fluke's attention and whisper my command. "Help him."

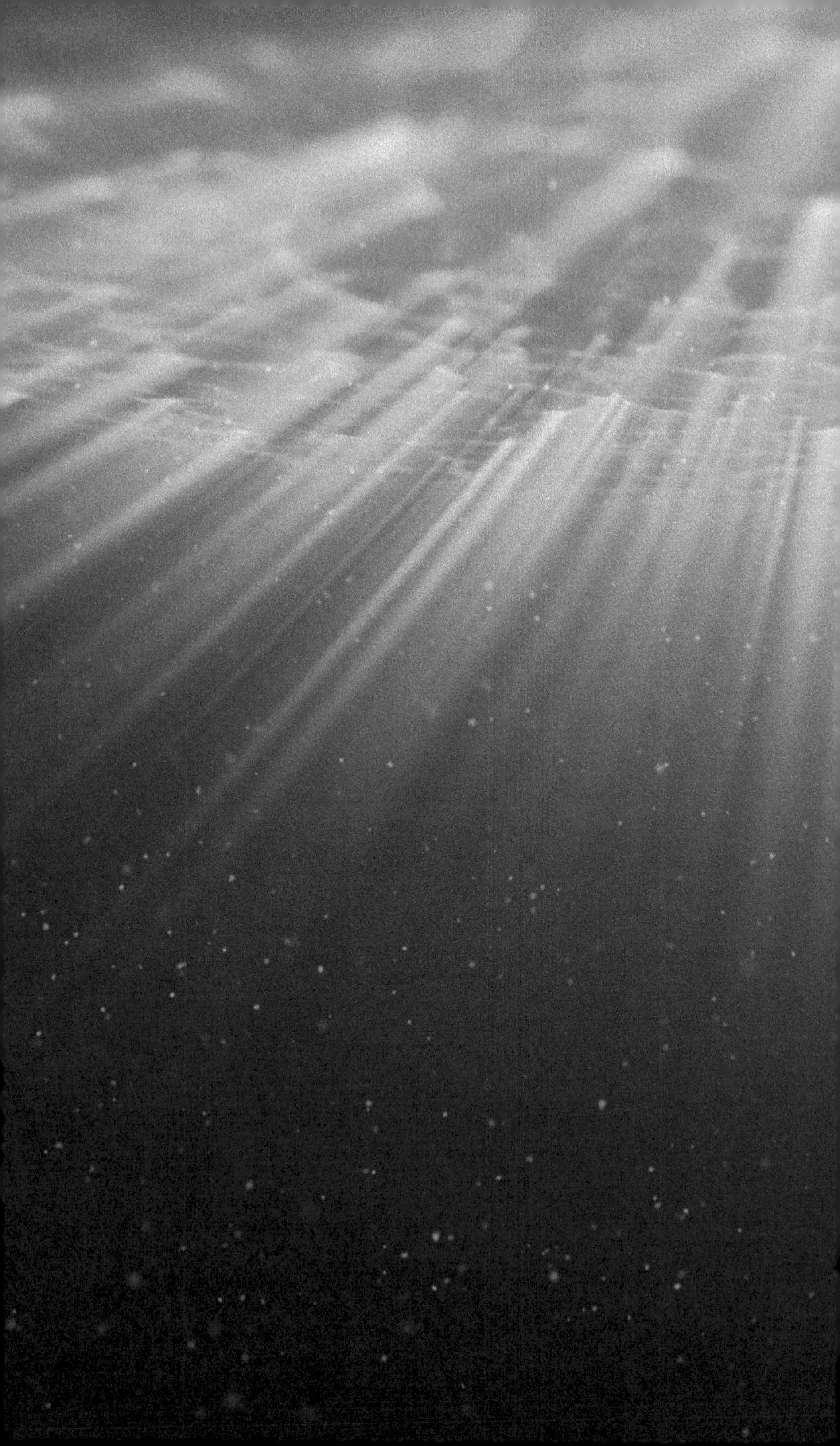

CHAPTER 8
ARIC

It's too bright. Thin, crimson veins pulse behind my closed eyes, and I hesitate to open them.

I'm not underwater anymore.

Water laps at my hips, splashing up onto my upper torso and face. My cheek is pressed against something hard and rough. I'm shivering. The atmosphere burns in my nostrils, smelling of salt and seaweed, and I can't remember my senses ever recognizing a distinction between the two before this moment.

I'm not sure I like the smell of the ocean.

When I crack an eye open, I'm momentarily blinded by light dancing across the surface of the water. I squint, and my sight adjusts.

Fluke lounges on a boulder adjacent to me, flicking his tail in the waves. That's where the droplets hitting my face are coming from.

The Violent Sea's soul-bound is an attractive mer—it's a striking truth in the sun. He has a feminine face with hard angles around his jaw, and a lithe torso. Light brown skin. And his eyes are as blue as a tropical sea. He belongs in the beds of nobility. Hell, I've bedded less in my boredom around court. How did he find himself in *her* grasp?

After how she hunted me, I don't doubt her ability to ruin anyone if it suits her desires.

I raise my head despite the pounding in it, and he snaps upright. "Finally. You're awake."

I'm not so sure about that.

A haze weighs on my mind, and I can barely keep my eyes open. My ears ring loudly. I touch the side of my head, noticing the lack of gossamer skin attached to my ears. They're smooth now, small and rounded, less bony. The last thing I remember is dragging myself out of the sea witch's ship and swimming for the distant surface with my ineffectual legs.

My legs...

I look at my lower half. Two hairy, muscular pillars of flesh replace my scales. One thought, and the ten toes at the end wiggle under my command. It's incredible, and strange.

Saltwater drips into my eyes, and I reach up to push my hair out of my face, wincing as my fingertips graze a tender spot on my temple. Ah, yes, I remember now. I was a few strokes from the surface when Fluke caught up with me and knocked me out cold.

My lips curl back in snarl, but when I open my mouth, nothing comes out. The air seethes between my teeth. I try again, a hand cupping my throat. Not even the slightest vibration.

My voice really is gone.

Fluke smirks and slips off his boulder to swim to mine. "I guess it's convenient that you can't interrupt me," he mutters. "Because I have much to share with you and little time to do it. I need you to shake your head yes or no, don't waste my time and don't lie to me. Do you understand?"

I glance around.

The ocean stretches out behind me, the water darker along the horizon. In front of me, there's a nearby shore, with a brief stretch of sand backing up to a cliffside. It's secluded, but well used, with an assemblage of human belongings crowding one side of the beach. A boat and fishing nets.

Fluke isn't blocking my way to shore, but he might if I ignore him.

Sea salt burns down my airway as I breathe in again. Yeah, I definitely don't like the smell of the ocean. There's something else beneath the salt and seaweed, something musty. Is that what fish smell like up here, what *I* smell like up here? Festering death?

Fluke clears his throat, impatience sharpening his gaze.

I might as well hear what he has to say. Slowly, I peel myself up into a sitting position and nod.

He braces his hands on my boulder, his webbed fingers rapping as he gathers his thoughts. Then he meets my gaze, and his eyes burn into mine. "Are you truly Triton's son?"

I don't want to think about what my father must think of me right now. A coward, a disappointment. *A waste.* I nod again.

He leans over the boulder and whispers, "And you want the witch dead as much as he does?"

I consider that question.

Father makes his disdain for The Violent Sea perfectly obvious to the public, with the humiliating plays and his grandiose speeches. I can't help but see it differently now. He may wish she were dead, but he's never ordered an assassination, and there's no shortage of paid killers in Atlantis. I do wonder now if there's a reason for his hesitation. I've been suspicious since the moment I met Viola, since I realized she was more beautiful and charming than Father ever let on. It's obvious he keeps his own secrets.

I think I may want her dead more than Triton ever has.

On the other hand, Fluke could be setting a trap for me, feeling out my loyalty at The Violent Sea's command. I try to recall his demeanor under the surface. He stuck to the shadows in that shipwreck, moved only by her orders, but I don't remember seeing a scrap of affection in his face. Shadows are for the reluctant, I know that well. Now, there's an eagerness in his stare, a spark that was missing in the sea witch's presence.

I cast aside the risk and incline my head in confirmation. Whatever this is, I have a feeling both our fates hinge on it.

His eyes flit to either side of us, scanning the surface before he leans in. "We have a chance to kill Viola," he whispers. "It'll take some time and human assistance, but I have a plan that will work. I couldn't do anything while her last soul-bound was alive." He shakes his head, a look of disgust marring his features. "The fool was obsessed with her, would have sold me out in an instant if he thought it would get his cock closer to her cunt. But now that she's killed him, there's no one left to protect her."

My fingers dig into the rock. Her last soul-bound actually *wanted* her, and she murdered him? She's insane.

Fluke's grimace twists with faint amusement. "She intends to spend most of the next couple days on land with you, so she'll be distracted. I just need you to ensure that she doesn't look my way long enough to figure things out. Keep her occupied, play her games, let her think she's winning."

His breath catches, and his brow creases as he seems to

think of something new. "And for Oblivion's sake, don't fuck her—this might be the only chance we have to be free, and if you die and mess it up for me, I'll search the foam for your passing spirit so I can kill you again myself."

I roll my eyes.

Me, fucking the sea witch? The creature who killed my mother and forced me to surrender my heart?

Yeah, he definitely doesn't have to worry about that.

Although, if I concentrate, I can still feel that foreign heartstring tugging at me. She's inside now, so deep and permanent that I'll never forget the feel of her. For as long as I live, I'll remember what it felt like to have her invade my heart, to travel along my veins and light them with her brilliance. It was terror. It was ecstasy. It was evil dressed in beauty and warmth.

How could a blue-blooded whore feel like that?

Fluke sees the aversion on my face and smiles. "All right," he sighs. "I can't share anything more with you, not yet." He pushes off the boulder, returning to the rock he was sitting on when I woke.

As the surface shifts under his hand, I realize there's a large piece of fabric there. A ripped sail.

Fluke tosses it at me. "You'll need this. The land-walkers don't appreciate bare skin, and you no longer have a scale sleeve to protect you."

He's right. My entire crotch is on display in a way I'm not used to.

I slip into the water with the sail in hand. It only takes a few moments to swim into the shallows, the water steadying me as I test out my legs. They're shaky, but strong. The sea witch gave me legs, but they still seem inherently *mine*. Without scales, my father's handiwork is visible. From my hips to feet, my skin carries the thin, horizontal scars from his lessons.

A part of me had hoped for new skin, but this magic must not work that way.

I practice bending my knees as I tie the sail around my hips. Waves pummel my lower back and I can barely keep myself standing against them.

Fluke slithers up beside me, one hand resting behind his head as he turns over to face the sky. "There's movement up top." He points to where the sun is cresting over the peak of the cliff.

Faint voices carry towards us, distorted by the drop. Shadows stretch outward, across the beach and ocean towards us as the bodies draw close enough to the edge to be noticed. Stone steps are nestled into the left side of the cliff-face. A staircase.

"I'm fairly certain this is palace grounds...so all *you* have to do is convince them to house you."

Without a voice? I shoot him a level glare.

"You'll think of something, siren. I have every confidence. We can't afford for you to fail—trust me, the sea witch will reap you at the first sign of negligence—so *don't*. Don't stop seducing the princess until we have Viola staked through all three of her hearts." He smiles wickedly. "I'll even help you get the humans' attention before I go."

Fluke slots two fingers between his lips and releases a pitch so piercing that I recoil farther onto the beach. In the next moment, he's gone. The ebbing wave ripples slightly where he dove into the tide.

Beastly roars erupt behind me, staccato and deep, completely unfamiliar and hair-raising.

I whip around to face the stairs, where the cries echo from. A cacophony of pounding steps follow. Louder and louder they come, until it seems as though the beasts might be right upon me.

What has Fluke done?

I twist, stumbling up onto the dry beach. Sand sticks between my toes, tickling the strange new skin there—but I ignore the wonderful sensation.

My eyes catch on the water vessel sitting on the far edge of the beach.

I clamber into the old, decaying boat. Stale water sloshes around my feet, cleaning the sand away and replacing it with slick, tacky mold. The sway of the half-beached hull knocks me off balance and nearly sends me over the edge into the water, but I catch myself at the last second. My hands land on a paddle, and I pull it into my grasp, turning it toward the four-legged beasts snarling back on land.

What are these things? They have slobbering mouths and sharp yellow teeth. Straggly hair all over. They're trying to clamber into the boat.

I swipe the oar, and they snap at the splintered wood but thankfully stay back. My legs are trembling.

It's difficult to keep my balance.

They say humans dance like this? How would one spin, how would they laugh and revel while focusing so intensely on staying upright? This is complete madness.

A feminine voice comes from the stairs, accompanied by the frantic clicking of what must be the woman's steps. "Tippet, Dash! Come back here, you dumb mutts. There's no one down there—no one!"

What she referred to as *mutts* ignore her shouting, and she lets out a high-pitched squeal. The sound echoes down the narrow staircase, and I cringe. It's truly the worst thing I've ever heard.

The female emerges on the beach.

I thought the voice seemed familiar.

Angel Face stumbles a step when her eyes land on me. Her frizzy curls are partially pinned back, but the rest of her hair tumbles down to frame her trussed bust. Green satin ribbons criss-cross the front of her bodice, and her skirt cascades with several layers of thin fabric, white and tan and dark red florals. The colors bring out her eyes, a lighter brown now than I've ever seen them, wide and illuminated by the daylight.

I prefer her night clothes. Just looking at the laces and ruffles I'd have to get past to fuck her makes me tired.

"What—who are—" she sputters, her fingers tracing the drapes of her dress. "Why are you down here? These are palace grounds."

I stare at her, maintaining my defense against the mutts and attempting to get a clear shot at her eyes. But she's surveying the beach around us. By the time she looks back at me, I have a mutt gnawing on the oar and swaying the boat by how hard it whips the wood back and forth. After a few moments of struggle, I manage to wrench it out of the beast's jaw.

Angel Face steps forward with both hands on her tiny waist, and I barely have a moment to catch my breath before she says, "Well, don't just stand there. Answer me."

I should be charming her, *somehow*, but I can't help but glare at her for that. Perhaps I prefer all of her better in the night, in the darkness of her balcony. When I have the upper hand, and she knows she's at my mercy. When she's afraid to speak.

Lifting one hand to my throat, I tap it with my fingertips, and then draw a line across with my thumb.

Her thin eyebrows pull together. "You can't talk?"

I shake my head.

"Oh. I see." She steps forward again, her expression pinched as she scans the ocean beside us. "Well, where is your boat?"

I have no answer for that, so I remain still as I continue to pursue her gaze.

She sighs irritably. "How did you get here?"

I grasp a handful of the sail and glance down at it, rubbing the silk between my fingers as I try to think of a plan.

Her small gasp lifts my head.

Angel Face studies the fabric in my hand from afar, her jaw hinged open. When she looks at my face again, her honey brown eyes are a little more liquid. "Are you—did you survive a ship wreck?"

Relief floods my veins. Yes, that's perfect. I nod eagerly.

"Oh, you poor thing." She lets out a high-pitched whistle, summoning the mutts back to her. "Let him alone, boys. He's harmless."

Well. I wouldn't say *that*.

They back away though, bowing their boxy heads as they return to Angel Face's side. One of the mutts continues to bare its teeth, but I get the feeling neither will attack without her clear order to do so. It's a keen reminder of The Violent Sea and her two bound hearts.

I'll be her third if I can't pull this off.

I approach the beached end of the hull, bracing my hands on the rough edges to keep from falling over. My wrestling with the mutt pushed the sinking vessel farther into the water.

"Here." Angel Face steps forward and wraps her hands around my upper arms. "Let me help you get out of that boat. Haven't gotten rid of those sea legs yet, have you?"

Honestly, she doesn't help me at all.

When I'm steady on land, she backs away, her arms crossing over her chest. Her fingers graze the religious pendant resting on her bosom, as if searching for answers on its surface.

"Well, let's see here," she presses her fingertips to her lips, rapping them lightly as her eyes scour my body, "I can't bring you up without a name." She nods at the oar in my hand. "Do you *know* how to write? Can you draw your name in the sand?" She exaggerates the last question, as if I were deaf as well as mute.

I wonder if she talks to everyone this way. It's deplorable.

I extend the mangled oar between us and draw an A in the sand. Then I hesitate. I can't tell her my full name. She knows it. Thankfully, I'd been smart enough to keep my face in shadow during our nights together, so she's yet to recognize me, but if she finds out I'm her mysterious visitor, it will complicate everything. She'll have questions I can't even begin to answer. I only have three days to get this right.

"A." She tests the letter in her mouth. After a moment, she slaps a smile onto her face and adds, "I like it."

No, she doesn't.

"My name is Hazel." She throws her hand toward me, palm down, fingers together and softly curved. A human offering, I think.

I cradle her wrist in one hand, considering the strange, thin covering on it. A glove, I suddenly remember. I've seen them in paintings. With my other hand, I pinch the material on her middle finger and tug the lace away.

"Oh," she inches back but I keep a firm grip on her arm, "wait, what are you—"

I slip her bare hand into mine, squeezing slightly, leaning in to meet her eyes with a smile.

Her breath catches, swelling behind her confined breasts.

A laugh bubbles out of her as she shyly cocks her head. "You know, you seem so very familiar. Have we met before?"

Looking into her eyes, I whisk us away—into her mind, a place I've become very well acquainted with—and turn her attention to a small speck of light in the nothingness. I form myself there, my unruly hair swept back in a bun, my body covered in a soft blue tailored uniform, medals pinned to my breast. From the light, that doorway that leads from my head to hers, I walk toward her until my features come into focus. Holding her gaze, I bow at the waist.

When I pull my mind back, Angel Face's eyes are alight. She's clutching my forearms in return now.

"I *do* know you. You're a captain of an ally brigade. We met at a ball or something, didn't we?"

Yes, in her mind, we have. In that new, sparkling memory.

I smile wider.

She scrambles to add, "Your service is *greatly* appreciated. Papa will be so troubled to hear of your tribulation on the ocean, but at least you survived to tell the tale—oh, well I suppose you won't exactly *tell* us, will you?" She giggles to herself. "Don't worry, Captain, we'll get you a bath and some food, and you'll be good as new."

What in Great Oblivion is a bath?

As we ascend the stone staircase together and I listen to her prattle on about things I can't quite understand, I wonder what it would cost to get The Violent Sea to take away *her* voice too.

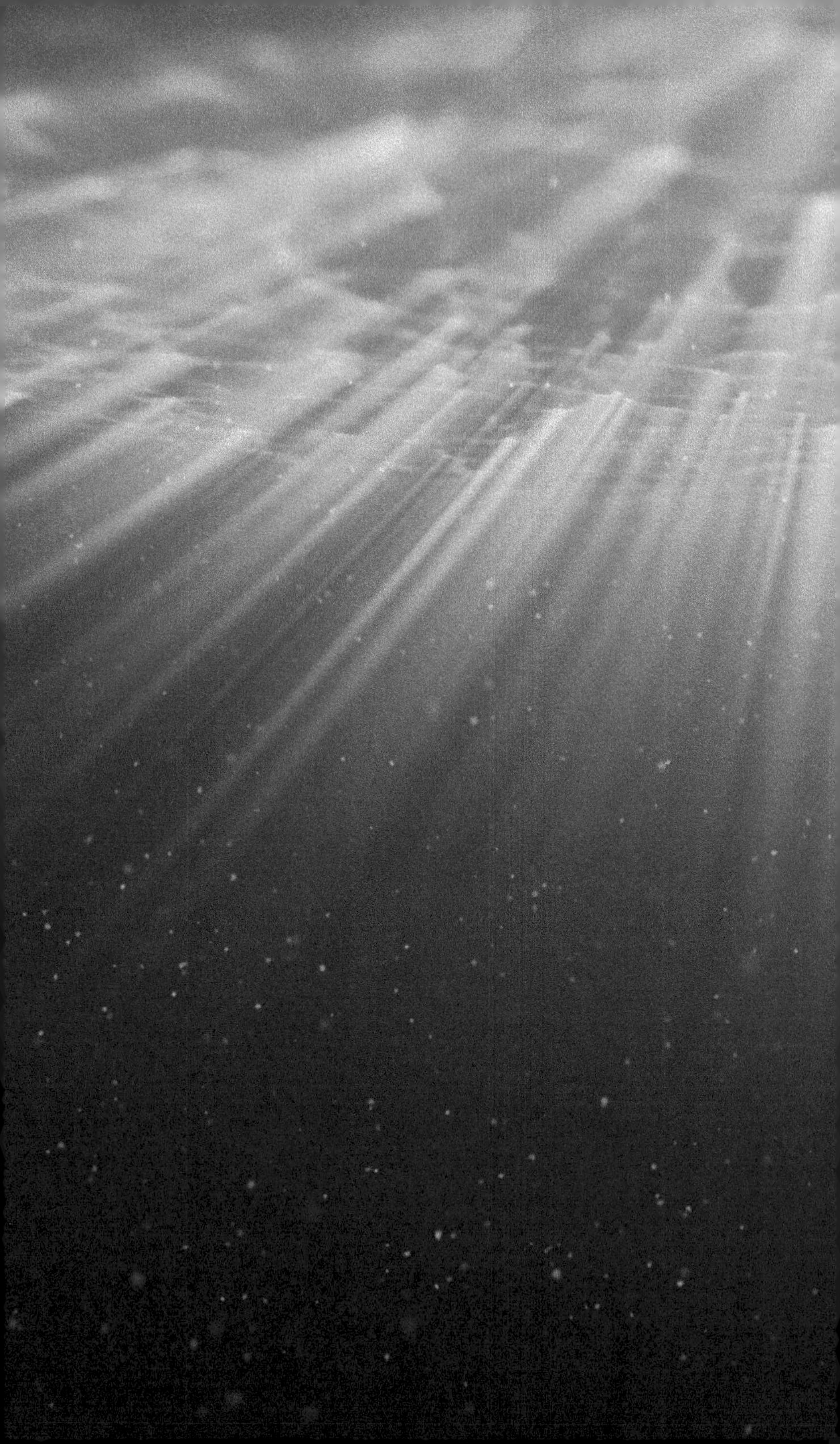

CHAPTER 9
ARIC

As it turns out, 'the bath' is simply a poor imitation of the sea, but without salt or fish or seaweed. The humans fill a boat-like shell with saccharine liquid, let it foam violently, and then expect you to flop around in it like a beached fish.

It was an odd experience.

I keep tugging at the clothes I was given. My pants suffocate me in all the wrong places, and the shirt is lined with the most confusing contraptions called *buttons,* which I only got halfway through before I abandoned the tedious task entirely.

I'm standing on the balcony of the room Angel Face led me to some number of hours ago.

My forearms brace the railing as I stare out at the sea and wait for her return. She ordered the staff to prepare me for dinner before she left to talk with her father, and I'm still buzzing with anticipation. If I lean over the edge of my balcony, I can see another terrace off to the right, one with small red rosebuds growing in a box on the railing. And beyond that, a crag I definitely recognize. That's *her* room.

A set of stairs and a few narrow hallways are all that stand between my bed and hers. This will be too easy.

I smile.

Though I come from the most ornate city in the ocean—a place of procured beauty and riches and luminous stone—I can't resist the architecture of human hands. The palace thrives on these warm, blustery cliffs. Just as life Beneath honors the night and all its starlight, this place celebrates the sun in all its spectacular, blinding glory.

The castle dances with the rocky ledge, in some spots pulling away from the cliff to allow for a garden of strange seaweed, which irritated my feet when I walked across it. In other spots, particularly on the left side of the palace, spires are nestled into the cliff-face. Like the one I stand on now.

With each new room I was led through on the way to this one, I grew in awe, inundated with such admiration that I struggled to form a clear thought. So many twisted columns and peaked, ivory windows. Floors carved into with delicate stones and walls pieced together with colorful tiles. Color everywhere.

Atlantis is grim and dark in comparison.

This castle is a priceless treasure, and I don't doubt that when the time comes for this wonder to fall into the sea or the ocean eventually rises to claim it, that it will be the new Atlantis. Nothing is forever—not even rock.

I walk a wide circle on the balcony before returning to the bedroom.

The sun is aligned with the opening of my veranda, washing the interior of the gilded room with brutal daylight. My feet burn against the red floor. The maids couldn't find a pair of shoes that fit me, so they sent someone away to fetch something suitable. I'm barefoot in the meantime.

My fingers skim the silken covers as I walk between two of the bed posts.

Honestly, I don't see much purpose for covering my feet in this place. It's all so soft. So level. I've been pacing for most of the sun's stretch across the sky. My hair is at last dry where I tied it back, and I'm no longer tripping over my own feet as much.

All there is to do is walk. And think. And wonder.

Since the maids left, I've seen no one, heard nothing. In all the ocean, I never felt this isolated. There was always something in the water beside me. Predator or prey. In Father's palace, I had my siblings and servants. Court life sprawling all around me.

Here, I'm just... existing.

I think of the mer I met in my gallery—how they bought novelties to fill up their homes, giving away precious happiness for beautiful things that could not speak or reach, that could not comfort beyond the eyes. Did they come to regret it? Did they ever look at their homes and wish for what they gave away? They gave from their finite well of memory for the endlessness of the physical, and yet I'd never seen a people who were so unsatisfied.

Perhaps it is the same for humans.

As the sun touches the horizon and spirits of color burst across the sky, a knock sounds on the bedroom door.

It opens, and several guards file in. I saw some of them shuffling around the halls as we walked through the palace earlier, but judging from the way they stare now—with thin mouths and stiff postures—they must be on new orders concerning *me*. One of the men steps forward and gestures for me to exit the room. No explanation.

It's not as if I can protest. I have no fucking voice.

I enter the corridor, and the guards fall into place around me. I focus on what I can see as we move through the palace, down flights of stairs and through foyer after foyer. The walls and ceiling are built in tiers of textured stone. Stories are created with shimmering tiles of cobalt and chartreuse, of viridian and scarlet and ebony. The decorative patterns are so intricate, I imagine it must have taken years to put it together. It's daylight encapsulated, room after room. Each archway is carved into an artwork of points and curves. The floor is a sheet of checkered black-and-white silk, the cold of it radiating up into the soles of my feet.

Fire sconces replace the windows and cast the palace walls in shadow for a brief time.

Just as quickly, the halls open up again to a large banquet hall. Glass lines the wall before me, looking out at the foaming sea and the distant sunset, water glittering beneath it. As we enter the room, the guards who accompanied me disperse, taking up position between me and who is already here, waiting for me.

A long, polished table sits in the center of the floor. Chairs with delicate backings and a handful of humans occupy the far end. The human king stands where the table comes to a head. I recognize him easily; the way he holds himself with authority and looks across the room with a thousand thoughts weighing on his expression. The crown helps too.

He's the root of his daughter, the earth that grew her, all brown skin and dark lines. Wild eyebrows and a thick beard.

He glares at me.

Angel Face refuses to meet my gaze, sitting with her eyes downcast to the King's left.

When one of the guards nudges my back, I realize I've

stopped walking on the threshold, so I continue forward to the table.

"Captain A, I presume," the King greets me in a cultured, resonant voice. "My daughter tells me she found you in the shallows below our home."

I halt in front of the King and bow. Angel Face doesn't lift her head. Something's wrong here.

Warily, I nod.

"How is that possible?" That question comes from beside me, from the chair to the King's right side. I twist to face the old man in it.

His back bends at an unusual angle. He wears dark robes unlike anything the others at the table wear, and his neck and fingers are weighed down with more fine jewelry than even the King. He leans forward on the table with his leathery hands and sneers, "How did you survive a wreck we have not heard head or tail about, *and* the open waters? How was *our* shore the first you reached?"

The King interjects, "How does my dearest Hazel remember you and I do not?"

"Well," the old man scoffs, lowering his voice, "I think there's an obvious answer for that, Majesty. Consider the way he looks at her. I told you Hazel would be better off at the convent, where she can't get herself into trouble."

Angel Face raises her head then, to squint at the robed man.

The lines of the King's face deepen. "You better not be suggesting what I think you are, Archibald."

"Of course not, my King," he replies at once, lifting a hand to press against his heart. I can't sense any true remorse in his eyes, though. I can't sense anything. His pupils swirl, cloudy around the edges. "I am simply reminding you that we have no proof that the Captain is who he says he is, or if Hazel has told us the truth. We can never be too careful when it comes to our country's precious flower, can we? We still have time to dedicate her."

The King grimaces; whatever dedication Archibald refers to, I don't think he likes it.

"I didn't lie, Papa," Angel Face murmurs. "I swear it. Perhaps you aren't looking close enough at him to remember."

The King's eyes search her face, the strong line of his nose casting a silhouette in the fading daylight. Finally, he sighs, inclines his head in assent to her request, and takes a step toward me. The guards to either side of him step forward too.

His consideration is shrewd.

I let him fester with his doubt for an instant, only a heartbeat, before I wrap him up in memories the way I did his daughter. I've seen enough of the palace to put together a setting now. He's sitting on a throne as I kneel at his feet. I've brought him and his daughter presents from a far-off shore.

"Why, my word, Hazel," he mutters as I pull away from his mind. "I think you might be right."

The chair beside me scrapes against the floor. I don't acknowledge the old man leaving his seat. "Majesty," Archibald protests, hunching close to the King. "We drew up all of our records, we *scoured* them."

Archibald glances at me briefly, and I return the stare, trying to lock him into it, trying to extend my song to him so that we can be done with his interference. But it doesn't work.

The King rolls his eyes and pats the old man's arm. "We must have missed him somehow. Your sight is not what it once was. I'm sure you would remember him too, if you could see him."

Ah, his sight is failing him. That's why my song can't influence him.

This is an inconvenience, but rectifiable. I turn the full force of my song back on the King, barraging him with images of the two of us drinking and laughing, getting permission to dance with his daughter. I paint myself as a perfect gentleman.

The King smiles and reaches out to slap me on the shoulder.

"Yes, I remember you perfectly now. I'm sorry for the misunderstanding, Captain. Let us blame the mead and the weight of your recent hardship—it's had a physical effect on you. My condolences on the loss of your ship and crew." He steps back and gestures for me to take a seat. "You must be starving."

Warmth floods my veins. I *am* hungry. My stomach's been aching for hours, and if the potent scents coming from the door on the other end of the room can be trusted, the meal is suited for royalty.

As I sit at the nearest open seat, across from the princess, I examine the wall to either side of the entrances.

Nude sculptures border the doors, man and woman, thin sheets rippling over their curves as if that were enough to soften the state of their undress. Paintings fill the wall, more of the human body on display in each one. For a *reserved* people, they certainly like to surround themselves with droves of salacious art.

I recognize what the princess once described to me as angels, stout bodies fawning across clouds and trees, round faces and moony eyes. Grossly childish.

I'll be referring to the princess as Hazel from now on.

The other members of the court converse quietly, building a hum around the table. None of them speak directly to me, but I'm certain they are speaking about me with how often they glance in my direction. I keep my expression pleasant, a smile strapped across my mouth. Hazel sneaks glances at me too, each too fleeting to return or properly enjoy.

They sip from goblets filled with deep, red liquid—wine.

On one of my earliest excavations with the gallery, I kept a container of wine for myself from a shipwreck and surfaced with it after the sun fell. For hours, I let the stars blur above me as I floated, succumbing to the wine's effects.

I accidentally wandered into a sea dragon's cave on my return home, and Father punished me the next day for being seen by a passerby who stopped to help. I swore never to drink it again. But I suppose there's no way for Father to sour the experience this time, is there?

I take a small sip from the goblet, letting the fragrant flower of the wine develop on my tongue. *Delicious.* It tastes even better on land, without salt water splashing in to dilute it.

Then, dinner is being served.

As plates are placed on the table, the humans make a motion with their right hand, touching their brows and chest, their shoulders. When I see Hazel mutter something beneath her breath with closed eyes and briefly touch her necklace, I realize it must be a religious ritual. I watch the King and the holy man echo it on either side of her, and memorize the pattern.

A maid's arm appears to my left, placing my plate on the table.

I'm momentarily fascinated by that arm. Her skin is pale and as flawless as the statues that guard the dining hall. The dark sleeves of her dress are rolled up to her elbows, her nails sharpened into delicate points. Lovely fingers. I can almost see those nails raking down the length of my back. Blood beneath them, *me* beneath them.

A cloying scent wraps around me. It rolls off of the maid in waves, filling my nostrils and gathering in the back of my throat, and I can't help but lean into it.

The bath I was subjected to smelled sweet, but not like this—not sweet enough to tempt me into sneaking a taste, a bite, a lick. I imagine the flavor melting on my tongue, clinging to my teeth. Pure sugar. Pure pleasure. I can't remember the last time I was so affected by a female.

As she pulls back, I catch her hand in mine without meaning to. I twist to gaze up at her, needing to see the stranger in her entirety, needing to know the face that belongs to that scent.

I meet a pair of purple eyes.

As I jerk back, the force of my reaction knocks my knees into the underside of the table and sends my chair scraping away from her. The Violent Sea. My freshly-filled goblet tumbles onto the linens and splashes into my lap. I seethe, turning the goblet upright and rubbing at my soaked pants as if I could push the wine away—but this isn't the ocean, and the air here is my enemy.

"What happened, Captain?" the King asks, concern in his voice. "Are you alright?"

"It was my own clumsiness," the sea witch says instantly, shooting a meek glance up the table. She's using that sweet voice that makes me taste bile. "I'm sorry, your Majesty."

She scrambles to soak up the spill with a towel from her apron.

I can't tear my eyes away from her—from this witch without tentacles. She looks every inch like a human maid. Her hips are broad, her waist is cinched, and her breasts are hidden away behind a leather corset. Not that I care much about seeing them again; I'm certainly not *disappointed* by her modesty. It's all an act anyway. Her head is covered by a colorful scarf, masking the purple hair that cascades down to her mid-back.

"Let me help you, sir." Before I can gather my senses, she drags her towel to my lap. There is nothing gentle or meek about her then. Not as she pats my thigh hard enough to bruise and leans in to whisper, "How's the silence treating you, dear Prince? Do you give up yet? Are you ready to be mine?" Her voice is unbelievably playful.

I feel a small but pointed tug in my chest, and I know she touched the heartstring connecting us. The reverberations continue to spread through me even after she lets go, like expanding ripples in a still pool.

A chill runs down my spine.

I have hair there now, hair everywhere, and they all rise from my puckering skin.

My awareness channels lower. The heartstring has no boundaries; her challenge evokes the most dangerous impulses in me, impulses I shouldn't have. She's so close, I'm sure her cycle is working against me too. That's why she smells so fucking good. I don't give a second thought to the traitorous strain in my pants.

It's the bond making me feel this way, folding me into her scent, causing this reaction in my body. Just the heartstring.

She's cruel and cold-blooded, and I don't want her.

I don't.

Her hands are still in my lap. She's inches from discovering the effect she has on me. I force myself back against the chair, out of the charged space I'd been leaning into. The wooden anchors of the seat groan. I grasp her wrists and wrench her hands off of me, snarling the best I can without use of my voice.

She squeaks as I shove her away and staggers dramatically into the chair beside mine.

A few gasps erupt across the table. I suddenly realize that my reaction might have been a mistake. To them, she's a maid. To them, I just physically handled her for spilling on me.

Damn it.

"I was just trying to help you, Captain." The sea witch's voice trembles.

Her eyes are large and coated with a sheen resembling glass. I've never seen eyes do such a thing before. All I know is that my stomach is twisting into knots, and even *I* almost believe her innocence. She plays her part well.

Charming, beautiful, treacherous creature.

I nod, containing my frustration long enough to smile tightly and wave her away. Then I turn to my plate and the wide-eyed stares surrounding me, their wariness and silent judgment clinging to me like mud.

They hurriedly avert their attentions.

I haltingly mimic their religious motion and pick up one of the utensils in front of me. The metal immediately bites into my skin. Seeping into my fingers and ripping at the skin.

For the first time today, I'm grateful for my lost voice… because I've touched pure silver. My answering curse is only a huff of air as the utensil clatters against the edge of my plate, and I'm once again cannoned with troubled glances.

My face burns.

I have little choice now, don't I? I lift a piece of fragrant, steaming meat from the plate and pop it into my mouth. I force myself to relax, picking at my plate with bare fingers as if it was the most natural thing in the world.

I don't look up. I don't interact. I don't acknowledge the whispers.

Eventually, the meal ends.

The room clears out, and I'm left behind in the hall with only flickering candlelight left to illuminate the art around me. The statues' eyes are dead. Displaced.

They look how I feel.

There is no place where I fit, is there? I was too soft for the palace in the ocean and I'm too rough for the one in the sun.

I'm struck again by loneliness. Even if I survive the sea witch's deal, if I win this game she wants to play and I help Fluke kill her, I might not survive the result—the reality I see as light slips from the horizon and my fingers continue to throb where the silver burned me.

I realized what might happen to me if her death does not return my tail.

Humanity.

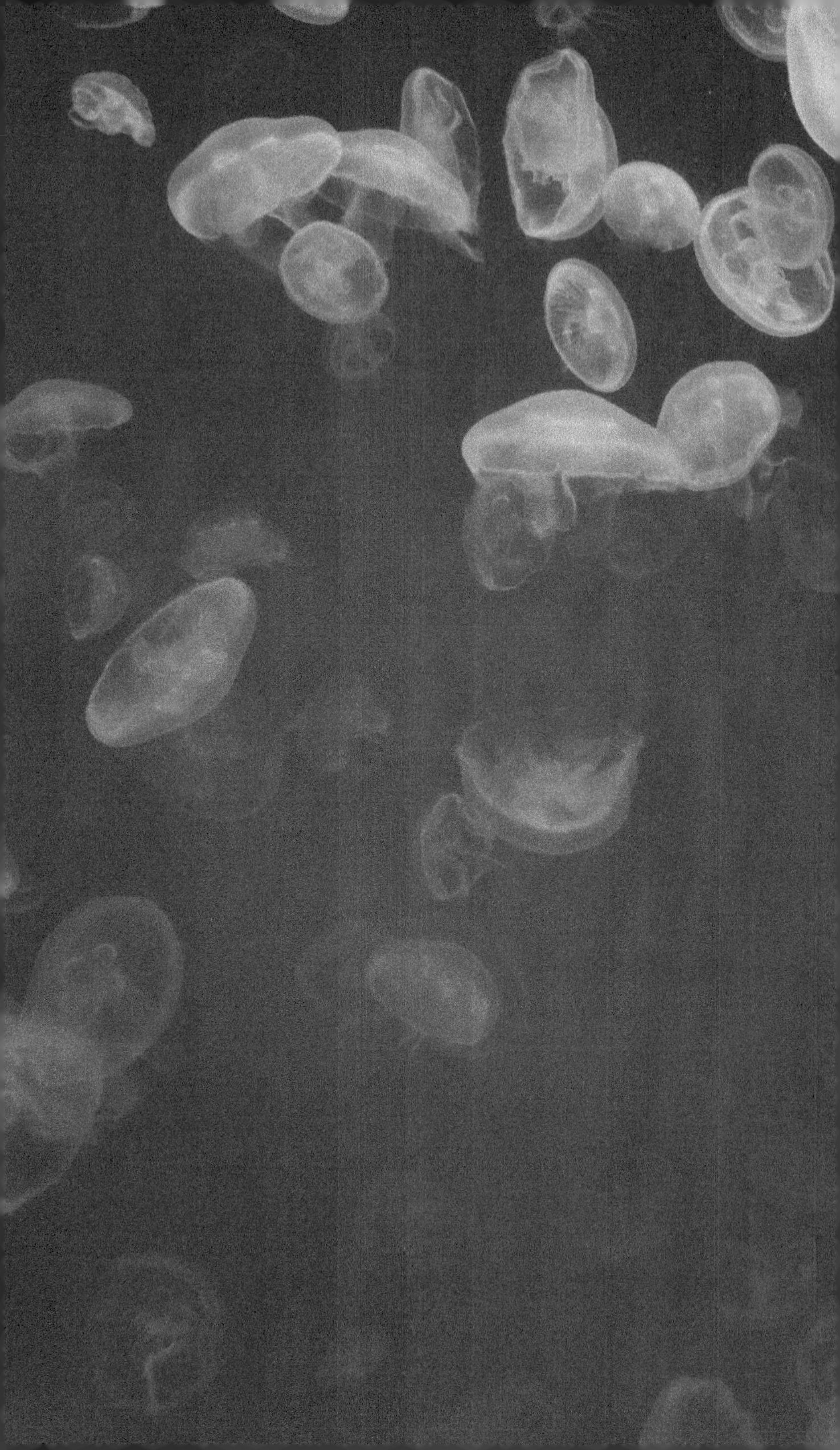

CHAPTER 10
VIOLA

I sit secluded next to a cluster of thin, arched windows, my human legs tucked into the bench seat beneath them. The wall curves around my perch, wrapping me up in the shadows.

My smile is a permanent devotion upon my lips.

I can't stop thinking of the look on Aric's face when he realized who I was and how he ruined his own night with barely any encouragement.

He's hopeless. Utterly hopeless.

I watch the tide crash into the sea far below, counting the waves. Each swell is another pebble rolling through my stomach. I've been above the surface for less than a day, and I already ache to return. I try not to, but that's like trying to bend wet bone—the efforts are laborious and futile. Such is my life. Or at least, that's how I felt until I met Aric. He's my way out of this torture, the only wave of luck I'll ever need.

I wait for him outside the dining hall, and I tell myself it's to bask in my victory. To keep him from chasing after the princess too soon. But there's something else inside me too.

A curious spark. I refuse to pay too much attention to it, to give it any opportunity to grow.

Indulging the heartstring won't do me any good, even if it feels right.

Aric doesn't notice me as he emerges from the corridor to my left—the long tunnel that leads into the dining hall. His gaze is locked on the marble floor. Overgrown tendrils of red hair fall around his face, cloaking his features. I think he might be speaking to himself. *Trying to.* As he passes by, the shadows shift enough to decipher the tension in his brow.

Yes, he's definitely saying something.

I reach for the heartstring connecting us, loosening his trapped voice so that it rattles down the string back into his chest. The words in his mouth rasp into being. "... *warped, hateful whore.*"

Thinking of me, obviously. How sweet.

Aric rocks back at the sudden expulsion of his tongue and falls still in the middle of the hall beside me.

I slide to the edge of the bench and croon, "Come now, *Captain*. Surely you can think of more creative things to call me than a whore."

Aric twists to face me. His eyes are wide, but that shock fades as I stand and walk to him. "But whore fits you so well," he replies, ever the courageous—foolishly reckless—siren. "Especially in that dress."

Why does he have to be so funny?

"Really?" I circle him. "I took this dress straight off a maid, an elderly one—all I had to do was relieve her face of a few wrinkles for it. She didn't seem like the wanton sort."

His eyes rotate in their sockets. "How am I speaking to you right now?"

"Well, you opened your mouth and used your tongue to form a combination of truly grotesque words."

He glares at me.

"I allowed you to." I shrug, pausing in front of him with crossed arms. "Your voice belongs to me. I can loan it out whenever and to whomever I wish."

"So why give it back?"

"Why not?" I can't contain my smile. "How will I relish in your suffering if I cannot hear it? How can I appreciate your colorful insults?"

He says absolutely nothing in return.

I step nearer, and he doesn't react. I love that he shows defiance in what little ways he can, this show of indifference, his silence. In another lifetime, another turn of the foam and sea where we weren't born enemies—where he wasn't the key to my liberty—we might have been friends. But here we were. He's fighting for his life, and I am fighting for my freedom. I will do what I must to make him mine. Sabotaging his chances with the human princess, making myself a constant irritation to him every second over the next three days. It's simply what's necessary. She can't marry him, and I need to make sure of it.

I draw even closer, prodding him in the chest with a sharp nail.

"Besides," I whisper, cocking my head, "it's fun to give you these small freedoms just so I can take them away again." His eyes tighten into slits, and I barely restrain a laugh. "In this way, I already own you. I'm the only one who gets your tongue."

My eyes instinctively drop to his mouth. Soft, pink, two sharp peaks. *Tempting.*

He does us both a favor and elbows past me, knocking me out of my brief bout of insanity. "Don't talk about my tongue."

"All right." I follow at a leisurely pace, threading my

fingers at the small of my back. "What about your legs? Do you like them? You're adjusting rather well for a mer. I expected you to flounder on the beach for a while, but no—you're *thriving* on two legs, just like I hoped you would. Isn't it remarkable?"

"Stop," he hisses. "Quit talking to me as if you've done me a favor."

There's a hint of desperation in his voice. And maybe a part of me wants to take pity on him, knowing he must be overwhelmed and a little bit volatile, but I can't. For the life of me, I can't stop. He's too restrained. I can't help but goad him past the point of no return. I need to know if that point even *exists*.

It's my damn cycle's fault...

I chuckle darkly, trying to distract myself. "Oh, dear Prince. Is the world Above not what you dreamed of? Does your princess act differently than you thought she would?" I lengthen my strides, coming up beside him to examine his burning eyes, his hard jaw. I continue to stoke the embers. "You can't expect her to spread her legs on the dining room table. She has the crown's mistress to think about."

His pace falters.

He spares me a scouring glance, his brow stitched and lips clamped tightly. A question, despite his stubbornness.

"Their faith," I clarify. "Once you see the cathedral, you'll understand." And he'll see it soon.

Aric looks away. He strolls down hall after hall, his features screwing further with every dead end he runs into, every corridor he does not recognize. He has no idea where he is. I putter after him with a smile so intense, my cheeks begin to ache. I don't know what it is exactly, but simply being close to him is something of a balm. It's as if my body can tell he's what I need. What I *crave*.

"Or," I eventually add, "it's possible she won't be interested in you at all. You have no voice to charm her with now, no history to rely on, and she saw how intemperate you can be with the help. An impatient man is not easy to love."

Aric halts and runs a hand through his hair. His next breath echoes in the corridor.

I stand behind him, watching his back curve in defeat. His hands fist. His ribs expand and contract unevenly. The lights burn low here, so I can't see his face, but I imagine he's breaking for me, crumbling and falling like brittle rock, crashing apart in the sea and turning to sand. I yearn to sift through him. To find that part of him that will make me whole.

It's there. It has to be.

I stride forward until my breasts press into the corded muscles of his back. Really, I'm impressed I can do this: touch him without wanting to crawl right out of my skin.

Maybe it's because I'm the one choosing it. Or maybe it's something more.

"Are you lost, Silver-Pipes?"

Maybe I expected him to continue ignoring me, maybe I was speaking only to hear myself gloat... because I didn't anticipate his reaction.

Aric spins and pitches toward me.

I recoil, my back slamming into stone, its rough surface catching on the silk scarf covering my hair.

Crack. His fists collide with the wall on either side of my head.

My hands fly up on instinct, bracing against his chest, keeping him at bay. I didn't need to, though; he doesn't move any closer. With the sconces dwindling to ash and pure rage dancing across his features, his eyes have darkened to a chilling black. Only two slivers of dark blue remain, pointing to the fresco ceiling.

Aric's chest heaves under my fingertips, and I suddenly want to press deeper. I want to get beneath his skin.

He growls, "You are a plague. And I will burn you out of my skin a thousand times, if that's what it takes. Give and take away, try to torture me—it doesn't matter. You will not win."

His arms bend, bringing his face closer to mine with his teeth still bared. I don't know what he wants, but I think I want it too. My hearts thunder. A tentacle slides out from under my dress to wrap around his ankle, suctioning his skin hard enough to bring him back to his senses. He has to know he wouldn't survive a brawl with me. Not here, not the way he is.

Aric pushes off the wall and drops his arms.

Weariness floods his face, driving out the anger, dulling his eyes. They become passionless, lifeless, exactly the way they were the night I met him. Where does he go in his head when that happens?

My hands remain tangled in his shirt. I can't let go.

He looks so broken that I find myself wanting to do something to make him feel better, even if it doesn't change anything. Even if it isn't real. Even if, in the end, I still need to destroy him. Perhaps that's why I feel a little bit sad for him. He never had a chance. Not with the father he was subjected to, and not with me.

"Go ahead," I whisper. "Worm your way into my head. Hurt me. That's what you want, isn't it?"

He stiffly shakes his head.

A chill spreads through my stomach. I can't imagine why he wouldn't take the opportunity, why he wouldn't attack.

My palm travels up the column of his neck to his jaw,

where the beginning of an auburn beard kisses my fingertips. I can't resist. He stops breathing, but he doesn't pull away, as though the gentleness of this touch disorients him. Hair growth is a human phenomenon. For creatures like us, in our natural forms, we only maintain what we are born with—our eyebrows and the hair on our scalp.

This, though, suits him.

It's easy to forget how deeply I should despise him. The whys and hows. The facts of it. The Goddess's gift has a fierce hold on my body, and this is what the heartstring is designed to do to both of us anyway: it convinces us of one another's significance, even if there isn't any. It binds, and sometimes, in moments like this one, when I'm close enough to those I'm bound to that I feel the pull of their lungs in my heart, I can't help but admire the malevolent.

Heartstrings were always meant to be given as gifts. A witch's ultimate gift.

The way I use them, the way I've deviated their purpose to suit my needs, has never been a truth I've felt comfortable acknowledging. But right now, I do it. Because the bond between us was formed without pain, and every tug I make on his heart doesn't hurt him, doesn't hurt me. Not yet.

"Okay," I breathe, brushing a knuckle under his chin. "Well, are you going to tell me why you think I'm a whore then, or shall I guess?"

He inhales sharply and tries to step away, but I have his ankle. "Let go of me," he rasps.

I do, and he stalks up the hall, back the way we came.

My tentacle shifts to nothing as I follow. "It could be the way I live below the waves," I muse. We ascend a set of stairs he's walked past several times and at the landing, we cross an indoor balcony leading to the western towers housing him. "But, in my defense, shells are enormously uncomfortable—I don't know how mer in the city do it—and fabric is downright irritating. If I could be naked up here too, I would. I don't see what's so whorish about that. The only reason breasts are covered in Atlantis in the first place is because Triton can't control himself."

Aric trips, catching himself on the banister as a laugh crackles out of him.

I pause. "What's so funny?"

He turns slowly, his eyes clouded with amusement. The change is subtle. He stands a little taller, looks at me more intently, and I *know*. He's found a weapon. "The plays tell your story well, Viola. You stand here trying to rewrite the narrative, trying to place the blame on my father when we both know it is *you* who could not control yourself, and still can't to this day."

That's ridiculous. It's always been my story to tell.

"I didn't take you for a courtly half-wit," I quip. "In fact, I was told many things about you, and none of them suggested that you care for the throne you're in line to inherit, or those miserable plays, or any of the other diversions Triton fills his city with."

"I'm not inheriting anything anymore," he returns.

"No. Because you took the way out I offered you. You barely hesitated." I quirk a brow as I wait for him to argue, but he doesn't. "Tell me, if you despise the city your father built so much that you can't bear to linger within its walls, why do you still believe in the foundation it sits on? Why do you believe the stories he spins?"

Aric eats up the space between us, and I crane my neck to meet his glare.

"Because a witch like you is still a monster, no matter the form," he spits. "You wreck everything you touch, and I don't need anyone to tell me that because I can see it. I *feel* it. The fractures inside you. The fragments. You rip people apart because you're not capable of anything else. All of Atlantis knows *exactly* what you are."

I withdraw a step.

Tingles engulf my body, followed quickly by brutal numbness. I knew all of that already, and yet—

Perhaps I still thought someone would remember me. I thought someone would hold onto the truth because it was the right thing to do. I hoped for justice. But that's the last starry-eyed dream I'll allow myself to have, allow myself to lose.

"You see?" Aric sneers. "That's what I th—"

I clench my fist between us, twisting counter-clockwise as I rip his voice away. He backs up with a wince.

"Good night, Prince. Don't let those nasty bedbugs bite."

I relish the look of confusion that crosses his face. May Aric spend the next several hours wondering if bugs will crawl out of his bed and eat him alive. May he lose as much sleep as I will. He might have been the one to get under my skin tonight, but I took the last word. I will take everything I need from him.

I will take it all.

I WANDER the cobblestone hills descending into the city. The steep streets wind between shops and homes. Cream brick soars into the sky, punctuated with iron stairs and gardens planted between shutters. Life has simmered to a low hum.

Laughter and the phantom scents of supper drift toward me as I navigate the streets.

As I leave the castle gates behind and enter the heart of the city, a larger shadow towers over me. The cathedral, in all its greed and beauty. The world is too dark right now to admire its banners and gilded edges, but the twin flames licking at the entrance is enough of a warning not to forget that the mistress of the crown is the one truly in control around here.

Homes crowd in around the cathedral, and I aim for the backside of the monstrosity, where a quaint chateau sits across from an elevated courtyard. The home is built slender and tall, with a narrow staircase leading to its worn door. Peeling red paint colors the doorway.

Boisterous laughter erupts inside.

I smile as I climb the steps. Pressure builds in my chest, rising high enough to swell in my throat. My hearts beat hard enough to bruise me on the inside. It feels as if my body takes on a will of its own when I reach the landing, as I step forward and rap on the door before I can second-guess the decision.

The laughter cuts off cold, and the chateau stirs. Then the door swings open.

The man in the doorway locks eyes with me.

His freckled face is lit from a candle in his hand, his green eyes glittering with surprise as he gasps, "Vi!" He sets the candle down on the table beside him and launches forward to scoop me up into his arms, spinning me fiercely as he pulls me into the warmth of the house.

My body tightens under his affection, but I endure the feel of his body against mine. I know it will only hurt his feelings if I try to push him away.

I force myself to laugh into his neck. "It's good to see you too, Guillermo."

Guillermo sets me back on my feet, and I release a sigh of relief. His smile is as life-altering as I remember, bright and careless. My chest threatens to burst just looking at him.

A second figure appears in the entryway, and my hearts sing in recognition.

"Jussi." I approach him with open arms.

He frames my waist lightly with his artist's hands, and squeezes gently. I cradle his face, pressing a kiss to one brown cheek and then the other as he mirrors the gesture. I pull back to look into his sparkling, storm-gray eyes.

I choke on a sob. "You look so happy."

He nods and kisses the tip of my nose. "Happy as a clam."

"All because of me," Guillermo interjects, slinging an arm around Jussi's shoulders. "Indeed, I am his sun and moon, I am the air he breathes." He lifts a hand to his heart, his eyes fluttering as he leans heavily on his partner.

Jussi snarls, but his lips are fighting a smile. "Be quiet, darling. Don't make me curse you for your vanity." He squints at Guillermo.

"Aye," Guillermo springs back, shoving Jussi hard enough to jostle his smile free, "you better not, you slippery fish. You fool around too much. You're lucky I protect our home enough for the both of us."

He touches an intricately braided piece of wood around his neck. Willow branches. I shake my head as I watch him perform a strange hand signal, first in front of himself and then over Jussi as the latter rolls his eyes.

I bite back a laugh.

Guillermo turns to me once he's finished, pointing accusatorially. "Vi, you tell him to get his head out of the ocean."

"I took his *body* out of the ocean," I reply dryly. "I think I've done enough."

He clicks his tongue, a look of disgust contorting his face.

I wink at Guillermo, then turn to Jussi. "Do you still bathe on the roof?"

Jussi's brows raise, surprise filling his eyes as he exchanges a look with his partner. "Always. I can draw some water for you, if you plan to stay a while?" He nods to the spigot just outside the front door.

"No, no." I brush his offer away with a wave of my hand. "I'll draw it for myself in the morning. But I will be staying the night, if you're all right to keep me."

Guillermo hooks his arm around my neck, pulling me into his side as he drags me farther into the chateau. Warm tones of wood and cream tile envelop us. We skirt around a dining table cluttered with paint and glass and brushes. "Nothing would make us happier, Vi."

He turns his head and whispers in my ear, "Don't tell Jussi, but I have a bottle of port hidden in the kitchen. We can drink it together once the old man passes out."

"I heard that," Jussi grumbles.

"Ay," Guillermo exclaims, launching away from me to wrap Jussi in an embrace. He starts crooning in a sweet, musical voice. "It's a miracle! My old man is not tired yet."

I pause on the edge of the kitchen and watch the two men blunder into it.

Jussi grumpily pushes at Guillermo, but the freckled man seizes his partner's shoulders and wrenches him into a deep, smiling kiss. All trace of their bickering evaporates. A part deep in my chest clenches, deeper than my strings and hearts and hunger. What I feel now is regret and loss and a second-hand drunkenness on love.

A greater longing than any curse could give me.

Aric doesn't know the lengths I'm willing to go to in order to break him. To win him. To take my life back. I don't play by the rules, I *bend* them. And I'm willing to bet he has no idea just how flexible a whore can be.

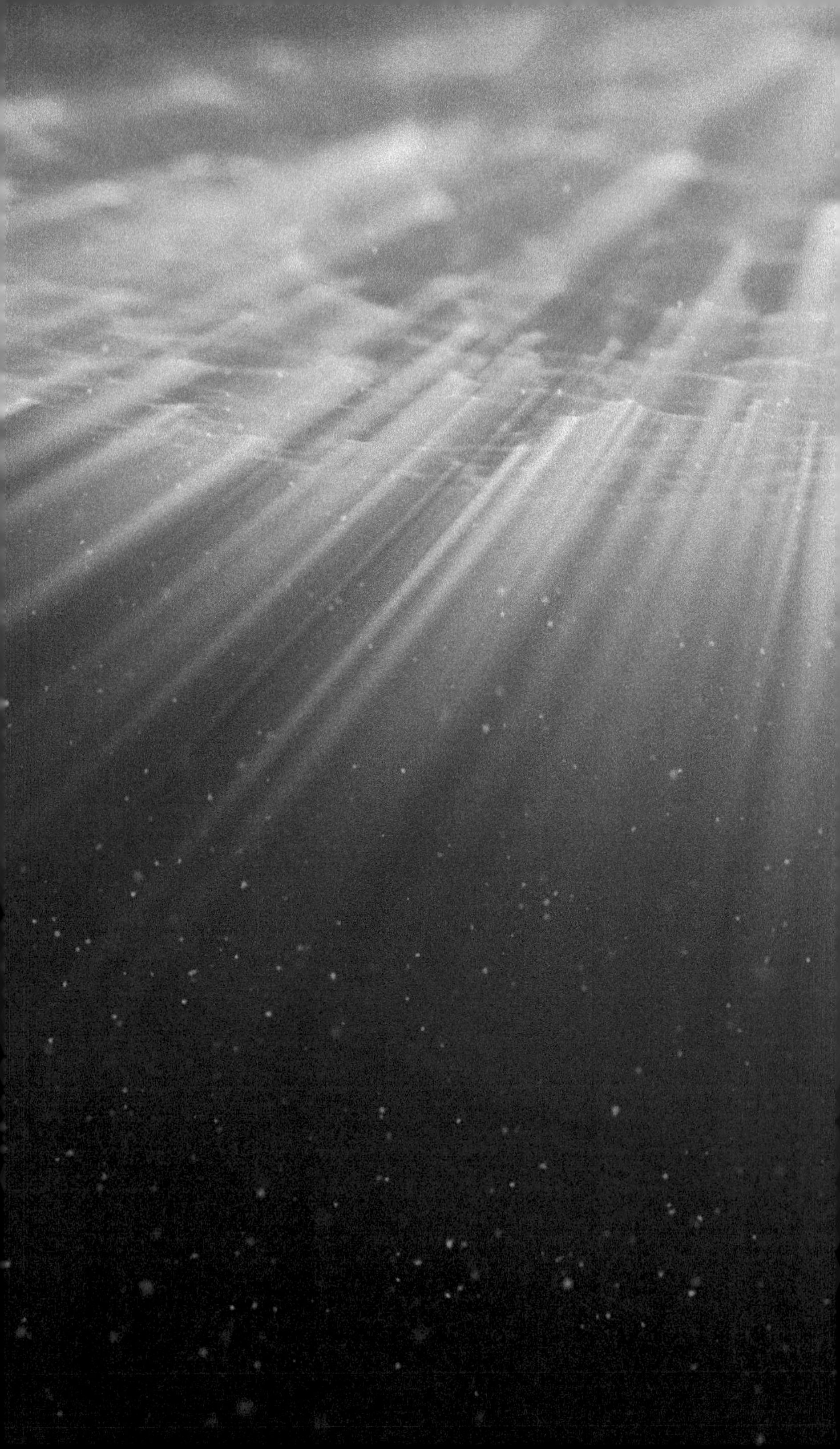

CHAPTER II
ARIC

Something is happening to my face... I think I'm growing a beard like the King has.

How annoyingly human.

I graze a hand over my jaw, the short bristles scratching my palm. The sensation helps me stay awake as I sit on a long bench in the cathedral. For all its garish construction, I expected the inside to be better illuminated—but the candles are few, and the windows let in little light through their colored glass.

Archibald paces at the front of the room.

He wears even finer robes than yesterday, the white seams glistening, the spectacles on his nose reflecting the golden hues of the candlelight to either side of him.

There has to be hundreds of people here. I don't know how they bear his lecture with such soft smiles and attentiveness. They do *this* every seven days? Listen to a man speak nonsense and sit perfectly still for hours? I've run out of things to look at.

Hazel's angels are everywhere, and the more Archibald talks, the more convoluted their beliefs get. A twinge spears through my arm, a companion to the dryness of my mouth and the ache in my temples. Dehydrated.

This is something I've never experienced before.

My eyelids stick together as I blink, my entire torso sliding against the wooden panels at my back. Last night, I tossed and turned after tearing the bed apart in search of what the sea witch called 'bedbugs.' It only occurred to me as the sun rose that she might have tricked me. That I *let* her trick me.

I should have known better.

Her smile as she left last night had been too smug. Too infuriating.

If I had any strength left, I would be stewing. I would be figuring out how to track the sea witch down and get back at her, but I'm too tired. The city's mistress is a dark hole—aptly named with its gold and jewels and idleness—sucking me dry as I sit idly in the center of it.

Hazel showed up at my room this morning and insisted I walk with her to mass. I figured it was a good sign—a sign of her forgiveness. Briefly, I'd hoped mass would be another meal and I could make up for my missteps from the night before, but no. I'm alone again. The princess sits at the front of the room with her father, who separated the two of us the instant we entered the cathedral.

Apparently, the front row is reserved for nobility.

It's exactly like my father's table at the parties he hosts in Atlantis. Only the best of the best. Humans are not so different from us at all.

They're being called forward by Archibald now.

One by one, they press their mouths to his rings and drink from a fine goblet.

My vision blurs. A choir of women sing...

<hr />

THE NEXT THING I KNOW, my shoulder is being shaken, and I jerk awake.

I register the emptiness first. Most of the cathedral has cleared out, and the atmosphere is stale in an eerie, regretful sort of way, as if the air itself wishes to turn back time. As if phantoms wait in the shadows for a chance to reclaim what they've lost.

Here, in this moment of waking, I feel them. The strange presence of something *more* in the walls.

And then the sensation gone.

I'm rested, aside from a knot in my neck that screams as I look up at Hazel.

She stands in the narrow aisle between the benches. Her cheeks are stained pink beneath her bronze skin, those eyes of hers dark in the dim lighting. The darkness does not make her beautiful. She needs sun and firelight. It's a sad realization, indeed, to know I cannot admire her any other way. I admire the sunshine more for what it can do to her.

"Are you feeling ill?"

I don't respond because, well, I can't.

She's shifting on her feet, nervous. "Papa said you can return to the castle now if you need more time to recover. Of course, you absolutely should if you're unwell, but they've also set up lunch in the courtyard. I know we don't know each other very well, but I'd like you to come. If you want to." She pauses, her teeth digging into her lower lip, and then she sits down on the bench beside me and stares ahead.

At the front of the room, near the massive erection of

crossing wooden beams, the King and the priest are engaged in conversation.

"Archibald is talking to Papa about the convent again," she murmurs, twisting her fingers in her lap. After a moment of silence, she glances at me from the corner of her eye. "If you sit with us, Papa won't entertain the conversation. He's tired. I'm tired. And the priest is relentless. Can you stay awake long enough to eat with me?"

It's not a question. It's a new beginning, and I'll take it, even if it means she's using me as a shield.

I stand and offer her my hand. Her face cracks into a smile as she slips her gloved palm in mine and leads us out of the bench seat.

The men at the front, a few nobility and loitering guards, see us approach and file out of a set of doors hidden to the side, behind a pair of purple curtains which have been pinned back. Hazel tugs me toward it.

Across from the doors, I catch sight of a long glass box. More than that, I *feel* it. It pulls me and my magic toward it in what feels like a current. Without meaning to, I step toward it, trying to follow the streams of power unraveling from me. The closer I get, the stronger it tugs. The more it takes.

I hesitate.

Hazel follows me, her hand still in mine. She looks between me and the case, and a soft smile blossoms over her face. "Do you have many artifacts in your country? Father prides himself on our collection—it's the most expansive one on this continent, and still growing. Archibald added another piece to the coffers just last year."

I take one more step, drawing close enough to examine what sits within the glass. A velvet sheet and a handful of items nestled on top. Each of them radiates with tangible power, but none more than a metal box situated near the center. It's a compact thing, no wider than my hand and half as tall. There's something inside, feeding on the atmosphere, bypassing glass and space and flesh. I want to find out what it is, and at the same time, I never want to get close enough to touch it. I'm afraid it'll swallow my song whole.

"Would you like to see more?" Hazel sidles up beside me, her arm in line with mine. Enthusiasm fills her voice; this is clearly something she's passionate about—these *artifacts*. She drops my hand and walks to a door beside the glass box, smiling at me over her shoulder. It's been left open a sliver. "Archibald allows me down in the catacombs to view them sometimes. I'm sure he won't mind, if we're quick."

Translation: he won't mind if he doesn't find out.

I smile back at her and follow her beyond the door. There's a pair of torches bracing either wall at the top of the staircase. Hazel removes one from its perch and leads us down into the dark.

The tug of that artifact behind us begins fading as we do.

At first, the staircase is only stone. Only dust and cobwebs and the flicker of firelight over sand-colored walls. Then the walls shift. Long, narrow clefts are carved into the stone, appearing in stacks, trailing upward as far as I can see. There's no telling how deep they go; the torch sheds only so much light.

I inch to the side that Hazel holds her torch and peer into one of the gaps. There's dark material covering something. A strange smell.

Reaching in, I grab the thin covering and tug.

I stagger back. My foot slips on the step, and I pitch into Hazel's back. We almost tumble down, but her hand flies out and saves the both of us by catching on a ledge of one of those clefts. The clefts that hold *human remains*.

Her eyes bulge as she looks at me, as I scramble to regain

my footing. "Be *careful*," she scolds me. "These stairs are not forgiving." No. And if we were to die down here, I have the most horrid feeling that our souls would never escape.

Those phantoms I felt up in the cathedral have returned, encroaching on every side of me. I realize now that they never left—they were down here, reaching up through the floorboards to greet me.

I steady the both of us, pulling Hazel back into the center of the staircase, and choke on the sudden acid breeching my throat.

We continue our descent until the staircase ends and a room finally spreads out before us. It's massive, turning Hazel's torch into a tick of light consumed by the darkness. Luckily, she seems to understand where she's going. She walks to the left, and as she reaches the edge of the room, something flashes. Glass.

More glass boxes line the wall, and she raises the torch over them to illuminate the contents, beckoning me closer.

"There are items here that bless in every way you can imagine. Marriage blessings and miracles for barren wombs. Artifacts that humble, and others that grant wealth. Even certain illnesses have been cured by touching these boxes. They've altered history." She continues talking, pointing out particular artifacts and listing their uses. But all I can see is what rests in the wall behind her.

Bones. Skulls, skeletons, dismembered and pieced back together in a staggering collage. I've never seen such a thing.

Curiosity possesses me, and I take the torch from Hazel to look closer. I don't even glance at the artifacts beneath me as I walk past them, absorbing every inch of the death embedded in stone as it continues on and on.

Something sinister pours from the bones, thickening in the dark.

"What is it?" Hazel asks from close behind me.

I think these human souls are trapped, suffering.

In the ocean, we understand our souls belong to the water. From water we come and to water we return. There is no fear of death because our spirits are never truly gone.

I wonder if it must be different for humans. They seem *furious* being here, so perhaps their souls are not meant to linger in the physical realm as well as the unseen. If that's true, what kind of magic has trapped them here? Why can't they leave?

These phantoms can touch me just as well as the ones in the ocean. They have their own song. One that I don't dare sing.

I watch as the light travels across each skeleton.

The wall dips into an alcove, and I'm brought face to face with a fully intact skeleton, standing like a guard in the inlet. Its body draped with loose, ratty clothing. In that moment, it looks both dead and alive, and it scares the curiosity right out of me.

In my terror, I drop the torch and it snuffs out under my feet as I recoil from the wall.

As I land on my back, Hazel screams. Then I hear her footsteps. "Captain, are you okay? What happened?"

I manage to make a snorting type of sound as I sit up. She finds me, her fingers grappling with my hair and then my shoulder as she helps me stand. She's so close. My hands spread out over her back, wandering the length of her spine. She stiffens in surprise, and it feels so familiar to me, to touch her in the dark. Her warmth and the silk of her bodice. Her scent, a potent flush of earth. I can almost taste her.

In the emptiness of my mind, I see a flash of purple. A vicious smile.

The Violent Sea.

I shouldn't be thinking of her when touching Hazel. I don't want to think of her at all, and yet...

Hazel clears her throat and pulls away, only keeping hold of my hand to draw me toward the faint light filtering down the staircase. "Come. I don't want anyone to realize we're missing and find us alone together."

We weren't alone at all.

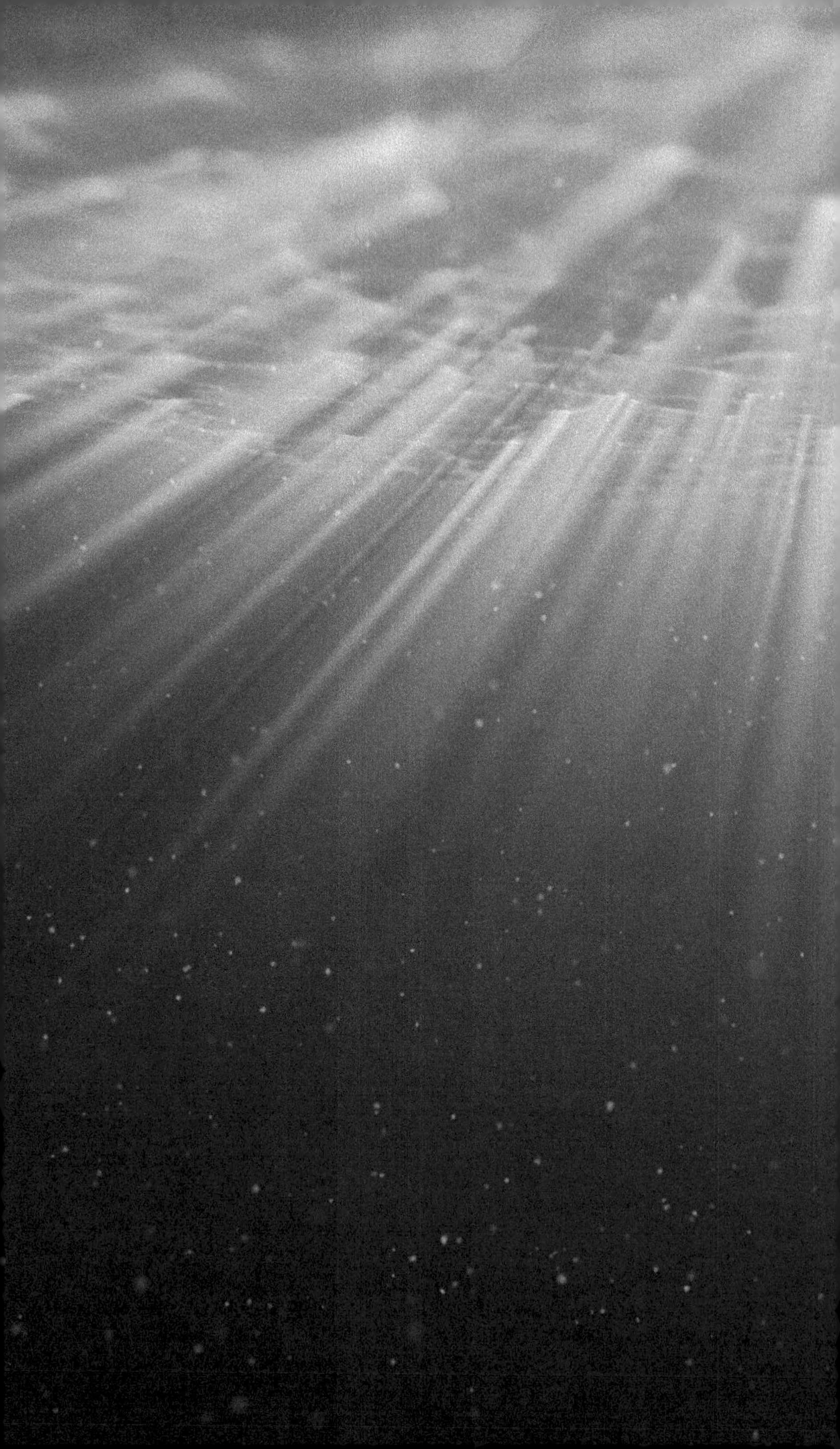

CHAPTER 12
ARIC

The courtyard is a stretch of warm-toned brick. Endless shades of rust and gold whirl under my feet and dainty flowers grow in around the pavers. Fruit trees line either end of the fenced-in space, iron grates and vines and the tops of square buildings closing in beyond that. At the center of the yard, a table has been set up with food and wine and baskets of steaming bread, the scents both welcoming and torturous to my stomach.

My gut gurgles. Do all humans have to eat this often?

Beneath, we only have to hunt for a meal every couple days, maybe a week if the fish are sparse.

Hazel keeps her arm looped with mine and guides us to the chair next to hers. The King sits there, on Hazel's right, and Archibald moves into place across from us. The old man is watching me intently.

I meet the King's wary gaze and bow, pressing a hand against my heart the way I've seen so many subjects do for him today.

He smiles tightly and motions for me to sit. "I'm glad you

joined us, Captain. I was worried we dragged you from your room too soon after your ordeal. I imagine civilization is something you have to ease back into." *He has no idea.*

I know he's referring to my outburst last night, so I offer him a look of cordiality and nod.

"He rested plenty during the sermon," Archibald interjects, shooting me a sharp look.

The other guests are women, a variety of ages, each wearing seamless white-and-black robes, their headdresses and collars reminding me of the checkered marble floor in the palace. Though, that floor seems warm and gentle in comparison.

They must live here if they haven't left like the others.

The crown's mistress? With all these women congregating, it looks like more of a brothel, and not the friendly sort. These were the women singing earlier. Is that their purpose here? Is that why they seem so unhappy? I know what that feels like—to discover my only value has been placed on my ability to sing. To lull. To seduce. Striving to please others does not satisfy. It's hell. They don't have to worry about going there after they die. They are already here.

The priest makes that same religious motion from last night, removes his spectacles, and bows his head.

As one, the rest of the table bows. I pause in the middle of copying the motion when I realize that they've all closed their eyes too, and Archibald begins speaking more of his strange melodic stanzas. The women down the table quietly echo him.

Blue birds sing in the trees ahead of me. They pick at the fruit trees, juice dripping languidly onto the ground. The phantoms of the cathedral loom in the archway. Tangible, but not quite visible. Watching. Waiting.

Their fury fills my chest, my head.

I hope I never have to come to this place again.

Archibald is still speaking when I sense another set of eyes land on me, but no one at the table has raised their head. I turn my gaze in the direction of that pull. My stare latches onto a building across the street from the courtyard, to the movement atop it. The courtyard is bolstered above the street below, level with the interior of the cathedral and all the roofs surrounding it.

It's close enough that I can see *her*.

A woman strolls across the roof of a narrow building. She holds a bucket of steaming water, and her strides are slow and graceful enough to undulate through every inch of her body. She dumps water into a bathing trough, and I trace her curves with my eyes. I can imagine her soft skin giving under my touch. I can imagine bending her over the edge of the tub and seeing beneath that skirt.

The woman sets the bucket down and tugs the scarf off her head, and I can't breathe.

I curse the ocean and its cruel spirits of fate. Of course it's her. Why else would I be thinking of sex at a moment like this? My desires have betrayed me once again, have drawn me to Viola. She's lured me in with that heartstring.

She's doing it on purpose. The smile on her face as she peeks over her shoulder says it all.

Her lips are painted a vibrant crimson. Her hair is the purple of a setting sun, of that moment when night eclipses day and the edge of the world dances with dusk. She is the personification of all the moments I surfaced for as a young mer, and for which I was severely punished.

The Violent Sea is a stunning creature. I repulse myself even thinking that, but I'd need to be a eunuch not to *feel* her in my body like coral attaching and building upon my bones. She holds my gaze as her hands reach up and push the cotton slip off her shoulders, and the swathe of fabric flutters to her feet. Leaving her bare.

I want to look away, but I don't.

With Hazel, I could only imagine. In our fantasies together, her body was always a little hazy, a little distant, because silhouettes were all she offered me. Human men, I knew. I've drowned hundreds of them at my father's urging, to bring honor to him and my name and my kind. Sirens wear murder as a badge. I killed enough to make people think I'd eventually grown bored of it, when really, I'd been sick of it from the very beginning.

But in all my life, I've never held a woman in my arms, never dragged one into the deep to examine her intimately. I've heard of only one or two that were kept in the city as trophies until they began to rot, but I never searched them out.

I didn't know the womanly form beyond marble and dreams, not until this second.

Viola turns. The planes of her body reflect the sun like a flawless, pale beacon. To any bystander, she probably blends into the stone around her. Her breasts could be mistaken for flowers clinging to the house's porous wall. She could be harmless at a cursory glance, but I know better.

Her body is a toxic spore, invasive and conquering, bearing down on my muscles. Crushing my lungs and twisting my gut.

My eyes are not my own. They're hers, and they follow the trail of her fingernails as they travel down the length of her torso, over her plump hips... and lower. I look between her shapely legs, where her fingertips pause at a tuft of purple curls. *Fuck.*

The breeze sifting through the courtyard is suddenly too cold, the food too fragrant. All I see is purple. Sunsets. Her red lips. All I can focus on is her string anchored in my chest, the tug telling me I'm hers, hers, hers.

For one heartbeat, I wonder what it might be like.

Viola steps back into the tub, and the submersion of her body breaks my trance. I swivel my head forward, shaking it to get her out of my eyes, out of my brain. Try as I might, she lingers, and her heart continues tugging. I won't look at her again. I refuse to give her the satisfaction. I'll simply distract myself with Hazel until she gives up and leaves me alone. Easy.

Even as she rises partially out of the water.

Even as she spreads her thick thighs and touches herself, and I can feel it as if I was touching her myself, her swollen purple flesh.

Stop it, I tell myself, as if it will work if I only say it angrily enough. It suffices for a moment, as Archibald finishes with his poetry and the table collectively raises their faces.

Food is passed around.

I keep my eyes fixed on Hazel, smiling as she blabbers about the dishes and tells me which ones I should try. When she leans over her chair to hand me bowls and platters, I sway forward to connect our bodies. It's a touch subtle enough to go undetected by the others at the table. The King and Archibald are occupied, conversing quietly over their corner of the table. I caress Hazel's hand in thanks as she hands me a basket of bread, and the tension in my chest increases tenfold.

Viola is watching. I feel her eyes on my face, but I won't look at her. *I fucking won't.*

Refractions of light bounce up from Hazel's white plate to dance across her profile. Instead of the smile I expect, as her eyes meet mine and she inhales sharply, the blood draining from her face. She looks at me as though I've suddenly regrown my fins.

Have I?

Glancing down, I don't see anything unusual for a human, but when I return my eyes to her, she emits a small squeak. The table hums around us, oblivious to her behavior—but they won't be clueless for long.

I know terror when I see it.

I scan everything around me for an answer. Behind Hazel, I catch a glint of red in one of the two polished knobs on the back of her chair. It's my distorted reflection. My eyes have turned a bloody crimson.

I blink a few times, thinking it must be a trick of the light, but the red remains.

Hazel squeezes her eyes shut, murmuring frantic drivel under her breath.

The sea witch must be meddling from the rooftop, changing my appearance to scare Hazel. I might not be human, but I'm not a devil. If there's anything I learned from the absurd ramblings of this morning and the paintings on the walls, it's that humans believe more in evil than they do good. They fear it. Honor it. Their 'devil' is a second god, worshiped with their hate.

Anyone with a modicum of sense knows that hate is more powerful than love, and that it is more easily manipulated to gain respect and control. That's why Atlantis bows to my father.

I won't let Viola turn me into that.

Before Hazel can flee—which her trembling limbs look prepared to do at any second—I reach beneath the table and brush my fingertips against her leg. Her eyes snap open and lock with mine, and I pull her in.

We're back in the cathedral.

My eyes aren't red anymore because Viola can't touch me in Hazel's head. I'm the one in control now. I'm standing on the raised section of floor at the front of the room, and Hazel kneels the way she kneeled before the priest when she pressed her mouth to his rings.

I kneel in front of her, and her lips part in a gasp.

I dig into her memories. That moment at the table when she saw the burning red of a devil's eyes. Simple to alter. She saw nothing then but the eyes she sees now.

Then my hands are on her. I push her back to lie on the floor and then I hitch her dress. She could pull back. She could look away because she learned how to on that balcony of hers, but I know she wants this. She accepts this as her own imagination and lets me settle between her thighs.

Now that I have a visual to work off of—now that I stole that glimpse of Viola's human form—I know what to put together in order to please her.

Mermaids have a similar anatomy, only with a sheer flap of skin that protects the gap in their scales. I like this better. Everything is easier to manipulate.

I flatten my tongue and drag it up her center, and she jerks beneath me. I twirl my tongue in wide circles. I don't move too quickly. I want to sear this moment into her mind, want her to remember how badly she wanted me to make her come every time she looks at me, even if she believes it was only in her head.

I feel the heartstring again. Tugging harder and sharper, more insistent, until I can no longer ignore the woman on the other end.

It's as if Viola has plunged one of her tentacles down my throat and wrapped it around my organs, as if she were planning to rip them out one-by-one. My vision ripples and I pull back from Hazel's mind.

The princess is still staring at me from her seat at the table. Her cheeks are bright red, and her breathing is labored. One of her hands is wrapped around her necklace so tightly that her knuckles are yellow. As her eyes clear, she tears her gaze away from me with a mumbled apology and pushes her chair back as she readies to stand.

The moment she pushes herself up, she faints.

The King launches out of his chair, and a few of the robed women crowd in too as I sit there. I'm secretly a little pleased that I stole enough of her breath to incapacitate her. She'll be fine in a moment or two, and she'll wake with images of me in her head. She's going to fall in love with me, whatever that means... it's only a matter of time.

The problem is, I don't have much of that time left, and Viola has the same amount to ruin it. She nearly did just now.

The sea witch wants me to pay attention to her? Fine.

I look to the rooftop as the rest of the table concerns itself with the princess. Viola's still up there, leisurely touching herself, and I think that makes it worse—knowing that she's not even *trying* to come, holding my gaze as if she's trying to make a point.

Through her eyes, I sink into a portal of the deepest violet blue, and I take her with me.

Suddenly, she's the one on her knees for me on that damn rooftop. Sunlight envelops us, hot and fierce and blinding. My cock is in her throat. I'm gripping her hair tight enough that a glassiness springs to her eyes. Moisture gathers and overflows. I laugh at the shock on her face, and at first, she jerks back. But just as quickly, she realizes where we are, and her surprise settles. She doesn't pull away. She smiles and takes me deeper between those red lips.

My desire doesn't let me waste it.

Her mouth is several degrees hotter than Hazel's, and I don't even know if that's my own imagination or if she's somehow influencing the vision. She's likely powerful enough to do that. The sea witch sucks me down like she has something to prove, and maybe she does.

I move swiftly, brutally, a prisoner to my lust.

It's been decades since I felt this desperate for release, this ready to burst apart at the seams. My skin bubbles with heat, and I hate that it's *her* doing this to me. I hate this heartstring and her bewitching eyes. I hate everything about her, but she won't look away, and neither do I. Her eyes are equal parts play and challenge. She bares her teeth around my cock, and I don't know if it's a threat, but I know I want to find out. She takes me deeper. *Deeper.* Until I'm drowning in sensation.

My hatred is a cyclone, churning and violent, inescapable. The red wax on her lips colors my length, and my spine shudders with the impending ecstasy.

I wonder in that moment, if it is possible for her to reach past my skin and change my very soul. I wonder if I have let her in so deep that she discovered a crevice, a weakness, and marked me in a way I'll never recover from. It might be possibly, because I find myself wanting to come undone in her mouth. Right now.

I want her to swallow me and make me hers. *Hers.*

Absolutely not.

I rip away from the vision and land back in my chair within the courtyard.

Most of the table is still crowding around Hazel, who sits on the ground fanning her red cheeks and answering her father's barrage of questions. One of the robed women is brushing a damp cloth over her brow. A few are reciting more of the same confounding nonsense—prayers, I suddenly recall them calling it.

Archibald stands at the head of the table, clutching his golden spectacles in one hand as his eyes flick rapidly between her and I. It's an unwelcome scrutiny.

Reluctantly, I peek up at the rooftop.

Viola has removed herself from the tub. Her wet body crosses the roof swiftly, bath water sluicing off her with every step. I can't see her face anymore. And I don't know why that bothers me so much. She descends into the belly of the house, disappearing entirely.

Without a second thought, I leave my seat at the table.

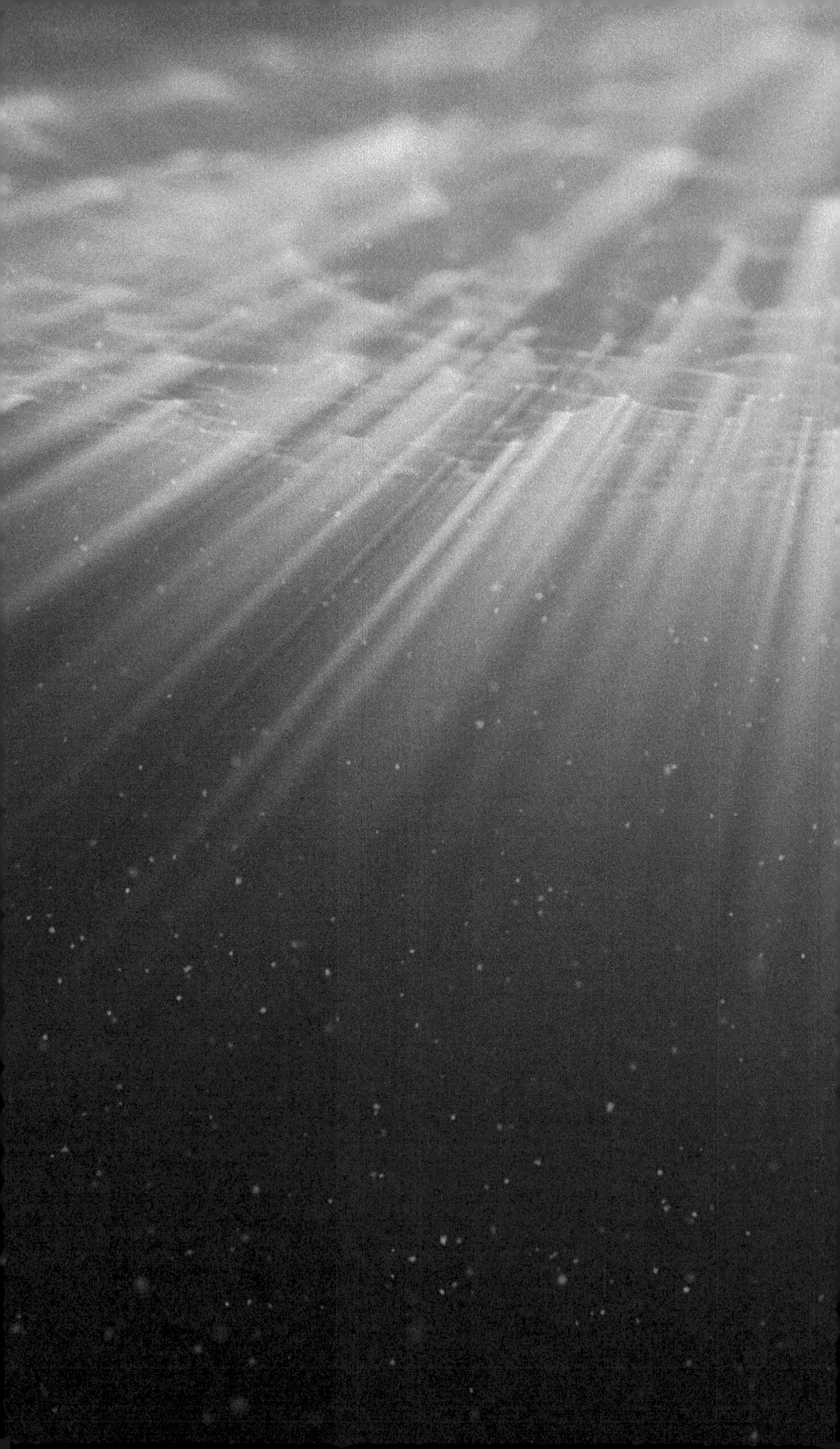

CHAPTER 13
ARIC

After descending a steep flight of stairs to the street, it's easy to spot the right building. It's not the kind of place I'd expect to find her in. I've spent a majority of my life collecting and selling art, and that's what this home looks like from the outside.

A masterpiece of craftsmanship.

Who did she have to hurt to claim it for her own?

I'm not sure what I plan to do once I cross the street. Break down the door, maybe. It's what comes after that which scares me—whatever this heartstring pulls out of me.

Thankfully, I don't have to find out.

About halfway to the building, the painted door opens, and I watch Viola slip out in a laughable excuse for clothing. She might as well be naked for all it conceals. She wears a thin, white shirt—a *man's* shirt—and her waist is wrapped tightly with bands of leather and dark fabric.

A skirt cascades beneath it, bunched in the front so that her legs are on full display.

I weave between citizens and a wagon drawn by skittish donkeys to get to her.

She seems to sense my approach without looking at me, without even being close enough for me to touch her. My throat tingles, and I know she's given me my voice back.

The breeze flirts with her head scarf. Her shoulders are bare, the fabric of her shirt falling off of them and bunching on her arms. I see the outline of her dark nipples shifting with every swing of her hips. She continues strolling down the street as I fall into step beside her.

There's too many people around us. I can't confront her the way I want, can't pin her in place and force her to look into my eyes.

"Silver-Pipes," she greets me with an impish smile on her crimson lips. "Did you enjoy the show?"

"What exactly were you trying to accomplish with all of that?"

"I don't know what you mean." She flutters her lashes. "It's not my fault you have as little self-control as I do. Who's the whore now?"

She *was* using that bath to make a point.

"You wanted me to see you," I snap.

"And once you did, you couldn't look away. I was in that vision you projected too, remember? When you rammed your cock down my throat. Who do you blame for that?"

Me. It was my fault that we ended up that way, but I hadn't expected her to do what she did. I didn't expect her change the game.

I lean in close enough to smell her ambrosial soap. A fragrance sweeter than crab, and more potent than urchin. Her essence caresses me like delicate fingers trailing down my body and I fight the desire to drag my tongue up her neck just to taste it. It's just her cycle. It's not me.

I reply slowly, succinctly, fully in control. "I blame you for *everything*."

Her eyes narrow before she spins away, stalking up the street in the direction of the square, but I still have my voice. She wants me to chase, to keep fighting. And maybe I have a fascination for suffering in her hands, because I do.

The square is a swell of bodies, surging from stand to stand, shop to shop, the air filled with haggling voices and laughter. A couple cuts between Viola and I. They're linked together at the elbow, similar to how Hazel walked with me this morning—a position of affection, surely. The man gazes tenderly down at the woman as they pass by. He bends toward her, and she rises on her toes, leaning into him as she slants her mouth against his.

I stumble, watching their embrace.

What a strange thing to do.

As I catch up to Viola again, I point to her face. "What did you do to your mouth?"

"My mouth?" Her eyes widen in feigned innocence.

"Yes. It looks like you've painted your lips with blood."

Her tongue flicks out over her top lip. "I'm sure the new friends you've made in the cathedral would be more than happy to tell you about this city's whores. Red is their sigil. Since you seem convinced that I'm one of them, I might as well live up to expectations." As we enter the square, she gestures at a shady corner. The corner where women with painted lips and darkened eyes loiter, strolling in and out of a stall surrounded on all sides by thick curtains.

Had I struck some kind of nerve by comparing her to them?

I return my attention to the witch, but she's already moving again. Viola approaches a stall, her fingers grazing the enormous piles of colorful flesh, each basket a cornucopia of fruits and vegetables. She picks up a plump red ball and turns it gingerly in her hand. After returning it to its basket, she moves on to the next cluster, then the next.

I'm about to intervene and ask her what she's looking for when a man appears from behind the crates.

The sea witch shifts in that moment, not physically, but in a far more shocking way. She greets him with a smile and dives into a lively conversation about the food between them. I watch them from a distance. They talk at a whirlwind speed, so I miss most of it, but I catch enough to understand that Viola has been here many times. And, perhaps most surprising of all, there's no trace of malice in her voice.

Is this how she preys on the men of this city? Does she charm them senseless so that they never see her coming?

Before she leaves the stall, Viola leans over the crates to press her lips to one side of his face, then the other, leaving behind the print of her lips on his skin. My traitorous cock twitches at the reminder. With a wiggle of her fingers, Viola turns away from the vendor and joins me again in the bustling crowd.

"What was that?"

She tilts her head in my direction as we navigate the square. "What was what?"

We walk past a sundial built up in the very center, the pedestal embellished with intricate carvings and more of the tile I'd seen in the palace. It's enough to remind me of my dwindling time. It's enough to make me angry again.

I grab Viola's arm and force her to look at me. The crowd blurs around us as I anchor my gaze in hers and hiss, "That thing you did to his cheeks."

She blinks a couple times. "I kissed him, Aric."

Kissed him. *Kissed*. I scour my head for a definition of that word, but come up empty.

Viola chuckles at my blank expression. "Don't tell me in all the years you've spent collecting priceless human novelties, you never learned from them what it means to kiss?" Then she cocks her head in a pitying manner, and my gut clenches.

Her hands brace against my chest. Those sharp nails of hers dig into the skin there, even through the material of my shirt, and ever so slowly, she rises up on the balls of her feet. I'm so gripped by my curiosity that I don't push her away. She tilts her head to the side and brings her lips to the hollow of my cheek.

The kiss is as light as air. Unbearably soft.

"It's the most human thing in the world, dear Prince," she whispers next to my ear. "It's how they show affection, how they greet each other, and how they say goodbye."

Her nose brushes mine as she shifts to kiss my other cheek.

I don't think I'm breathing. I've forgotten how. I swallow the saliva gathering in my mouth, the *embarrassment*. I feel as though I've just been told the world has two suns.

Beneath, I had considered myself an expert in human matters, but the way she looks at me now takes all that pride in my heart and crushes it to dust. Perhaps I knew nothing. But then, how could I know anything for certain, when I was stuck in the ocean?

Viola's eyes drop to my mouth. "And lovers," she adds quietly. "Lovers kiss each other on the mouth, with teeth and tongue."

Flames flicker under my skin, burning up my neck and prickling the back of my skull. This idea is so bizarre to me. It would be to *any* mer. The form we keep Beneath requires flexible jaws and sharp teeth, to tear through thick skin and sinew. Our mouths are weapons, not instruments of pleasure. The way Viola talks about kissing makes me want to try it for myself.

I suddenly realize that I'm jealous of Viola, for knowing everything she does and for her ability to walk among the humans like this. To be like them. And I despise her for rubbing it in my face.

Before I can do something exceptionally foolish, like close the distance between us, Viola throws herself into the traffic of the square, and she takes my voice along with her.

I watch her go, knowing she doesn't want me to follow, knowing that I *shouldn't* now that she's sown danger into my thoughts. Now that she's sown *doubt*. The sea witch isn't what she should be, what I *thought* she'd be.

I may have awakened the true monster inside of her, one more exquisitely adorned than any mistress Above or Beneath.

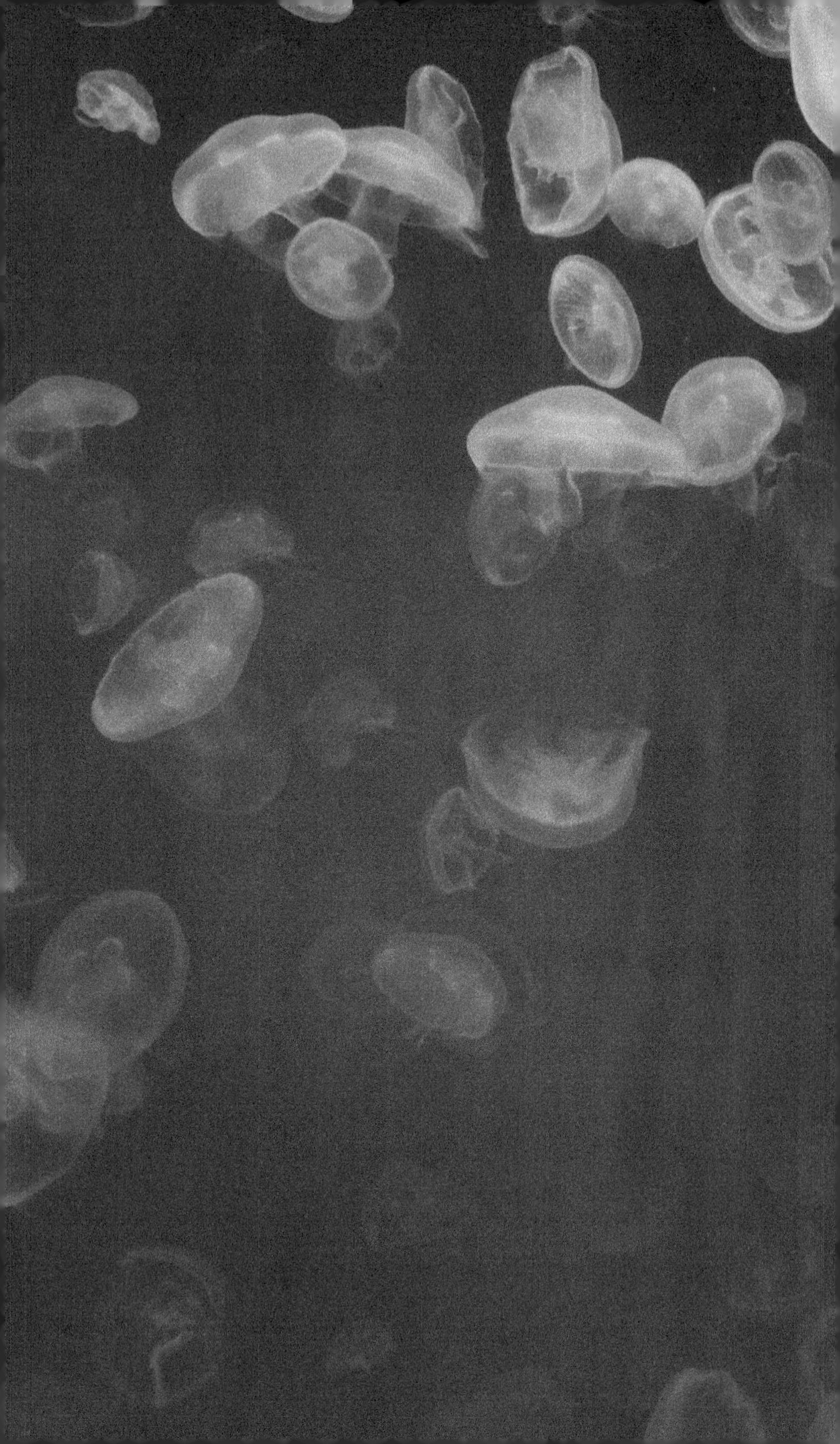

CHAPTER 14
VIOLA

The gray pavers under my feet glisten. They smell of lemon and soap.

I cling to that detail, let it ground me and ease the pressure in my body as I lace my way between the stands.

The tension in my core has become unmanageable. I nearly took Aric right here, in the middle of the square. What a display that would have been. With my cycle sharpening and the curse weighing on my chest, I can't think clearly.

Multicolored awnings blur above my head as I stride through the marketplace, the canvases stitched together in strips and pieces. Baskets of bright yellow, orange, and red fruit. Fresh vegetables. Pastries and vials of golden oil.

The scent of it all calms my hearts.

By the time I glance back, Aric is gone—either returned to the cathedral or palace, the two most ornate but barren places in the entire city. Those halls don't dance with children or music. Though I brought him above the surface, he found himself in the same place: a lovely cage.

This is where life is. In the streets, along the canals, with humans that have more to gain than lose. Aric didn't see it and he never will. I push away the heaviness that realization gives me—there's no reason to pity him for what he is, or for what I am. I'm not his salvation.

I deliberately remind myself of all the reasons I shouldn't care about him, all the reasons I need him to die for me.

And it works for now.

Spotting the vibrant stand sitting near the edge of the canal, I approach Guillermo's back as he talks to a customer. His arms wave wildly as he gestures to the painted canvases and scrolls and containers of pigment. Behind the wares, a large curtain separates Jussi's artist stall from his completed works. I've seen him lead hundreds of people behind that curtain, each of them departing with smiles and memories imprinted in parchment.

I watched from the canals as he and Guillermo built a life together, as they fell deeper in love every year and slowly coalesced into one being instead of two. That's what love does best. It blurs lines and sways minds, combines souls like streams colliding.

I linger at the edge of the stall as Guillermo finishes up with the customer, and glance around at the fresh art pieces. Jussi has entered another brief obsession with charcoal landscapes. A shadow passes behind the curtain.

He paces when he's stuck, either emotionally and creatively, which means he must be working on something personal right now. He's alone.

Good.

I slip between the crates and through the linen curtains. As I enter the room and the curtains close behind me, I blink to adjust my vision. The walls of the tent are layered to carefully control lighting. One curtain on the left side of the room has been pushed back, allowing daylight to fall upon the table in the center of the space. Jussi's easel is set up in front of it, and an unfinished replica of a bowl of fruit takes up the canvas.

It's an exceptionally dull reference, even for him.

Jussi turns to me from where he stands against the right wall, his profile cast in shadow.

I ignore him and cross the room to the bowl of fruit, lifting a peach to my mouth. The fruit touches my lips, and the sensation of its fleecy skin pulls what happened with Aric to the front of my mind. The tip of my tongue darts out. Firm. Velvety soft. I should have bit him in that vision for what he dared to do, but instead...

Instead, I lost my mind.

There's no other explanation for it. No other excuse. My cycle has driven me mad for sex, and all this time away from the ocean is getting to me. I'll return to the sea tonight, at least for a little while—Goddess forbid that things get worse.

"Viola," Jussi rumbles.

I sink my teeth into the fruit, garbling around the succulent flesh, "Oh, come on, Jussi. We're in a market. You can replace it from the vendor next door."

"Viola," he repeats, his tone uncompromising.

I turn and survey his tense posture in front of the shifting flaps of the tent. This isn't about the fruit.

"Please don't tell me you've involved yourself with the crown prince of Atlantis."

My hearts skip. Jussi saw him, *recognized* him. I should have known it was a possibility, considering his previous life as a chair-holder on Triton's court.

I shrug and take another bite, but the juice turns sour in my mouth. "He can't inherit an underwater kingdom without gills, can he?"

A harsh breath leaves Jussi's mouth and he shakes his

head. "That's the problem." The frustration in his voice draws my full attention. "Do you have any idea how many dreams are hanging on that boy?"

My back straightens as if a rod had been thrust through my spine. I slam the fruit back into the bowl and soft, white tissues fly out from the bite I made, spattering the bronze bowl and the table beneath it. I take a step forward, baring my fangs. "I know it's been a while since I plucked you from the ocean, Jussi. Your mind has aged. You can become confused, as a human does. So I'll do you a favor and pretend I didn't just hear royalist bullshit spew from your mouth."

Jussi closes his eyes for a long minute, standing perfectly still. When his eyes open, he walks to his easel, removes the half-finished canvas, and replaces it with a blank one.

He waves at a pile of pillows. "Sit down, love."

"No."

Jussi returns my glare. "Plant your ass on the cushions so I can paint you. Please?"

I consider the offer. It's rare for him to waste words in an argument. He has something more to say and he's trying to find the right way to say it. As much as I fear what it might be, a part of me respects him enough to listen.

I drop myself onto the pillows, arranging myself in a casual manner even though my organs are twisting. "If you make my nose look crooked, I'll give you a tail."

It's an empty threat, and so he chuckles as he perches on his wooden stool. "Guillermo would be secretly delighted."

"Precisely. There's a method to my madness."

Jussi looks at me. "I've never doubted that about you, Vi. You're a good witch."

I don't know what to say to that because, honestly, I'm not sure if it's true. All the souls I've punished... I had my reasons, but were those reasons enough? I still inflict suffering upon the world. Most of the time, I'd say yes, my reasons are enough, but if I were to ask my coven—if my coven was still *alive*—I can't be sure they would agree.

Selflessness has never been my strength, not then and certainly not now. So I keep my mouth shut and wait patiently as Jussi prepares his pencils and brushes.

Once he begins, a hush coats the room. There's only the sound of scratching on parchment, our disjointed breathing, and the hundreds of thoughts twirling in Jussi's head. His brain has always been loud that way. Deafening even in the silence. When he speaks, his voice is soft.

"Do you remember the night we met?"

It all comes racing back to me—those early days after I pieced my world back together. The curse was fresh. I was starving. The soul-bonds I made were short-lived, and I couldn't keep a power source alive for longer than a few days at a time. I was hunting for a new target in the outskirts of Atlantis and I saw a mer. Quiet, peculiar.

"Of course I do," I mutter. "You were hopeless."

He nods solemnly. "But you saw more than that, too. I wanted love. You saw that desire in me, and clung to it instead of my allegiances. Why?"

Truthfully, I expected him to be an easy meal. A chair-holder of Triton's court, unhappy enough to spend his time roaming the slums and desperate enough to trade his tail for a pair of legs? It was a shock.

I watched him forsake Triton and all of his responsibilities, and then I watched him fall in love. I didn't hope for a friend, but he became one.

It was only right to release him from the bond after that, to give him this life.

I stare at the canvas ceiling, willing the tingles under my skin to pass. "I know what you're trying to do," I murmur.

He exhales. "Vi."

"Stop it." I squint at the sun.

Jussi stills in his chair, the stick of charcoal dangling between his fingers. His compassionate stare triggers an ache in my chest. It's the same one that won me to him.

"I love you and Guillermo," I continue, briefly surrendering my anger. "I would never do anything to hurt either of you, but that doesn't mean you should take advantage of our friendship and tell me that what I'm doing here is wrong. You can't possibly understand."

Jussi grimaces. "I would be doing our friendship a disservice if I didn't tell you the truth."

He can't be telling the truth because if he is, then that would mean I've done the unthinkable. I lift a palm to stave him off. "Don't. I don't care."

But he's already begun, so he'll finish it despite the consequences. "I was there when Triton capsized his father's court for you, when he terrorized the city into submission. I know what he is capable of, Vi, *I know*. There isn't a day that I don't regret helping him rise to power, that I don't regret allowing—" Jussi's voice cracks, and he pauses a moment before continuing on in a dry rasp. "Triton is an evil mer— you're not wrong for believing that—worse than his father and his father's father. The worst of them all. But as much as you've lost faith in Atlantis, I know our people see it as we do. They see it and fear speaking up, fear being struck down the instant they try to rise above the city he's built. And they also see that Aric is different. For the first time in centuries, the city hopes for a better world, because of *him*."

I shake my head, my thoughts reeling from all there is to disseminate in that. "You're a fool," I rise to my feet, my cheeks burning, "and so are they."

"What if you're mistaken?"

Forget running to the sea. Forget baths and fantasies and harmless tricks. I'm going to settle this. "I'm not," I snarl. "He may be young and charming and clever, he might have sung the entire city into a false sense of security, but he's the same as his father. And I'll prove it."

Aric *is* a monster. All I have to do is push him to the brink, and he'll prove me right.

The curtains at the front of the tent suddenly part, and blinding sunlight invades the room, curling around Guillermo's broad form. "Vi," he beams at me as the curtains close behind him, "I thought I heard your voice. Why are you two barking at each other?"

"She's the one doing the barking," Jussi grumbles.

Guillermo frowns, leaning in to whisper, "What put him in such a foul mood?"

"I'm sorry, Guillermo." I reply, because I am sorry to leave Jussi like this for his partner to deal with. "I'll be returning to the house late tonight. Keep the door unlocked for me?" I place a hand on Guillermo's arm, and his calloused fingers fly up to squeeze mine as I pass by.

Jussi's stormy eyes darken further as they slide away from me. "Test him as long as you need to, Vi, but that will not show you his heart."

I scoff, closing the last few steps to the exit. I'm not quick enough to miss the way Jussi drags a hand over the canvas, smearing the charcoal and casting a silent but final judgment.

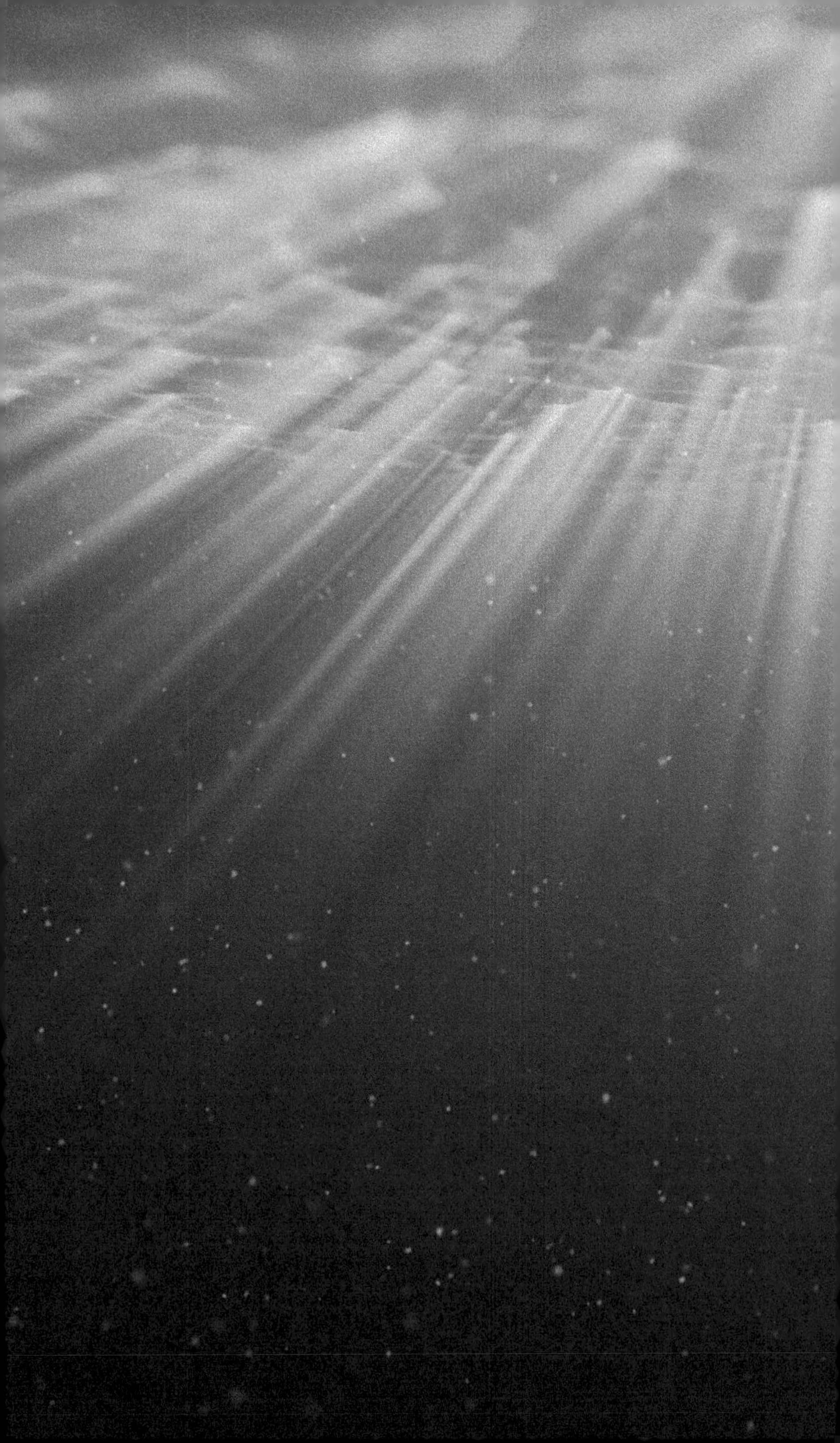

CHAPTER 15
ARIC

Sleeping in a human bed is what I imagine lying on a cloud feels like, imaginary or real bugs be damned. I'm too tired to worry about the biting tonight. And yet, I can't drift off.

I toss and turn. Moonlight shifts through the open shutters of my room. The sea sings.

I can't get her out of my head.

Every time I close in on oblivion, the nothingness parts and I see her. I shouldn't, but I do. My shattered conscience has plenty to say about it, filling my ears with their vindications.

The whispers eventually drive me out of bed and into the cool air of the balcony.

I can't breathe deep enough to clear her scent from my memory, my teeth aren't sharp enough to scrape it from my tongue. Sticky sweetness edged in salt. My body has become a slave to the fantasy of tasting her.

I don't know why I do this.

Why do I make decisions with my body before my mind

can catch up? Why do I desire what's bad for me? I drop into a crouch, tugging on two fistfuls of my hair.

Pain helps clarify the voices.

I hear the warm treble of my mother—the memory of her so faint, it's barely a vibration. *Open your eyes*, she whispers. *See what I see.*

Folly. That's all her voice offers me. Never an answer, always a question. The comfort of her presence doesn't compensate for how lost I feel. Not this time.

The other side roars in reply.

It affirms everything I already know, urging me to take matters into my own hands.

The sea witch makes herself vulnerable around me. For whatever reason, she lets me inside her head. With my soul hanging in the balance and nothing more than the heart-string connecting us, I can still hurt her. Until she reaps me and possesses my soul, I still have that option. She admitted as much.

Perhaps it's time to try.

End this, it says—that piece of myself most like my father.

If there's a chance for me to prove my worth to him, it will be in this. In her. I'd be doing the entire ocean a kindness by killing her. So why is my stomach in knots?

See what I see, she repeats, as if it would make any more sense the second time.

I pinch the stars embedded in my skin, trying to muffle them, trying to find a single moment of peace. One moment of clarity. This decision, for the first time, must be entirely my own. Feelings can't have anything to do with it.

A different voice carries to me, then, calling my name... but it's not from beside me or within.

It's coming from below.

I stand and inch to the edge of the balcony.

When I peek over the side, I see around the curve of the tower and down onto Hazel's balcony. She's there, leaning over the railing, both forearms braced on the stone banister.

Her voice echoes again.

"*Aric*," she cries. "Tell me you're here."

She's right here, within my grasp. Waiting for me. Maybe the only solution is to show her who I am.

Today was a failure, and I only have two more days before The Violent Sea comes for me, before she drags me Beneath with her beautiful claws and makes me hers. If Fluke doesn't follow through, that's exactly what could happen. I loathe how little I feel about that. It's as if I've already accepted it.

This is how I felt about most things before Viola: unwavering apathy.

About my father and my position and the courtiers I used to call friends. Even about *sex* a lot of the time.

Maybe I need a little release now. A purge of this tension the sea witch has instilled in me—instilled *on purpose* for whatever twisted reason in her head. I suppose she's proven her point. My body has been affected so deeply by her, I'm sure I could find my pleasure if I tried. Why shouldn't it be with Hazel? I'd take care of two problems at once—placing myself in her affection and perhaps cleansing my thoughts of the witch at last.

I don't give myself a chance to change my mind.

The hallways of the palace are dark, empty, eerily silent. These human royals must feel especially safe within their palace because I don't see guards roaming the halls or standing at Hazel's door.

How wonderful that must be... not fearing for your life at any given moment.

When I reach Hazel's quarters, I carefully open her door and slip into the front room. One by one, I blow out all of the candles. With the lantern at her side, she won't notice the gathering darkness at her back—and that's the point.

I want her to see me emerge from dark.

I want her to come to the truth of who I am on her own, to realize I'm the creature she's longing for. That's the only way forward, the only way I'll possess her heart completely enough to convince her to marry me. I can't tell her, but I can show her.

By the time I reach the balcony doors, I'm sufficiently settled in the shadows. I turn the brass lever on the door and push the shutter open. The creak startles Hazel, and she spins to face me in her red gown.

Candle light glows around her waist.

Her jaw slackens, and she tilts her head as she considers my silhouette. "Aric?"

I step forward.

Hazel recoils as the moonlight hits me. "Captain? What are you doing here?"

I don't respond. I just stare at her, my eyes hooded and darkness swimming around the edges of my vision.

She licks her lips. The delicate knob in her throat bobs.

Then, she shows tremendous bravery and pointedly looks away. A dismissal. "If you've come to apologize, you're too late. You were supposed to stay with me, to help me ward off the priest and his incessant campaigns about my future. But you left. Now he's trying to convince Papa I'm sickly because my soul isn't dedicated enough to God."

I stride forward, and her eyes snap to mine.

She shies back, hitting the banister, but I continue my pursuit even as she starts to tremble. I halt in front of her, debating whether or not I should whisk her to a more intimate place, to a corner of her mind where I can control every breath.

Hazel's gaze searches my face, her eyes pinched with cautious wonder. I'm the only man who has ever stood with her here, like this. She should know me.

I brush my fingertips over her cheek and into her hair, imitating the tenderness I saw in the square when that couple embraced each other. Her eyes flutter, but she still doesn't seem to understand. She doesn't see me. Have I really been so distant, so abstract a presence, that she can't recognize the feel of me?

Has anyone memorized me? I don't think so.

Her voice drops to a whisper. "I *fainted*. Do you not care for me at all?" Before the last word even finishes rolling off her tongue, I kiss her.

I watch down the line of my nose as her eyes flutter closed, as her lips mold to mine. But my heart doesn't respond. I search for a flicker of happiness or excitement inside me, anything that would give me a glimpse into the worth of a kiss and what it meant to that couple in the square.

It's nice, but that's all it is. Warm. Soft.

My body is vibrating too intensely to be content with nice. I want to *burn*—so I take Hazel's bottom lip between my teeth, and bite it. She whimpers. My hands roam up her back, pressing her closer as I graze my teeth down the column of her neck and close them again on the skin of her collar. She's too surprised, too frightened to move, to reciprocate. And that just doesn't work for me.

Patience lost, I take one of her hands and place it on my crotch, where my length strains against the cotton. I nibble a tender spot on her shoulder.

She gasps, exhaling in a moan. Her other hand rises to thread in my hair.

I guide her fingers to curl around my cock and push into her hand, a soundless groan rumbling through my throat as I teach her what I like. After a few strokes, she gains the confidence to work my length on her own and I let her, even if it isn't quite rough enough. I seize the material around her thighs and start to hitch them so I can get to the heat underneath. I need to sink into her and forget the confusion of this day.

I need to forget...

Wildflower eyes. Alabaster skin and purple curls. Musical laughter.

My cock engorges to the brink of bursting, and a phantom twinge of pain spears through my length—oh fuck, no, that's *real* pain. A ripping sensation travels down the center of me. There's too much pressure.

What in Oblivion is happening to me?

I lean back with a hiss and look down. The considerable bulge in my pants, cupped in Hazel's hand, is... shrinking.

I suddenly recognize the tingle in my back. The sense of being watched. I know what I'm going to see before I even turn my head.

My eyes catch a streak of movement on the balcony outside my room.

She's here, using her magic to humiliate me.

As my cock retracts to the size of a newly-hatched turtle, Hazel's face reddens, and she withdraws her hands to press them against her chest. She averts her eyes.

I hate to imagine what she thinks of this, thinks of me.

The pain finally ebbs and I can stand up straight, but I don't have time to control the damage, to catch her up in a vision and fix this.

A voice echoes from below us, down on the rocks, the tone so familiar, my entire body prickles. It doesn't speak coherently—only mumbles and a low, fluctuating hum. If I didn't know better, I might have mistaken it for a song.

Hazel certainly does.

Her breath catches as she hears the voice too—my voice, given to some random fish swimming near the surface from the sound of it. Viola is trying to distract her.

The princess bursts into motion, bracing her palms on my chest to push me back.

"Leave me," she orders. Her eyes flick between me and the railing as she guides me towards the inner rooms. When my back hits the balcony door, she steps away and folds her hands together in front of her stomach. "I won't tell anyone what happened tonight, but you need to go now. Thank you for, uh... for apologizing."

I want to take her in my arms and force her to look at me, to see the truth, but this is delicate. If I push and she calls for the guards, then I'll lose what little advantage I have. I'll probably spend the next two days in a dungeon. I turn on my heel and exit her quarters, heat ravaging my organs as I stalk back through the tower.

I slam through the door to my room, passing through it back into the night sky.

The balcony is empty, but she isn't gone. I feel her here still, nearby, imminent like the charge in the ocean before Father sends out a storm. I can *smell* her. Burnt sugar drifting through the night. My nose follows that scent until I see her.

She's not on the balcony anymore, technically.

She's hanging onto the side of the palace by her tentacles, just beyond my reach. Vining, purple blooms grow across the stone edifice and blend beautifully with her arms. I suppose that's her gift. She fits in anywhere, as anything. I don't think she could look out of place even if she tried.

Viola smiles. "What's the matter, dear Prince? Feeling *shorted*?"

I stalk up to the edge closest to her and slam my fists against the railing. I try to reply, try to voice how deeply I hate her in this particular moment, but she withholds my voice. She snickers. And that's when I realize that I'm giving her exactly what she wants by reacting this way. The more I react, the more delight she draws from it.

She needs to be taught a fucking lesson.

With a deep breath, I step back from the railing. I calmly lift a hand and beckon her forward with one finger.

Her eyes shift, but she doesn't hesitate to crawl across the wall to me. I wait, motionless, as she slithers her way over the railing and lands on the veranda beside me, her tentacles propping her up like several legs.

Her scent overwhelms me in a cosmic wave.

Then I strike.

Grabbing a fistful of her hair, I rip her forward, cupping her throat firmly in my other hand as she falls into me. She begins struggling. Her nails tear into my hands. Her tentacles wrap around my legs and torso, trying to pull herself free, but I don't let her go. I let the pain clarify my will, let it pierce through the influence of her cycle.

She smells so fucking *good*.

Viola tries to speak, but I'm squeezing her throat so that nothing can come out. I glare down into her amethyst eyes.

My intention isn't lost on her: if she lets go of my voice, I'll let go of hers. Her power tingles down the inside of my throat and my voice returns.

I loosen my grip on her neck and grind out, "You treacherous viper. You're not playing fair."

She smiles, a cruel glint in her eyes. "We never established any rules for *me*." Her voice is a brutalized rasp. "Besides, I'm of the opinion that all's fair when someone is starving."

My upper lip curls. "You're a monster."

"If I'm a monster," her eyes narrow as she leans in, "it's because that is what Triton made me."

"Ever get tired of blaming others for your problems?"

"The *Bastard of Atlantis* is my problem. He did the same to you as he did to me, and surely to your brothers—sculpted you after his image from birth."

The warmth drains from my face. She grins triumphantly, raising a brow. She's digging for something, I can tell.

"What does that matter?" I snipe.

"It matters." Her smile looks positively painful. Not quite as painful as having my cock condensed to the size of a thumb... but close.

After drawing a halted breath, I admit, "He sees what I want him to see. And I suppose, so do you."

I can tell that's not the response she expected. The muscles in her shoulders and down her back turn rigid. Her lips part, and she tips her head to the side as if looking at me from an entirely new angle.

"You hate him."

The skin around my nose wrinkles. I push her away from me and back up into the center of the veranda. "I didn't—"

"I see it now," she states, "in your eyes."

I blink, measuring my breaths. I don't reply—because what could I say? Yes, I hate him. But I've certainly never admitted it before, to other people or myself.

Her skin is glowing an almost-silver under the moon.

Grappling again with the vines, she pulls herself up off

the balcony. She turns to look at the flowers, and my eyes trace the line of her profile, softer than it should be all swathed in shadow.

"You know," she murmurs to the wall, "sometimes we have no choice but to fit into the skin we are given. Once we're in it, we lose ourselves to the surroundings, surrendering piece after piece until there's nothing left of us. I've met so many mer like that."

She bites her lower lip, red wax transferring to her teeth.

"What are you getting at?" I rasp.

Her eyes flash to mine, the purple deepened to a near black by the distance. Horrifically beautiful. "When I made this deal, I assumed you were already empty." She pauses to swallow. "So, I guess I want to know... am I wrong? Is there something left inside of you that I missed?"

It doesn't sound like a question. At least, not one she expects me to answer.

My ribs clench.

If I didn't know what she was, what she's done to my mother and me, and what she plans to do to me still, the look on her face could have been tender.

"Think on it," she murmurs. "You can convince me one way or another tomorrow."

The sea witch glances behind her, down at the sea. She rearranges her tentacles. A tingle sparks at the base of my throat, and my crotch remains forgotten.

I lurch forward before my voice is ripped from me. "Viola," I growl.

She pauses to meet my gaze.

"You're forgetting something."

"Am I?" Her eyes sparkle. "Do you wish for me to kiss you goodnight, Silver-Pipes?"

My stomach turns.

How long did she watch me from up here? She must have seen the kiss. Or... my horrible attempt at one. That's more embarrassing than the rest of it somehow—those moments down there with Hazel felt like a personal failure.

A *human* failure.

"I swear upon the seven seas," I say tightly, "if you leave me here with my cock like this, I'll make you regret it."

She laughs. "And what could you possibly use it for between now and tomorrow? Judging from the look on that poor princess's face, I'd say you sufficiently snuffed her curiosity."

I growl, slamming my fists against the stone railing for a second time. I wish I still had them fisted in her hair. "When I get my hands on you—"

"*If* you get your hands on me..." she taunts, smiling brightly. "What could you possibly do about it, *little* Prince?"

Her emphasis on *little* has my face burning.

I forget my place, the significant drop to the sea below, and start reaching for her. I'm a heartbeat from falling over the railing. Before I can plummet to my death, an iron rod of fire erupts in my crotch. I hiss, staggering back from the edge, leaning over my knees as my cock engorges, stretching inch by inch by inch. I watch in horror as my body settles with the new length. I was already a male of considerable size, but now if I tried to fuck the princess, she'd probably break in half.

That conniving witch.

I glare up at her.

"Don't say I never did anything for you," she croons, and then she flings herself off the palace.

I peer over the edge quick enough to watch her crash into a patch of wave between jagged rock. I'm left alone again, prisoner to my thoughts.

What would have happened if I never went to Hazel's room? What had The Violent Sea planned to do with me if she had found me here alone?

I almost wish, out of curiosity's sake, that I'd been here to find out.

CHAPTER 16
ARIC

I wake to a celebration overtaking the city.

Which, unfortunately, ruins my plans for the day. I had planned on stealing Hazel away somewhere to fix the travesty of last night.

Instead, the King summoned me to the banquet hall to explain the holiday over breakfast. Today is what the city calls *carnevale*, a day of dancing and feasting, with a rich history that the King was all too happy to describe in exhausting detail. I tuned out most of it. Something about dead soldiers and a human war that was won at great cost to their country.

My biggest takeaway: everyone wears masks. *Everyone.*

When Hazel finally emerged from her room, we traveled into the city together so that the King could make an appearance.

It's disorienting to see painted porcelain masks instead of faces. On the bright side, the sun feels exquisite on my skin as we walk through the square, and Hazel—as abnormally quiet as she is this morning—has her arm looped in mine. The square is more chaotic than when I saw it yesterday, and I didn't think that was possible.

Music plays from all corners of the market. The melody rises and falls in waves, playing off one another, each having a turn at the forefront of the revelry. People dance in groups and pairs, wearing veils and plaster and desiccated wood. Anything and everything to hide their faces. The whores don't congregate in the shadows today, but instead weave through the party with smiles on their crimson lips. Bronze platters travel the crowd, distributing food and drink without a hint of coin being exchanged.

A true celebration.

Even Atlantis has never held such a party.

Watching it unfold around us stirs a longing in me. I want to dance, and drink, and eat with these strangers who should mean nothing to me. I want to be consumed by their laughter. I want so much to be with them, and even more to *be* them. Just for a day.

Apparently, the nobility doesn't partake with peasants here either.

The guards at the front of our promenade cut a line straight through the square. Citizens scatter out of our way. I stare out at the masks as we pass through, wishing to stop but knowing I mustn't. Not when I have a bride to win and a soul to preserve.

Hazel is touching me but remains distant. She's barely looked at me since leaving the palace, so I bide my time until we get a private moment.

My eyes catch on a trio of children.

They weave between people, squealing. It takes another minute or so to realize that one of them is actually crying: a little girl with dirt on her skirt and cheeks. The two other children playing with her aren't really playing—they're taunting her, tossing a doll back and forth over her head, and the poor thing is falling right into their cruelty. She gets so worked up that she starts screaming at them, attempting uselessly to snatch the doll out of the air.

She reminds me of... *me*.

Me, reaching for the surface as a child, growing bitter and angry with every piece of my future that was ripped out of my hands and tossed without mercy above my head.

The boys guide her closer to the King's procession.

I can see what they plan to do even before they follow through with it. One of the them teases the girl by holding the doll directly above her head and the other sneaks up to trip her from behind. I intervene before making the conscious thought to do so.

Barreling between two guards, I catch the little girl before she can collide with the ground and be trampled.

When I look up, I take the lead from Viola's instinct back at the cathedral and toss a vision of red eyes peering out of my mask into both the boys' minds. Their eyes practically bulge out of their skulls. The doll falls to the ground as they scramble away with high-pitched squeaks of fear.

I pick up the doll and offer it to the little girl.

Her big brown eyes study my hand, then slide up to my mask. I smile even though she can't see it. Quick as lightning, she snatches the doll out of my grasp and clutches it to her chest. She doesn't speak, but a small grin flits across her face before she turns and disappears into the crowd.

Thankfully, Hazel decided to wait for me.

Her guards shift uneasily. They're frowning at me, and I know it's because every second of this delay separates us more from her father up ahead. Returning to our position within the guards' protection, I squeeze Hazel's lace-fitted fingers between mine. She lifts her eyes to my face, considering me with renewed interest. My own face is obscured by a blue fish mask gifted to me by the King, so I lean in and nudge the underside of her chin with one finger, tilting my head in question.

She sighs, shaking her head. "I'm sorry, I know I'm not the best company right now. I didn't get much sleep last night."

No, because she'd been waiting on her balcony for me, for the creature I used to be. When I woke this morning, I spotted her sleeping there.

I elbow her playfully, and that earns me a small laugh.

The corners of Hazel's eyes crinkle. "A proud man, aren't you, Captain?"

She thinks I'm teasing her about my visit, but I'll be whatever she wants me to be, whatever it takes to fix this. Now that the memory of last night is brought to the front of her mind, I scramble to lure her in, to affect the memory. I look into her eyes and infuse shadows into her thoughts to make her doubt what she remembers.

Maybe my cock *didn't* magically shrink under her touch. Maybe she was so tired that she simply imagined that, and imagined my voice below the balcony.

I lift her hand and press a kiss to her knuckles through my mask. When her neck flushes, I know my mental manipulation is working at least a little bit. Enough for her to walk nearer to my side as we're led to the canal.

Gondolas bob there, dressed in gold and red satin.

As Hazel withdraws her hand from my elbow, I suddenly worry she's going to step onto the first boat with her father and leave me on my own. That would be just my luck, wouldn't it? But then a large man boards the gondola beside the King—a guard, if the badges lining his chest are any indication. There's not enough room to seat more than two passengers, especially not with the driver balancing on the end.

The next boat is boarded by the priest—he's the only one *not* wearing a mask. I didn't see him during the procession, so we must have joined us in our walk through the city streets. When we passed the cathedral.

He beckons to Hazel with a grimy grin.

Hazel's hand returns to my arm, clutching tightly as she drags me to the last vacant gondola. Thank oblivion the mask covers my mouth... because I don't think the priest would be pleased with my smirk.

I tug her arm at the edge of the canal and step forward onto the boat first, turning around to help her board. My wandering hands graze her upper arm, her waist, anything that could be disguised as a gentleman's touch. If she dislikes my affection, she doesn't act like it.

We sit side-by-side in the cushioned seat, and when we finally set out, Hazel's verbal dam breaks.

She describes each section of the city as we float through them. The rest of the market. The tradesmen's districts. All of the historical and meaningful landmarks. Exploring it like this, by canal, makes the city seem bigger than it was from the palace. Everything had been diminished from above. Down here, level with them, the individual homes are significant.

Citizens toss flowers from cast-iron balconies and the red petals fleck the water ahead of us like trails of blood. Cheers echo off the walls of the canal. The King is barely visible at the front of the procession, his dark blue tunic and golden crown glistening.

Our boat falls behind the others.

Whether a poor pick of gondolier or a sign of my own turning luck, I'm grateful for it. My right knee settles against

Hazel's leg. I stretch an arm behind the seat, brushing my fingertips against her upper back, tracing the collar of her dress.

Truthfully, I'm not listening to her anymore.

My head is spinning with all of the ideas of how to get her alone and secure her affections. Maybe I should kiss her again. Maybe I simply didn't do it right the first time. There was so much kissing in the square when we walked through. I want to feel what *they* felt.

I'm determined to understand.

As we turn another bend in the canals to face the cresting sun, I shield my eyes. Hazel prattles on with her tour of the city. Her eyes are molten again, exceptionally pretty in the daylight. I let them distract me from the weight of the heart-string in my chest as the gondola rocks back and forth.

I don't realize how dramatically the boat is leaning until the sun suddenly disappears.

Blinking rapidly, I drop my hand.

Our gondola has been separated from the rest of the parade, veering into a narrow canal. The buildings are taller here, blocking out the sunlight. The cobblestone platforms to either side of us look dirty and abandoned. Whoever lives in this part of the city does not care for its condition.

Hazel twists in her seat to face the gondolier. "Why have we turned here?"

I look back in time to see an iron gate slice down in the archway behind us, cutting us off from the main canal. Shouting echoes on the other side; the soldiers floating with us have noticed our departure. The tip of another gondola appears in the archway, but we're turning another bend, steering us out of view from the guards.

Our masked gondolier picks up the pace, his brown arms pumping to propel us through the water.

"Where are we going?" Hazel's fear is apparent, threading through her voice like the invasive ivy climbing the walls to either side of us. When he continues navigating the canal without responding, she screeches, "Answer me!"

Nothing.

Hazel turns to me and rips her mask off, her face bright red. "Are you behind this?" Her voice trembles. "If you are, I demand to be returned to my father this instant. This area of the city isn't safe."

I shake my head, trying to sort out the situation.

I can't think straight.

Hazel shakes my arm. "Don't just sit there. Do something!"

That's right... I can do something.

My entire life, I've been told to do nothing. I've been told to know my place, to play my part, to support my father as he sculpted me and the rest of Atlantis into exactly what he desired. And when I was caught disobeying, I learned what it felt like to be truly paralyzed. I learned to fear rising, doing, being.

Below the surface, I never had a choice.

I have one now.

Tearing my own mask off, I stand up and climb onto the back of the boat with the gondolier. He's solid, with broad shoulders and long legs. His fingers tighten around the oar's darkly veined wood.

He leans to the side and the gondola collides with the canal wall. The entire craft shudders. I flail my arms to restore my balance, but when we bounce off the building, the other side ricochets into the wall as well.

The oar in the gondolier's hand shatters like crystal, leaving us to drift without direction.

Glancing behind me, I see Hazel curled up on the bench

seat, her necklace clutched in both hands. The walls up ahead fall away and a platform appears.

Hope and relief sweeps through me.

Swiftly, I grab the gondolier by his shirt and try to throw him into the water, but he grapples with me and we both slam into the wall. The boat spins out into the center of the canal and I catch myself on the tail jutting out the end of the gondola, barely keeping my whole body from toppling head first into the water.

Waves slurp at my legs like a maw from the great dark.

The gondolier lurches for the cabin seat, his hands reaching for Hazel, and I swing my leg up to trip him.

That knocks his mask free.

Every organ in my body leadens. Of course. How had I not guessed it earlier? I rise up off of my knees, my thoughts and nerves dazed.

He grimaces. "Brace yourself, Prince."

"*Captain.*"

A screech rips through the air as the boat's side continues to grind against the canal wall.

Hazel scrambles back from the bow of the ship, her gaze locked on a snake creeping up from the water, wrapping around the farthest peak of the gondola with iridescent, ivory scales. The beast is so large that the boat tips forward from the weight of it. Its diamond head slithers around the bow to peer at us, two bright purple eyes meeting mine.

The sea witch is behind this.

I leap over Hazel, drawing the shark tooth from the sheath hidden beneath my shirt. I land and slam the sharp point into the serpent's body and a deafening hiss resounds through the canal as the snake unfurls. I don't retreat quickly enough. The snake whips around and buries her fangs into my arm.

Heat explodes under my skin. My stomach turns. I stagger back, falling into the seat beside Hazel as the snake slips back under the water.

"Oh, God," Hazel whispers as she stares at my wound. "Vipers are venomous."

Viper venom. That would explain the sudden cloudiness of my head. It figures Viola would take that form. I called her a viper last night, and she loves to prove me right.

A slight rumble in the water around the gondola is our only warning.

Then several white snakes shoot out of the water at once, their jaws unhinging to latch onto one side of the gondola. Stringy mucus drips onto the red and gold interior. The boat begins rocking. A splash sounds from behind us, and when I turn to look, Fluke is gone.

He abandoned our doomed boat.

My head is a haze of disjointed voices, the ones on either side of my head and my own within. I stand, and the world tilts around me.

I reach out to grab Hazel, but my limbs are too heavy. She loses her footing, flailing, and her head hits the cobblestone platform with a sickening crack.

The gondola flips, submerging us both.

Murky water fills my vision, acrid particles flooding my mouth. A bloom of darkness appears in the corner of my eye. It takes a moment for my mind to recognize it as blood. *Hazel.* I swim into that fog, fumbling right into her.

I wrap my arms around her waist.

She's far too heavy to carry to the surface in my current state. Belatedly, I realize that my hand is still holding the shark tooth. I move quickly, cutting off her corset and petticoats, stripping her down to her undergarments, and then we finally break the surface.

Someone else is there, at the edge of the platform. I can't see them. I can't see anything, really. The venom is in my eyes.

Hands grapple with Hazel's arms.

I'm not stupid enough to fight them off. Hazel isn't breathing. As I tread the water a little closer, I see that Fluke is the one pulling her up. As I hoist myself out of the water and crawl to them, I watch him press his mouth to hers, his cheeks shifting in and out as he *breathes* into her.

I return my shark tooth back to its sheathe and clamber forward, my chest burning with jealousy.

It looks like he's kissing her better than I did last night.

Grasping his shoulder, I try to rip him off of her. He throws an arm out and knocks me over, making my head spin faster. The venom swirls and pulses in my veins.

"Stop," he snarls. "We can't let her die."

Fluke returns his mouth to hers. Again, pushing his breath into her. Breathing... he must be helping her breathe. My envy dissipates. He lifts his mouth, rests his ear against her chest with a distant expression, and presses a hand against her upper abdomen.

When he breathes into her the next time, Hazel's body convulses. Water erupts from her mouth. Fluke wrenches back with a look of utter disgust on his face, spitting out what made it between his lips. Then Hazel curls up on her side and vomits.

Fluke crouches in front of me.

I try to focus on his face, but it's all a blur of dark and light, shadow and sun. His voice, at least, rings clear in my ears. "Viola wanted to ruin your chances with the princess, but my orders pertain to what happened in the canal, not *this*. Not after. I can help, but you need to hit me."

I blink, the spots in my vision clearing enough to see the outline of his jaw. Hit him? Why?

A crash and clang echoes from far away.

Voices split the silence of the abandoned platform.

Fluke grabs a handful of my shirt and pulls me closer. "*Hit me, you dumb fucker.*"

I do as he says.

Though my limbs weaken more with every heartbeat, I manage to punch him hard enough to split his lip. The smell of iron taints the air. I can't tell if it's the fresh cut I smell, or if the shadow pooled around Hazel's head is actually blood and not her hair.

"I'm sorry," Fluke shouts loudly, his voice echoing off the cobblestone and carrying farther than I can see. "Forgive me, Captain. *Please.*"

No sooner do I start crawling towards the princess when dozens of bodies pour onto the platform. Guards surround us. Two of them wrench my arms behind my back. If I had my voice, I would be screaming at the hot pain that rips through the bite wound and up into my shoulder.

The King appears beside Hazel, his ornate golden mask hanging from his neck.

Hazel begins weeping when she sees her father. She spouts unintelligible words as she flings her arms around his shoulders.

The King's eyes scour the abandoned platform and land on me. If Viola's sole intention was to sow dissent between me and the King, it seems to have worked. In a voice as dark as the ocean, he demands, "What happened?"

"It was me, your Majesty." Fluke's voice warbles, ludicrously frail for the size of man he is. "I lost control of the gondola—I have a condition, you see. Sometimes, I just... forget myself. When I came to, we were drifting down this alley, the gate had been tripped, and spirits were rising from the water. It's all my fault."

He then descends into a fit, clutching his head and moaning mournfully as his body rolls all over the ground.

The King's expression shifts as he glances behind him, to where the priest is carefully studying the situation.

"Possession," the old man mutters to the King. Then he turns to address a guard beside him. "Run ahead to the cathedral—tell the nuns to prepare a bed."

Hazel's weeping parts long enough for her to form real words. "There were vipers, Papa. They—they bit—"

The King's eyes bulge, and he pushes her back from where she's been soaking his tunic. "Vipers attacked you?" His hands start assessing her shoulders, her arms, looking for any evidence of a bite.

"Not me," she sobs. "The Captain. He protected me."

The King's eyes flick to me again, gentle surprise warming them. He opens his mouth to speak, but before he can say anything, Hazel faints. Again.

The King waves off a guard that attempts to intercede and then he lifts his daughter off the ground himself. She looks peaceful there, *safe*. It's so odd that anyone could feel those things in the arms of a father. My world has become so small in the light of this one.

The King barks orders at the guards to prepare for their return through city street.

"Let him go," he tells my guards.

Pain swells when they release my arms, blood pumping unfettered in my veins again. The platform undulates beneath me.

I grit my teeth and bear it.

The King says, "You have my humblest gratitude, son. When we get settled back at the palace, you and I will talk."

He turns to the guards. "Escort him back to the castle, take him to the healer and see if there's anything to be done."

My limbs are stiffening—the venom spreading deep and wide.

Poison doesn't affect oceanfolk quite the same way as humans, and for all the changes Viola made to my body, I'm still mer. Silver still burns my skin and venom is only an inconvenience.

A human would be dead by now.

I struggle my way to my feet, swaying precariously. I don't know how I'm going to walk all the way to the palace to sleep this off.

Fluke falls into step beside me, leaning into me under the guise of helping me walk as we make our way out of the smaller city streets. He whispers in my ear, "She's waiting for me down in the canal, in one of the half-drowned shops. Ditch your escorts and keep her busy. I have a holy man to talk to."

He pulls away and winks. This is part of his plan somehow.

I grimace, but incline my head as he walks into the beckoning arms of the priest up ahead. As we emerge back in the square, the canal reappears beside us. The guards are talking to each other behind me, not paying too much attention to me, but why would they? My death is practically certain to them. I'm nothing to them but a task to be completed, a body to be delivered or death to be confirmed.

Maneuvering the crowd, I make it seem as though the traffic is what's pushing us closer and closer to the water's edge... and once we're close enough to the canal, I throw myself in.

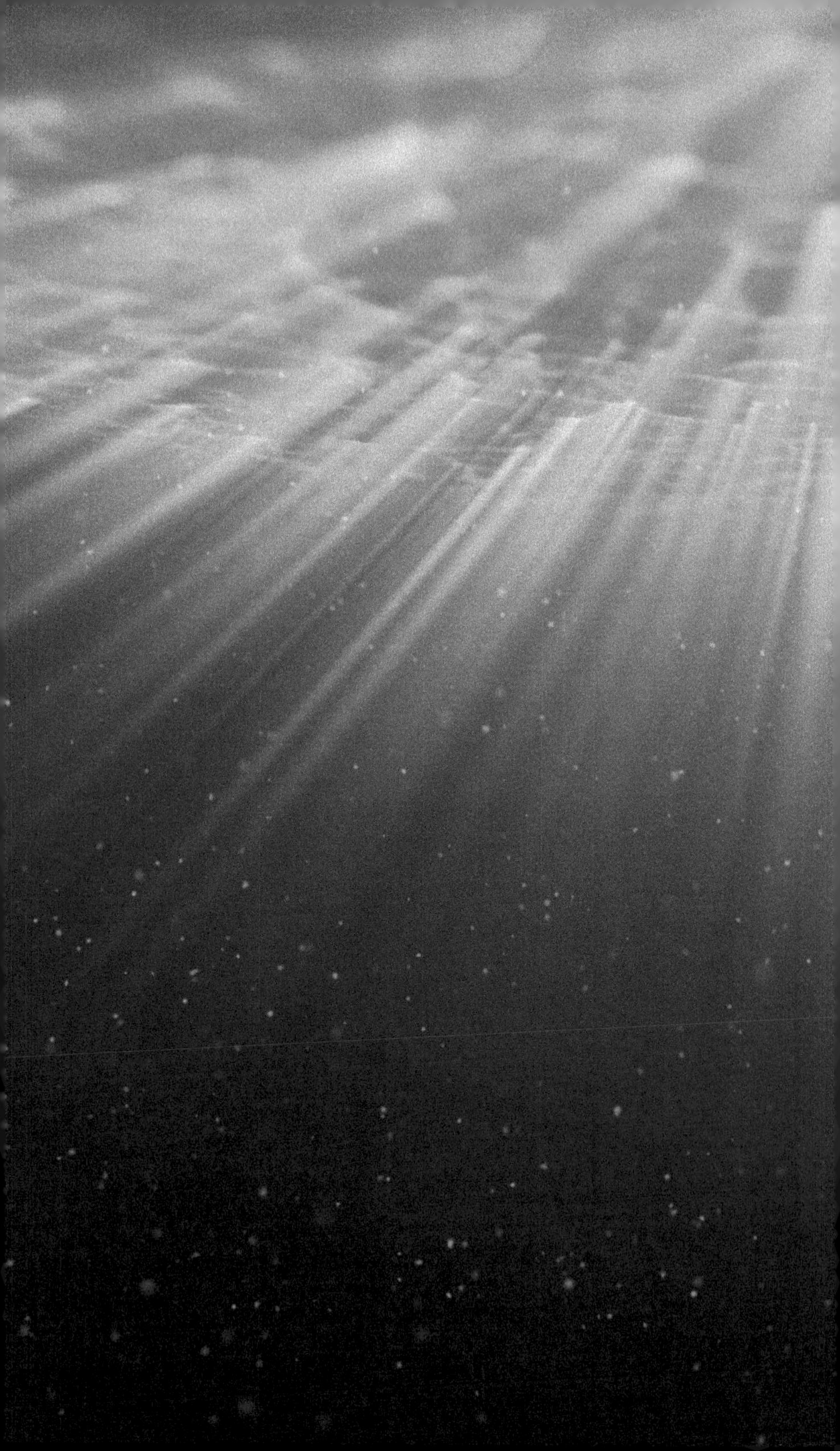

CHAPTER 17
ARIC

Viola is holed up in what looks to be a small, abandoned bookshop.

It's not the first place I looked. Not the third or the tenth. I've been dragging myself along in the canal, using the wall to keep my head above water. My limbs are too stiff to swim properly.

Soaked, musty parchment shifts under my fingertips as I grip the edge of the room's floor. The canal feeds directly into the small space, a shallow level of water blanketing the floor. The shelves are in disarray, some lying on their sides with their books scattered, the wooden panels bulged and decaying from constant moisture.

Viola's other soul-bound is here, sitting on a stack of books in the corner, his shoulders slumped and his eyes sagging. He has legs. Peasant clothes. He must have been tasked in the city, maybe as the one who tripped the iron gate. I imagine the trigger was somewhere up in the turrets.

I'm also guessing she recently fed on him.

Viola paces between the aisles that are still standing. She

hears me flounder my way out of the canal and says coyly, "Well, you aren't the fluke I was expecting."

Her steps splash in a distinctive, even pattern—she has feet right now. I do my best to stand straight and raise my chin, not wanting her to know how weak I'm feeling, but when she turns the corner into the belly of the room, my composure slips.

Her skin is not her own. The shade is too dark, her cheeks too sallow.

The princess, Hazel, stares back at me. She's just been carried back to the palace, so it can't truly be her. These eyes are too bright, a luminous shade of violet.

Viola looks at her soul-bound. "Leave us. If I sense you within even smelling distance of this place, I'll rip your heart out and feast on it tonight." It's so strange to hear her speak, because her voice is the same dusky alto that should belong to the sea witch.

Her power only camouflages appearances, so it would seem.

Viola's soul-bound lurches off the stack of books, hitting the water at the same time as his tail returns, ripping loudly through the seams of his pants. His grimace as he drags himself out of the room tells me everything.

The sea witch is in a terrible mood, and her touch was not gentle.

I lean against the closest wall. My head is spinning, the blood in my veins moving too sluggishly to stand up on my own much longer. I'm too tired to demand my voice. If Viola doesn't want to give it back, she won'; it's useless to expend my energy playing these games.

Please, no more games.

Viola seems to understand without me telling her.

Without another word, she waves her hand, and a tickle climbs up my throat.

"Why?" I rasp.

Her head tilts in that unnerving, predatory way as she draws closer. "Why *what*?"

Something trails in the water behind her. I squint, using my shoulder to anchor me as I slog forward for another look. It's one of the tentacles sprouting from her back. I think it's bleeding.

Bleeding dark blue.

That must be where I cut her, and she must need to keep it in a natural form to heal. Good. I'm glad I managed to leave some kind of mark.

"You hurt her." I whisper. "Now you're wearing her skin. What happened to you not wanting to drag innocents into your personal business?"

She stares at me for a long moment.

Then she shrugs and says, "If Fluke didn't butcher his orders, she'd be fine right now. I only wanted to scare her."

Somehow, I was beginning to think better of her than that. I'm actually *disappointed*. There's no reason for me to feel that, or to feel anything at all towards her besides hate. She doesn't deserve the benefit of my doubt.

Her injured tentacle sweeps forward into the space between us, "This is my mask, Aric. I thought you'd like it."

Viola lifts the tentacle to my face, its ivory tip grazing my cheek. She's instigating again, prodding at me to get a reaction, trying to prove *something*.

I won't stand for it anymore.

Before she can pull away, I seize her tentacle and wrap it around my wrist. With vicious movements, I wrench her toward me. "Fix me," I growl.

She smirks.

The voices of my conscience are deafening. They scream their desires, their differing motivations working me up to one thing: getting the sea witch closer to me, getting my hands on more than her tentacle.

Me, all over her.

One more tug and our noses brush. I stare into her eyes, the only part of her that feels familiar, feels right.

"Fix. What. You. Hurt."

Black spots swarm my vision. I'm going to collapse soon if she doesn't do something. I'll lose precious hours with Hazel, and Viola will be that much closer to claiming me.

Maybe that's what she wants.

But is she that vile? That unfair?

Her eyes sweep down to my arm, her tentacle sliding across my skin to reveal the bite mark under my wet shirt. The wound is black and blue around the entry points.

Her smile fades. "Okay."

Viola takes my wrist and lifts my arm to her face. She meets my gaze again, only for a moment, and bares her front teeth. Her pupils thin into delicate, serpentine slits. Milky white fluid begins to seep from her gums, flowing down her canines. She uses her tongue to gather the anti-venom off her teeth, and then drops her mouth to my arm.

Her tongue drags over my skin.

She licks at the bite in small massaging circles, her teeth grazing irreverently. I want to push her away. I shouldn't feel this way about her touch, about her tongue.

The effects of her venom are already fading, and by the time she lifts her head, I feel steady. Solid.

But I stand there totally captivated by her.

Her scent is in my nostrils. Her saliva is on my skin, in my bloodstream. *She's inside me.* "You're welcome," she whispers as she tries to walk past me.

My grip tightens on her tentacle.

Her wound is nearly finished healing, the white skin regenerating at a rapid pace, sped along by her magic.

"You're not going anywhere," I tell her.

She looks me up and down. "And why not? Do you want something more from me?"

I search for the right response. I need to stall her for an indeterminate amount of time, and that means engaging in even the most ridiculous conversation if that will keep her occupied in this room. "I want you to stop meddling." I feel a nervous vein feathering in my temple. "I need you to give me a real chance."

She folds her human arms over her chest. "Well, maybe I should stroll through the streets with you in this skin, Aric. Word of mouth is a powerful thing. A scandalous rumor about you and the princess can permeate the city and compromise her purity, and then the King will be forced to give her over to you."

Her eyes glitter with malice as she leans in. "Or perhaps they'll send her off to a convent and cut off your head."

I yank on her tentacle, spinning her around in my arms as we careen into the wall. My full weight lands in the center of her back. She turns her face to the side, blue blood trickling from her nose, down over her red lips. I emit a low growl. Because she's *smiling*.

At once, I have my shark tooth in hand. I don't recall drawing it.

Biting fury. Confusion. That's all I have. I don't quite know what I'm doing. All I know is that this feels *good*. I press the tip of the shark blade to her neck. "If you don't take her face off your skin this instant," I warn through gritted teeth, "I'm going to fuck you until you're too tired to keep up with the charade."

Viola tenses.

I'm not proud that this is my leverage, that *this* was where my head went to as a last resort. But if she wants to threaten me, I'll do the same to her. It has nothing to do with the traitorous ache in my core, the heat spreading through me. My body very badly wants to fuck her. The words simply fell out of my mouth before I could stop them, dropping out of the fog her cycle stirred up in my head.

I don't mean it.

I could never hurt her like that, *any* female like that. The idea makes me sick. She doesn't need to know that, though. We're all playing into our parts, playing into the skin we're given, like she said last night. I suddenly wonder if I have ever seen the real Aric that hides beneath all these lies. Chances are, I wouldn't recognize him.

"I'm not the safest creature to threaten with that right now," she whispers.

I scoff. "I can handle you."

She's quiet for a moment.

And then, just when I think I finally have her pinned down, she has to open her tempting mouth and ruin it. "Is that supposed to intimidate me, dear Prince?" she says in an airy voice. "You'd better keep that blade of yours firmly against my throat if you try, or you'll wind up as flotsam in my arms. Do your worst."

I scramble to retain some measure of power, of sense... but she's taken it. With three words, she's stolen it all for herself. *Do your worst.*

My worst is far less than what I've threatened.

Where do I go from here?

In my silence, she chuckles. "That's what I thought. You're an empty mer, promises and all, *exactly* like your father."

Those words hurt more than I want to admit. More than the venom, and more than a thousand cuts between my scales.

My need for her fills my chest and plucks that heartstring until I feel like I'm vibrating. Pressing the tip of the tooth to the underside of her chin, I tilt her face toward mine. Her eyes are cloudy. I can't tell if this is another test, another game. What does she really want?

This?

Because if she truly wants *this*, that changes the game, changes the rules. Changes what I'm capable of doing to her.

"It's almost as though you *want* me to fuck you, witch," I say softly.

She doesn't respond.

That ache in me grows, touching every muscle in my abdomen, burning away every speck of lingering hesitation. I want her. In this moment, it doesn't matter why, or who we are, or what we've done to one another. What we might do yet. I want her more than I've ever wanted anyone.

And I'm finally starting to believe she wants me in return.

With her purple eyes anchored in mine, I'm sure.

"Kneel, then," I command, my voice a husky whisper.

She blinks, her eyes losing their predatory sharpness.

I press the knife harder to her neck, breaking skin. Her essence is too sweet to resist. I lean in and breathe her scent deep into my lungs. It's liquid smoke, choking my hatred. All that's left behind is my desire, and she's *not moving fast enough*.

"Kneel on the books before I cut you open and make you bleed all over them." I'll mark the entire room with her scent if that's the only way I can be inside her.

Viola decides to obey me.

She guides her knees to the piles of books lining the wall

in front of her, breathing shallowly. Delight spears through my gut at every erratic little gasp. As her sex parts, more of her essence drifts up to envelop me.

I'm caught up in the sticky-sweet resin of her.

This isn't the most stable position in the world, but I have a firm grip on her. I won't let her fall and ruin my fun. I trace the curve of her ass with the shark blade, grazing the beckoning part of her legs.

"Wider," I breathe. "Open your legs and let me in."

A noise stirs in the very back of her throat, bubbling across her vocal cords as she listens to my instruction. That was a *trill*.

Her arousal is intensifying, and so is mine.

I want to see what she looks like when her other mask fades, the one she dresses with smiles and hatred. The one she puts on for Atlantis.

I want to break her open and see the truth.

Dragging the shark tooth down the length of her back, I smile as she shivers. "That's it," I mutter.

I let the shark blade slip between her legs from behind, and I'm careful not to cut her. Her body trembles. This must be torture for her, indulging her cycle but being unable to follow through on her Goddess's bidding. Being unable to eat me.

Leaning in, I glide my knuckles along her center.

She's utterly soaked, and we both know it has nothing to do with the water at our feet. It's an earth-shattering awareness. Her slickness. My eyes drift shut, because I can't look at her when she looks like this, like Hazel. I memorize her with my touch instead. The exquisite sculpting of her, the peaks and folds and soft curls.

She moans, and I suddenly realize I'm being far too gentle. Her pheromones are in my head.

As quickly as possible, I rip my pants open. Then I'm banding my forearm over the front of her hips to tilt her ass back and up. I notch myself at her entrance and her breath catches, but I don't push inside. Not yet.

"Now," I whisper in her ear, fisting my free hand in her hair.

As I bring the tooth back to her neck, I can't stop from turning my face into her hair. Her arousal has stained my knuckles, stained my soul. She's too delicious. Too enticing and soft and warm, too *everything*. I didn't know it was possible to want someone this much and hate them in equal measure. To hate them for making me feel so desperate.

"Beg for my cock."

She hesitates, that hint of a smile on her face turning into an effervescent grin. "I don't beg for what's already mine. You could learn a thing or two from that."

My heart thunders, and warmth flushes my body.

I wrench her head back by her hair, and as her back arches, I push into her. Her opening tightens, making it near impossible to continue. She trills again, the sound pathetic and needy. I hate how much I like it.

"You prepared my body to your liking, witch," I snarl, "so stop your whimpering and take it like the precious whore you wish to be."

Her hair is velvet in my hand.

I slam my fist against the wall to keep from burying my nose in it again, and she cries out. Even so, her body softens for me, obeying the order. I continue my claiming, and her moans drown out the sound of the canal lapping at the doorway. Deeper and deeper.

I give of myself until there's nothing left.

An unbelievable pressure bears down around my cock, and I gasp for reason as I acclimate to the suction of her inner muscles. I try to withdraw and shudder as tension coils in my length. It's as if my cock has been anchored into the core of her. I can't pull out.

Reality hits me. What have I done?

Viola's body shakes with amusement, sending tremors through the muscles of my stomach. She has no right to be amused right now. Maybe it's because she knew this would be my demise.

I'm not feeling so confident in my ability to handle her anymore.

Viola's visage rolls and shakes, shimmering like sunlight. She's close to letting the disguise drop. She's close to *losing control*. If she loses control and shifts form to top me, I won't stand a chance. She'll kill me. She was being serious earlier, about me keeping her in line.

I bring the tooth to her cheek, cutting her shallowly in warning, before letting the knife drop back to her throat. I press it firmly against her soft skin.

Viola's eyes open in alarm, and I latch onto them.

In the fantasy, I'm still inside her. She looks like herself, pastel hair and lavender eyes, skin so flawless I want to devour it. This is my world, and I am its god. *She. Will. Bow.*

I slice her throat open.

And perhaps I'm still feeling some sort of fucked up way about her because I don't make it hurt. I don't infuse any sensation into it whatsoever.

There's already enough pain between us.

Blue blood gushes over my hand, ethereal and downright lovely against the backdrop of her alabaster skin. Every part of her is beautiful. Spheres of pleasure roll up my spine, until I'm practically bursting with the force of it. The sea witch doesn't fight me. She doesn't push me away. She *laughs*, the sound twining with her gasping breaths.

It's unthinkable. There's such joy in these sounds, such pleasure, that I nearly drop the blade.

I allow the more pleasurable sensations to overtake me. The warm blood trickling over my hand. Her cunt, hot and tight, sucking and squeezing, milking. The slick slide of my cock inside her. I'm lost to her, each thrust a surrender to her magnificent pull.

Viola throws herself back into me, her muscles clamping me harder. And that's when a terrifying thought occurs to me. Will I be able to detach myself now that she's accepted me, with her secret suctions and vibrating tissues and a heat that suggests her release is imminent too. If this is what her cunt can do when it's aroused, what will it do to me when she comes? Can I even survive it?

I throw the vision off of us.

Viola is Viola again—every trickery of her magic gone. Her tentacles are splayed over the books and my lower abdomen. I hold her up as she rakes her nails down the wall in front of us, as her eyebrows furrow. Those red lips part in another guttural moan.

Any second now, she'll detonate, and I can't allow it.

I lower my blade to where her hearts glow a bright gold. "If you come," I snarl. "I'll drive this blade into your chest, and there will be nothing false about it."

"Do it, then," she retorts breathlessly. "Show me who you really are."

As if she doesn't already know. As if that's not exactly why she targeted me in the first place. She thinks I'm weak, vulnerable. I dig the tooth into the skin directly above her open wound. I should finish this. Maybe if I do, my tail will return and I can go home. Back to my father. Back to the place that made me so... *indifferent.*

Blue blood runs from the cut I make above her hearts,

dripping across the swirl on her chest. The evidence of her curse and treason.

Still, she chases her release. It's as if she *wants* to dance with death, would rather *die* than cut this pleasure short. The sea witch might be as lonely as I am, as depraved and miserable and restless in all the same horrible ways.

Damn, that changes everything.

Viola loses her rhythm, collapsing against the wall as a violent shudder rolls through her body. Her release radiates into my cock. All that heat gathers at the base of my length, and I'm tugged *deeper* somehow—stretched and twisted up inside her. Something velvety soft rubs against the underside of my cock.

Sparks race down my spine.

I can't let my guard down. The instant I do, she'll eat me alive. "*Fuck*," I seethe, pulling the shark blade away from her neck and driving it down into a book beside us so I can use both hands to free myself.

With an almost painful pull, I manage to pull out of her. Her human legs are gone, so as I break free from her ivory tentacles, she tumbles into a heap of parchment and leather.

I fall back on my ass.

She's already twisting, reaching for me, rising on the shaky pedestal of her tentacles.

"What are you doing?" she asks.

There's a hundred questions behind that one.

"I'm done," I say, trying to disentangle my arm from her grasp. Another tentacle wraps around my wrist, and one around my leg.

"We're not," she argues. "The princess isn't going to marry you after what happened in the canal. Sunset tomorrow, you'll be mine. You might as well give up now and come home."

It's both a request and a command, but a deal is a deal.

This day and the next is mine, no matter the end. And if there's one thing I know for certain, it's this:

"There's no home left for me under the sea," I tell her. "Not with you."

I try to pull away again, but her tentacles make it impossible. Another one suctions to my left leg. There's no chance of making it away from her unless she lets me.

"Admit it, Aric," she says in a low, fluttering tone. "You aren't finished. Shall we take a closer look at the evidence?" Her eyes flick to my arousal, her tongue darting out to wet her lips. My cock twitches. "Shall I serve you this once before you return the favor for all eternity?"

Icy flames spread in my stomach, prickling into the surface of my skin.

There's nothing I desire more than to feel her mouth on me, to feel the reality and compare it to what I fantasized. The sight of her on her knees for me is the kind of fantasy I could live in for the rest of my life.

I can't resist her in this.

Silence stretches between us. Life and death, communicated in a glance. Her hands move to undo the buttons I struggled with this morning. She parts my shirt. Viola tucks her fingers beneath the band of my pants and pulls them down my legs. Her eyes are on mine, and neither of us dare to look away.

I'm going to file this memory away for a day when this is inevitably over, when she's gone or I am, and I perhaps return to a life where no one is powerful enough to move me.

And if not...

I'd rather die than let her reap me. I'll toss myself off a balcony back at the palace if I need to make that happen. This might be one of my final pleasures.

What an incomparable pleasure she is.

She leans over me, her breath caressing my crotch. It takes everything in me to keep my hips from arching up to meet her. I fist my hands to keep from threading them in her hair.

I hold my breath, waiting for her to envelop me in the warmth of her mouth and push me over that brink.

But her gaze drops at the last second. She traces her fingertips over my collection of razor-thin scars embedded in my flesh.

Gone is the fire from her eyes, the liquid seduction from her body. She takes in the full tapestry of cuts stretching down my legs, and a wetness rims her lashes. "He hurt you," she whispers.

My stomach hardens.

I don't want her to know about this. It's just another thing for her to wield as a weapon against me, or worse, *pity* me for. I dig my nails into her wrists to peel them off my legs, but I don't have enough strength or hands to detangle myself completely, and that enrages me even further.

I bring my face close to hers, not showing an ounce of the dread I feel as I snarl, "You have no idea what you're talking about."

Her eyes flash, glowing lilac as her hearts flare with anger. "I have no idea? That's what you think?"

Then her tentacles are all over me. My wrists, my thighs, my chest. I feel her everywhere. She crawls on top of me with burning eyes, her free tentacles propping her up as she straddles me.

My cock notches at her entrance without any guidance.

I can see her cunt better from this angle—the plane of white, translucent skin between her ivory tentacles, in the same spot a woman's entry would be.

I half-expect her to lower herself onto my throbbing length just to prove her point, but she doesn't.

She just hovers there.

I think that might be worse, to be stuck in this state of *almost*. To feel her arousal dripping down my length, the scent of her covering me like a blanket and making me absolutely feral with desire all over again. "Do you want to know what *I* think, Silver-Pipes?"

I glare at her, cursing my hips for twitching at the sound of her voice. Not that it matters. She's not letting me budge an inch. I impatiently wait for what she has to say.

The sea witch leans in until our noses brush again, and I can smell the herbal wax on her lips. "I think you're a fool for making this deal with me," she says softly. "For provoking me every chance you get when you clearly have no intention of protecting yourself. I have plenty of ideas about you. You're not what you should have been. You fight just to bleed. You fuck instead of drown, dream instead of wreck. I'm certain that makes you the worst siren that ever existed."

She chuckles humorlessly.

My heart aches for more.

"Maybe you're not a siren at all," she muses.

I pull against her hold on my wrists. I don't dare move anything below my waist, not with her cunt threatening me like the blade I held to her throat. In my heart, beneath the tug of her heart's string, I know I'm willing to die for this too.

She drags the tip of her nose across my cheek to whisper in my ear. "But that also makes you a better mer than your father ever was, or ever will be."

I stop fighting, stop breathing.

As she lifts her face to meet my gaze, I feel something melt in my chest. Melt and burn, burn, burn. Her eyes flick back and forth between mine.

"And you know what else?" she murmurs, her voice opening like a door, like the sky at dawn. "I think despite how often you dream of killing me, you dream of touching me even more. It was *my* eyes you brought into that vision, *my* face. You don't want a princess sitting in an ivory tower above the sea. You want something that can't be broken. You want someone like *me*."

My chest dissolves into all-consuming flames.

When I tug on my wrists again, she releases them.

It's my intention to shove her away. That's what I *should* do. But as my hands slide over the curve of her hips, I slam my cock into her instead.

Her mouth falls open on a groan, and I grit my teeth.

I sit up, raising her hips between my hands to impale her again. "I don't want you," I growl, thrusting into her over and over. "I hate you with every fiber of my being."

Her cunt is madness. Unholy pleasure. My darkest desire and unraveling at once. And the smile she gives me as she takes the brutal pounding... her amused, knowing smile is the most grotesque thing I've ever seen.

"Keep hating me then," she whispers, looping her human arms around my neck and pressing her chest to mine. Surrendering. "Hate me forever, if you do it like this."

Four of her tentacles shoot out to either side of us, crashing through books and into the fragile wall and floor. The ivory arms brace her upright as she starts to move, as she presses forward to gain the leverage she needs to dominate our rhythm.

I give myself over. I let her fuck me.

I've never let anyone fuck me before, and it's a *revelation*. Her eyes, her hair, her nipples—they're wildflowers, growing and blooming, beauty I can't bear to pluck. Those scarlet lips are painted with sin. It might as well be my blood. I'm half a second from slicing myself open just to be on her mouth.

She should have killed me by now.

Viola notices me looking at her breasts and gasps out, "Go ahead. Suckle, if that's what you want."

I don't let myself argue. I eagerly lean up and take one of her breasts in my mouth, sucking hard on her puckering purple areola. The sweetest elixir coats my tongue—the barest trickle of essence that drives me into a frenzy. I'm touching her everywhere.

Lecherous heat wrangles up my spine, inch by inch, bone by bone. Release is so close, I can taste it. It's the bond. It's her Goddess. There's no way I'm coming because of *her*.

I can't.

"Yes, you can," she moans.

I must have said some part of that out loud. How much, I'm not sure. She gazes down at me with vicious determination. She rides me harder. I've made things that much worse by telling her I don't plan on coming. I might as well have begged her.

"I won't," I say again.

Her tentacles writhe against my legs. They suction and tug, manipulating the bend of my legs until I realize what she's planning. I open my mouth to stop her, but it's too late. One of her tentacles prods my asshole. I lose control of my body as it responds to her. I buck into her cunt even harder, groaning as she pushes in an inch. She's found yet another way to get under my skin, to take up space inside of me and make me hers, and I *fucking love it*.

Release spears through me like a storm permeating the sea. Hazy, immersed, drifting at the mercy of lights on a distant shore. I open my eyes and see her. Her hearts, shining brighter than the sun as she comes again above me.

Who would have guessed that a creature of the deep could rival the greatest wonder of the surface?

Beneath our ragged breaths, the world falls still.

I wonder if this is how I'll feel when she reaps my soul: helpless, warm, expectant. I raise a thumb to her lips and smear the wax across her cheek. I won't kiss her. I'm terrified of kissing her. "If I'm not a siren, then you're not a whore."

A shroud of ice coats my organs as I realize that I'm *feeling* something. Beyond reason and rage, beyond my comfort. Here it is: sensation. And I'm still alive to feel it.

How the fuck am I still alive?

Her eyes twinkle like the stars did on that night so long ago, when I floated on the surface with only a bottle of wine and my dreams, when everything felt possible and my happiness probable. The strange emotion in my heart rises up between my ribs in a helpless attempt to touch her, hold her. But the sea witch climbs off of me before I can decide what to do with it, her tentacles rippling away.

I stand and tug my pants up, grimacing as the wet material clings like a leech to my skin.

The shattered voices of my conscience are silent, their influence absent. They've left me to the reality of my actions. I did it again. I made a reckless decision with my body before my mind could catch up.

Viola shifts into her human form.

I envy her nakedness, but I knot that if I'm going to make it back into the palace, I need to be clothed. As I start fussing with the buttons on my shirt, her bare foot flicks water at me.

"How in the world are you going to fall in love with a princess after fucking me like *that*?" she teases.

"Our deal doesn't require that I love her," I reply flatly,

"only that *she* loves *me*. And I still fully intend on making that happen."

"You think it can be true love if it's not reciprocated?"

I scoff and give up on my shirt, walking backwards toward the mouth of the canal. "True love isn't real. And if it is, then I'm not capable of it. You said she'd have to agree to marry me; you *had* to quantify love with action because you can't prove it exists any other way."

The sea witch blinks, her eyes darkening as she shakes her head. "Love is real, Aric."

I click my tongue, a flood of brutal cold filling my abdomen. "Well, if even *you* have experienced it, I must be more broken than I thought." I say it as a joke, but I don't think my smile fools her.

She takes a small step toward me. "There's a drier path back to the city square," she says, looking at the rickety door on the back wall. "I'll show you, if you think you can trust me long enough to guide you there."

I'm not particularly eager to swim in the canal again, especially against the current.

"I will never trust you, witch," I reply. "But lead the way."

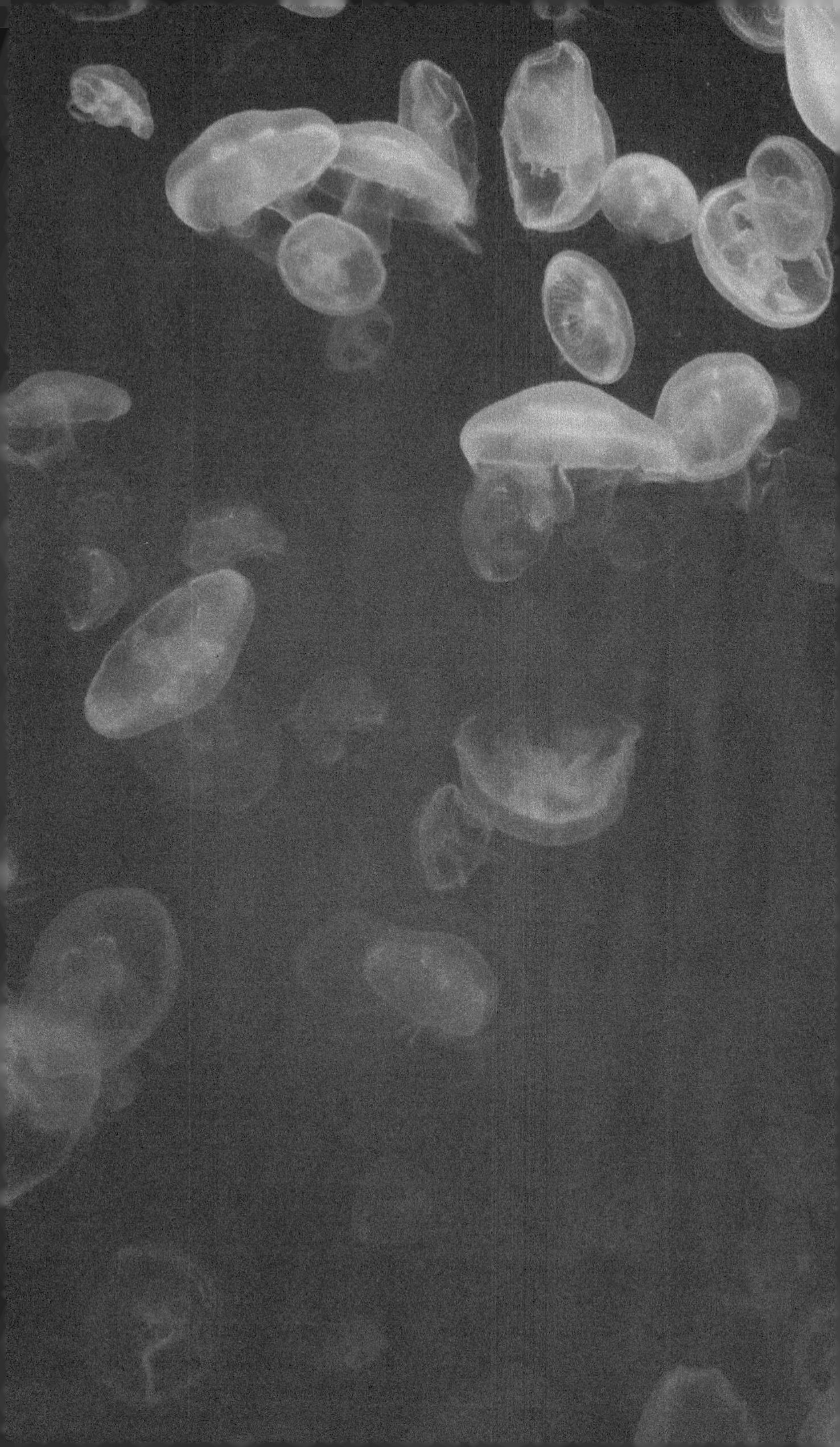

CHAPTER 18
VIOLA

I claim a thin, cotton dress hanging from a clothesline. It's not much, but it's better than being naked; my skin is smoldering like white coal in the afternoon sun.

The streets narrow and grow more crowded as we near the city square, filled with masks and stumbling drunks and suffocating happiness.

Aric follows me into the mayhem. He hasn't said anything since we left the drowned shop, even though I allow him to keep his voice a little while longer. I'm hoping it encourages him to follow me for the rest of the day. So far, it has. There's so much I want to show him.

I pluck a scarf off a woman's costume and wrap it around my hair. When we pass a particularly intoxicated man, I slip the red mask off the top of his head and settle it over my eyes, the fragile material barely stretching down to my cheekbones. We turn the next corner and plunge into the heart of the market, every inch swimming with movement and music and color. I walk with purpose, reaching back to tug Aric forward as we slip between the bodies.

We approach a tent with open curtains and I turn to smile at him, but he's too distracted by the activities happening within the tent.

Humans gather around large vases, brass necks engraved with sacred markings and spitting out thick, white clouds. The whole tent is shrouded in a veil of smoke, like ocean foam dancing in the air.

I snag another mask from a passerby and offer it to Aric. He considers it, utterly still.

"You don't have to leave yet," I tell him. "You could stay and join the real celebration... if you think you can keep up."

I don't want him to go.

The memory of what we did together curls tightly in my chest, making me want to eliminate as much of the space between us as possible. Not for the sake of the cycle. I've fulfilled it, and the mating ache is slowly seeping out of my body. Now that I'm coming down, I see the significance of Aric surviving it.

Goddess Mora spared him.

That, in and of itself, is a miracle. It can't be a coincidence that Triton's son is the only male to survive my cycle, or *any* witch cycle entered into under the surface, as far as I know.

Everything clarifies for me as I look into Aric's eyes. That night we met, when I followed his song. The rune of favor he pulled for our binding—*The Gift*. Those arrows in his eyes. *The Goddess drew us together.* Not for the reason I thought initially—not to *punish* him—but for some greater purpose.

One I still don't fully understand.

I want to understand. I want to understand Aric.

He fucked me senseless back in that shop, just like he promised... but there had been moments, *fleeting heartbeats,* where he'd also been unbelievably gentle. *It's almost as though you want me to fuck you, witch. Kneel, then. Open your legs and let me in.* Aric had needed to know I wanted that as badly as he did, even if he did spout empty threats beforehand. It was the opposite of what I'd expected him to do, had urged him to do. I wanted him to show me who he was.

One last test, I told myself. His response was not evil, not his father, not even a little bit.

He forced me to admit how much I wanted him, if not in words then with the submission of my body. I wanted it badly enough to kneel when he asked me to.

And before, when I watched him walk into the square... I saw the way he treated that child. He didn't stand by and let her get pushed around or trampled. He stood up for her, protected her.

I'd refused to accept it for what it was then, but I feel the truth of it now—proof that the Prince of Atlantis is a *defender*.

The same as me, or close enough.

Close enough that when I saw his scars, everything shifted. He was marked by Triton too. His wounds just happen to be less obvious than mine. After what I did to his gallery and his friend, why *wouldn't* he be angry with me? I pushed him. Taunted him. Hurt and sabotaged. So he grew even angrier.

Jussi was right—anger is the most convincing mask, thicker and stronger than painted porcelain.

Aric steps forward, ignoring the mask in my hand.

He lowers his face to mine and warmth swirls in the space between us as he whispers onto my cheek. "You want me to stay? Would you like me to drink and dance and feast with you? Shall we search for a hidden hollow in this square so I can fuck you again?"

There's something vicious in his voice, so faint I almost don't hear it.

Aric traces his fingertips along my jaw, and I lose track of my thoughts. His thumb caresses my lips. "All you have to do is ask, *Viola*."

I hesitate, my throat working. There's something wrong, but I so desperately want to believe he means it, that he wishes to be here with me. That he feels the significance between us as powerfully I do.

"Stay," I breathe.

Aric smiles then, but it is not kind. He chuckles darkly, peeling back from me as he says, "There is nothing I desire less."

I feel my body go cold, my eyes hardening beneath the mask. Every limb in my body stiffens beneath his cruelty.

Of course he hates me. Of course the sex meant nothing to him. How could it be any other way, after I ripped him from the ocean and punished him at every turn? Punished him for things he didn't do. I filled his veins with venom and nearly drowned the princess. *His human princess.*

I went too far.

Perhaps I wasn't so wrong that night I saw him singing to her. Perhaps he does care for her, as much as he can care for anything.

The porcelain offering slips from my fingers and shatters at our feet. I clench a hand in front of my chest, reclaiming his voice. "Enjoy the desolate palace, Prince."

Then I walk away and start formulating a new plan.

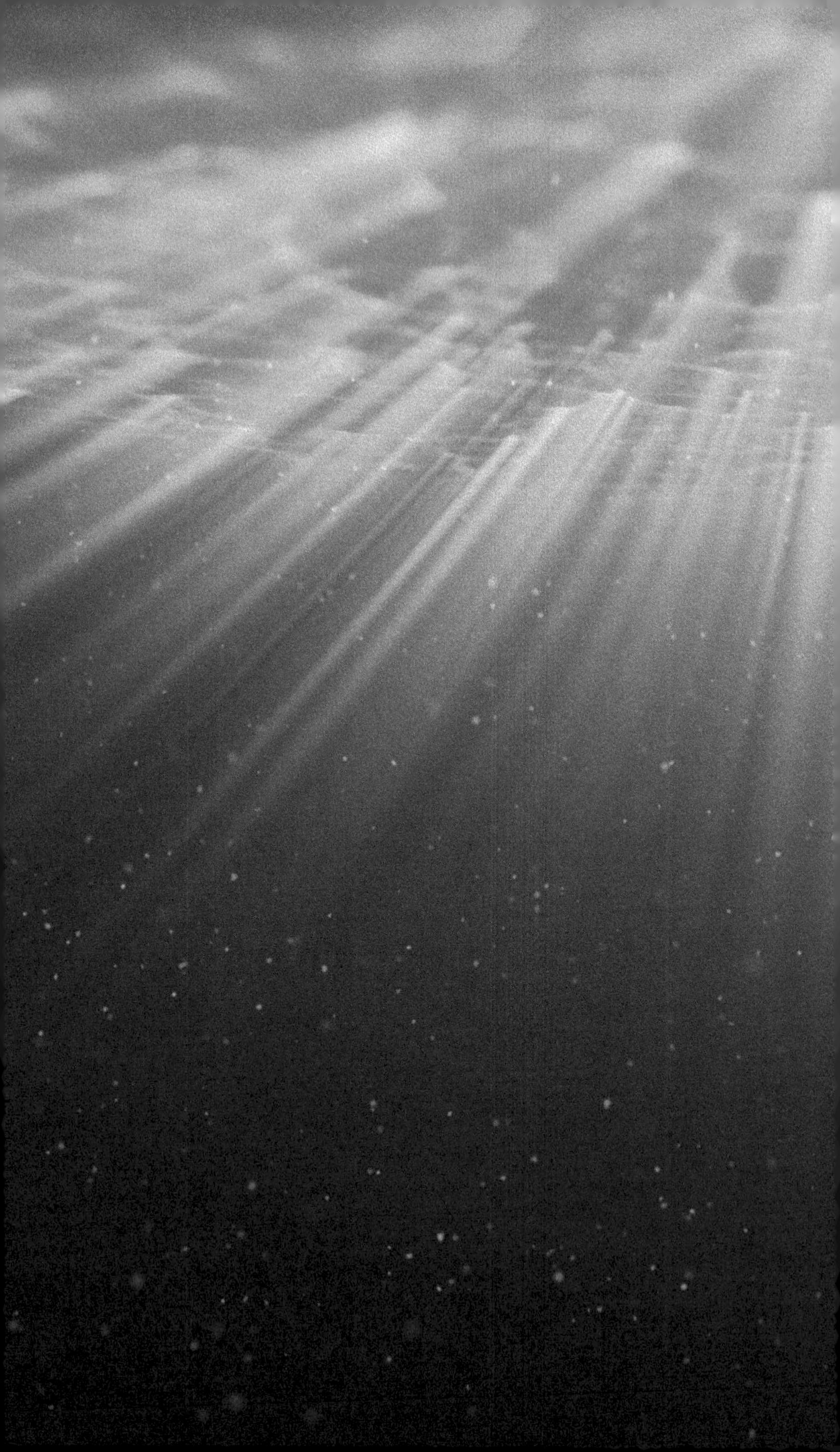

CHAPTER 19

ARIC

Hazel was angry with me the last time I disappeared on her.

This time, I report directly to her room.

The entire walk back to the palace, I curse the dampness of my clothes and the treachery of my body. Not only for what I did, but for what I still wish to do. I wanted nothing more than to stay with Viola, to indeed revel and feast and fuck her for a second time against the wall of some narrow alley. My eyes couldn't help but mark every place we could have done that on my way out of the square.

That feeling in my chest lingers. The reaching, uncomfortable ache I'm now all too aware of.

What does it mean? I wish I had a word for it. A name.

I curse the sea witch, because I don't know what else to do. I was cruel and cold to her because every irrational part of me—and there's not much left of me that *is* rational—wanted to be the exact opposite. And I can't afford to be anything but her enemy right now.

One day.

That's all the time I have left. I refuse to waste that time thinking about her, or what I might feel towards her. Nothing will change the fact that she intends to gorge herself on me when my time is up. It won't change the fact that she took my mother away from me.

Even if the feel of her is imprinted on my soul.

I halt beyond the corner leading to Hazel's room. There are guards at her door, which suggests that her father is with her.

Taking a breath, I shut my eyes.

When I was a child, I *lived* at the theater. The best memories I have of my mother were ones that occurred in that old amphitheater. It was her place.

I spent my childhood there, playing in the underdwellings, surrounded by stories of love and tragedy and triumph, watching my mother write and direct some of the best shows known to the ocean. Her passion for those stories is etched into my heart.

Today, it might be my salvation.

As I roll my shoulders and open my eyes, I become the man worthy of a princess. The man who fought a viper for her and made it out the other side by the grace of heroism. I become a man who is capable of love. One last performance.

The performance of my life.

I turn the corner and will my body to visibly tremble as I approach the door.

The guards spring to attention.

"Announce yourself, my lord."

Without a voice, my intentions have to be conveyed through action. I wave my arms wildly, mouthing nonsense and raking fingers through my hair. I plead with my eyes. They aren't focusing on my face long enough to pull them into a vision, even if I wanted to—they're assessing my damp clothes and exchanging glances with one another. I try to scream, letting the effort bulge the veins in my neck, making my hysteria obvious to them.

"Wait," the second guard exclaims, wagging a finger in my direction. "Yer the mute Capt'n the palace's been whispering 'bout all morning. Aren't you s'posed to be dead from a spider bite?"

"No, the princess wailed about a snake, remember?"

"Ah, yes. A viper. Def'nitly dead then."

I reach for the door between them and they close in, blocking off my advance with their arms. The one that demanded I announce myself shoves me back.

"Captain or not, you ain't getting into this room. His Majesty brought the priest in to perform a cleansing, and we were told not to let them be disturbed by anything."

That wrinkled-up old man is in there doing Oblivion knows what to Hazel and *I'm* forbidden? After everything that happened to me in the canal? The King told me we would talk. Sure, he probably thought I'd be dead by then, but I'm not. I'm still here.

We're going to talk.

I back away slowly, considering the stretch of hallway to either side of us.

Then I seize a pot of flowers sitting on the table to the right of her door and smash it into the hard marble floor. Damp dirt scatters everywhere.

The guards stare down at the pottery in shock.

Well, that didn't have quite the desired effect.

Before they can recover, I walk to the nearest stone statue and slide my body behind it so I can brace my feet on the wall and *push*. The statue is heavy. It's like wrestling a massive boulder.

I push even harder, until I finally feel a slight give.

"What's he doin'?"

"I think he's trying to knock it over."

"Ha! Idiot."

My chest rumbles as I funnel all my remaining strength into my legs. Sweat breaks out over my forehead. I'm fairly sure I pull a muscle in my back in the process, but the statue at last topples, and the marble head of the statue shatters as it collides with the ground.

I hear the guards curse in tandem. As the shards skitter across the floor around me, a rough hand catches me by the arm and wrenches me off the ground.

At the same moment, the door to Hazel's room snaps open, and the King steps out.

"What is all this commotion?" he demands. His eyes sweep across the wreckage, then land on me.

He blinks, as if in total wonder, and staggers forward a step. "You're alive," he breathes, shaking his head in disbelief. "We were worried that—Hazel was so sure that you had—oh, for heaven's sake, *release him*."

The guard handling me does as he says, stepping back but resting a hand on the hilt of his sword. Yeah, right. Like I would be stupid enough to attack a king.

"Please," the King gestures for me to walk ahead of him into Hazel's room, "join us."

A maid greets us in the front room, wringing her hands and craning her head to look in at Hazel's bedroom. I stalk across the fine, colorful rug of the sitting room. The human princess is lying in her bed, her complexion pale and eyes tired. The priest stands close by, a few of his cloaked women gathered around him as he swings a ball of fragrant burning herbs in his hand. The air is filled with smoke.

Hazel turns her head and sees me, and her eyes widen.

"Captain," she squeaks, her eyes overflowing with moisture as she tries to sit up. "You're alive."

I drop to my knees at her bedside, cradling one of her hands in both of mine. The King looks between the two of us, obviously uncomfortable with our sudden proximity, but he doesn't say anything.

He cares for her happiness.

I don't know if I will ever get used to that.

I don't move from my position or let go of her hand, I don't even look away from her face for the entire cleansing. A man fooled by love wouldn't. Even after the ritual is finished, and the maids open the windows to clear out the smoke, and the priest asks the King for a private audience in the corridor, I remain.

After several minutes, the King returns and beckons me to join him at the threshold to her room. I concede to his request after giving Hazel one last lingering look. She's already succumbed to sleep.

By the time I meet the King in the corridor, he's officially brooding. He runs his fingers down the breadth of his beard. His eyes trace the lines in marble beneath us. I wonder if he saw through my performance, if he can see the dark desperation swelling in my heart with every moment that slips through my fingers. The priest is nowhere to be seen. He likely returned to the cathedral, to Fluke.

Could the sea witch's death be cresting the horizon?

The idea of playing my part in that is less appealing than it was before. Before I touched her, filled her.

Viola's right. I'm a terrible siren.

"Captain," he begins. "I'm grateful for your sacrifices and concern for my daughter. She's clearly fond of you." His voice is calm, the thoughts measured. "I've been considering how I might reward you for your heroics, and the priest had an idea

I think you'll be delighted to hear about. Would you walk with me?"

I don't think delighted is quite the right word for anything when it comes to the priest, but I know better than to question a king.

Nodding, I allow him to lead me down the hall. He leads me down unfamiliar corridors, past banquet halls and multiple foyers, into a wing of the castle that overlooks the city. Hundreds of windows appear to our right, opening up to the crowded buildings and the distant towering presence of the cathedral. Here, above the sloping streets with the sun setting behind us, it looks like a sea of smoldering candles and shifting shadows.

We walk to the far end of the wing, where our view shifts from the city to the crescent bay far below.

A ship is anchored there. The flag attached to the mast head bursts with shades of blue and purple and red. It's the same flag I wrapped myself in on the beach my first day on the surface.

The King gestures to the ship. "It's yours, if you want it. We've been supplying ships for your country, as our treaty entails, but I'm happy to gift this one to you alone, out of gratitude for your saving my daughter. It would take months for your people to come retrieve you, and even longer to recoup your losses. Take this back to your country instead. I'll even send along some of my own men and supplies to help you make it there safely. Everything can be ready by tomorrow evening."

I stare at the ship.

He doesn't want me to marry his daughter. I don't need to hear the explicit words to understand why—he thinks I'm beneath them. The same prejudice exists in Atlantis when it comes to the underlings, to those born outside of noble rule. I've just never been on the wrong side of it before.

As I suspected, it doesn't feel good.

Sailing across the sea on a ship? That's a better idea than tossing myself into an assemblage of sharp rocks below the palace, and it gives me a slightly better chance of survival too. The sea witch could decide to hunt me down, but I can't just stay here and wait for her. She will come for me, that much I *am* sure of.

I lift my head and return the King's warm expression, nodding my agreement.

"Wonderful," his voice booms through the hall. He squeezes my shoulder, and I have to bite the inside of my cheek to keep from flinching. "Rest up while you can, Captain. You have a long journey ahead of you."

I hear the words he doesn't say: I *don't want you to return to my daughter's room. Not now. Now ever.*

He tries to beckon me into the banquet hall for a late meal, but I decline. As much as I know that the King is right, that I *should* rest, I can't help but lie awake.

I stare at the shutters of the balcony, anticipating a shadow or trill of laughter. I wait for Viola to come for me.

And when she doesn't, I find myself... disappointed.

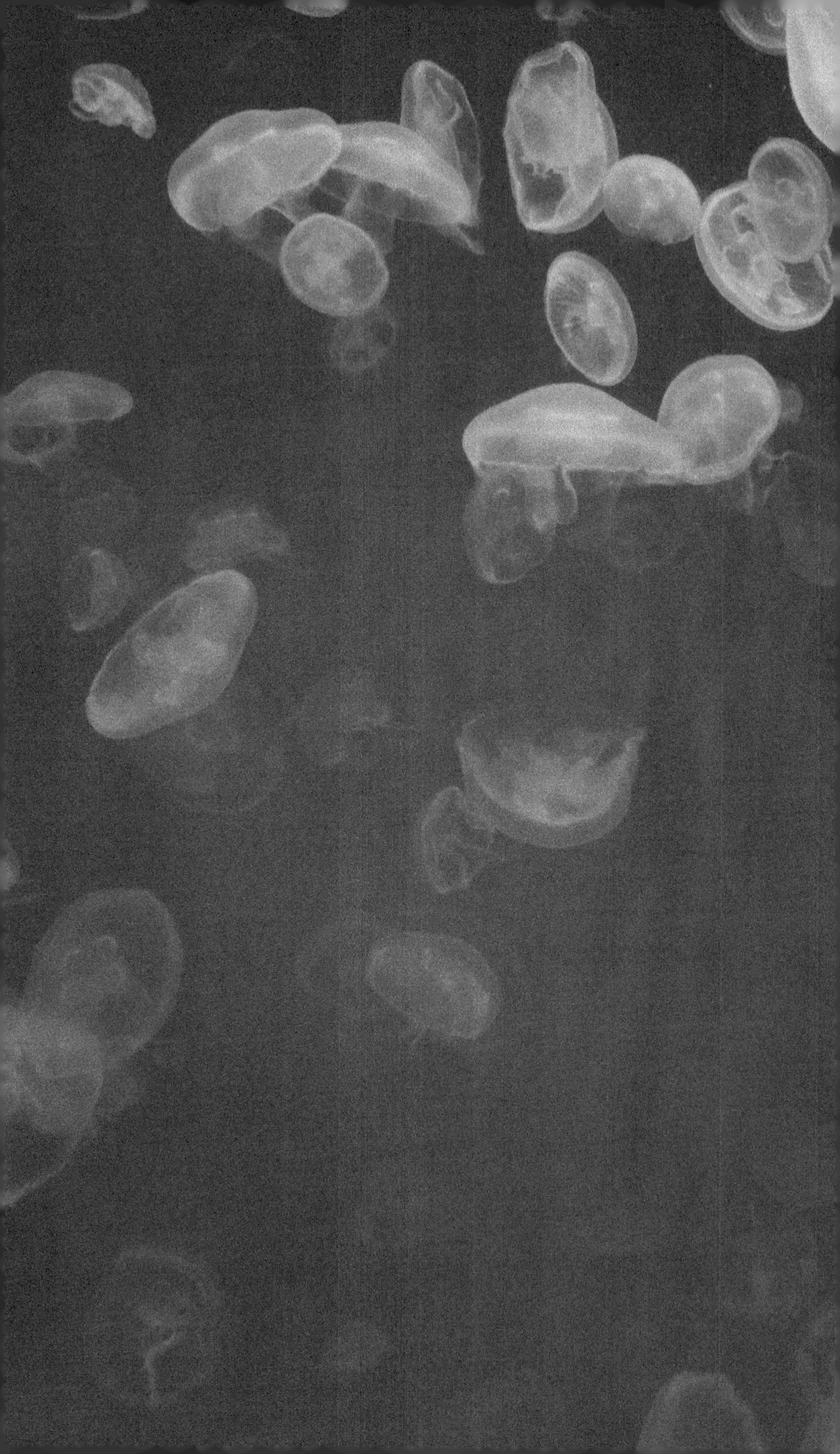

CHAPTER 20
VIOLA

Panic gnaws on my heartstrings.

Aric violated our agreement. I feel it, the decision he made hours ago. I don't know what it means, exactly. Maybe he finally gave up on the human princess, or maybe the human princess gave up on him.

Either way, my body urges me toward him.

Both of my soul-bounds are elsewhere, too far away to accidentally summon, and for that I'm grateful. I've folded myself into a shabby cabinet of the shipwreck, my tentacles shielding me from the greater interior of the captain's quarters.

My hearts flicker erratically, and I'm shaking. *Hard*.

I can't reap Aric. I knew it the moment I asked him to stay with me back in the city square. He preyed on my vulnerability. He was rough and calculating and cruel, but I fell into him anyway. The moment I saw his scars. I felt the hesitation in his heart when he considered hurting me back in the shop, when he chose to prove me wrong. I see the hope he's given to Atlantis: a merciful reign to soothe the wounds of his father.

Restraint, even against enemies.

How could I destroy the futures of so many for the sake of my own freedom? How could I destroy *him*, now that he's touched me?

I don't know how long I've been here, how long it's been since I left the carnevale and surrendered to the call of the ocean. But I do know why I'm cowering.

If I can't follow through on the original plan, I'm left with only one option. I need to go to Atlantis. I have Triton's first-born son, and that's a powerful kind of leverage I've never had before. I need to get into the castle and confront Triton, demand my freedom in exchange for Aric. It could work. Everything in me recoils at the thought of seeing Triton, of being in that throne room with him again.

So here I sit, trembling like a child in the only place I feel remotely safe.

"Viola?" a soft voice calls outside the cabinet.

I close my eyes and slowly wrangle control of my limbs. As the veil of my tentacles part, I see Perla's face peering in at me. The glow of jellyfish dances across her cheekbones, the slant of her jaw as sharp as a blade.

"What are you doing in there?" she asks.

I run a hand through my hair, my claws raking across my scalp. "Resisting the shriek of existential dread."

"A noble undertaking." She chuckles softly.

A deafening silence fills the water between us. She waits for me to break. I wait for her to leave through the hole in the floor, to the lower levels of the ship where the other mermaids lounge and sing and eat.

But she doesn't, and neither do I.

"I have to see him," I explain. "Talk to him. How can I do that without protection?"

She frowns. "You are protected."

Perla has been kind to me from the first moment we met. She knows more about me than most do, piecing together my life from passive conversation, gleaning truth from my silences. I'm not particularly secretive, but it's rare for anyone to show an interest in truly understanding me, to see me for more than what I can do for them.

Perla is one of the few.

She's also the only one who has ever refused my offer for a fresh start above the surface. The ocean is her home, as vicious and perilous as it might be.

Perla knows about Triton. Knows I live bound to him in a way that is similar to how my soul-bound are fettered to me. It has nothing to do with my soul. There is no heartstring between Triton and I that lends affection, because I never gave him any part of myself willingly.

He used a heinous magic. A magic that preyed on my body while my mind and my hearts remained my own.

I can hate him. I just cannot hurt him.

I've never been able to work out whether his is a worse binding than the ones I deal out. Hating without the possibility to move on. Possession without consent.

"The spirits are silent," I mutter as Perla leans into the opening of the cabinet. Better that I look at her than the collection of runes and bones on the floor behind her. I've been seeking direction from the spirits and Goddess Mora all night, but they aren't answering. And I know why. "They're as helpless against Triton as I am."

The ocean picked sides a long time ago, with Triton's great-great-grandfather.

My spirits are stingy with the details.

Whatever manner of magic Triton inherited from his ancestor goes beyond storms, and it's powerful enough to put the rest of the ocean in subservience.

An impatience hangs over Atlantis. A darkness clings to it, as if Oblivion itself is waiting on a debt.

There are terrible, invisible, impossible monsters that live beneath the ocean floor, and I'm more than certain one of them ascended to Atlantis when Triton rose to power. It's yet another reason I avoid the city. Passing through the gates feels like entering a prison—a sparkling, deadly fish net.

"I wasn't talking about the spirits, or even the Goddess," Perla whispers.

When I glance up at her, she gives me a smile and pushes away. She drifts to my wall of glass containers, reaching into the shelf to withdraw a cloudy jar. A half-eaten heart bobs within its vessel as she returns to my side. She sets it in front of me on the decaying wood, her thoughts seeming to swirl like whirlpools behind her eyes.

Eventually, Perla says, "Do you recall what you told me the night you brought *him* back home with you?"

My newest soul-bound, her abuser.

I do remember, but I let her continue to speak without interrupting.

"You can't change what's happened to you," she whispers. "But you can become his worst nightmare if that will heal you, if it will make you whole. Monsters only exist without history to pardon them. Be a monster if you must, as long as you are a great one."

It's true, even now.

I hold tightly to that wisdom, especially now that I've seen a glimmer of it inside Aric. How foolish I was to turn a blind eye to his past, to judge him by the life he was born into. *I* was born to a shitty father that gave me up to the streets, wasn't I? And that had nothing to do with me.

Aric hates me now. *Fix. What. You. Hurt.*

I can fix the wrong I've done to him. I can fix what I hurt and return him to where he belongs. If I play the game just right, I might even be able to place Aric on the throne before dawn. Once my curse is lifted, anything is possible. I can hurt Triton, kill him. And killing Triton would make me whole.

Wouldn't it?

I take the vessel from Perla and shatter it against the wall of the cabinet. The heart is spongy in my hand, soft. My fingernails cut into the gray tissues with the slightest pressure. It's not an appetizing meal, but evil men never are. They are only a means to an end. As my teeth sink into the corroded flesh, threads of remnant magic swirl lavishly on my tongue. My mouth tingles.

The rest of my body catches up in the next heartbeat, all of my muscles tightening and coiling.

Until time itself slows to a near standstill.

CHAPTER 21
ARIC

Striding off palace grounds, I follow the city map the King gave me before sending me on my way.

He fitted me in the finest clothes. The insides of the navy tunic and pants are lined with silk, the structure of every piece giving me a sense of armor, of power—even the embroidered cuffs around my wrists are stiff.

Hazel didn't come to supper to see me away. Whether her own decision or the request of her father—I was glad for it. My decision had already been made.

Tonight, I set sail for my own world, come death or hellish waters.

As I turn into a section of street that will lead me down to the bay, hands grip my shoulders and wrench me into a narrow side alley. I struggle at first, elbowing my assailer in the stomach hard enough to make him grunt, but then I look up and see his eyes.

Vibrant blue against light brown skin.

It's Fluke.

I shake him off and he chuckles, "Don't worry, Prince. I'm

but a humble subject, and I crave a few minutes of your undivided attention."

I shoot him a lethal glare and straighten my tunic.

Fluke reaches into his trousers and pulls out a lump of metal hanging from a chain. The surface of the pendant is tarnished brass, carved into with tiny letters and dark gemstones. It radiates that same unpleasant mortal magic I sensed in the cathedral.

This must be one of the priest's artifacts.

"This is our freedom," he says, holding up the necklace between us. "Thanks to you, I got some time with the holy man to explain who I was. *And* I told him all about Viola. Apparently he's been trying to rid her presence from the canals for over a decade now. When I explained I could help him, he gave me this."

I give him a look that says what I cannot. *What the fuck is it?*

His smile turns barbarous. "All you have to do is get this necklace close to her, and then keep it with her until the holy man initiates his hunt."

Hunt?

Fluke sees the confusion on my face and explains, "This isn't the whole artifact. It has a twin. The priest has the other half and a strand of Viola's hair to attune it to her presence."

My stomach lurches. How did he get strands of her hair without her realizing it, and how long has he been carrying them around with him?

What else does he have of her?

I wish I had my voice so I could ask.

I try to tell myself I only want to know because I'm curious, but really I know it's because I feel sick about it. He's taken pieces of her without consent. He's giving her up to that slimy old man.

Abruptly, I realize that I'm feeling *protective* of the sea witch.

What has Viola done to me?

"Give me your hand," Fluke demands, presenting his hand palm-up in front of me.

I think about refusing, but the look on Fluke's face warns me against doing that. There's a wild gleam in his eye, a blood-thirst. I have no desire to pick a fight with him so close to my liberation, so I place my hand in his.

Fluke closes his fingers around mine.

Then, quicker than I can anticipate, his other hand flies to his side, withdrawing a blade from the waistband of his pants and slashing it across my palm. I don't even have time to react before he presses the pendant of the necklace into the weeping wound. It zaps my skin at first contact. I feel it wiggle into my flesh and tether to something deep inside me, until suddenly my entire body starts to hum.

That hum continues to rattle my bones as I look up.

Fluke smiles. "There. Now it's attuned to you too."

My mind goes eerily quiet for a few heartbeats. What does he mean? What exactly is attuned to me? I hope he didn't stick my hair in there alongside Viola's.

He wouldn't do that, would he?

I think of his treachery, and I don't know. The extent of his scheming, collecting whispers and cannons to fire at will... He hates Viola more than I do—perhaps more than I ever have or ever could.

Fluke continues, "When the holy man hunts her, both sides will hum as he gets closer—it's like a talking compass, guiding him to wherever she is. He showed me how it worked with my hair first. It's a fascinating charm."

He starts backing up down the alley. "Now go do your part and occupy her."

I look down at the necklace, my heart pounding.

There's no way to tell him I won't be here to do what he's asking of me. I mean, I could *try*. Or I could hand it back to him so he can do it himself, but—

I suddenly don't want to give it back.

That tingly new magic rooted in my bones recoils at the thought of being separated from me.

Not so soon. We've only just met, it sings.

I can't bear to set it down, to let it go.

Besides, I'm the only one who can stand between Viola and Fluke's plan. I'm the only one in the whole world who can protect her. I know I shouldn't want to. I shouldn't feel relieved that my leaving will keep her as safe as it will keep me. But my fingers close around the pendant anyway.

I stuff it into my pocket.

Let Viola terrorize this city and the ocean and my father. Maybe by sparing her, she'll eventually bring Atlantis down and set my siblings free. I convince myself it's that and *not* the confusing feelings that I've come to harbor for her that urges me into the busy bay.

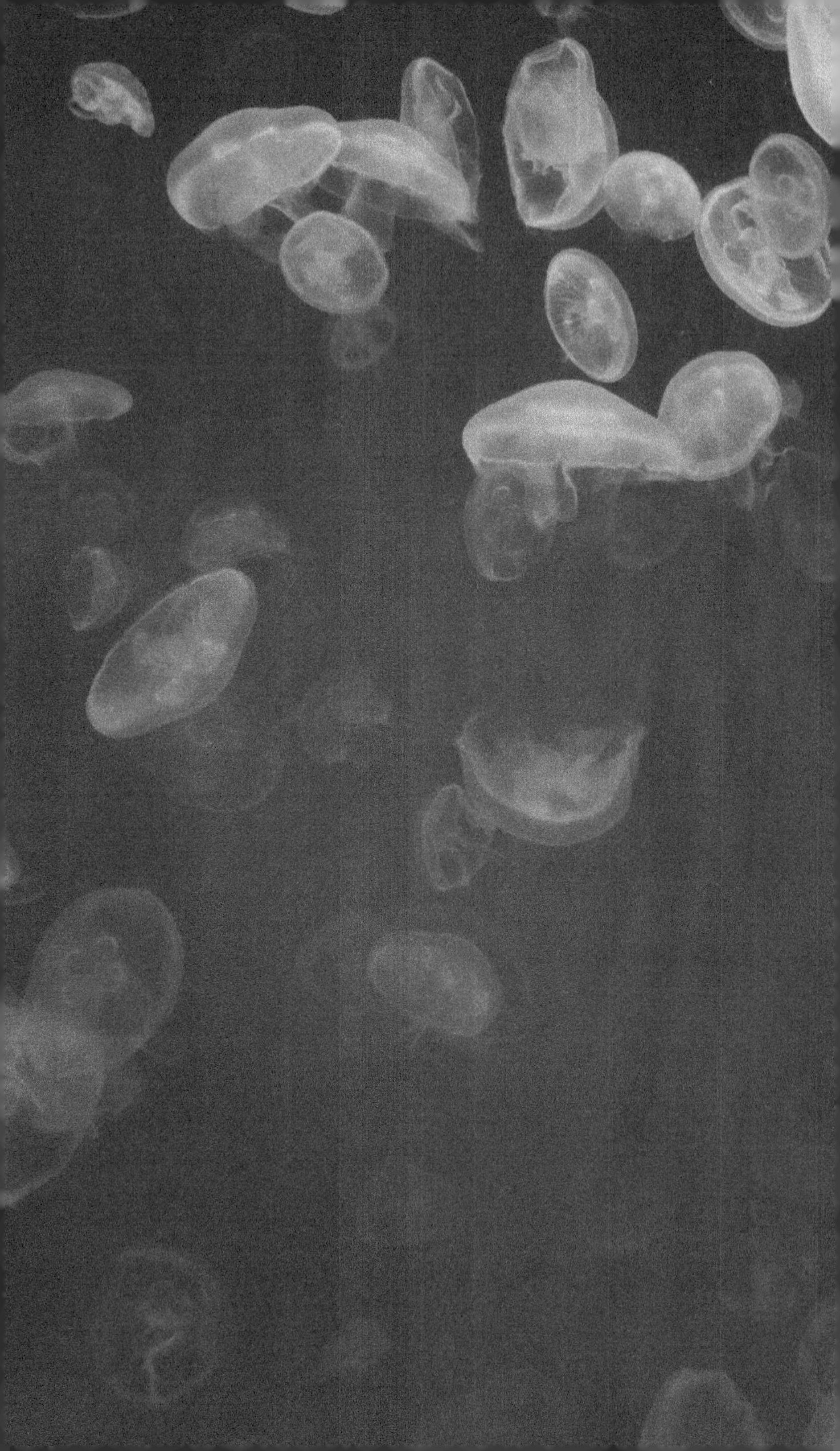

CHAPTER 22
VIOLA

There are layers to Atlantis.

Beneath the central city are open-mouthed caverns called the underdwellings, and they belong to the underlings—all the creatures that exist beyond mer: eels and sea rays and whalefolk; even mer who were disgraced and had their names scratched from the city walls. My father was one such mer. He ran gambling rings in the city for bored nobles, until one of them decided he was favoring an opponent a little too often.

I remember him well. His bitterness. The sickly color of his tongue. I remember the way he didn't take care of me in the slums, or himself.

When our family name was erased from the walls, we were forgotten. That's how all entry is controlled—by living, breathing, magical stones erected throughout the city. They used to be a symbol of togetherness.

Atlantis used to be a fortress against the harsh realities of the ocean, according to scrolls I once read in the library at the heart of the city.

Now the walls are smeared daily with the guts of jellyfish until they glow and weigh upon the suffering of hundreds.

It's a horror.

My gaze catches on a half-whale, half-mer as he leans out of one of the slums to dump bones into the abyss. Another death, another non-funeral, moving at an agonizing pace. It'll take days for it to hit the bottom of the chasm. Days before the spirit will rest.

The procession seems to move even slower due to the gift currently surging through my veins.

I take it all in for what feels like the first time, even while a thousand memories work to cleave my hearts open. Time is at my mercy, thanks to the heart I saved for a day such as this. I knew a day would come when I needed to move faster than light.

As I spear towards the first towering gate, I scan the city's current defenses.

Two guards float at either side of the entrance and a couple more patrol just within. Nothing too extreme for the lower class neighborhoods. Still, they're supposed to be on watch for creatures the stones don't guard against.

Creatures like me.

The stones were imbued with magic by witches. There's no way to shut us out—which is probably one of the main reasons Triton opted to kill my old coven instead of driving them away. He couldn't be sure they wouldn't return.

I crest a rising current, coasting dangerously close to the iridescent barrier that protects the city. Electric fragments skitter across my skin.

Faster, I dive.

The guards don't see me grasp the inner peak of the arch above them and launch myself through the first gate. If the guards patrolling inside notice me, I don't linger long enough to find out. The outermost ring of the city is the smallest, housing the families that are closest to ruin. Only another minute of swimming, and the second gate comes into view. The increased guard presence doesn't catch me there either. Time is moving too slow. The same goes for the third and fourth gates.

Until, finally, I'm darting between lush underwater gardens and sprawling estates. The walls glow brighter here; guts are brushed onto the buildings grotesquely thick.

Triton's castle looms, the spires of coral filed down into smooth curves.

That's the final gate—making it into those pastel halls.

There's a good chance I've been seen by someone by now, but no one will beat me to the throne room. No one will move fast enough to warn their king.

Instead of swimming to the front entrance, I slip into one of the crevices chiseled into the back, above the gardens. These halls are dark, unguarded and free of luminous guts. I follow the reverberations of music coming from the heart of the castle. By the time I reach the throne room, my skin is prickling with apprehension.

It's exactly the same, even all these decades later.

Coral cascades down the tall walls. Fish dart in and out of the habitat, clams are burrowed into the vibrant growth—Triton's personal pearl-makers. The room is filled with mer, his court and the city's additional nobles. Musicians slam into enchanted drums and pluck strings. Scales glint as mermaids dance naked in front of his throne.

The mermaid dancing for Triton looks like I used to, before I received Goddess Mora's gift. She has purple scales and long amethyst hair, a smile as shy as an anemone.

Seeing him watch her like this makes me want to tear my skin off. *You can't change what's happened to you, but you can become his worst nightmare.* I force my hearts to calm, the gift in my veins to quiet.

I shift my skin and swim down.

Triton's eyes focus on me as I halt in front of the throne and force time to return to a normal pace. He looks between the two of us, confusion furrowing his brow. I've made myself a perfect copy of her.

My intent is to unsettle him, and it works.

"What's the meaning of this?" he demands, half-rising from his throne.

I tilt my head and drop the illusion.

The drumming cuts off cold. Silence falls as the entire room turns to acknowledge me.

The maid beside me gasps and darts away, but the only sign of Triton's surprise is a slow blink. Then he smiles bright enough to make my stomach churn.

"A visit from The Violent Sea," he muses. "To what do I owe this terror?"

I ache, not because I recall his voice from so long ago, but because I can almost hear Aric in it. The same deep hum, the drifting syllables. A hint of crass amusement. But there's a hardness in Triton that isn't in Aric. I should have seen it sooner—the differences.

"I have the crown prince of Atlantis in my possession," I declare. "I've come here to trade him for my freedom."

His fingers tighten on the throne as he leans forward, his grin mangled. "Really? I don't see him with you now." He glances upward. "Is he hiding in the ceiling somewhere like the coward he is?"

My skins prickles with anger.

"He's in a safe place, for now. That won't be the case for much longer if you don't give me what I came here for."

"I've already erased his name from the city stones."

My stomach dips. *Great Goddess.*

If his name has been scratched from the stones, the rift between him and Triton must run deeper than I thought.

My eyes drift to the seats on the right and left of the throne. The court. A young, white-haired mer lounges in one of them. The recognition is immediate. It's one of the other princes, his eyes dark and narrowed, his tail still as bones. The crown of coral and jewels on his head answers my silent quandary.

My upper lip curls as I return my stare to Triton. "You can't do that. The throne belongs to him."

"My first son was never committed to this court. Not like my second-born is." He nods to the mer without taking his eyes off of me, his face shifting between a smile and snarl, one and then the other, both at once. "There was not much to forget. Aric spent his free time doting on bottom-feeders and wasting away in that disgusting little gallery. He wasn't worthy of the throne. And his weaknesses, his inability to resist *you*, proves it."

Jussi was right.

Aric is the kind of king I could support, that I could respect and even love—the king I dreamed of as a little girl, before foul fingers and fouler words ruined it all.

The only hope for this city, dashed. Because of me.

And perhaps I'm furious that I refused to see it sooner, maybe I'm dying to be punished for it, because I can't keep my thoughts to myself. "I find it funny that you think his inability to resist me is a sign of weakness. Why then, are *you* still sitting there? You should have abdicated the throne ages ago." Because he wants me, even now. That's why he holds onto my curse, and why he hasn't struck me down for trespassing and trying to ransom his son.

He wants me, and he always will.

His eyes darken. "Be careful what lies you spout here, witching."

"Why?" I croon. "Afraid someone in this room will believe me? Have you ruined your guards' trust so completely? They remember the treachery of your youth—they *must*. They know exactly what you are. And that terrifies you, doesn't it?"

Someday soon, his rule will collapse. Atlantis will demand a better king. And when that day comes, I will ensure that change is made.

Triton sees that promise in my eyes.

He releases the arms of his throne, pushing chains of gold off his lap to rise completely from the seat. "I do not fear anything," he says. "Use my first-born up and spit him out if that's what you want. He's already dead to me."

This visit was a failure, but I won't let him see it.

I cross my arms over my chest, "You know, now that I *know* you want him dead, I'm inclined to do the opposite. Maybe I'll keep him forever."

Triton frowns, his face twisting into that half-hearted snarl once more. Before he can say anything in response, his body jerks. All evidence of rage slips from his face. "Perhaps I'll take matters into my own hands then."

I've missed something. He has a secret, and I have a feeling I'm going to hate it almost as much as I hate him. "What are you talking about?"

"I can sense him on the sea right now. Can't you?"

It can't be.

I reach out blindly for those strings inside me, the connections I carefully set aside before coming here. I'd forced them completely out of my mind. I didn't even realize that one of them had drawn closer than the others. *Too* close.

What the hell is Aric doing on the sea?

The look on Triton's face is a harbinger of disaster. The water electrifies around us, and I know I need to move. He's summoning a storm.

I lurch for an exit.

Bolts of radiant lightning cut me off. They spread in a grate over every crevice of the room, and my body recoils. I feel the memories of his last trap lift to the surface of my mind, of when he forced me to watch as he tore my world apart. "Ah." Triton's taunt slithers around me. "And where do you think you're going?"

I spin to face him, my chest heaving, my composure cracking. "If you try to keep me here, I'll bathe these walls in blood," I tell him.

He laughs again. "You can't kill me, Viola."

Gasps ripple through the room. Because he said my name.

My tentacles lash out, lengthening and sharpening as I point them strategically around the room. Against the necks of several guards and one at Triton's favorite son. "No, but I can kill your son and every guard in this room. Except for one. I'll ensure one makes it out of here alive to tell the truth: that you care nothing for the good of this city or those that protect you. How will you explain their deaths?"

Triton stares at me with the same stillness of his second-born, the stillness of fury. Maybe he'd like to kill me, after all.

But then he erupts in hearty laughter, relaxing back in his throne as his lightning starts sputtering out. "What violent stories you thread, witchling."

My skin prickles at that word. I want to vomit.

My gills flutter, my body straining for a breath when I know there isn't one to be had. There will never be clean air for me again.

Triton knows...

He knows that I care too much, and that's why he wants to ruin it. He will stop at nothing to ruin me. "Go if you wish to race the storm, but it's really no use."

A savage smile twists his mouth. "You're already too late."

CHAPTER 23
ARIC

The ship sails beyond the scope of the bay, and the city becomes a speck behind us as the sun sets.

I take a bite out of the apple in my hand and admire the fingers of red and orange painting the sky. I'm back on the water and it feels... *strange*.

I stand on the stern of the ship, leaning against the railing as the crew steers us into the open waters. It's been fascinating to watch them work. I never had a chance to before—my role has always been one of ruin. They're exuberant. Passionate. Each human is a partner to the next, in both tasks and humor. It's a good crew, I imagine.

They don't include me in their camaraderie.

I think they suspect the truth: that I have no clue what I'm doing. I do my best to ignore them.

In a matter of weeks, I'll be in a new country and they'll return home, and I will never have to see them again. With the decent weight of coin in my purse—another gift from the King—I'm sure I'll be able to make my own way. Perhaps I'll find a crew and replace the flag above me with a black one

Pirates do well for themselves. They get to see all that the world has to offer.

Or perhaps I'll sell the ship and settle in for a comfortable, human life in this mysterious country.

My hand drifts to the pendant in my pocket. I keep thinking the same thing, over and over. *I'm carrying a piece of her with me.* With nothing to do and no one to talk to, my thoughts drift as well.

I wonder what my life would have been like if we were both born human, if we had lived above the canals together in the quaint burrows of the city. She wouldn't have been the worst person to kiss and touch. She'd have made a pretty little wife.

That's to say, if she wasn't a murderous witch in that fantasy.

I even think of what it might have been like to have her with me now. If instead of devouring me, she wanted to run away at my side. She would never, obviously... but it's an interesting distraction.

My skin prickles at the thought of hearing her trill again, of seeing her silken purple hair in my fist. I could have taken her into my captain's quarters and bound her heart to mine in a different way.

My body jolts at the unexpected thought.

I hope the rest of the journey isn't this boring—or I might convince myself that I actually care about the witch. And I don't. My fingers twitch around the necklace in my pocket. Why did I bother protecting her? She would have never done the same for me.

The sailor standing in the crow's nest bellows down to the rest of us, tearing me away from my thoughts.

"*Batten down the hatches!*"

At that command, the deck erupts in chaos. Sailors shout

to one another. They run to the sails. Some begin to tie items down or toss them under the deck, and as I walk into the commotion, I hear it.

I look up and finally understand.

Clouds are moving in. Dark, foreboding, angry.

There was no trace of a storm when we embarked, but now they're rolling in on all sides, as if the four winds have communed to target us. Faint light crackles in the dark. It isn't stars. That is blue lightning.

Who the hell pissed my father off this time?

I stalk across the deck to the bow of the ship. The wind whips at my hair, loosening it from the tie at the nape of my neck. Waves swell and spike across the expanse before us. A hum echoes beneath my feet, and I know it's radiating up out of the sea. There's no evidence that the rest of the crew can hear it. They're too focused on the sky. The sun slips away, leaving us at the mercy of lanterns the crew managed to light before starting their card games.

Blue light flashes at my back.

A distant rumble.

Light hits again to my right side, and the sky growls louder. Waves crash into the sides of the ship and water sprays the deck, and then the sky begins to weep.

I leap down and help the crew shut the openings into the main hull. Once that's finished, someone shoves the end of a length of rope in my hand. A tether. The rest of the crew does the same, clinging to the other ropes and the sail posts, our only anchors. As one, we turn towards the storm.

As one, we sail into the heart of it.

It soon becomes impossible to see more than a few foot or so in front of me. The wind is strong enough to make my feet slide over the slick surface of the deck, so I wrap the rope around my waist and follow the end to a post it's attached to, letting it take the brunt of the storm. A couple men continue to run around the deck, and an older sailor has strapped himself to the wheel.

Lanterns snuff out as the rain becomes a tempest.

The ship teeters. The air around me pulses with electricity. I taste fear, a bittersweet film coating my tongue, and it comes from everywhere, from the entire crew—I don't need to look into their eyes to understand it.

A deafening crack rends the air.

The bolt of lightning cuts through the clouds and rain and collides with the center of the deck. One of the lanterns shatters on impact. Fire catches, clinging to the oil and growing as the center of the deck fissures. Both ends of the ship begin to tilt inward. Beneath the flames, I see the hole. The hole that will condemn us all.

One shout reaches me over the din. *"Abandon ship."*

I remove the rope from my torso and follow the crew to the far edge of the ship, where a set of smaller boats hang. They swing precariously, but the crew handles them with impressive dexterity. Within a minute, we're boarding them.

When we hit the water, the sailors fight against the dragging currents.

Sinking ships take down what's immediately surrounding them—I know this, and I've seen it at least a thousand times. We need to get out of here *now*. The rest of the crew knows this too. Sailors to either side of me start to shove each other and point back at the wreckage. Some blubber religious songs that I first heard back at the cathedral—singing their frantic prayers.

But when I glance back, I see it.

A kraken is overtaking the ship.

Its black tentacles unfurl like ropes from the ocean, shooting into the sides of the ship with such force that planks and beams fly out in every direction. Canvas rips. The dark tentacles snake and whip, desperately searching through the empty belly of the ship.

The kraken's cry tears through the night—agony incarnate, so loud that the boat we row trembles from it.

The sailor to my right screams at the others to move faster, but his commands are cut off when the sky cracks again. A rod of jagged, blue lightning strikes our boat.

Wood fractures.

Screams.

Sizzling.

The scent of burning flesh.

We're thrown into the ocean, and one of the sailors collides with me, pushing me under. I shove him away and surface. He doesn't follow me back up.

The surviving crew swims away from the sinking ship, their eyes wide and voices frantic. Sour terror crackles on my tongue. One of the older sailors sees me as our paths merge and he shakes his head as he starts swimming away.

He calls me cursed.

We aren't swimming fast enough. As the whirling current of the ship drags me into its orbit, water rushes into my mouth, and I truly believe that the sailor is right. I am cursed. There's no one out there who could see me in my entirety and choose to care. I'm unloveable. It's a fact that's been proven to me over and over, carved into my scales. I turned away from it. I didn't want it to be true.

But now, facing suffocation in the ocean that had once been home to me, I see it.

I'm spinning faster and faster. I grapple for something, *anything*—some life line that might pull me back to the surface. There's only splintered wood and iron nails. My head collides with a beam, the impact sending stars exploding behind my eyes.

I gasp for air that isn't there.

Salt water burns its way down my throat.

I feel one of the kraken's tentacles brush my side, and a dozen purple, blurry eyes seem to surround me, each iris centered in the suctions. Is this real? Another screech rings out, shuddering through my entire body.

My vision wavers.

Between shards of the descending wreckage, I see a flash of light in the distance. It speeds toward me, weaving so quickly that I wonder if it must be a star, a dream, a wish. I wonder if it's the desire I voiced that night so many years ago, when I floated on the surface with a bottle of drowned wine in my hand. I wonder if it fell to earth to finally answer my question.

Is there anyone out there who might change my world? Send them to me. Please.

There was no way out of the world I was born into. No escape. When I dared to wish for anything, it was for some kind of salvation to come find me. Is that what this is? There's a silhouette forming in the center of that sphere of brilliance. A goddess, as golden as the sun. The only warmth in this cold sea.

I want to feel her, know her, just once.

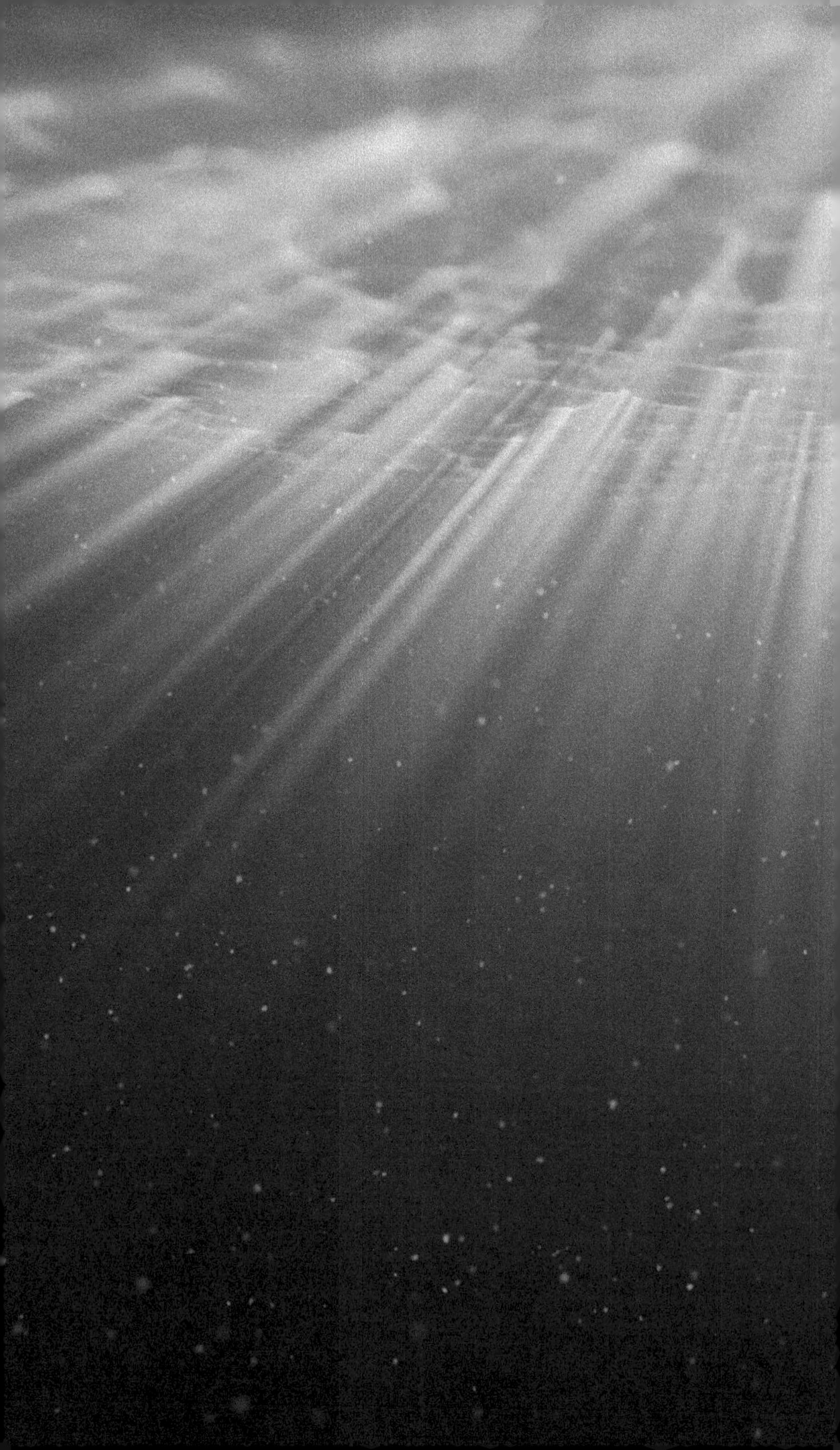

CHAPTER 24

ARIC

Voices gurgle in my periphery as I rise, my mind swimming with colors and half-formed dreams. My body is heavy, and a soreness crawls up out of the darkness along with me. Somehow, I know that if I move even an inch, I'll regret it.

Where am I?

Those voices around me clarify, as if they'd entered the forefront of my mind. Or maybe they'd only entered the room where I lay. Because I *am* lying down.

The weight I feel is the heaviness of gravity pressing me into soft cushions. I'm back on the surface. In a bed.

A male voice curls into my ears, soft and silken. "This is all I could find for clothing that might fit him."

"That's fine, Jussi. Thank you." The sea witch.

My last conscious moments come flooding back. The shipwreck. I hit my head. Light streaked toward me in the water—that must have been her, coming to collect me after I ruined my only chance of escape.

I wish I had died.

The male, Jussi, speaks again. "Guillermo is nearly done cooking. What can I bring you?"

"Nothing."

A stretch of silence. Then he replies, "You should eat something. You're paler than usual, which I didn't think was possible."

"I'll eat when he wakes up."

"Vi—" *Vi?*

"Please, Jussi. I can't right now."

"Okay, but I'm an hour away from pouring stew down your throat myself."

A small, weak laugh. "Consider me warned."

It's strange to hear her talk this way—with affection. Whoever this Jussi is, he means something to her.

A soft thud sounds across the room, and I peel my eyes open.

Directly above me, the ceiling is carved and painted with whorls of radiant color, similar to the eccentric palette of the palace. Deep shades of sand and clay accented with the jewels of a sunset. There's a subtle contrast here to what I saw on the palace walls, though. An unreliability, a *wildness* that suggests it was a work of passion rather than of measured beauty. There's no pattern, no reason.

I discover it to be the loveliest work of art I've ever seen.

Fighting the tightness of my neck, I turn my head to look in the direction of the door I heard shut earlier. My eyes gorge themselves on Viola's silhouette.

She stares emptily at the worn wooden door, her shoulders hunched and arms crossed tightly over her chest. Her fingers rub at the sleeves of her dress, the blue fabric billowing out from her elbows and bunching tightly around her waist.

Another stolen garment.

This one looks lovely on her.

She lifts a hand to her mouth, running her thumb over her lower lip. No red stain. Only her mauve skin, darkened by the scratch of her teeth and pinch of her nails. Her hair is piled on the crown of her head, falling around her face in thin tendrils. I've never seen her look so unhappy, even in the moments when she loudly hated me.

The sea witch looks tired, and I'm struck by the sudden, profound urge to pull her into bed beside me and crush her to my chest. To find comfort in her as well as give it.

I must have hit my head real damn hard.

Attempting to sit up, a sharp ache bursts through my skull and radiates down into my neck. My vision blurs. I groan, the sound rattling painfully in the back of my head. It's only after I've collapsed back into the mattress and regain my breath that I realize what that sound means.

I have my voice.

Viola whirls, her purple eyes brightening as they land on me. "You're awake."

"No, I'm not." My voice is rough from the salt water I swallowed. "I must be dead. And if I'm with you, the humans were right—I've been sent to hell."

She snorts. "I'm glad you maintain humor even on the brink of death."

"There's little to do but laugh at my life."

Her lips twist with wry amusement. She draws nearer to the bed. "You could thank me for saving you instead."

A painful heave of my chest—not quite a laugh. "You shouldn't have."

"You would have rather drowned?"

"I was ready to. I prefer that to being toyed with."

Her brow furrows. "How are you being toyed with?"

My hands fist in the sheet covering my body, covering the

scars she once cried over. She looks ready to cry again. She's the most beautiful liar, a gorgeous feigner of emotion... seducing me with her misery, even now.

I watch my accusation finally dawn on her. "You think I'm to blame for your ship wrecking?"

I don't reply.

Her confusion gives way to anger, and her body starts trembling. Her hands form fists as she steps forward. "How do you imagine I did it?" It isn't anger I hear in her voice, but shock. "Last I recall, *I* am not the one who possesses the ability to summon or control storms. That terror belongs to your father."

The storm came out of nowhere. It was violent and pointed, and I simply assumed it was her from the moment I came to, but maybe I wasn't thinking clearly enough.

Back in the ocean, when the storm began, I thought it might have been one of my father's temperamental fits.

"What are you suggesting?" I growl.

"You aren't blind to what happened last night on the sea," she says quietly. "You were there, and I think you're clever enough to put the pieces together."

"Why would my father try to kill me?"

"Why does he do anything?" Viola huffs a laugh. "You were a loose end. I incited him, and he found a way to retaliate, a way to hurt me."

"So it *was* your fault."

She hesitates, considering that. After a long moment, she shrugs and mutters to the wall, "As much as the cruelty of the human race is the fault of a devil, I suppose."

I can't find the words or reason to contradict her. Is she trying to compare herself to the humans' devil?

I'd believe that one.

Slowly, I say, "They do believe the strangest things."

"And so does most of Atlantis," she counters, sighing as she sits on the bed beside me.

Viola reaches out, as if on instinct, and runs her fingertips through my hair. Her eyes meet mine, and as we look into each other, I'm reminded of the day we met. Her emotions reach out to me, grazing my senses. She tastes of blue mourning and enduring iron.

She gives herself up so easily, like she did that first night, as if she's suddenly decided to trust me.

But why?

I ask the only thing I want to know. "Why did you save me?"

A small smile flits across her face.

"Because," she whispers, twirling a piece of my hair between her fingers before gently sweeping it to the side of my face. "I am the only one who gets to swallow you whole."

That shouldn't feel like the most significant thing anyone's ever said to me... and yet I'm burning to touch her.

Her roaming fingers send sparks scattering through my skin as they descend the column of my neck. She's the sunset of my life, the fading horizon I've chased since I was old enough to breach the surface on my own. And now, she's here. My death and oath and transformation.

If this must be my ending, at least she is a beautiful one.

I wish I could blame it on her cycle, but that impulsive urge is gone. The pheromones are gone. Her cycle is fading now that we've touched each other. I want to keep touching her anyway.

"Well, you did it," I admit to her. "You won me."

Her hand settles against my chest, over my pounding heart. She stares at her splayed fingers. I don't push her away, don't touch her, even as she looks at me like she can see through skin and bone to the heartstring connecting us.

She refused Jussi earlier—refused his human food.

I wonder if it's because she plans to have her fill of me instead. *Will I satisfy her?*

A twisted, mortal part of me hopes I do.

"Yes," she murmurs. "I did."

Her eyes mark the bob of my throat.

Eventually, I venture, "How badly will it hurt?"

She rises from the bed and steps away, and I find myself instantly missing her proximity. How fucked up is that?

"I'm not reaping you, Aric."

My heart stops. The entire world halts.

"What?" I ask in disbelief.

Viola shakes her head, wrapping her arms around her chest, clutching tightly to the sleeves of her dress as if to anchor her fingers. I wish she were still sitting beside me, burying them in my hair. It felt so right. "If it wasn't for the storm last night, I would have let you go," she explains softly.

"Then why am I here? What are you doing with me?"

That mischievous smile of hers appears again. The one I used to hate. "I'm going to make you King."

My thoughts eddy, empty.

"King of what, exactly?"

"Of *me*. Of all of us under the surface. I'm going to place you on the throne you are owed. Atlantis will be a better place with you leading it."

Why does she want me on the throne now? I thought she ripped me from the ocean to explicitly *prevent* that.

Though, perhaps the target on my back was never truly meant for me. It's my father she wants to destroy. With every moment we spend together, that truth becomes clearer. It's also becoming clear to me that he deserves it. Deep down, I think I always knew that.

"How?" I demand. "My father will never give up his

throne to me now. The only way I'll have it is by taking it, by killing his entire court and starting over. I won't do that."

Her eyes narrow, her lips tightening into a white slash. "He didn't hesitate to kill *you*."

"I'm not him."

She surveys the length of my body. "I know you're not." A flush of purple colors her cheeks.

I don't know what the sea witch's angle is. I trust her in so much that I believe she wants to help me get rid of my father, to place me on his throne, but nothing beyond that. I have to be prepared for when she tries to use me. Because there's certainly a plan. I see her mind spinning with it now.

I look away before I can admire her too long.

She's too beautiful. Dangerous and tantalizing and utterly beautiful.

To quell my desire, I turn my thoughts toward my father and all that's been confessed. He tried to *kill* me. I know what she said is true. He's given up on whatever familial honor kept me in his good graces for so long, but those graces had always been fragile at best.

With Viola at my side, I could survive facing my father and his brutal court. I could probably destroy them if I wanted to, through sheer force and cleverness. But there must be another way. Something that won't perpetuate the bloodshed of my father and his father's father. The generations of treachery.

The spark of an idea catches, fanning to a flame in my mind. I lift my eyes to Viola and mutter, "Maybe we can trap him instead."

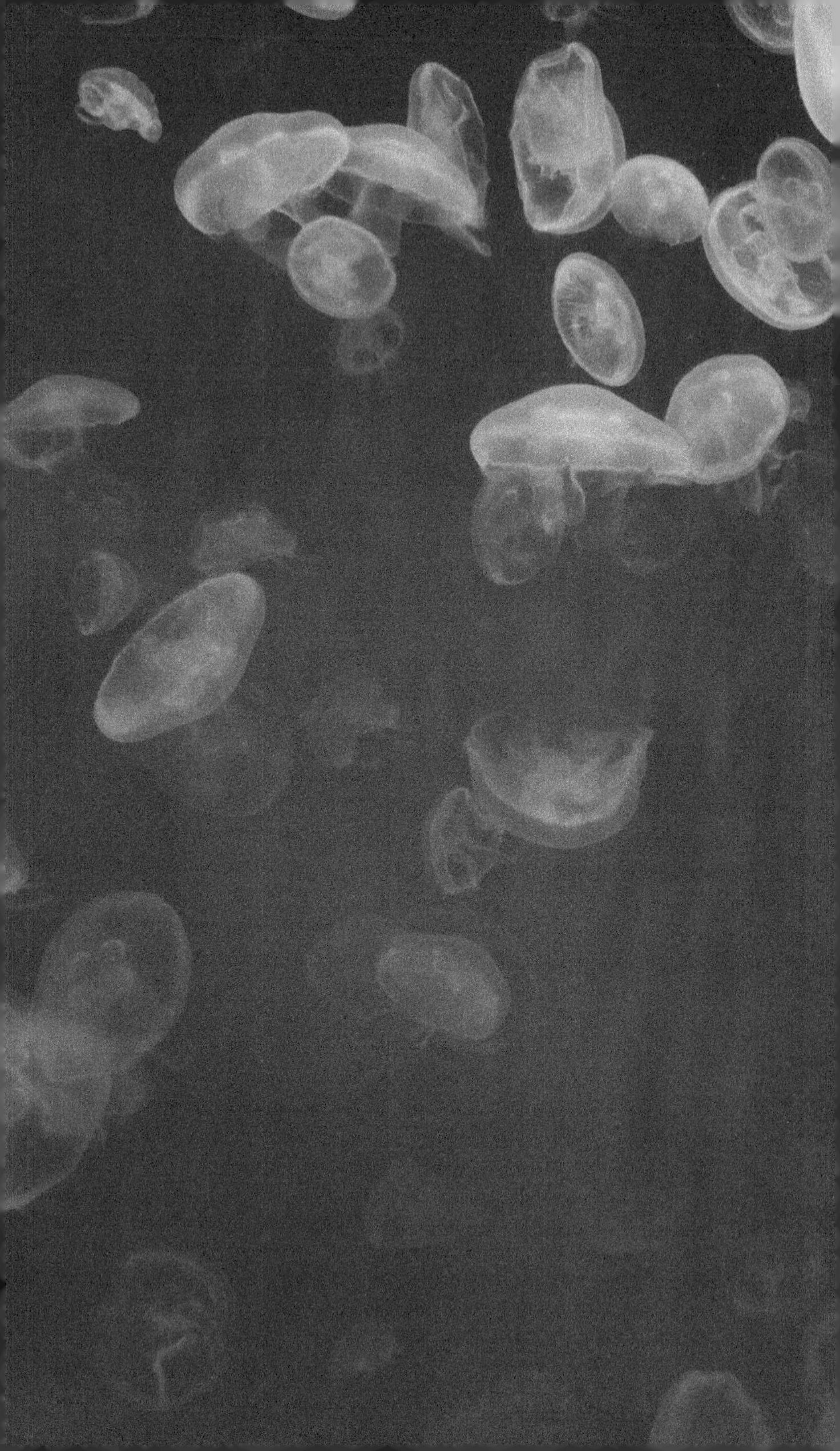

CHAPTER 25
VIOLA

I peer at the cathedral from where we watch it in a nearby alley.

All day, Aric and I have been working out a plan to nullify Triton and his poisonous influence on Atlantis.

Aside from ensuring we ate the stew Guillermo made, my old friends have been absent from the house, giving us space and quiet for our scheming. Truthfully, I think they're a little nervous about housing a prince of the ocean.

But I had asked for their help, and they were so shocked when I showed up with him hung over my shoulders last night that they instantly acquiesced.

It's best to get this ruse over with tonight, so Aric and I can get out of their way.

The priest closed the church doors a few minutes ago, and the stream of departing devotees are finally slowing.

"Now," I mutter.

We slip from the alley and approach the trellised platform of the courtyard. It's dark enough now that we don't run the risk of being seen. The world is a deep, cloaking blue despite the house lights peeking through windows above us.

Not that I think anyone would care about someone breaking *into* the cathedral—I'm pretty sure the city cares more about those trying to escape it.

I grasp at the vine-grown trellis, metal digging into my palms as I heave myself up. This close, I can smell the rust coating the iron, transferring sulfur to my fingertips. I ignore the bite of thorns as I slot my hands into new points and climb.

Aric spews a string of curses as he follows me up, encountering the same prickly branches, and we swiftly rise through the night air together.

Close to the top ledge, a bar beneath me gives as I reach for another crevice, and I slip.

Before I can react and grapple for purchase, Aric catches me around my chest. He pins me between the trellis and his arm. Thorns dig into my cheek as I look at him.

My skin tingles, blood slowly seeping from a laceration on my temple, but as I glance beneath us, I feel nothing but hot relief. The drop would have hurt far worse.

He's still holding me tightly, keeping me in place.

"Thank you," I whisper, reclaiming my grip on the wall.

He inhales sharply. "Well, we still need each other, don't we?" Then he peels his arm away and continues climbing.

Once we vault over the fence at the top, I survey the area—the gate on the other end of the courtyard is weighed down with chains. Shadows shift beyond the iron grates, where soldiers are stationed, vigilantly guarding the base of the staircase.

I slip my hand into Aric's as I shift us both.

His stature shrinks and shrinks until he's slightly shorter than me, his red hair lengthening until it falls past his breasts, which are growing into heavy peaks. He glances down, fondling them with an airy chuckle of amusement. I roll my eyes, but fight a smile of my own as the edges of his face take on a more feline quality. By the time his body is finished settling, his clothes are falling off of him.

Perhaps I didn't need to dedicate so much effort into making him look pretty, but I couldn't help it.

I look pointedly at his shirt and he removes it. His pants too. The only thing he keeps on is a leather strap holding his shark tooth. He kicks the rest into a shadowed corner of the courtyard and dons the dress I hand him, then the hood we stole from the nun's laundry line, twin to the one I pull over my hair now.

As we approach the double doors leading into the cathedral, I let one of my tentacles curl up from beneath my stolen skirt, shifting the tip narrow enough to slide into the lock.

It's easy enough to inflate the tissues, to feel for and manipulate the tumblers to let us inside.

Aric's eyebrows twitch, the only sign of his appreciation as he walks past me into the dark church. As I follow him, my entire body begins to hum.

It may be dim inside, but the festivities aren't over.

The scent of burnt wicks assault my senses. Smoke curls amidst the benches. The nuns linger, watching. At the front of the cathedral, where the last candles flicker, the priest paces in front of a citizen—a woman with dark, frizzy hair and fine material bunched around her knees as she kneels. Her hands grip tightly to a bar erected on the raised platform. Her knuckles are *bloodied*.

The priest extends his arm out to his side, drawing attention to the tendriled whip in his hand.

He's performing a flagellation.

The young woman cries out as he whips her hands again,

and I realize with a jolt that this isn't just *any* citizen. This is the city's princess. *Aric's* princess.

The priest must have finally convinced the human king to surrender her to the convent.

I've seen so many female royals given to this hell over the decades, all forced to endure a similar fate. Young ladies cloistered away, surrounded by the silence of nuns and the rule of a strict priest until they're given away in an arranged marriage.

None of those priests were ever as cruel as this one.

I hoped perhaps that *this* king, *this* father, would be the first to spare his daughter, but I was wrong. I should have known the crown's mistress would have her way.

It always does.

Aric realizes her identity the same moment I do, and a growl radiates from deep inside his buxom chest. He cares for her, that much is clear, regardless of how much he says in dissent. Perhaps he simply does not recognize love when he feels it. As he steps forward, vengeance in his eyes, I place a hand on his chest. His eyes flash.

I shake my head and step closer, launching up to murmur in his ear, "We'll save her. Another night, after we retrieve the artifact and deal with Triton. We need to take advantage of the priest's distraction."

Aric's jaw clenches, but he nods. He jerks his chin in a silent command for us to continue with the plan.

When we turn and weave between the columns, taking the long way around the cathedral, I'm sure we look like we belong. I've darkened my eyes and softened my facial features. If any nun dares glance our direction, they'll see their own kind. The priest is still whipping the princess's hands as we reach the door to the basement, where Aric said the artifacts are stored.

The hum in my body intensifies as we near the priest.

I hate males like him. Males who think they can create good with pain, obedience from punishment. It's all so backwards.

"Say it again, Princess. Let God hear your repentance."

The princess murmurs her prayers.

The whip sounds again, colliding with her skin with a grotesque slap, and oily guilt settles in my gut. I meant what I said to Aric—we'd save her, and the priest would get what he deserves. Just not yet.

The case Aric told me about is open and half-empty.

The door beside it, leading to the basement, is ajar. We watch as one of the nuns lifts a golden box from the case. She turns and disappears down the staircase. It looks like we caught them in the middle of their locking up.

I stride to the case and reach into it, lifting the next boxed artifact from its blanket of black velvet.

Aric follows my lead, taking up the next and trailing after me down the stairs. He told me what to expect from the descent. So I carefully remain in the center of the staircase as we make our way underground, his warmth a welcome comfort at my back. Several of the sconces are lit on either side of us, leading us down into dust and forgotten graves. The walls soon transform into a mosaic of bone.

I can sense Aric's unease as he shifts to descend beside me rather than behind, inching closer with his eyes trained on our surroundings.

"Are you afraid of death, dear Prince?"

He jumps at my whisper and grimaces. "No, I'm afraid of any dead who are not at peace."

I scan the bones. "You can feel them?"

After a long moment, he nods.

I knew sirens had a predilection for spirits, but I didn't

know it extended to human souls. I imagine his sense of them must be similar to the one I developed for Goddess Mora and her helpers: an awareness that allows communication and sensation, sometimes to my own detriment depending on the spirit's mood. I pity his vulnerability; these tortured souls must wreak havoc on his psyche, especially considering he would be the first to have heard their cries in centuries.

The end of the staircase comes into view below us.

The front of the room is exceptionally lit, allowing the nuns to move easily around the many obstacles spanning the floor. There's skeletons arranged against every wall, turned to face the altars erected throughout the room. Macabre marble statues adorn the altars: bound women with covered faces; thorny braided crowns suffocating animals; angels holding lanterns and weapons. Beyond the altars, interspersed through the deeper recesses of the room, are bookshelves. Hundreds, maybe thousands of tomes sit on their shelves. This is more than a graveyard. This is a hiding place of *knowledge*.

The nun we followed down here turns from her position in front of a glass case, jolting a bit when she sees us.

I keep my head down and aim for the next case, maintaining a sense of purpose in my steps, hoping Aric is doing the same behind me. By the time we pass by her, the nun has looked away from us and returned to the staircase. The boards creak as she ascends the steps.

No hint of alarm, thank the spirits.

I drop the artifact unceremoniously in the case and spin to the ones beside it. "Which one?" But even as I ask, I feel the pull, tugging at my magic, drawing me forward.

Aric stares at the source, but backs away from it and me.

He nods at the amber glass masking a gold and silver box in the centermost case.

I submit to the pull. With every step I take towards it, my chest tightens. The drumbeat of my hearts slow. And miraculously, the constant uneasiness of my body, that call from the ocean, becomes smaller and smaller until I can barely hear it. Warmth blooms in my veins. It's as if all the cold is being sapped from my limbs, siphoned away into that little box, leaving me more human than I ever thought possible.

By the time I halt in front of the case, my chest is shaking. The pressure bubbles into my mouth, and I laugh quietly to myself, tracing my hands over my torso, relishing in the weightlessness of my skin.

"What the hell is wrong with you?" Aric demands, inching to the other side of the room.

"Nothing," I whisper, reaching for the lid of the box. "I feel *wonderful*."

Aric shuffles away, his light footfalls fading as he turns a corner and delves into the seemingly endless room. I don't bother stopping him.

My eyes are trained on the box as I finger the edge of the lid and pry it open. The metal is heavier than I expect. And that's another thing I realize belatedly—that the silver doesn't burn my skin. Clumps of wax fall away, the drip having served as a seal. I push the lid out of the way, and the interior of the box is revealed.

Lying on a felt cushion, three shards of ivory bone wait for me.

They feed on power. This close, I sense the hunger in them, like three anchors dragging my magic into an endless void. My power is unending. I spool out more and more, as much as the bones desire, as quickly as I can regenerate it. I think they would happily feed off of me forever.

Maybe I should let them.

I scoop up the bones, their ivory clattering together in my palm. My skin settles into place, and I doubt I could shift out of this disguise even if I wanted to.

I don't feel Triton right now. I don't feel his curse. If I take these bones and disappear, I could forget Aric and our plight to take Triton's throne. I could forget Atlantis altogether. I could be free of the ocean, and that is all I've wanted since the day *he* set his eyes on me, since the day he declared my body was his and stained my soul to prove it.

But... it wouldn't be real, would it?

These bones feed on what exists. I could leave this continent and the ocean, I could flee far and pretend to be free, but I'll carry a reminder with me in the form of these remains. I will never be able to forget. I will never be free until Triton is unable to hurt me, unable to hurt anyone else ever again.

Maybe I'll never be free if I stay with Aric, but at least I won't be alone.

I'm not sure when he became someone I desire to be with. That spoiled, chronically unsatisfied siren with daddy issues. I care for him, and I know that's a stupid thing to do, but it was too late to turn back the instant I kneeled for him. The moment I let him drive away the wounds I'd let fester for centuries. He replaced my pain with pleasure, my fear with desire, my suspicion with a tentative trust. He changed everything.

So, yes, I care. And I know it's a mistake, because he will never reciprocate. I know I've destroyed him too thoroughly.

The door at the top of the stairs thumps shut, and I stagger back from the case, my fingers tightening around the bones. Those footsteps are heavy. They're calculated. I turn and run in the direction Aric disappeared.

He wandered farther than he should have, past the stacks of ancient tomes and dusty relics forgotten to the hive mind of the church. I find him huddled over a case in a far corner, between an altar and a tower of ripped robes.

"We have company."

He spins to face me, his face ashen.

I wave him towards me. "What the hell are you waiting for? Let's get out of here."

He joins me as I turn back to the front of the room. By the time we enter the aisles of tomes, we catch a glimpse of lights peeking through the shelves. The priest isn't the only one searching for us down here.

The entire cathedral is on alert.

A low curse slips off Aric's tongue, and his hand fists in the bodice of my dress as he veers us in the opposite direction, away from the bobbing lights.

We keep moving, weaving between the aisles until we escape every hint of lanterns. Aric slumps at the end of a stack, his eyes glazed. I lean against the stack beside him, our shoulders brushing, and wait for him to gather his thoughts.

When he looks at me, his brown eyes burn into mine. "Did you get it?" he asks, his voice the barest whisper.

I nod.

Relief slides across his face, followed by a grimace. "The priest knows we're here."

"That nun likely went straight to him after she left us down here." I press the fist holding the bones against my lips. "I'm so stupid, I should have knocked her out or something."

Aric shakes his head. "Neither of us did the right thing."

He turns the corner, his hand closing blindly over mine to pull me along. A strange hum permeates the room, growing louder until it feels as if it's rattling the walls, rattling my bones.

Aric leads us between stacks until we finally find the edge of the room. It's filled with clusters of altars and statues. Broken pieces of a false god.

The footsteps return. They're impossible to track at this point. There's so many different ones, echoing from every direction. Every noise bounces off the several pillars of marble, splitting and dispersing. The only constant is that infernal hum. I think it might actually drive me mad if I have to listen to it for much longer.

Ahead of me, Aric suddenly stiffens.

His fingers tighten on mine as he wrenches us both to the side, behind a statue of a woman holding a terrible imitation of a heart. He seizes my wrists and raises them, arranging the position to match the shape of the statue. Then Aric's slender body pins mine in place.

That's when I see the lantern light swinging back and forth across the marble floor. The footsteps that accompany it are light and swift. A nun.

My mouth had been parted to voice my annoyance, but I clamp it shut.

Aric's face is so close to mine that I can smell the sweat beading his brow. Salty, spiced, and slightly sweet. It makes me want to lean in closer. I want to press against him and get the scent all over me. His cool breath puffs against my collar. His chin tilts up, and his lips nearly brush mine.

My eyes meet his.

He's staring at me already, the feminine angles of his face doing nothing to mask the bestial slant of his brow. My mouth parts again. Our breathing mingles. The sliver of blue at the apex of his irises glows faintly.

Wait—no, that's my heartslight.

Shit.

I suppose the bones can't steal away *all* magic. There's still my inheritance, and nothing I've ever encountered on land or at sea is capable of silencing that. And nothing will close that hole in my chest, no matter what form I take.

My hearts will always be vulnerable.

Aric's hands release my wrists and press against my breast as that lantern light dances to our other side. It slowly fades as the nun turns away and slips into the stacks.

I wonder if Aric can feel how hard my hearts are thudding.

He reclaims my hand and leads us onward. How he maintains any sense of direction in this place, I have no idea. That hum under my feet is completely disorienting me. Aric drags us through a shorter stack of shelves and brings the staircase to the cathedral into view.

Pacing in front of the stairs, a whip in one hand and some strange vibrating pendant in the other, is the priest.

Aric expels a harsh breath. His glare is molten earth, blood and stone. I've seen that look aimed at me before. He turns to me, his eyes simmering with resolve. "Okay," he mutters, bracing a hand on the shelf beside us as he leans in. "I'm going to draw him away from the staircase. When he comes after me, get out."

What? "I can't leave without—"

"Yes, you fucking can," he snaps. "You have to. Get the artifact out of here—if they catch us both under the influence of that thing, we have no way of fighting back. If you get out, at least I have my song. I'll follow you as soon as I can."

It makes sense. This is the best option, the smartest option. I don't want to leave him behind, but he's right—if I leave with the bones, then he'll regain full use of his power.

Neither of us are safe with this relic close enough to feed on us.

I swallow the dread tickling the back of my throat. "Fine. But if you get killed—"

"Yeah, yeah." His mouth quirks into a smirk. "You'll search for my spirit in the ocean foam so you can punish me a second time. I'm aware."

I can't help but smile. "Good."

Aric walks down the stack, pausing just before the corner. He twists to say over his shoulder, "If I don't make it out of here, give my father hell for the both of us."

Before I can tell him that there's no world in which I would allow him to die, he slips beyond the shelf, putting himself directly in the priest's line of sight.

The priest looks up from the pendant in his hand, a chilling smile spreading over his mouth. His spectacles reflect the candlelight. "Look at you. You've climbed right into your grave, little spirit. Now you're too far from the canals to escape."

The canals...

The priest must believe Aric is the spirit haunting their city, the one killing men who troll for prostitutes and abuse them. He thinks Aric is *me*. But I'm aware of *his* evil as well, of how he abuses the women of this cathedral in the same manner. I've heard the suffering he causes. The suffering that ripples out and touches every corner of this city. It seems he's been waiting for the moment when I finally come for him, the way I definitely would have eventually.

He steps forward, the whip in his hand shifting in preparation. But Aric is already running into the stacks, his feminine figure swallowed up by the dark.

I hide myself at the end of the stack as the priest approaches, and the humming deafens me as he passes by.

Infernal human magic. My hands lift to muffle my ears. I bite my lower lip to keep from whimpering—I only barely manage it.

The tension eases as the priest follows Aric between the aisles of parchment and leather. With every resounding step, I feel that hum slough from my limbs.

Peering through the last stack to the base of the staircase, I see that the path is clear.

The string connecting me to Aric strains with longing as I leave the shadows, clutching the bones against my chest. As I race up the stairs into the silent and cavernous cathedral above, I can hardly believe what I just witnessed.

A siren committing the most selfless act imaginable.

Risking his life for an enemy.

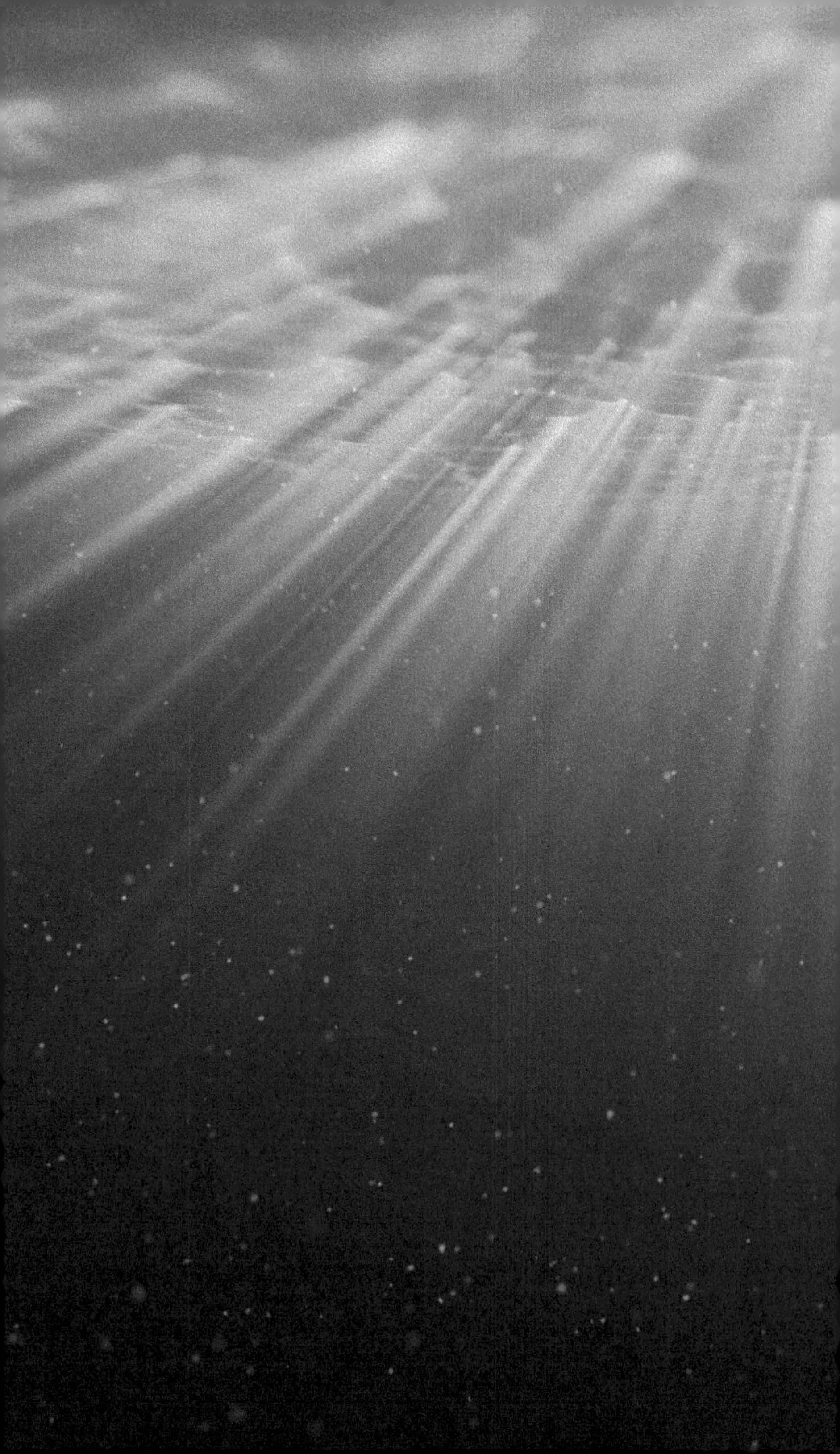

CHAPTER 26
ARIC

A whistle slices through the air behind me, warbling through the room with as much force as the vibration of Fluke's pendant against my stomach.

The bobbing of lantern lights close in.

I slipped the pendant Fluke gave me into the holster for my shark blade.

Fuck, if this isn't the stupidest thing I've ever done. From the moment we entered the church, the pendant came to life with a faint burring. It didn't intensify while we were upstairs. I don't think the priest had it with him when he was punishing Hazel.

Hazel.

It's my fault she's in this place, that her father gave her up, that she's now being subjected to the priest and all of his cruelty. I used her, and she dealt with the consequences.

Archibald's voice echoes faintly from behind me, "Come out, little spirit, and face your god."

I tried to rid myself of the pendant. I retreated to the farthest corner of the basement to avoid alerting the sea witch to what I'd carried in, and fully intended on abandoning it in that dark corner... but I *couldn't*. My hand refused to let it go. That's when I started to truly understand what Fluke must have done when he said he attuned it to me.

The pendant was given my blood, and so it was given permission to use my body for its bidding.

Permission and possession, the way of magic. This necklace won't let go of me until its purpose is fulfilled. And when Viola found me, sickened by my realization, I knew I couldn't risk telling her. We might have formed this tentative partnership, but that won't last long if she finds out what I'd been willing to do to her.

As the hum slowly fades from the necklace, relief shimmers in my veins. Viola made it out of the cathedral.

I attempt to veer away from the impending lights, but it's impossible. There's too many of them. I just have to buy myself enough time for my song to return, so that when I'm caught, I won't be defenseless. My power is slowly trickling back in, but it's slow, like waking after a long sleep to find the strength in my limbs isn't quite there yet.

The reality of my situation crashes over me.

I let her leave me here, and she escaped with the bones. The sea witch has everything she needs. She has her weapon against Triton. There's no reason for her to come back for me, or to hope I make it out of this—no reason except the one she's already given me.

I am the only one who gets to swallow you whole.

Those words fill me with a quiet, ravaging flame. They weren't empty words.

I'm hers to consume, and she is mine to surrender to.

Gritting my teeth, I align myself in the direction of the fewest bobbing lights. I'll have to face the cloaked women in this small body and hope I triumph.

I turn the corner of one of the bookshelves and stagger to a stop in front of the woman. Every horrifying detail is illuminated by firelight. Her eyes are a clouded blue. Her expression is blank, her jaw slack, and the religious pendant hanging from her neck pulses with a faint cobalt light. In her hand, she holds a broken wine bottle, the jagged edges glistening.

There is no emotion, no sentience in her eyes as she slices at me.

The lantern swings between us, casting violent shadows as I duck under the attack. Retreating up the aisle, I grapple with the thick volumes and begin launching them at her.

She doesn't react, even when the hard bindings hit her in the face and she starts to bleed. Her steps are rickety, as though her limbs are disjointed or she's not really in control of them.

Ice fills my stomach as I realize what's happened...

Archibald has taken over their bodies somehow.

I give up trying to hurt her and turn to retreat, but collide with another body. Another cloaked slave. She tries to grab me, but I knock her arms away. The lantern in her hand drops, and its glass erupts, flames catching on her dress and the books beside her. She doesn't even scream as her skin starts to burn. I stagger back, looking for another way out.

I feel a tug on my chest. The heartstring. Even when Viola's far away, our souls touch.

The womanly robes pull tight over my chest. My legs lengthen and the muscles on my abdomen tighten. Viola is shifting me back to my male form. I didn't realize she could do that at a distance.

Maybe she's closer than I thought, maybe she abandoned the bones somewhere and doubled back to help me.

She must have.

That soul-stirring witch was never going to leave me behind.

This sudden revelation makes me want to get on my knees and kiss her feet, kiss every inch of her from toe to crown. *I want to kiss her.*

But she can't come back into this cathedral right now.

If she comes back, the pendant will know, both sides of it. The priest will know. She needs to stay far, far away, and there's no way for me to tell her that.

The women to either side of me survey my new form blankly, then turn to attend to the rapidly spreading fire. I no longer look like the female they'd been sent out to seize. Another two lanterns appear in my peripheral, turning into the stack on both ends.

I drop to my hands and knees and shove myself through one of the lower shelves. I scramble over dusty leather and clamber to my feet in the parallel aisle.

As I spear into an adjacent stack, I accidentally ram my shoulder into the shelf, and the wood shudders.

I pause, backing up to consider the shelves and their chaotic arrangement throughout the room. They aren't properly anchored down. The way these shelves are set up...

Before I can change my mind, I slam into the stack with all my strength.

As the first shelf careens forward and collides with the next, I can see that my idea will work. They all start toppling. That'll at least provide an obstacle. I try not to feel bad for the mindless women getting caught in the middle of it. I spin on my heel and return to the back of the room. I thought I felt a breeze back there, and while Viola and I didn't have time to search for cellar doors or a window, they might be my only option left for escape.

I skid to a halt as I leave behind the maze of books.

A lone figure stands here, waiting for me. Archibald. His wolfish smile falters when he sees me without Viola's magic disguising my body. "Captain?"

I glare at him from across the room, making myself as large and intimidating as the holy gown I'm wearing will allow.

Archibald scoffs. "You're part of her trickery. I thought I sensed something wicked about you."

"You're one to speak about hidden wickedness," I snarl.

His eyes flutter in surprise. "Ah, so he *can* talk. Very good." He tilts his head in consideration. "Hand over the witch, boy, and I'll spare your life."

The fury in my chest swells. "You would do well not to call me 'boy'."

"Because you are a demon?" he retorts.

"Because I've been alive longer than you *and* your predecessor, and I'll happily rip you to shreds to prove it."

Archibald's confidence slips, but only for a second. "Whatever you are," he says carefully. "I don't wish to go to war with you today. I only want the witch."

My power inflates beneath my ribs, announcing its full return. I smile.

"Well, that's too bad. She's already gone."

"Hmm." His hand tightens on the necklace as he stuffs it into his robes. "That would explain the behavior of the pendant."

His eyes flick to somewhere beyond me, and he nods.

Searing pain ruptures across my neck as a heavy chain curls around it. The links sear into my skin. Pure silver. I twist and discover a cloaked servant had been waiting beside me in the stacks. She was so quiet, so still. Did she even bother to breathe? Does she need to?

Are any of these women truly alive once their body is taken from them?

She steps on the chain to bring me to my knees.

The priest stalks forward, now wholly unafraid of me, and demands, "Where is she?"

I glance up at him, my vision hazy.

I try to unwrap the chain, but the skin of my fingertips burn away the instant I touch it. My neck is sizzling, the veins erupting, my organs refusing to function under the weight of the silver. But beneath that, a rush of power. My song. Without hesitation, I open my mouth and force a melody out through my constricted airway. It's strange... different. And I think that's because the spirits rushing through me aren't ones I'm familiar with. The spirits singing through me right now are the ones in the walls around us. Human and furious.

Amethyst tendrils spark off my tongue. They curl and most fall to the floor prematurely, but as I sing louder, they grow stronger.

Archibald notices and snaps his fingers to get the cloaked woman's attention. *"Gag him!"*

She wrenches on my chain, sending me sprawling. Then she kneels on my chest, twisting the hem of her skirt up into her hand and shoving it into my mouth. I try to push her away, but the chains are too vicious. I'm too weak.

I try to send my song spiraling into her eyes. She's looking at me. But her eyes are cloudy like the others were, and when I grapple with her mind, it's empty. Just a large, white expanse.

She's not inside it anymore.

This is it. This is how I die. At least, that's what I believe as Archibald closes the space between us and kneels at my side. There's no use trying to influence him either. He's not wearing his spectacles, and I get the feeling his immunity goes beyond flawed vision. This human uses a worse magic than even the vilest ocean spirits dabble in.

"I know you're only one of her prisoners," he murmurs, grazing a thumb over my cheek.

I jerk, hissing when the movement makes the chain dig in. My vision bubbles.

I can barely hear him as he continues, "Don't worry, I know your nature will not allow you to harm her. Your fellow slave told me everything."

He pauses, scrutinizing me.

I keep every hint of emotion from my face—luckily, I've had plenty of practice.

"I will spare you just as I spared the other, *if* you swear fealty to god and help us rid the city of her. We will rid the entire world of evil, in due time."

Someday soon, I'll get my hands on him. Once I do, I won't stop tearing until his blood becomes a second skin over my hands. I'm glad for the gag because a smile threatens my composure as I nod. Invisible gods don't have to keep promises, and neither do I.

He pushes the woman off me and unwraps the chain from my neck.

"It's my responsibility to protect the men of this city," he mutters, gripping the back of my neck to pull me into a sitting position. He doesn't let me go right away, instead drawing closer on his knees. His face is too close to mine, his clouded eyes too intense.

Bile churns in my throat, and I find myself wondering if it will seep through the still-healing holes in my neck. If he were born under the surface, he would have made an excellent siren; the look in his eyes makes me think he'd be all too glad to cut open my stomach and examine the contents.

"She's killed men. Good men. She targets them and will not hesitate to turn on you too." His lip curls in disdain. "Remind yourself of that the next time you feel the urge to protect her."

As much as I want to rip his tongue out, I hesitate... because I see the truth in his eyes. I know with certainty that she is capable of it—that she could kill above the water just as easily as she's killed beneath it. All this time I've spent with her, I almost forgot.

I almost forgot about the innocents she killed beneath the surface, members of Father's court and citizens of Atlantis. Hundreds. My mother included.

It would be foolish of me to trust her, to allow her to gain even an ounce of power over Atlantis.

I can't say anything, can't *do* anything. I'm paralyzed. The voices in my head scream at each other, the darkness swirling in agreement with the priest, drowning out every thought of *her* and what she's done to me—the way she's softened me in all my sharpest places. Another part of me hopes that the priest is wrong. That he's wrong about her just as I had been, and that she might be so much more than our fear of her.

Archibald smiles and finally lets me go.

As he stands, he says, "The hunt will happen soon. Just keep the amulet as close to her as possible, and I will do the rest. There may be redemption for you yet, son."

Redemption? Never. Not for what I have done, or for what I'm about to do.

Archibald offers me his hand, but I ignore it and rise to my feet on my own. I feel another tug on the heartstring—she's much closer now, nearly back to the cathedral.

"Stay down here," I rasp. "She can't see us together."

He takes a small step to the side in assent.

I return to the stacks, giving the mindless slave waiting beside them a wide berth. She stands there, unblinking. She might as well have been one of the statues, one of the altars. Forgotten.

As I weave my way through the shelves, I encounter more of them. All unseeing and still. Waiting. Waiting. Waiting. Waiting for nothing. Even the ones trapped beneath the wreckage are silent as I climb over them. They aren't their own. They barely feel real.

Once I'm past the last of the toppled shelves, I race up the stairs and into the cathedral.

Night has painted the room a dark blue. Moonlight peeks through the windows and dances between the long seats, guiding me straight to the massive double doors. I throw them open. Fresh air fills my lungs, and as I rush down the front steps, I catch a glimpse of the silhouette emerging from the alley up ahead.

I struggle to get another full breath.

The hood she stole from the cathedral is gone. Her amaranthine hair flies up around her head from lingering static, creating a halo that looks all too fitting. She's what I imagined an angel would look like when Hazel first told me about them. Powerful. Beyond beautiful, dangerously and deceivingly so. A being that defies all sense, that defies every rationale of the universe to exist.

She is the sort of vision I would have painted on ceilings, that I would have admired for all my days.

And I am going to be the death of her.

She deserves it, doesn't she? She deserves every horrible thing that's happened to her, and everything that will come in the future. She's a liar. She's a murderer.

Her every emotion is feigned, even the look of radiant

relief she displays when she sees me bursting from the cathedral—it must be.

Because the alternative is that *I* am the real evil.

I meet her at the corner and we run down the alley—going where, I don't know. She grabs my hand and leads me into an adjacent street. We pass several narrower roads, but then she skids to a stop and leans into one of them to snatch clothes off a line.

As she tosses clothes at me, I dress, and my head turns with everything that Archibald said to me and everything that Viola has revealed to me herself. I try to fit them together, try to make sense of the confusion swarming my thoughts. There are cracks in my resolve. Not deep enough to come clean, to tell her what happened in the basement and what I'm carrying and put myself at her fickle mercy, but something bothers me about what the priest said.

She targets men.

Of all the victims attributed to her, how many of them were women? Only one.

Centuries she's been killing, and yet even the priest knew she exclusively hunts men. Triton never made that distinction before. Now that I think about it, I realize that she has a particular taste in souls.

And the one woman she's been accused of killing doesn't fit her pattern.

"Viola." I whisper her name, and there's no hatred in my voice. No violence. I think it might be the first time I've ever said her name like this—as an equal. As a friend.

She looks up at me, her brows pulling together.

Curiosity pulls her nearer—or maybe that's me tugging on that string between us. Maybe she's tugging too.

"You didn't kill my mother." It's not a question because I already know. Somehow, I know it beyond the shadow of a doubt that has plagued me from the moment we met, when she laughed in the belly of a kraken.

Her eyes shutter.

I see the cranks turning in her mind, the understanding of why I hated her so intensely, so quickly. The reason I let her hate me in return. The lies she was not even aware of until this moment.

Could things have been different between us, if I knew?

Could I have looked past the fact that she has killed so many, that she ruined me for her own selfish reasons? That she continues to use me now?

"No," she replies, her voice barely audible. Then her throat bobs, and she rolls her shoulders back as though in preparation. "No, Aric. I didn't. Your mother was the first mer I ever turned human."

SHE LIVED.

I stand in an olive grove hidden in the gnarled hills just outside the city, staring at the home my mother created for herself.

A family gathers on the patio of the house. Children run and scream, a father chasing after them. A young woman rubs sleep from her eyes, a woman so familiar she could be a mirror. Red hair. Skin kissed with the faintest undertone of brass. A wry smile as she watches her children squeal.

Mother smiled like that. Maybe I smile like that too.

She lived, and loved, *without me*. My mother is dead now, of course—humans only live for so long. But she lives on in this woman and her children.

The sea witch took my mother from me, but not in the way I believed. Not the way Father swore to me and Atlantis she did. Seeing it for myself, I don't know if this is better, or if it's worse. For my mother, certainly this was a better ending, but—

"Even my mother knew I was hopeless," I mutter.

Viola is silent for a few long moments.

I sense her moving closer, her body heat encroaching on my back. I wait for her to touch me and wonder how I'll react when she does. I wonder if I'll lash out and hurt her as badly as I am hurting, or if I'll put my hands on her and pin her to a tree and kiss her until I can no longer think of why I should hate her. I don't know if there is any reason to hate her left. I want to thank her for what she did. I want to hate her for hurting me, even indirectly, but I can't.

"She saved herself," she whispers. "She was scared, and perhaps a little selfish, but that's no reflection on who you are. Or what you are."

"You thought it too." My eyes slide to her. Whatever she sees in my face makes her grimace. "You thought that my father ruined me. Maybe he did."

"That was before I knew you."

I shake my head. "You don't know me now."

"Well, that must be because you are *so* forthcoming." Her playful tone is so at odds with the moment that I blink in surprise. Then I smile. I can't restrain it.

But that smile fades, leaving behind nothing but a false sense of happiness that I know won't last—like those pearls our gallery collected, offering fleeting and brittle relief. I turn from her, facing the hills and the humans that carry the last trace of my mother. When Viola tugs on that connection between us, I ignore her.

Eventually, I feel her leave my side.

I hear her steps retreat, slow and soft against the acidic soil, and then they pause.

"Not all humans are like the ones you met in the palace and its mistress."

Viola speaks as if in a confession of her own.

I glance back and see her standing under the bough of an olive tree, the greenery standing out against her alabaster skin. Somehow, she looks at home here, on land. I see the longing to remain here in her eyes, in the way she sways in the gentle breeze. That's why she was so comfortable in the market. Why she pretends to be human, walking and talking among them... because that is the one thing she cannot have. The only thing she truly wants.

We are so alike in our desires. How can it be?

"Some mortals are bright and generous. If you watch them, they will teach you new ways of breathing, new ways of living. There is goodness up here, dear Prince, if you know where to search for it." It sounds like a promise, but I don't have the confidence to be sure.

Then Viola leaves me there in the grove, alone with my endless thoughts and a radiant dawn cresting the horizon.

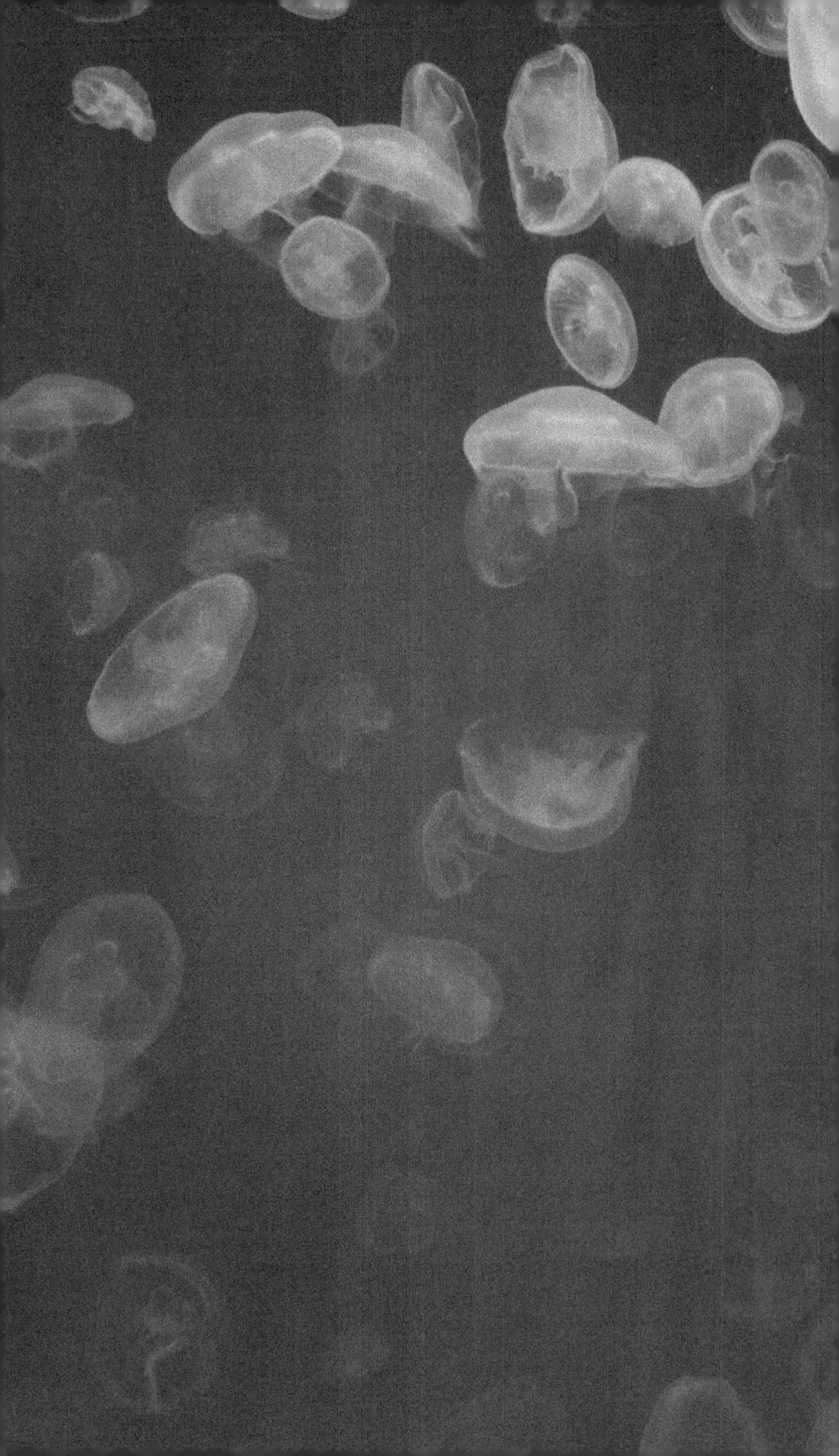

CHAPTER 27
VIOLA

Guillermo's family is gathering for their weekly meal together by the time I return to the city.

I trail after Jussi down the smaller, more intimate streets of the city, lost to my thoughts. Lost to the memory of Aric's reaction when he found out about his mother. I've come to realize that when he feels any strong emotion, he shuts down.

I couldn't think of a way to comfort him, so I left him to sort out those feelings.

It was the right thing to do. I just wish I didn't feel this way as a result—like I abandoned him, no better than his mother who left him in that dark, unforgiving ocean. I would have turned them both, would have turned *all* of her children if she had asked me to. But then I never would have known Aric. Because of that, I can't quite wish things were different.

I lengthen my steps to catch up with my old friend.

He carries a canvas under his arm. Blue paint sweeps across it from top to bottom, the colors shifting with endless shades of sky and ocean. In the center of the canvas, a stone edifice rises out of the waves, water spilling toward it from every direction.

I cock my head, trying to see more. "That's an interesting landscape."

Jussi's head swivels to mark my attention, and then he lifts the canvas between us, allowing me to admire it upright. "I found this place on one of my boating trips, just a few miles off the coast. It's this sinkhole where boats like mine can get drawn in and destroyed. Fishermen call it the Pit. A direct funnel into their human hell," he chuckles, "can you imagine?"

I grimace, reaching out to finger a hard ridge of paint. He perfectly captured the sensation of being towed toward it. "No, I can't."

"Really, it's just this old, abandoned castle that no one's seen in decades. It has a chasm underneath the foundation, so when water falls in over the walls, the hole creates this pull on the ocean around it. With the condition of the canals and barges this year, it brought the whole structure to the surface. It won't last long. The King has already sent workers to the barges to adjust the water levels, and once the rainy season starts, the river will overflow—so I wanted to get a good replication on canvas before it disappears for who knows how long. Guillermo's mother wanted me to bring the painting tonight to show her."

I squeeze his arm. "You've outdone yourself."

"Thank you, love. I'll be back in a minute." Jussi kisses my temple before walking ahead, toward one of the many open doors lining the street.

Guillermo's family bustles back and forth, and I hesitate to join them.

Rarely, over the years, I would watch these gatherings from afar. It was lovely to me how they coalesced, how they became this *one thing*—a family. I watched them eat together, love and dance and laugh together. I longed for the day when I might take part, when I might experience it for myself. This might be my last chance before returning to the ocean for another few decades or longer.

And yet, I can't help but feel like a piece of me is incapable of it, the way I always do. That hunger inside me is alive and wanting. The artifact remains where I hid it, safe and beyond affecting me.

Maybe I should retrieve it before—

A hand suddenly appears on my back and slides over to the dip of my waist. Every inch of my skin erupts in goose flesh, my stomach churning. I spin in place, reaching up to blindly grab a fistful of the stranger's shirt, my sharp nails prepared to scratch their eyes out.

Molten brown eyes, with blue slivers pointing to the sky.

"Oh," I exhale, my entire body unraveling. "It's only you."

Aric doesn't step back and neither do I. He glances at the fingers I tangled in his shirt. When he piques an eyebrow at me, I release the material and attempt to smooth out the wrinkles. But his *hand* is still on my *waist*. I swear I feel his thumb moving, caressing me in soft strokes.

"Yeah, only me," he murmurs. "Look, I'm sorry for earlier. I shouldn't have let you walk back to the city all by yourself."

For an instant, I'm struck dumb. Is he *apologizing* to me? More than that, apologizing for something that seems inconsequential in the face of everything else between us, everything we've said and done to hurt one another.

This could very well be a trap. He could be lulling me with his touch and kind words before he strikes. He must be angry with me, about his mother.

"I'm perfectly capable of protecting myself, Aric."

"I know, but it was an awfully long walk. Boring, too."

"Since when do you care about my loneliness?" I return with a chuckle.

He shrugs. "I suppose since you started caring about mine."

My body heats beneath his stare. "Well then," I breathe. "I guess I forgive you."

Aric smiles sweetly, then turns to survey the street. "What's going on around here?"

"That depends on why you've come."

The voice startles both of us.

I take a step out of Aric's embrace and face Jussi, who's considering the prince with a grave look, slender arms crossed over his chest.

Aric catches my hand before I can fully disentangle.

My chest tingles, and I know without looking down that my hearts are glowing again. Thankfully, it's too bright outside for anyone to notice.

Aric returns Jussi's stare for a long moment, then he looks at me. The corner of his mouth twitches. Quietly, he explains, "I'm searching, I suppose."

The words fall into my heart like waterfall, pummeling the tissues, soothing the hunger in me for the briefest of seconds. I say without looking away from him, "I invited him here, Jussi."

Because I had, in a way. I invited him to look for the good in humanity, and where better to search than these streets?

Jussi scans the space between the two of us, the space that seems to be growing smaller and more unbearable with every passing moment. Slowly, he nods. "All right," he says gruffly. He waves a hand to signal that we should follow him. "Let me show you around."

Aric seems apprehensive of the offer.

He looks to me—perhaps for reassurance—and I shrug. He makes his own decision and follows Jussi into the gathering crowd without a word. Jussi guides us, introducing us to the men tending to the coal pit and young children darting from house to house, so many cousins that I lose count of them. At some point, someone hands me a glass of wine. I help some of the women arrange tarps and cushions on either side of the street, and Jussi and Aric walk ahead to where Guillermo is setting up an activity for the children that involves some old horseshoes.

I quickly finish up with what I'm doing and catch up to them, watching the introductions with a tumbling stomach.

Guillermo greets Jussi with a sloppy kiss on his cheek, then turns to face Aric and drags a fierce stare over Aric's body. I fully understood Jussi's reticence earlier, expected his coldness and general unpleasantness when it came to bringing Aric into his world, near his family. I didn't expect Guillermo—large and soft, utterly *joyous*, Guillermo—to mirror it.

I reach their little trio in time to hear Guillermo say, "So you're the annoying bastard that's been troubling our Viola."

Gaping, I lurch forward and slap that giant of a man right in the stomach. He doesn't react, of course—I didn't put a whole lot of strength or nails behind it. He just keeps staring at Aric with a remorseless smile.

"We don't get to see her as often as we'd like," Guillermo continues. "I'm sure you can imagine how frustrating it is for us that even for this brief time we have her, her time and attention continues being wasted on you and your father and all the other selfish assholes in your city that don't know how to stop ripping good people apart."

I'm beyond gaping. I think my jaw has fallen straight through the ground at my feet.

I drain my wine glass, wondering if I made a mistake by letting Aric remain here, wondering if mistakes are all I know how to make.

Jussi snickers, delighted by this sudden turn in the conversation. "A blunt man, my husband." He slaps him on the shoulder, then squeezes slightly, a subtle display of his appreciation.

I step in before the boys decide to devour Aric entirely. "Guillermo, be nice."

"It's all right," Aric interjects softly, effectively neutralizing all three of us. We turn to him. "I have been a bit of a bastard recently."

Guillermo huffs a laugh, at a loss for what to say next. He eventually manages a quiet, "Well, good. I'm glad we agree."

"For what it's worth, I would like to show you I can behave. I promise you that I can." Aric glances at me and traces an X over his breast, where I had carved that rune into his skin. "Cross my heart."

Guillermo's eyes lock with mine.

He must see something there because he cracks a smile. He returns his attention to Aric, grasps his shoulder, and pulls him in for a crushing hug. Aric stiffens. Before he can fully react, Guillermo shoves him away with a boisterous laugh.

"Trust me, we'll see precisely how *genteel* you can be," he sneers, turning to the wall of homes behind him. Guillermo places two fingers in his mouth and whistles loud enough to make my ears tremble. "MAMA!"

In no time at all, Guillermo's family folds Aric into their routine.

Guillermo's mama took him into the house where they are preparing the food, and put him to work. The siren prince who spit venom after venom at me, who fought and fucked me like we might bring the entire world to cinders together, is now sitting right outside their back door, *washing dishes.*

I don't bother hiding my smile as I lounge in the doorway and watch him.

He's keeping to his word. He hasn't so much as uttered a complaint as the dirty pile beside him grows larger and larger. The kitchen to my other side is absolute chaos. Women scramble to and fro, mixing and cutting and tending to the brick oven. Several bowls and platters scatter the room and every one of them adds a note to the euphony of smells filling the air.

The temptation of sneaking a bite or two is overwhelming, but Guillermo's mama is not a woman to test, especially at a time like this.

She's a fierce little red-head with the hands of an elder and the eyes of a hawk, and she runs this family around like a queen would her troops.

I guzzle the bottle of wine in my hand and stay neatly out of everyone's way.

As much fun as it is to watch Aric, it's fun to watch them too. Their bickering and affection. It means something to be accepted here. To be loved unconditionally. To be given trust to the same measure you offer it. That's part of what makes this city beautiful: the families.

My eyes burn. I have to turn my face outward, to the darkening sky above the alleyway, before I lose control and cry.

I think it's going to rain.

No one pays the warning any mind. These citizens never

do. They continue to cook and fill the streets with their instruments. What's a little rain in the face of such love?

A throat clears beside me.

Guillermo's mama shoves a dead chicken into my arms. "There's no dawdling in this house," she snaps. "If you're going to take up space in the kitchen, then the least you could do is be helpful. Gut and pluck this chicken outside, then ready it for the coals." She takes the wine from me and replaces it with a knife as she herds me through the doorway.

She shuts the door behind me.

I sigh, grimacing at the limp chicken in my hands.

"You're supposed to say 'yes, ma'am' or 'whatever you say, ma'am,'" Aric stands up in front of his steaming trough of water and smirks, "and then follow it up with an earnest, 'it's my pleasure to serve you, your most splendid majesty.'"

He grabs the back of his chair and kicks it toward me, an offering.

Before I can refuse, he returns to the trough and drops into a crouch, plunging his hands back into the water. My chest warms at the gesture.

Hitching my dress to keep it from getting dirty, I sit on the edge of the chair and begin ripping feathers from the bird's wings. "You've put a lot of thought into that, Prince," I retort mildly. "If I didn't know better, I might think that's another fantasy of yours—surrendering mind, body, and soul."

I thought it to be a harmless taunt, but Aric pauses across from me. He glances at me. "Can it be a fantasy if that's also my current reality?"

He means me, and the bond between us. Does he think that's what I want?

"I would never demand that of you, Aric."

He frowns, silently scrubbing at a bit of burnt food.

After a time, he replies, "It doesn't matter. It's like you promised me Beneath: you *own* me. At any moment, you could tug on this cord between us and reap my soul, and then what do I become to you? What do you become to me?" He glances at me sidelong, genuine worry in his eyes.

What will we become? It's a good question.

A better one is what we are to each other at this moment. Are we still enemies? Or are we friends now that we've saved each other, now that there are no secrets between us?

Does he still hate me?

I will be whatever he wants, whatever he needs. "That's not going to happen, Aric."

"Then what *is* going to happen?"

I tear at the feathers faster. I don't respond until the entire carcass is bare. "I will release you."

"When?"

I meet his imploring stare, fingering the handle of the knife as I take it into my hand. It's worn and smooth. Aric wants to be free of me, but I already knew that. Wouldn't I wish to be free too? Isn't freedom what I wish for every second of every day?

I've grown used to the constant sensation of him, through the connection between us. He has been the only good in too many decades of wrong.

Cutting the chicken open, I say, "Eventually."

After Triton is dealt with. When it doesn't hurt so much to think about.

Blood spills from the bird and splatters the ground between my feet. The head was already severed when Guillermo's mama handed it to me, so it really shouldn't have this much blood inside, but it gushes like a fountain.

My upper lip curls as I continue digging. Then I set aside the knife and start pulling the innards out with my hand.

One by one, they drop to the cobblestone alley. Lungs and spleen. Gizzards. Then I grasp that all too familiar organ in its chest and tug. Before I can toss it away, I notice something strange about the feel of it, something rough in the tissues. The chicken's heart is deformed.

A lesion has formed down its center, and a small mass protrudes from the other side.

Goddess Mora appears suddenly, hovering close behind me. She rakes her nails down my back. She urges me to listen. The blood was her doing, to get my attention. I've read entrails only once or twice before, when I felt the need to search for direction in the guts of mer I reaped, but I only know enough to understand that a defective heart is the illest of omens.

The hair on my neck raises.

"What is it?" Aric's question makes me jump.

I drop the heart like it's a live snake. "Nothing. It's nothing." I kick the entrails away from me and quickly finish scraping out the inside of the bird.

Maybe I should have looked closer, maybe I should have attempted to decipher what the Goddess wanted to tell me. But truth be told, I'm scared. One thing my coven mother never explained to me is how terrifying it is to be connected to spirits, to have access to the future and the past.

It makes the present a harrowing experience.

Just one day. That's all I want. One day to ignore the ocean and my commitments, to be blissfully, obliviously human. If something terrible is coming, I'll deal with it tomorrow.

Rising from the chair, I return to the doorway, but I pause before retreating into the clamor of the kitchen.

"I know you must be feeling confused and betrayed right now," I say. "I know that doesn't lend you a lot of trust and you aren't sure what to believe, but there's more than one side to every story. And if you ever want to hear mine, Aric, I will tell you *my* truth."

Aric goes preternaturally still.

I don't linger long enough for him to turn around and dig into the past.

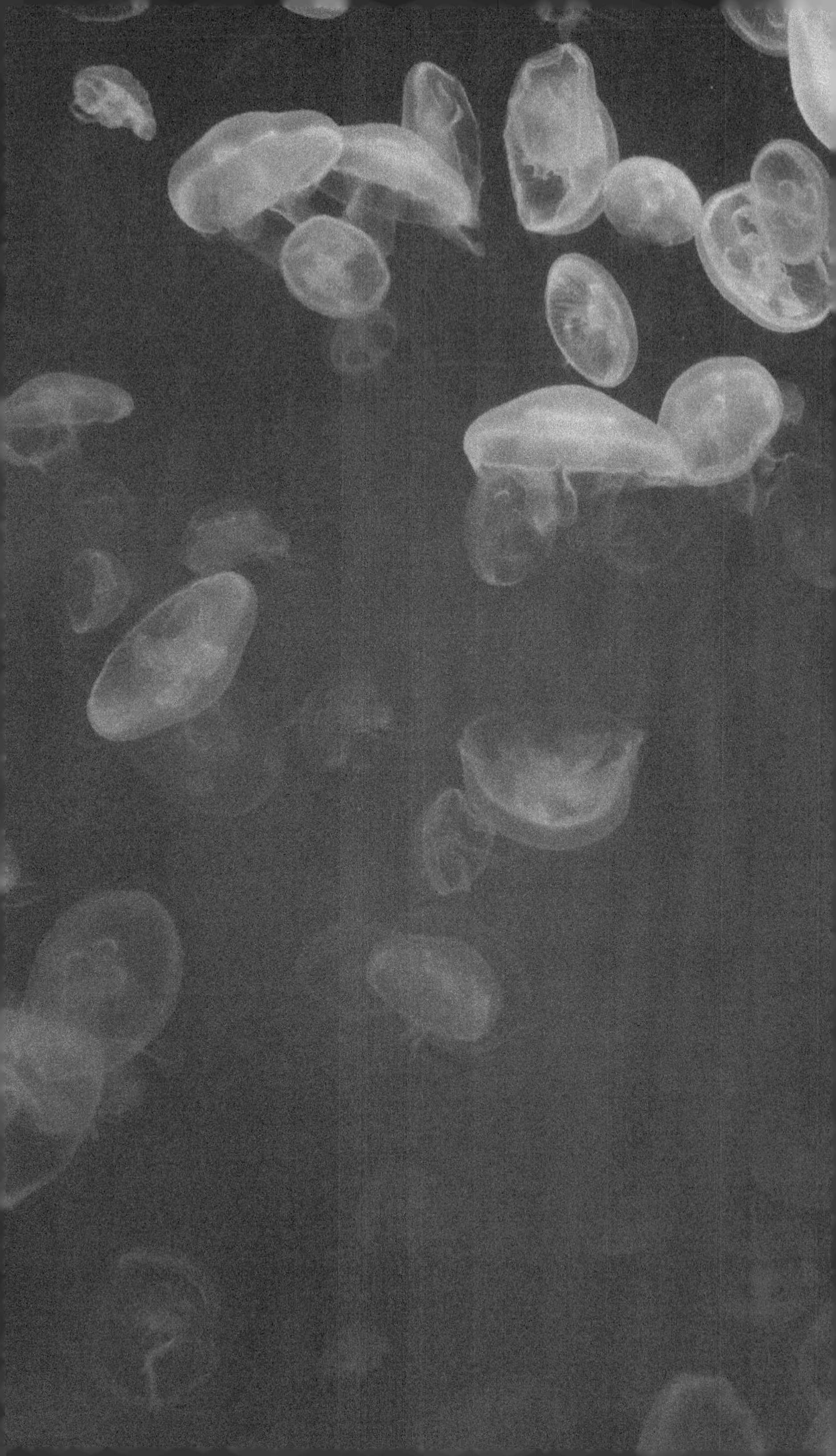

CHAPTER 28
VIOLA

I recover my wine bottle from Guillermo's mama, thank the Goddess.

The alcohol swirls languidly in my veins, dulling the call of the ocean just enough for me to enjoy myself. I survey the several jars of herbs on the table before me and pluck one after another up to inhale their scent. Thyme. Rosemary. Marjoram.

I tear a leaf off the mint plant sprawling in the windowsill and chew on it as I tinker with the blend in my bowl.

Truly, the diversity of the earth fascinates me. I could probably experiment for several lifetimes and never learn all there is to do with them. *Especially* in food. Forget the spells.

I'm so distracted by my task that I don't anticipate my visitor before their warmth touches my back. Hands appear, gripping the edge of the table on either side of me. "What are you stirring up in here, witch?"

Aric's voice is low and gravely. It sounds like he snuck some wine for himself.

I ignore his invasion of my space. "I'm sorry, are you talking to me? I didn't hear my name."

Though, if I were being honest with myself, I don't mind him calling me that anymore. He's stopped saying it in a derisive tone. I wanted him to see more than that when he looked at me. I wanted him to see all of me because I knew he might be the only one who would understand.

Aric steps even closer, squashing me between him and the table. He nuzzles the back of my neck and slurs, "*Vioooola?*"

I shake him and the threatening shiver off my back, spinning to face him with the bowl in hand.

"I'm blending herbs to sprinkle on the chicken once it's done. Smell." I stick the bowl directly under his nose. He has definitely been drinking. There's a warm, sleepy haze in his eyes. A looseness to his body. His reaction to my command is belated, and his nose dips a little too much as he takes a deep breath of the blend.

He accidentally inhales some of the smaller particles, the peppercorn I'd crushed.

Aric recoils with a sneeze, then coughs as it hits the back of his throat. I grimace as he tries to hack the stuff back up, his brown eyes watering as he rubs his chest. "That's, uh... very *penetrative*," he finally rasps.

A giggle rattles out of me as I spin back to the table. "Admit it, you like being penetrated."

I hear his shock before I feel it. He goes utterly silent as I pretend to occupy myself with the jars, and I bite my lower lip to keep from giggling again. Maybe I've had a little bit too much wine if I had the gall to say *that* out loud.

He responds with his body, locking me in with his arms again.

"You want a real confession?" His chest rumbles against my back.

I lean back, relishing in his hard angles. Giving up the illusion of being unaffected, I let my eyes flutter shut and nod.

He lowers his mouth to my ear. "Everything in this room smells incredible, but none of it is as delicious as you."

"Me?" I whisper.

I hear his smile. "And the taste of you is sweeter than my kindest fantasies."

Craning my head, I look at him, my head resting on his shoulder. I believe him. And maybe it's the way he's looking at me or the slow poison scrambling my thoughts, but I say, "You say that as if you want to taste me again."

For a moment, I think he might kiss me. I want him to kiss me.

My eyes catch on starfish attached to his earlobes. I notice that they're *vibrating*. "What are those?" I point at the earring closest to me. "Are they enchanted?"

"Oh," he reaches up and tugs on the one I pointed at, "uh, well, sort of."

"Usually the answer to a question like that is yes or no."

"It's not an enchantment, exactly. When I was younger, I had my conscience extracted."

My brow furrows. "I don't understand."

"I sought help from a witch in a neighboring ocean. She helped me imbue the starfish and set them into my skin."

It takes all of my self-control not to burst out laughing. "Let me guess, it cost you a great deal of gold?"

"Well, yes."

"I'm sorry to be the one to tell you this, dear Prince, but that witch swindled you."

His head bobs back. "What? No, she—it *worked*."

"Sure. She trapped a couple lost spirits in those starfish and told you the voices belonged to you. You understand them because you're a siren. But the conscience can't be separated from the body any more than your heart or brain can. Even when I reap souls, they don't become something I can hold in my hand."

Aric's mouth falls open. His eyes flick to the left and right, as if he were trying to absorb what I just told him, as if the truth was now twirling in the air around us.

After he regains some semblance of composure, he mutters, "I feel painfully stupid right now."

"It's not your fault you didn't know any better. If the witches of Atlantis hadn't been massacred, you never would have fallen victim to a hoax like that."

Aric only replies with an incredulous, "Your people were killed?"

He looks truly horrified by that admission.

I should have known Triton would lie about that too. The truth wouldn't have made him look good in the eyes of the public, especially the underlings, who are already close enough to revolting against the city that they support with their blood and labor.

I rake in a deep breath. "It's a long story we shouldn't get into right now. Later, I promise."

Aric considers me. After a moment, he peels away from me and offers me his hand. "Alright. Will you dance with me?"

My eyes flick to the open doorway behind him, to the couples turning in furious circles and matching pace with the melody out in the street. I don't see a way I wouldn't make a fool of myself. I shake my head, my mind swaying with the force of that motion. "I've been drinking too much."

Aric shrugs. "So? Dance badly with me." His hand

remains there, under my nose. A temptation of the most dangerous sort.

"I should finish what I'm working on."

"I doubt the herbs or the chicken will run off while we're dancing."

"You don't know that. Don't you have dishes to wash?"

He flashes a wicked grin. "I bribed one of the children to take over for me."

"Bribed, or intimidated?" I framed my hips with my sweaty palms.

"I swore I would behave, didn't I?"

"So you did." I smile.

But my mind returns to the carneval, when he lured me in and stoked my desire, then crushed me like a bug under his foot. So much has changed since then. Impossibly, there's more desire for him now, more want and need and feelings I can't even begin to sort through. It has nothing to do with a cycle this time. It has nothing to do with the heartstring.

If he crushes me again, I don't know what will ooze out.

I search for anything to spare me. "Do you even know the steps?"

"Not at all," he says brightly, "but we can learn them together."

I'm too inebriated to resist admiring him. His straight teeth and sculpted cheeks, his narrow chin that sends my eyes trailing the length of his neck to his chest.

The shirt I stole for him is just slightly too small.

Aric takes my hand before I can come up with another excuse, and I sigh as I allow him to drag me out of the house. He leads us down the street, where the dancers and musicians are playing. He's smiling as he slides an arm around my back, as he glances around at the other dancers and imitates the quick steps of the dance. I stumble along, unable to do more than follow the pull of his body.

"You should have asked one of the other women here to dance with you," I mutter. "They would have been more helpful than me."

"I didn't want to dance with anyone else."

"You just didn't want to be the only one looking a fool."

"Maybe." He pulls me against him, shortening his steps to skip like the others around us. "Or maybe I just *really* like touching you."

The dance quickens, and the couples begin to spin and stomp in a driving rhythm. Aric's eyes burn into mine, and I have to look away. Which turns out to be a mistake, because I'm still too inebriated to keep my balance.

Bile turns in the pit of my stomach.

My discomfort must be apparent because Aric slows down and pinches my chin to bring my eyes back to his.

"What's wrong?" he demands. "Are you feeling alright?"

No. I'm scared of him. I'm scared of how sweet he's being to me. I'm frightened that it won't last, that it's not real. I swallow against the thickness of my throat. "I don't know what to think about this. About you and me."

"I'm Aric and you're Viola, and we're dancing. Stop thinking so hard about it."

The music clashes over us, its melody urging us faster.

I suddenly realize that this is what Aric has always done for me. He turns off my thoughts. He moves violently, swiftly, and I can't control our direction or the destination or what I feel along the way. That's how I ended up on my knees for him, twice. Thinking too much has never been a problem around him. So he's right, why start now?

Aric wraps his arms around my waist.

His face burrows in my hair as he inhales my scent deep

into his lungs, and I feel so beautiful, so weightless and human in that moment.

There, in his arms, my head turns with the realization of one thing and one thing alone: I'm falling in love with Aric. I'm falling for the son of the mer who ruined my life, and there's nothing I can do to stop it.

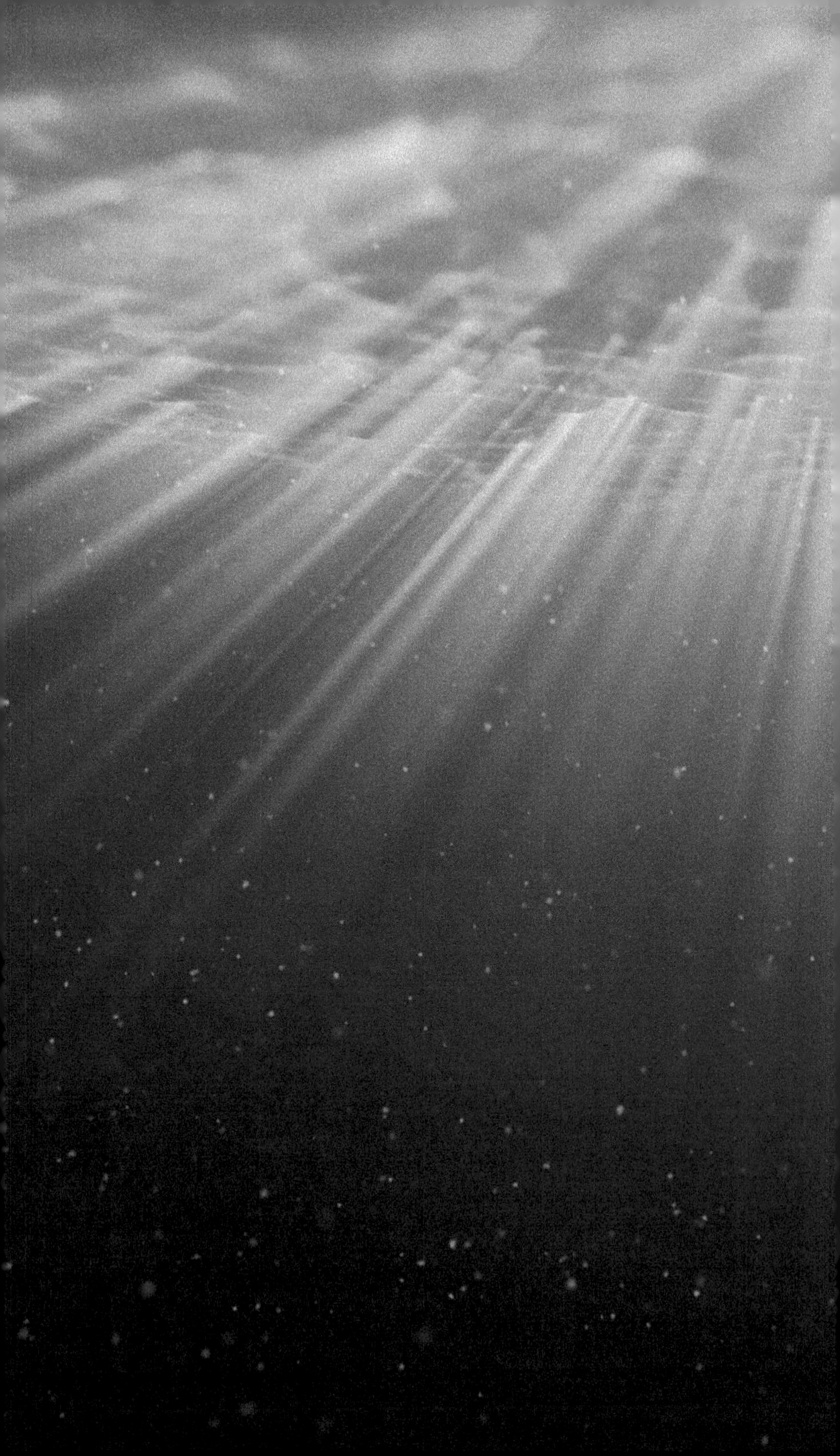

CHAPTER 29
ARIC

The sky opens up. A sudden downpour pummels the street, drenching us and the other couples dancing. Still, the music plays.

Howling erupts from the crowd, echoing off the walls and the colorful pavers under our feet. Everything gets louder. The drums. The stomp and slap of the dance. Viola's laughter.

Every thought that sifts through my mind at this moment is wholly my own. Every urge to hold her closer. Every tenderness that grows for her, like spores multiplying on my heart as they feed on her smile. I want nothing more than to keep her smiling like this forever.

My witch.

The dance sends ripples through the flood coursing over the street. Thunder cracks, and the music is barely audible as the rain falls in heavier sheets. Dancers begin to abandon the rhythm. They run for cover. The musicians seize their instru-

I remain with Viola as she spins out of my arms and turns her face to the sky.

She embraces the rain like an old friend. The cotton dress clings to her every curve. She twirls like she might never stop, like she might die if she does.

I run a hand through my hair, pushing my hair out of the way as I circle her.

We're the last ones left out here. The rain comes down hard enough that I can no longer see the doorways to either side of us, and I'm glad for it. I'm glad to be the only one looking at her. My chest starts burning, deeper than the heartstring, deeper than anything I've ever felt for anyone before.

The Violent Sea hunted me, ruined my life, claimed my soul. I was her prey. Yet here I am, believing with my whole chest that *she* belongs to *me*.

She knows me better than any friend or lover I've ever had, and I'm beginning to understand her just as completely. She isn't what my father says she is. She isn't the monster Fluke and the priest thinks she is. She's something more, something beyond all that.

Just as quickly as it came, the storm recedes. The rain lightens around us to a slow drizzle.

Viola staggers to stop, swaying as she gets her bearings. Her eyes are glazed as they scan the street. When they finally land on me, a smile blooms across her face and I return it without a thought.

She tilts her face back to the sky, squinting as if to search for some miracle beyond the clouds.

"The water's clean," she says. Her head straightens, and she raises her arms in front of her, the limbs trembling. She surveys the rain hitting her skin. Her eyes flick back to mine, fat silvery tears welling in them. "I feel clean."

I don't know nearly as much about her as I should, as much as I want to.

"You're perfect," I whisper.

She takes a step toward me, her body vibrating with intention. But before she can follow through on whatever idea she had, a clanging interrupts us.

Guillermo's mother stands in her house's doorway down the street, clutching a large bell in one hand and a narrow, wooden rod in her other.

A frown tugs at my mouth.

I want to stay here. I want to ask her the questions festering in my gut, the ones I should have asked her a long time ago—but she retreats to the stone building ahead of me. And maybe that's for the best. Nothing good will come from getting between a hungry witch and her next meal.

I follow her into the small home.

Half a dozen tables take up the open space between the kitchen and living room, chairs cluttered all around. Most seats are already occupied. Jussi waits for us just beyond the threshold, and it's impossible to hear what he says to Viola as we enter. But I watch her snarl at him in return, and his body shakes with laughter.

Jussi leads us to the right, to a smaller table settled near the front of the room.

He slides into a seat beside Guillermo. It's comical to see the two of them settle into place at possibly the shortest table in the room. Viola slips into the far seat without issue, the short thing that she is, but I'm quite a bit larger than her.

I hesitate.

Viola is already filling her plate and the one meant for me from the small baskets set in the center of the table. Bread and chicken, and portions of the dishes I tasted earlier while helping the women cook in the house. She glances up when I don't sit down, waving me forward impatiently.

Jussi dips his bread into a bowl of cloudy oil, watching me. Guillermo tries to hide his own curiosity as he digs into his plate, but I can tell that they are both scrutinizing my every move.

They care deeply for Viola, and I think that more than anything else slips past my pride and gets me to sit down in that tiny chair. I settle in, having barely enough room to sit with my feet flat on the ground. My knees are bent to the same level as my navel.

When Viola glances over at me with an encouraging smile, I forget my discomfort.

She places a second slice of bread on my plate, this one soaked in golden oil and bits of white fragrant herb, and nudges my arm with her elbow to tell me to eat.

Who is this woman? This sweet, smiling woman who filled my plate before eating from her own?

My heart blooms with warmth as I lift the bread to my mouth. I don't think I've ever tasted anything so delicious. I only make it halfway through the slice before Jussi brushes crumbs off his fingers, leaning forward in a way that tells me he has something to say to the table.

"So, Aric, when do you leave?"

I struggle to swallow the bread in my mouth, as moist and soft as it is. I glance over at Viola. She strips meat from the bone in her hand, her eyes pointedly averted. "Soon."

"How soon is 'soon'? Days? Weeks? Surely, you have an idea in mind for when you'll trade those legs in for your fins and swim on home."

I didn't expect him to know this much, to know what I am or what Viola was, and I certainly hadn't expected him to say something about it here, in front of all these people.

Apparently, neither did Viola. She leans over her plate, her eyes flicking to the tables beyond ours. "What are you thinking, Jussi?"

He smiles dryly. "It's fine, love. Do you really believe anyone beyond this table can hear me in the state of this room?" He pops another piece of bread into his mouth.

Viola's hands fist in the linen tablecloth. She looks ready to launch herself across the table.

I pry her hand from the linen and place bread between her fingers. Then I guide her wrist up until the food bumps into her mouth. Her fierce glare slashes to me, and I bump her mouth again.

"Eat, witch," I grumble. "You're hungry."

She blinks at me, but then her lips start to curve upwards. She huffs a laugh as she takes the bite.

I let go of her wrist and return to my own plate.

Glancing up at the table, I see Jussi and Guillermo wearing near-identical expressions of surprise. I clear my throat and say, "Look, I don't know what you two know about me, but if my staying in your home causes an issue, I can find somewhere else to go."

Guillermo sets down his fork and throws an arm over the back of his partner's chair. "We don't want you to find anyplace else—that's not what we're saying at all, is it, Jussi?" He squeezes Jussi's shoulder.

Jussi's brow furrows, but he doesn't say anything in opposition.

I glance at Viola. She's avoiding my gaze again. "How do you three know each other so well?"

"You mean, how do we know about Viola and all her tricks?" Jussi smirks. "Really, Prince, I'm surprised you don't recognize me."

I look at him a little closer. And after a minute, I see it—if his hair were shorter, and if silver gossamer fins framed his face. "You're one of my father's advisors."

"I was," he amends, nodding. "I advised your grandfather and shifted loyalties when I found out about your father's plan to wipe out the established court. I was one of the few he let live through the massacre, because I made myself invaluable to him."

"But then—how?" My gaze flicks to Viola, who finally lifts her face to stare at Jussi, her jaw clenching with the tension of a hundred silent pleas.

Jussi smiles at her and shrugs. "How does anyone find themselves at the mercy of our girl? She thought I was an easy target, a willing disciple of Triton's cruelty—and she was partially right. But I wasn't what she assumed. When she found that out, she let me go."

If it wasn't for the storm last night, I would have let you go.

She was telling me the truth.

Guillermo reaches across the table and grasps the sea witch's hand. "Viola gave my Jussi a new life. Without her, we never would have met, and I never would have fallen in love. We owe her everything."

"Hush," she mutters, her cheeks coloring with a faint purple blush. "You don't owe me anything."

"You're too modest, love. That's your biggest problem." Jussi glances at me, anger flashing in his eyes so briefly that I almost miss it. "You let the entire population of Atlantis misunderstand you. You let them trample you at every opportunity."

She shrugs.

"Don't you care?" I turn to Viola.

I know it's entirely my own fault for believing the lies, but I'm upset they existed without any opposition. That she never objected to them. That she never fought for herself.

"Why would you want Atlantis to believe those lies about you?"

"It's not my responsibility to make anyone understand me. That's not a war I would win. It's not a battle I want to waste my time fighting."

"You will win," I argue. "I'll see to it."

Guillermo chuckles, the entire table shaking as he slams a hand down next to his plate.

"Well," Jussi raises a brow in Viola's direction. "Would you look at that, Viola? Maybe you should have stolen the crown prince from Atlantis years ago."

Viola peers at me from the corner of her eye, her fingers twisting in the material of her skirt. There's a smile dancing beneath the surface. She's not letting me see it, but she's thinking the same thing I am: that she wishes we'd met years ago.

All this time I spent on my own, biding my time, occupying my mind with meaningless novelties and females.

Waiting for her.

"If only I had been so clever and brave," she murmurs, more to herself than the table.

But I heard her. I heard everything in those words.

"You are," I reply quietly.

She looks up at me then, her eyes searing into mine with a tenderness I never imagined her capable of before today.

Jussi and Guillermo turn their attentions to their meal, leaving us to this moment. All the things I want to say, that I need to say, rise up. I know it's not the place or the time, but I hope she can see the truth in my eyes. *I see you. I understand now. I'm sorry that I believed the worst, I was wrong.*

Her smile is the fading sunlight, touching me with color and warmth and the deepest sense of dread for the darkness coming once it's gone.

She turns to her plate and picks up a utensil.

I try to return to my own food, to assuage the incompleteness ravaging my body. But then her hand finds my leg under the table. She tugs on the heartstring, sending my mind spiraling and making my cock throb.

Every inch of my leg tingles as her fingertips graze higher.

I wish I could lose myself in the affection, but I still have the pendant with me. I couldn't leave it back at Jussi and Guillermo's house like I had my shark tooth, thanks to the magic gripping me. It's in my pocket.

The same pocket Viola's hand is slowly drifting towards.

Dread seizes my gut, and before I can think of a better way to distract her, I shove her hand off my thigh. Viola winces. The heartstring vibrates.

She stares down at her plate of untouched food for a long moment before pushing her seat back from the table.

"Excuse me," she mutters. "I need some air."

I catch her wrist.

She's leaving because of me, because I can never get my head on straight when it matters. I should have taken her hand and held it instead of pushing her away, done something to show her I want her. I need to say something to make it better, to get her to stay.

All my stupid mouth manages to blurt out is, "The door is already open, how much more air could you need?"

She glares at me and rips her wrist away. "I'm going for a walk."

"What?" I call after her as she stalks to the door. "It's pouring out there." Another brilliant statement, really.

She ignores me and disappears into the fresh downpour. My chest heaves as I stare after her. She didn't even get a chance to eat before I pissed her off, and I hadn't meant to do that. I *want* her to touch me, and to touch her in return, to be so close to her that nothing will get between us again, especially my own foolishness.

There's too much that I need to know.

It didn't seem like she wanted me to follow—in fact, I'm pretty damn sure that exit made it clear I'm the last thing she wants to look at right now. I wish I knew the right way to deal with her, to deal with my own shortcomings. I wish I knew what it meant to be good and do good. Just this once.

"Well?" Jussi leans back in his chair, folding his arms. He lifts an eyebrow at me and nods at the open door. "Are you just going to sit there and let her walk away?"

Guillermo tears a piece of meat off his fork without averting his eyes from me. "What a shame that would be," he says through gnashing teeth.

These men are fucking terrifying. I like them a lot.

I shoot out of my chair and head into the rainy street. When I catch a glimpse of her turning a corner, I follow her to the beach and the docking bay. I follow her, not attempting to catch up just yet—letting my head clear and prepare the words I'll need when she finally stops running.

As she starts descending the long stone staircase to the beach, the voices wake to either side of my head.

My earlobes itch from how loudly they rumble. The darkness brings attention to the pendant in my pocket, its words twining around the presence like fingers, clutching tightly to my last opportunity to get rid of Viola and protect myself. The other voice urges me to find a way to abandon it now on the rainy beach, even if it rips my soul to shreds in the process. I ignore them both, letting their opposing screams become as meaningless as the constant crash of waves out at sea.

There's a right way to do this.

She doesn't stand up for herself. She never has, and that means she has a story she's never told. I'm going to listen to it, if she'll let me. I'll find out the truth about what happened between her and my father, and then I'll show her the pendant Fluke gave me.

I'll tell her everything.

And if she decides to swallow me whole afterward, at least I'll know for certain that I deserve it.

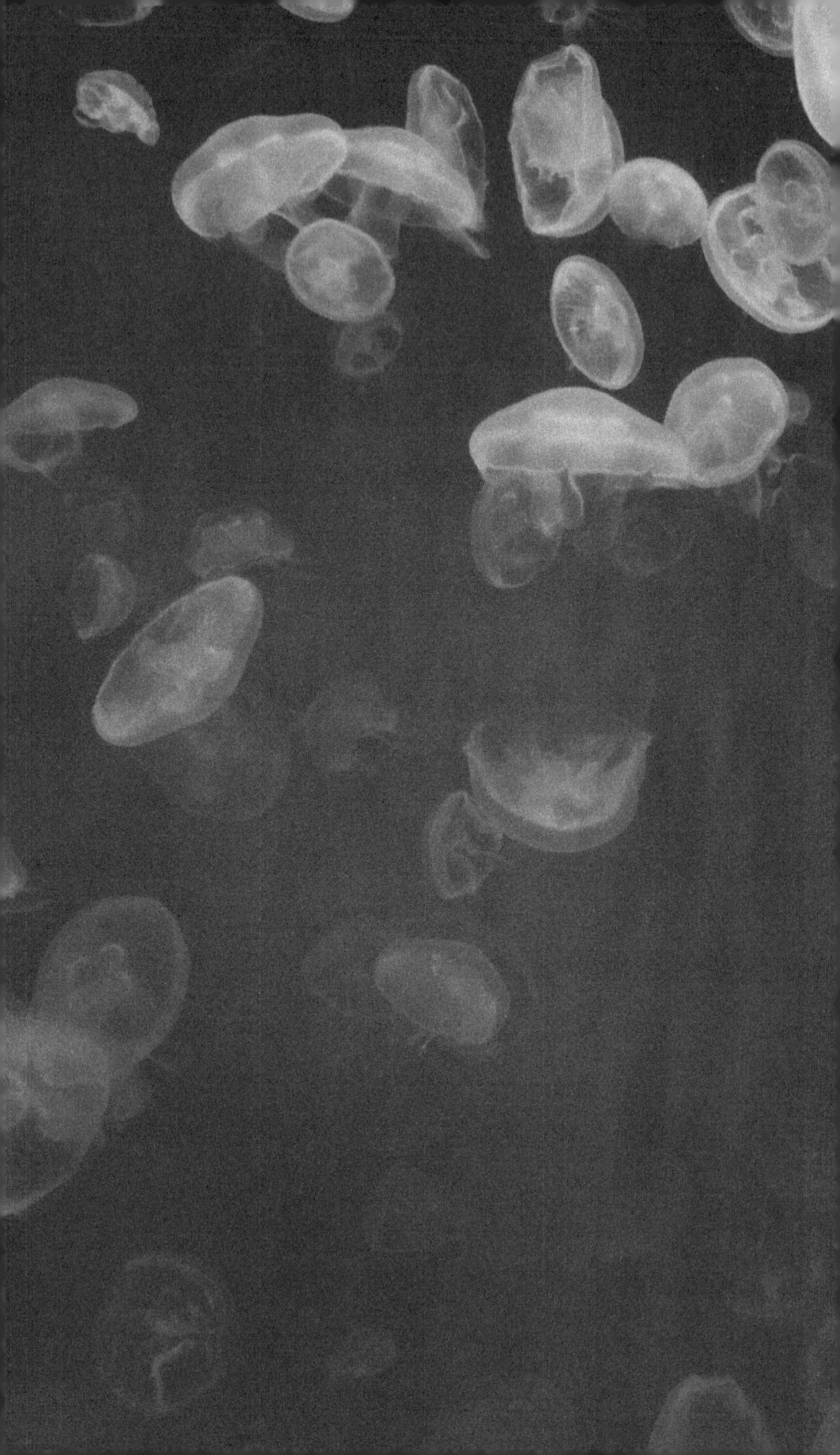

CHAPTER 30
VIOLA

*chapter content warning: there is (non-graphic) reference to childhood sexual abuse in this chapter (page 335 & 336)

There's a special place for sea witches.

A sacred place.

It holds the power to connect the physical realm with the spiritual, and it served my old coven as the place where we initiated witchlings.

We called them the Waken Whirlpools.

They're set apart from the ocean, and our kind always had to shift in order to gather there, as it requires walking and climbing to reach it. The coast beneath the city curves and winds, battling with the tide, sometimes dangerously, but if one were to walk long enough, they would eventually stumble upon a multi-arched opening that leads into that place of magic and tranquility.

The rain has stopped falling by the time I enter the cave.

I walk in along the outer edge of the room, avoiding the center where tides crash in and eddy with the ocean's rhythm. The sun seeps away, disappearing beyond the horizon and I glance up at the ceiling of the cave, which gapes in circular sections to a blanket of stars.

Moonlight spills in over the stone, illuminating my path.

The shifting tidepools touch a deeper and wider reserve of water, fed into this place by a trickling water wall on the far end of the cave. Run off from disrupted and barged rivers, presumably. A dark pool spreads through the belly of the cave. There's no explanation for how the water swirls with hundreds of cyclones and the jagged walls burst with flowers that usually only exist on the ocean floor.

My fingers affectionately graze the blue and orange tendrils as I pass them.

I've always thought it was the spirits' doing, that they sprout and thrive here, reaching out from the ocean, desperate for any semblance of existence beyond the unseen.

I pause on the stone ledge, looking out at the pool and the island of stone sitting in the center of its surging waters. Then I hold my breath and step off.

As I'm swallowed by the nearest whirlpool, the current tugs on my dress and hair until my feet catch on the bottom. I straighten my legs and resurface instantly. It looks more terrifying than it is. The currents are strong enough to drag me under if I submit to them, but they aren't harsh enough to drown in. When I stand up, the water barely reaches my breasts.

I wade between the swirling pools toward the island.

As I swipe excess water from my eyes, I hear a scuffle behind me. Aric walks along the ledge I just jumped from. He followed me for miles to this place without bothering to make me aware of his presence. It would have impressed me if I wasn't so concerned as to *why*. He made it clear earlier that he feels the same way he always has—repulsed by me.

Searching his face, I can't find a trace of malicious intent, but of course, that doesn't mean it's not there.

He smiles shyly, starting to unbutton his damp shirt. "How's the water? Warm?"

"Why did you follow me?"

Aric shrugs his shirt off. "Why did you run?"

I don't respond to that. I only watch as he paces the ledge, his head tilting one way and then the other, considering the distance between us.

Aric takes a small step back, raises his arms, and dives at a shallow angle into the water. I take a few slow steps back. Waiting.

He doesn't resurface right away, and the water froths too heavily to see him beneath until he's right on top of me. His hand wraps around my ankle and with one harsh tug, he sweeps me under the water.

I manage to suck in a breath before I'm totally submerged.

The whirlpools batter my body, dragging me into a nearby current and directly into Aric's chest. His arms wrap around my waist, pressing me against him. His fingers caress my back as he drags me upright and we break the surface.

He laughs as I sputter, his chest vibrating against mine as I push my hair out of my face. And then I'm fighting back.

My claws rake over his chest, and a struggle erupts between us as I swear at him and he scrambles to pin my arms beneath his. I do my best, but I'm battling a smile too. My hearts want to return all his enjoyment back to him. I want to forgive him without waiting for an apology. Not that he has anything to apologize for, really.

Eventually, he succeeds in overpowering me and tucks my arms tightly around his chest.

We float in the whirlpool, around and around. He gives me an easy smile, piercing through the glare I front, peeling away my hardness layer by layer. I unravel in his arms and allow him to just hold me. I could shift, could tear and rip at him in a thousand other forms to get out of this embrace, but I don't. That's not to say I trust him, or trust this. But his arms are a welcome reprieve from the tumultuous emotions I experienced on the walk here.

I've been drowning, and this moment is air.

Fully aware that this could be another attempt to humiliate me, to reel me in only to cruelly cast me away, I repeat in a whisper, "Why did you follow me? This place isn't meant for you."

He glances at our surroundings, his expression thoughtful and a touch awed.

"No, it isn't. I can feel the magic. It's warm and safe. It feels like you. I understand why you must feel protective of it." His eyes meet mine, wide and honest. "But I swear to you, I'm not here to do anything but talk."

My traitorous body melts further.

"Talk about what?"

My voice is barely audible over the trickling down the wall and the frothing pools around us, but he hears it. Because he's listening. Aric's entire focus is centered on me, those brown eyes darkened by the night unfurling above us, so dark I can no longer see those slivers of blue. He's damn beautiful.

His grimace is answer enough.

I disentangle from him, frowning. All that precious ease he gave me slowly slipping away between my fingers. "You know most of it already."

I dip beneath the surface and swim to the stone island.

When I surface and drag myself out of the water, I find Aric right behind me. The moss is soft and thick under my fingers. He pulls himself onto the island as I get to my feet, as I pace to the other side, attempting to get as much distance between us as possible.

Aric shakes his head, water slicking from his auburn hair and flying out in every direction. "I don't. All I have are lies that my heart now refuses to believe."

My hearts stutter at that confession.

"Please," he pleads. "I need the truth."

I train my eyes on the water trickling into the cave, and sit on the edge of the island. He quietly sits beside me. "What do you want to know?" My voice is quiet, guarded.

He inches closer to me, mirroring my posture: legs bent, arms wrapped around his shins.

"What really happened to you back in Atlantis?"

I smile bitterly. "A lot of things happened to me, Aric."

He doesn't say anything in response to that.

I swallow the sour taste in my mouth, the tang of blood as I chew on my inner lip. "I was tossed to the underdwellings with a father who couldn't take care of me, and I wasn't old enough to understand that not every mer is worthy of childlike trust. When my coven mother found me, I was still that child."

I glance over at him and shrug. "And when Triton met me, he took advantage of my innocence."

Aric pales. "When you were—"

"It happens more often than you think," I say quickly, matter-of-factly. It's easier to explain if I pretend we're not talking about me, if I consider the horrors others went through. So many dealt with worse than I did. "I ran into others who experienced the same at the palace, as I grew older and tended to the city with my coven. I was far from the first, and I'm sure there were others after me, too."

Aric looks disgusted, horrified.

I return my gaze back to the falling water, trying to push away the spikes of embarrassment and anger that ravage my gut. Already, he's looking at me differently. Thinking less of me. I'm not less.

Aric's legs straighten in front of him, dropping them down into the water. I watch from the corner of my eye as he rakes a hand through his hair, tugs on it. "Viola—Great Oblivion, the things I said to you, the things I *did* to you—"

He's *pitying* me, regretting the things we've done together. As if I hadn't been a completely willing partner.

I raise a hand to halt his concern. "*Stop*."

He clamps his mouth shut.

"I let you do those things to me," I say firmly. "We both know I could have stopped you at any point if that's what I wanted. I'm not a defenseless little maiden anymore. I've never felt that way with you."

He blinks once, twice.

Then his hand reaches across the space between us and wraps around mine. "Okay. Tell me the rest of it."

I stare at our clasped hands, letting the sight of it anchor me. "I didn't return to the palace for several years. Our coven mother forbade it when she found out what happened to me. But then she died and passed her inheritance on to me, and I was the only one Triton wanted to attend his palace. I was forced to return. It was the longest hours of my life, being in the same room as him, having to look into his eyes as he smiled at me.

"Triton wanted me even more after being kept from me for so long. He decided to claim me. He demanded my presence at the palace beyond my weekly visits, assigned me a seat at his parties so that he could publicly stake his claim on me as his new mistress. Even though I constantly refused him, he forced me to sit beside him, night after night after night. And then it didn't matter if I was truly his or not. No one would touch me. No one would look at me, knowing that he wanted me for himself. I knew then that I would never have a regular life, or a mate.

"My coven did what they could to comfort me. But we were all frightened of him, and of what he might do should we attempt to extract our coven from Atlantis and run. We feared things he eventually proved himself willing and capable of. So, instead, my coven gifted me with an eel companion, to comfort me on my visits to the palace and offer me a fraction of protection from his powers should he decide to hurt me. The eel was resistant to Triton's magic, and I had bound myself to it with all three of my hearts. I could siphon its abilities if I needed to.

"But then Triton got worse. He tried to bribe me by promising to share his throne, thinking that would sway me. Your mother was queen then, and I knew what that meant. That he would kill her. He swore that he would have me though, and I *know* I wouldn't have survived it if he did."

My throat swells, and I have to pause a moment to let the tightness pass. "Maybe it would have been over quickly if I'd submitted to him. One night, and then he would have forgotten about me like he did the rest. But I couldn't let him.

"I decided to do something I thought would make it all stop." I swallow again, hard. "I turned the eel I was bound to into a merman, and I allowed myself to love him, even if it wasn't entirely real. Even though I knew I wasn't in the place to truly love anyone beyond friendship. But I needed a way out. I needed a partner that would finally claim me and make me theirs, and, well, Francis was..."

I trail off, and the silence carries for a moment.

Aric clears his throat and mutters, "He was safe."

"He was safe," I echo, nodding. "I thought if Triton saw I'd moved on, he would let his obsession go, but I was wrong.

"He felt I had betrayed him, and that I needed to be punished for it. He gathered my coven, trapped me in a cage of lightning, and slaughtered them right in front of me. He used their blood to curse me. He ripped Francis apart with his bare hands because he couldn't do it with his magic, and then he bound me to him and to the ocean, and I feel him calling for me all the time. I can't be Above for more than a few minutes without feeling as though I'm crawling out of my skin to return."

The world feels so incredibly quiet to me then, so cold. "I'm terrified that someday, he's going to win. I'm going to grow so tired that I can't fight him anymore, and he'll take me at last."

Aric's hand squeezes mine.

"He will never have you," he says fiercely. He lifts my hand and kisses my palm. "I wish I could have protected you back then. I wish I could have kept you safe."

I smile, my lips trembling. Aric means it. He means it for me, and he would mean it for any innocent hurt by his father in Atlantis. He would protect all of them, if he could.

Because he is so *good*.

"Safe was what I thought I needed for the longest time, but when I met you, Aric, I... I just *needed*." I hesitate, my lungs burning. "You were vicious and rough, and as angry as I was. For the first time in my life, I knew what I wanted. I wanted *you*."

There's no fear in his eyes as he looks at me, no pity or judgment. "I understand."

"And you need to know that I only interfered with you and the princess because I had a suspicion your soul would free me from my curse. I think you might carry enough of Triton's blood to fool the magic into releasing me. But that's not what I want anymore. After we take care of Triton, I promise I'll do everything in my power to help you get the princess back, if you would rather stay here than return to Atlantis. We can make you look like a prince worthy of her hand. You can be with her."

His eyes widen.

I inhale shakily. "I let my hurt bleed on you when you were as innocent in what happened as I was." I flip my hand over and thread my fingers between his. "I'm sorry."

"I don't want Hazel," he whispers.

It suddenly feels like my entire chest could burst open. That connection between us tightens, and I'm not the one tugging on it this time.

It's him.

"And I don't accept your apology because you don't have *anything* to apologize for." Anger—that's anger in his voice. "*I'm* the one that should be sorry."

He moves then, kneeling in the sand in front of me.

"Take whatever you need from me, Viola." His hand pins mine to his chest, and I know what he's offering. "Take everything. I'm yours."

Aric bows, pressing a kiss to one of the knees I have bent between us. My ribs clench as he proceeds to rest his forehead there, his body trembling and surrendered. And I can't think of the words for what I feel for him then. For this siren who is willing to give himself up for me, willing to pay the debts of another, willing to right unspeakable wrongs at much too high a cost.

My song, my air.

I move, lifting his chin as I kneel along with him. "I'm not taking your life. Not for anything."

"I wish I had known I was your villain." His voice is a rumble, radiating into my bones and circling in my gut.

He studies my face, as if searching for regret.

I smile, knowing he won't find any.

"You weren't." Not even close. I lean up without hesitation, without a thought in my head, and press a kiss to the corner of his mouth. He stops breathing, and so do I.

I linger there, barely breathing, wanting to swallow this moment so I might keep it forever.

Reluctantly, I begin to pull away.

Before I can retreat more than a few inches, his hand flies up and cups the back of my neck. Our gazes latch. Lust drugs his pupils and darkens his features.

"Kiss me again," he whispers.

My lower abdomen tightens. Desire, hot and furious, skitters across my bones, and every inch of my skin begins tingling. I can't feel anything but my want for him; even my power lust fades in the face of such viscous need.

"Is this real?" I murmur, drifting closer.

The heartstring pulls taut enough that I'm sure it's capable of rending straight through my chest.

When he replies, his lips brush against mine—so achingly close to a kiss that I whimper. "As real as you wish for it to be." And maybe it's a mistake to fall for his tender words, to put myself wholly in his hands while knowing how easily he could shatter me, to believe that he has forgiven all that I've done to him.

Perhaps it is a mistake to think he might learn to love.

But I don't care as I wrap my arms around his shoulders and crush my lips to his.

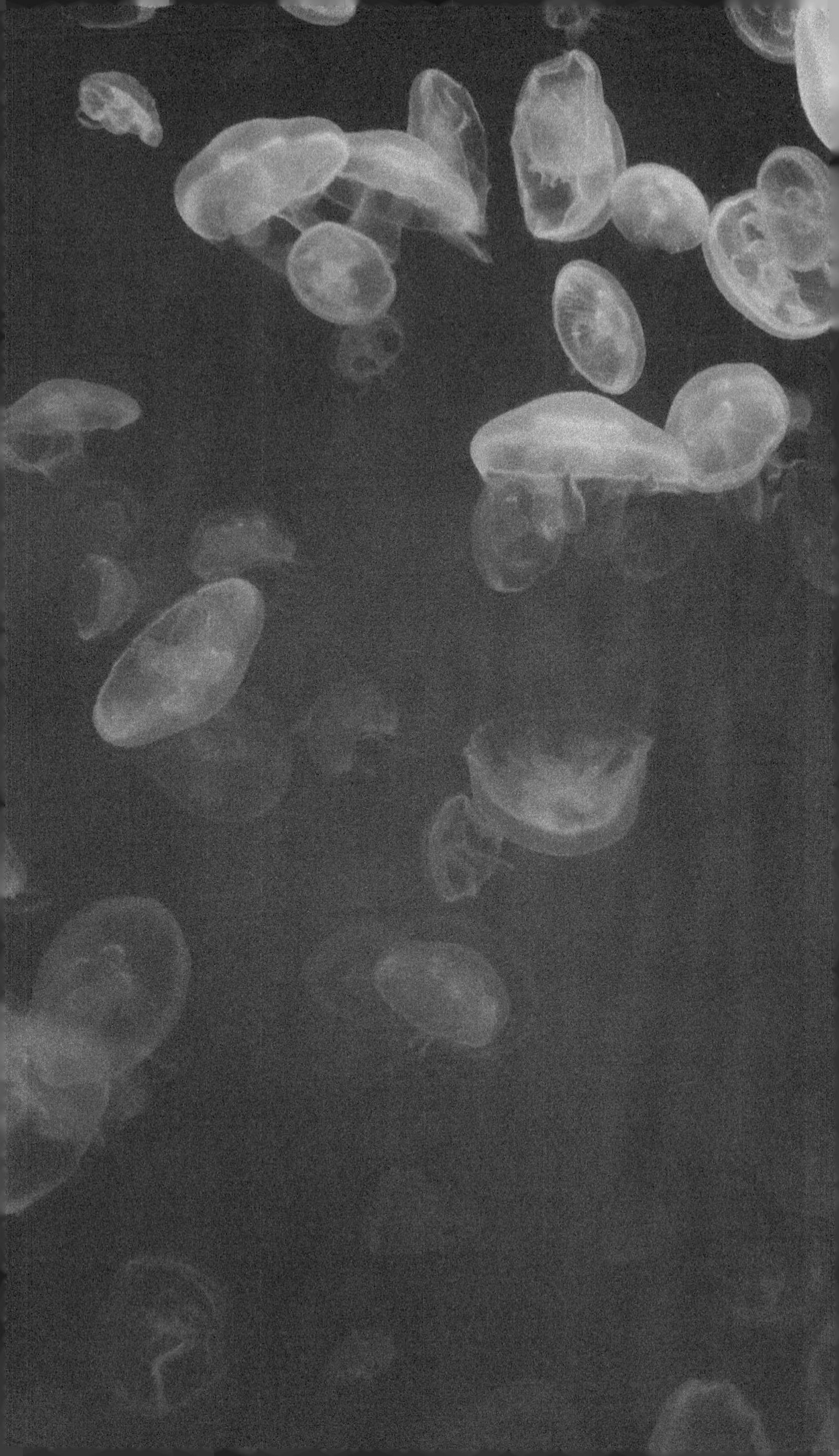

CHAPTER 31
VIOLA

Aric's throat makes a low rumbling sound as our lips marry. The scruff of his jaw scratches my cheeks, and it's all I can do not to gasp at the brutal sensation.

I love that about him—the hollow brutality. Because there's so much tenderness hidden beneath it. He's being so gentle right now, hesitant. I tug his lower lip between my teeth, urging him to take control.

His face angles above mine as the rumble in his throat turns into a groan.

Aric deepens the kiss, his hand fisting the damp hair at the nape of my neck. I part my lips and his tongue slips in, flicking the roof of my mouth. I press closer, adhering myself to his body. My fingers skim across his collar and up his neck. But then he pulls back.

His hands squeeze my thighs, fisting in the wet material of my dress. "Can I?"

"Please," I breathe, running my fingers through his auburn hair as his hands tug my dress up.

"Fuck, don't you dare beg for anything right now." Aric groans onto my neck.

He peels my dress over my head and tosses it aside, and I lie back on the stone, letting my legs fall open. Aric's chest expands with a great inhale. He exhales slowly as his gaze consumes every inch I laid bare to him.

"How do you want me?" I smile, my body shifting from one form to the next, legs to tentacles and back again.

My body vibrates in my human form as I tilt my head, waiting for his answer.

His eyes feast on me as he prowls over top of me, his gaze fixing on my mouth. "I just want you, it doesn't matter which form."

My choice. Always my choice.

Aric's lips crash into mine, and my spine arcs off the ground to feel more of him. His hand slides under my back, trailing down my spine, gliding down over my hip as he lowers himself on top of me.

I moan at the glorious weight of him.

His lips break from mine, and he starts kissing a line across my jaw, down my neck. He nips at the tender skin between my neck and shoulder, and I whimper again. I'm helpless. I'm lost. When he reaches my breasts, he nuzzles my nipple until it hardens. His tongue works in slow circles, drawing closer and closer to the peak until he finally sucks my nipple into his mouth.

Another groan erupts from him, vibrating my breast. "So fucking delicious," he says around my flesh.

My body undulates, desperate.

Aric doesn't indulge my silent plea. He repeats the unhurried exploration with my other breast, his kisses reverential.

My mind is already in fragments, but it shatters as he finally moves lower, kissing my belly.

"Oblivion..." he growls. "*The scent of you.*"

When he looks up at me across the length of my body, he hooks a leg over his shoulder and his lips quirk in a lopsided grin. One of his broad hands drags down the center of my torso, his nails scratching slightly.

I squirm.

"I know I said I didn't have a preference," he murmurs, his eyes sweeping down to admire the glistening core of me. "But I like your human body."

With precise movements, his hand slides between my legs and spreads me. He leans in, his breath caressing.

"Aric—" I rasp.

"This sweet little slit." Aric drags his tongue up my center, and a strangled moan rips out of my throat. "How soft the inside of these legs are." His teeth suddenly graze my inner thigh, and my hips twitch. "The way you drip for me."

His mouth returns to my center. His tongue twirls and flicks. He explores my entrance, circling and driving into it until I'm shaking from the clench of my muscles around sour emptiness.

I moan again, but the words are incoherent.

All I can think of is the broad flatness of his tongue as it travels upward, then of my desperation as he pulls back again, humming thoughtfully. "You know what, I lied to you. I don't just like it. I *love* it."

I writhe, my stomach tightening as he finds the apex of my pleasure.

When my hips jerk, he huffs a laugh. "Who knew a tiny bud like this could elicit such a spectacular reaction. I think I love this part of your human body best of all."

The throbbing in my center is too powerful, too overwhelming. I can't endure it. I reach down and thread my fingers into his hair, tugging, silently begging him.

My breath catches as he unsheathes his teeth and bites down on my swollen clitoris.

I loosen my grip on his hair.

"Patience," he growls, "or I'll give you a reason to cry."

Before the threat can sink in completely, his tongue lashes my flesh, hitting that electric spot just perfectly. Again and again. Faster and faster. He groans as though he's never tasted anything quite as sweet and the sound of his ministrations drift through my subconscious as I thrash, my arousal loud and wet against his tongue.

My nails scrape over the stone island beneath us, ripping through the crawling moss.

I cry out as release spears into me, and I feel it all the way down in my toes. It thunders through my chest and up into my head. I can't move. I can't think.

Aric leans up, grabs me around the waist, and hauls me up against him. He lifts me into his arms and drags me into the whirlpools, and I loop my arms around his neck, embracing him tightly as my trembling legs settle over his hips. He slides his hands under my thighs to support me, and then he turns his face into my hair, inhaling deeply as the water laps at our waists.

I'm already coming back to myself. I'm already starving for more.

I drag myself higher on his chest and kiss him deeply, but Aric doesn't make a move to impale me, even as his hardness twitches beneath me. I wiggle my way back down until his cock nudges my entrance. I bite his lip again, communicating my urgency. He groans softly, but still, he hesitates.

And I know why.

I rip away to glare at him, my nails digging into his

shoulders. "Stop treating me like I'm going to break," I snarl. "Fuck me like you mean it, like you did before."

Before he *knew*.

I'm not less.

He blinks rapidly, studying me. Then his hands tighten on my thighs. Intoxicating lust curls through his brown eyes and forms a smirk on his lips. He leans forward, possessing my mouth with his teeth and tongue as he begins walking.

Every step has us rising higher, subjecting my naked body to the cool night air, and I shiver.

Aric chuckles into my mouth.

My skin erupts in gooseflesh as we leave the whirlpools behind entirely, and I barely have time to register the sound of trickling water before my back collides with hard rock.

Hot water glides over my shoulders and down my chest, combating my chilled skin and drawing my focus back to the warmth gathered low in my belly. The wall is relatively flat and slick—which is good because Aric isn't gentle as he hoists me higher, pins my legs open, and notches himself at my entrance. Then he enters me with a sharp thrust.

All the air evaporates from my lungs.

Aric echoes my gasp, burying his face in my neck as he revels in the moment, in this connection. The heartstring vibrates, wrenching on us both.

Closer.

I'm too impatient, too eager to chase away the confessions of earlier with more of *us*. I grind down on him, uncaring of the sharp edges digging into my back as he starts moving with me. Rivulets of water stream between us, exacerbating each slap of his wet skin on mine. He peels back and looks down to watch. His eyes lock on my sex, bared. He watches his cock, glistening with my arousal as it withdraws and slams into me up to the hilt.

I lean forward to try and pull him back to me, but his hand finds my throat and pins me to the wall.

Water seeps across my scalp, trickling into my eyes.

Aric smiles, his gaze taking on a sinister gleam as he fucks me harder. My cunt convulses, trying helplessly to hold on to him as he hits that delicious spot deep inside me. His hands are gentle as they hold me in place, even as his fingers tighten enough to send my focus scattering into Oblivion. There's only him. His body. His smile. His voice.

"Are you still starving, my pretty witch?" he purrs in my ear. "If you won't take my life, shall I fill your sweet cunt with my cum instead—will that ease your hunger?"

"*Please.*" My plea comes out in the form of a trill.

That pushes Aric over the edge. His hands seize my hips as he rams into me, his chest rumbling, his grip on me turning painful as he tumbles into his release. He swells almost imperceptibly as he erupts, gushing forcibly inside of me, filling me to near bursting.

And it indeed feels as though I'm whole, for just that fraction of a second.

As I tumble after him into warm, twining ecstasy.

We slide to the ground together, his arms wrapped tightly around me. The water falling down the wall splits around us, coursing around our legs and down the slope into the whirlpools.

Aric tucks me even closer as he nuzzles my ear.

"You're so fucking perfect," he murmurs.

He presses a kiss to my neck, and I feel *cherished*. No one has ever made me feel this way. Like his soul is a match to mine. The edges sharp and the defenses hardened by years of hurting in total and complete silence. And yet, he nurtured this tenderness inside him.

He kept the goodness that all too often flees the ocean's great deep.

I realize in that moment that I *do* trust him, and I don't know if I've ever truly trusted anyone before. The words rise to the tip of my tongue, burning like stars in the darkness between us.

I love you.

Like a coward, I refuse to say them.

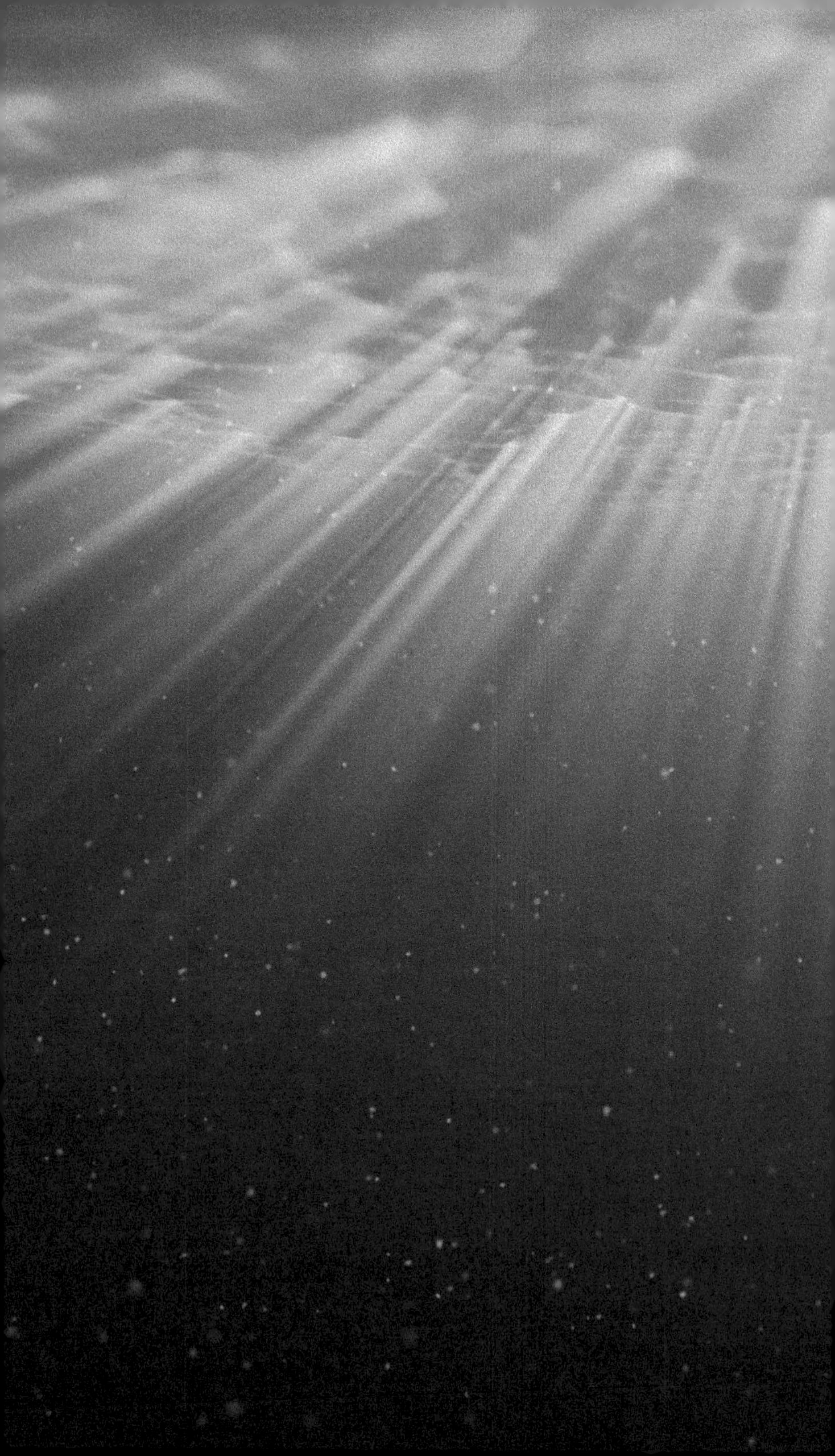

CHAPTER 32

ARIC

I wake to the sun peering through the cave's ceiling and a sea witch sleeping peacefully in my arms. I admire her slumbering form, sorting through the emotions I've experienced over the last day and a half. They crash into me again—gnawing worry and blooming warmth, the urge to hold her close enough that there's not one inch of her body that isn't touched by some piece of me.

All the horrific lies I have believed, all the horrible things I have done to this female, is a testament to how dangerous Atlantis has become. How broken.

In another life, I might have asked Viola to make these human legs permanent. I might have asked her to join me.

How could I do that, when my father is free to terrorize Atlantis and steal the innocence of those that cannot defend themselves, when she is bound to the ocean as permanently as my heart is bound to her? I need to keep him from hurting anyone else. I want to kill him.

There's no hesitation in my heart now. I want to rip him apart like sea nettle for what he did to Viola, and for what he's been doing to the whole city, but *especially* to her. If I do not rise to the throne afterward, who will? Simon? The mer who's been instructing a child to torture peers for fun? No, I can't allow that.

Viola wiggles in my arms, a sleepy trill emanating from the back of her throat.

My cock throbs against her backside. Our legs are tangled together, and I can almost pretend this morning is the first of thousands more just like it. My wildest fantasy.

A human life, with a human wife.

I press kisses to Viola's hair as I reach down and hook a hand under her knee. Gently, I spread her legs, slipping a thigh between hers to hold her open. She smells like me. I bet if I touched her now, she'd still be slick with our combined arousal. I bring my fingers to my mouth and spit on them anyway before I skim them across her breasts.

Her back arches as I near the purple thatch of curls between her thighs.

"Good morning, sweet witch of mine," I whisper.

She moans softly, and it's almost a word. A response. I think she's finally waking. So I kiss her hair again, and gently slide a finger through her slit.

Her chest starts rattling like a thunder storm.

Then Viola rips my wrist away from her, whipping around to straddle me before I can even blink fully. Her eyes are as fierce as I've ever seen them, a purple so light, they could almost be blue. She snarls with her entire body, her tentacles bursting from her hips and promptly shriveling, here and gone so quickly, it's as if she isn't awake enough to control the shift. Her claws sharpen into teeth-like points, drawing blood on my wrist and chest.

I still beneath her.

I know better than to make sudden movements in the presence of a predator in need of a meal.

As her gaze focuses more, her pupils dilate. Her claws retract. As she finally shakes off the haze of sleep, her features soften.

A couple of the tentacles she summoned in sleep endure, writhing between us, sliding across the planes of my stomach in comforting caresses. Eventually, they retract too.

"I'm sorry," I whisper. "I thought you knew it was me."

Her voice crackles as she says, "It's okay."

"You're starving."

She nods. "I've been away from the ocean for too long as well. It's affecting me. I should go home and feed." Feed... on her soul-bound.

We never got around to discussing them last night, why she'd targeted them or what Fluke has been doing behind her back. We were too busy *kissing*.

Her fucking kisses—they're earth-shattering. Her lips are weapons I want to bleed on again and again.

The imagery flashes unbidden in my mind: her claws touching someone else, her fingers raking through their hair as she angles her mouth over theirs, her tentacles clinging to their scales...

"Not a chance," I growl, my eyes narrowing.

Viola frowns. "I don't have a choice, Aric, and neither do you. There's no telling what trouble those mer have gotten into without me around to monitor them. I have to go."

I grimace, glancing at my clothes and her dress piled up on the other side of the island. I should tell her about the pendant *now*. It's past due time, and the longer I wait, the more it will seem like I'm trying to hide it from her.

I'm terrified. Not of what she might do, but of what she might think of me.

She scoots back as if to stand up, but I catch her again.

My lips part to confess everything. But then she smiles. She's so lovely, the words catch in my throat.

"Prince Aric," she purrs, running her hands up my chest and over my shoulders, "are you *jealous*?"

I squeeze her hips, my heart pounding. "I am."

Viola kisses the corner of my mouth the way she did last night. Soft and sweet.

My resolve crumbles now as it had then, and I lean up, nuzzling her nose, returning the almost-kiss. Maybe my worries could wait just a little while longer. Maybe we could have this one day, before I ruin it all.

One day to fill my soul with her kisses.

As she pulls back, her smile falters. "Well, I don't know what you expect from me. I certainly can't feed on *you*."

"Why the fuck not?" I demand.

She glares at me. "Because I'm not going to suck life from you like some leech."

"Don't view it that way."

"What other way *is* there?"

Wrapping my arms around her waist, I say, "I want to be your only source. I want to be the one you run to when you need something, and the one you walk to when you simply *want* something. It just so happens that what you need right now is a little bit of life, and I can spare it."

She chews on her lip. "This isn't a good idea."

"No, it's an *excellent* one. Look at you, you're practically salivating at the thought."

Her eyes flash, her claws raking gently over my chest. "Hush," she snaps, but her eyes are sparkling. "You're a great pain to me sometimes, you know that?"

"Oh? Last night made me think I was a pleasure."

"Pain can be pleasurable, as our time together has generously proven." She hesitates before slowly settling her body over mine, chest to chest. "Alright, I'll feed from you, just... just hold me while I do it."

The worry is clear in her eyes. She doesn't want to feel like she's taking anything from me. She needs my touch to remind her of what we are, and what we're not.

She wants me to hold her tighter, to hold her in my heart.

I reply in the thinnest whisper, "I'll hold you forever if you wish it."

Viola reaches up to frame my face between her hands. She studies me, considering what may lay hidden in my eyes, and then she leans in, pausing just before our lips touch.

The heartstring pulls taut, and I gasp.

The moment my lips part, she starts pulling, reaching into me with invisible claws to grasp a piece of me buried inside. She pulls my life force to the surface.

It doesn't hurt like I expected—and maybe that's because she has no desire to hurt me. I feel the drain on my power. A tightening, twisting, squeezing. My head spins, my vision wavering. It's all I can do to stay awake, to keep falling into her eyes as she feeds on me.

Falling into sunset skies.

Her fingers dig into my chest again, her eyes shutting as she finally lets go of my inner life force and peels back.

Exhaling sharply, she sits up, shaking her head. I can't move yet, but my spotty vision catches on the spiraling wound on her chest.

The wound that's *closing*.

"Viola," I gasp. "Triton's mark—"

Her head whips down, and her eyes widen in delighted surprise. "It's working," she rasps.

She looks up at me, her eyes glistening and bright.

But as quickly as it began, her skin starts curling inwards

over the mark. The healing collapses, reverses, and the wound retreats to its original form.

"Well," she breathes. "It worked for a moment."

All these decades, she existed in this state of brokenness. It isn't fair. I swallow my exhaustion as I say, "Viola."

She turns her eyes on me. "No. Don't you start."

"But—"

"I said *no*," she snarls. "I said never, and I meant it."

When I don't reply, she continues quietly, "There's no guarantee the rest of you would be enough anyway, that the mark wouldn't open back up the way it's doing now. And if it's all for nothing, Aric, I won't be able to endure it. Even if I take your life and manage to gain my freedom... I won't survive it. So the answer is no. It will always be no."

She won't yield to her hunger.

I don't deserve that mercy, but I say, "All right."

Viola starts to lean back, and I grip her around her hips before she can stand up, a brilliant and fiendish idea tickling the back of my mind.

"I'm curious," I purr. "You can shift me into anything, right? Does that mean you could give me tentacles like yours if I asked nicely?"

Her brow furrows. "That is a sacred form. The spirits only bestow them on witches once they take their vows."

"Hmm," I brush my hand over the bristly growth on my jaw. "Not a tentacle then. How about suctions—could you give me just one, right here, on the pad of my finger?" I hold up my pointer finger.

"I suppose I *could*, but why would you want that?"

"Am I not allowed to surprise you? You love to surprise *me*." I pique a brow in challenge, wiggling my finger in front of her scowl. "Do what I asked, and I'll show you why."

She leans forward, her eyes on mine, and closes her

mouth around my finger. Her magic tingles into the pad of it as she sucks. That tingle travels up my arm, hurtling through my tissues, creating a new muscle for the suction.

Then she pops my finger out of her mouth, smiling.

"Now," I rasp, the blood in my body rushing maniacally behind my ears. "Turn around and lay down on your stomach."

Viola blinks, but I don't give her a chance to be confused. I sit up and lift her off my lap, setting her down beside me. I nod at the ground. "Obey me, witch, and you'll be rewarded."

She can't hide her excitement as she obeys. Her body forms a perfect hourglass shape, the luminous alabaster of her skin glowing against the gray stone. I cup the back of her knee and bend it until she's half-kneeling, half-sitting. Then I arrange her other knee forward as well, spreading her legs so she's straddling the air.

Her sex is now gloriously exposed for me.

I move into the space behind her, my hard cock resting on her lower back. Exercising my new muscle, I watch the suction undulate, its shiny tissues shifting at my will. Her skin visibly prickles as I slide my arm around her pelvis, pinning her between me and the island.

Her legs are arranged in such a way that my thighs trap her. She can't move.

"What are you doing?" she murmurs.

I kiss her back, dragging my tongue over her spine. She shudders. When I reach the nape of her neck, I reply, "You should be worrying about what I'm *not* going to do."

I slide my hand lower and drag the suction across the sensitive skin at the apex between her thighs.

Her hips jerk, and she cries out, but I continue teasing her, skirting my suction around the place she really wants me. I feel her grow impatient, grinding the air. She peeks at me over her shoulder, eyes blazing. "Touch me, you fucking monster."

"Monster, huh? I think you *like* how monstrous I can be."

My suction closes over her swollen bud, and her resulting cry echoes through the cave. I experiment with the pressure, determining which of my movements affect her best. The pitch of her voice deepens as she draws closer to coming, and I quickly move away when that happens. Growls join her trills, dancing off each other as I push her closer to that edge.

Her pleasure is an aphrodisiac, dragging me to the precipice along with her.

She digs her fingers into the moss as I press my suction in that perfect angle that has her gasping. "Don't stop. Oh, please—"

I reach up and clamp a hand over her mouth, silencing her. "No begging," I rumble. But I love it when she begs. It's just about the prettiest thing I've ever heard.

To reward her, I let her come.

Viola tips over the edge, but I don't remove the suction. Her thighs shift against mine as she tries to straighten her legs, tries to remove herself from my touch. Her voice vibrates through my hand, tears spilling down her cheeks and kissing my skin.

Fuck, she's beautiful.

I lean forward, pressing my mouth to the soft skin under her ear. "It feels wrong to be gagged, doesn't it?" Her breath comes faster. I nearly lose myself right there, but I bite my cheek and growl, "Maybe that's your real temptation: your ability to drive me out of my skin, possessing my voice and heart, making me feel *everything* when I'd grown so damn content with feeling nothing. Now it's my turn."

I send her soaring into pleasure a handful more times, until her crying turns to sobbing, and then turns to muffled screams. I pause as the last orgasm rocks her body, because I can't feel her breathing—but when I remove my hand from her mouth, she laughs through her tears.

My chest aches at the sound.

I reach down and notch my tip at her drenched entrance, and slowly push inside. Inch by inch, I disappear into her, body and soul. Her moans set fire to my blood. I fuck her to the rhythm of her gasping, to the beat of her pounding hearts.

The heartstring shakes with the force of it.

My head balloons as release closes in, and I'm not even fully aware of the words before they fall from my lips. "I love being inside of you. You are my happiness, my sanctuary."

I tip into blinding pleasure, ramming into her hard and fast. She comes with me, her legs spreading, lifting off the ground to swallow me even deeper. Eventually I still, wrapping my arm tight around her waist to embrace her from behind, barely catching our body weight with my other hand before I crush her.

Viola pushes back against me and we collapse, curling up together on our sides.

She pulls my hand to her mouth and kisses the suction, and the muscle reignites with a sore ache, dissolving under her pull. "You are mine," she whispers.

Entirely hers.

I hold her there for long minutes, breathing in the scent of her. I wish I could hold her like this for hours, but her stomach has other plans. It growls loudly, echoing through the room.

Inky guilt spreads through my chest. My hand glides down to press against the grumble. "I'm sorry. You didn't eat dinner last night because of me."

She turns in my arms.

When her eyes meet mine, they're warm and satisfied despite the hunger she must feel... the hunger she must *always* feel. "I ran into a rainstorm because I was upset. Technically, that was *my* fault."

I kiss her, deep and soft.

Her stomach growls again, vibrating against my ribcage, and I pull away to reach for my pants. "I'll go grab us some food," I say as I tug the damp material up my legs.

"I'll come with you."

"No." I stop her from grabbing her dress and flash a dastardly grin. "I don't plan on sharing you with anyone today."

Her knees are bent between us, skin red and rubbed raw from the stone. I lean forward and kiss each one.

An awed and somewhat shy expression ripples over her face and I smile, lurching forward to kiss her once more. "Don't you dare get dressed," I say onto her lips.

Then I turn and dive into the pool.

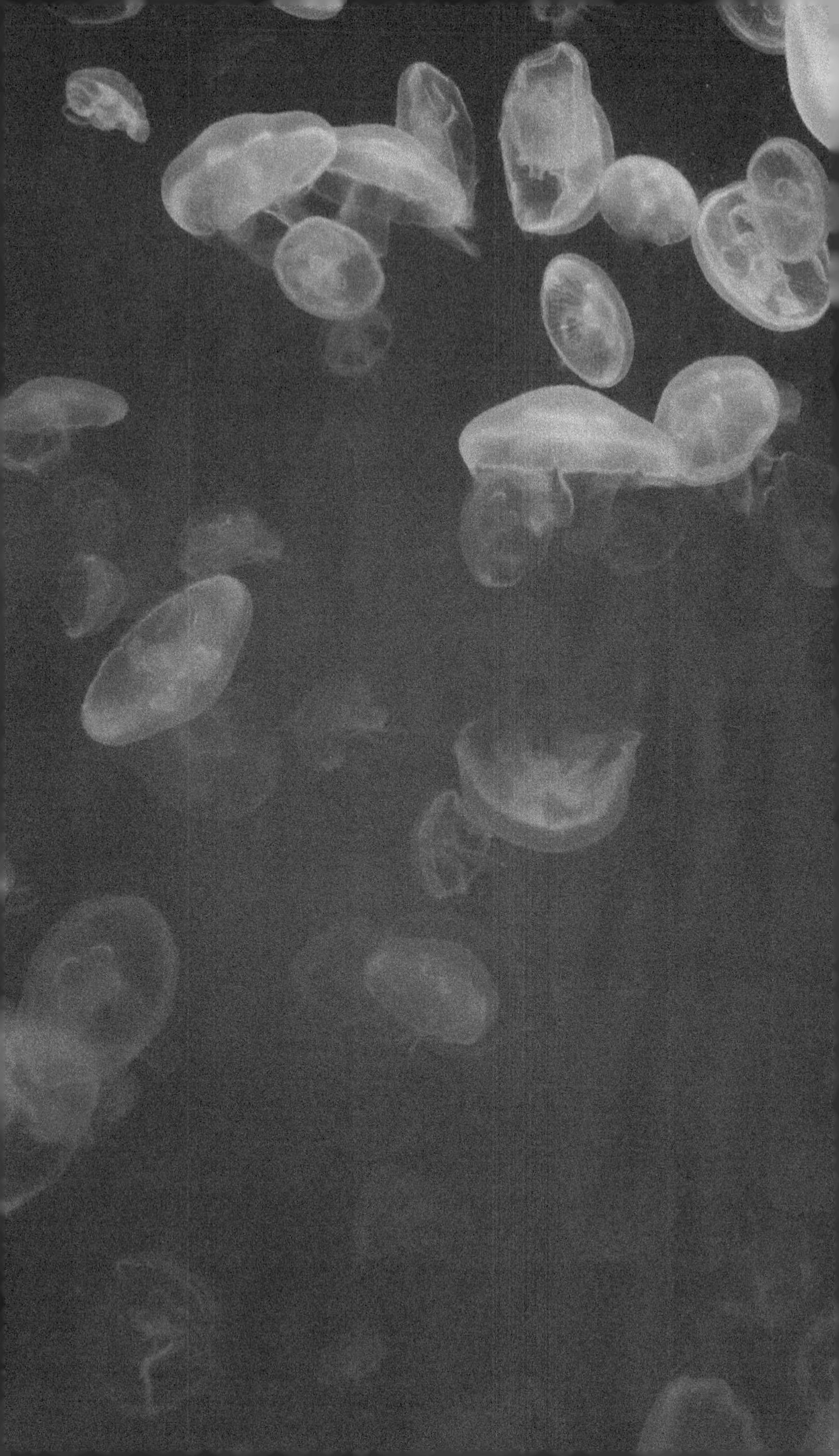

CHAPTER 33
VIOLA

I *love him.*
    I say it in my head as Aric swims out of the cave. Then again, when he's gone, I whisper it to myself. I try to familiarize myself with the way it feels in my mouth, in my heart. I grow accustomed to the sound of it in my ears.

I've never told anyone that I love them before. Not *this* sort of love.

The intimacy of it is more terrifying than I imagined. I feel as though my hearts are trying to leap out of my chest, and I grow more impatient with every moment that passes without him here. The words remain within me, driving me mad with their incessant pounding. Now that he's left me with my thoughts, all I want is for him to come back so I can confess this to him. So I can get it out of me.

There's nothing I can do now except wait.

I distract myself with memories of what he's said and done to me. I lie back on the island and let my hand drift between my legs. I'm still wet with his cum and my own, and there's a pleasant soreness radiating from deep within me.

My fingertips brush over my clitoris and I gasp at the reaction it spurs in my core, the tenderness Aric created with that clever little idea of his.

Before Aric, I never let any male master me. Command me. What few copulations my cycle led me into after Francis were swift and purely animalistic in nature. It's a relief to be taken over, *controlled*, to be so driven out of my mind by lust that the only thing I can focus on is him. In those moments, there's nothing but us. I can't feel anything in his touch but the pleasure he offers. The safety of his arms.

I love him.

My eyes flutter closed, shutting out the morning sky and the dripping moss above me. For a moment, everything in my world feels right. More right than I ever imagined possible.

That's when Goddess Mora makes herself known.

The whirlpools go absolutely silent. I open my eyes and find that they've gone totally still. Just *stopped whirling*. They've never done that in my presence before. I didn't even know they *could* do that. They've stopped churning so I might hear *her* better, and hear her I do.

Or, at least, I hear *something*.

A hum.

Goddess Mora grips my shoulder with her ethereal claws. She squeezes enough for it to hurt, just a little. When I turn toward that side of my body, I freeze—because she's brought my attention to the source of that hum. On the other side of the stone island, my dress is vibrating.

Go, she whispers. *You must look.*

The dread from yesterday returns with a vengeance, making my bones cold and my skin hot. My stomach twists as I crawl across the island. I don't trust my legs enough to stand. Fear strips my limbs of their remaining strength and

I'm not sure what to expect, only that it can't be good. This is what she tried to warn me about yesterday, I'm sure of it.

I raise the dress, and a small bronze pendant drops to the stone with a resounding thunk.

Then it's not just my bones that are cold. It's my entire body, down to the blood in my veins, the thoughts in my head. I lift the pendant. I mark my hair encased in its glass center, the symbols etched into the tarnished edges. It's vibrating so hard that the fingers I use to hold it start itching. I understand then, without knowing what it is.

It can't be. But it's true.

I love him, and he has betrayed me.

CHAPTER 34
ARIC

The city is eerily calm as I return through the streets. It's still early—the sun has just barely begun to peek between the buildings, and I can't shake the unease from my limbs. I feel as though every step I take towards the heart of the city has my heart beating faster, beating harder.

The entire walk I fought the voices assailing me from either side of my head. I'm beginning to hear a whisper beneath them. A whisper undeniably *mine*.

I'm beginning to believe nothing beyond that matters.

I peer at the cathedral looming tall above me. It looks harmless in the first streams of daylight. Clean and strong and beautiful. It gives away none of the ugly inside of it. Yet it creates prisoners, breeds evil, keeps every trace of magic brought through its doors in a basement, hiding it from the rest of the world.

My gaze catches on a glimmer of light coming from the corner of the building, and I pause.

Brows stitching together, I slowly approach the cathedral. There's something lying here, at the corner.

An *arrow*.

I kneel to examine it. I reaching for it, but stop short. The reason it was glimmering in the sunlight is because it's crafted from pure silver. Silver, to use against someone like me.

Someone like *Viola*.

I haven't felt the pendant hum the entire time I've been in the city—and I should certainly feel it *now*, so close to the cathedral. Unless the priest isn't inside.

Running around the side of the building to the front doors, I find them closed. I yank on them, but they're locked. The cathedral is absolutely barren. Their hunt has begun, I'm sure of it. That's why I feel so exposed walking these streets this morning. I can sense *him* prowling out here.

And I left Viola all alone in that cave.

My hand drifts to my pocket, and my entire body jolts as I realize that it's empty.

"*Fuck*," I choke out.

I scramble off the front steps and run through the streets, throwing myself around corners and across bridges as fast as my legs can carry me.

The pendant must have fallen out of my pocket—I must have left it behind in the cave, which holds a naked sea witch who has no idea what's coming for her.

Could the priest track her that far outside the city? Is his magic that powerful? There's no telling what those artifacts are capable of, assisted by his twisted dark magic. By the time I'm sprinting across the golden sands leading to the cave, my imagination has gotten the best of me.

When I see Viola climbing down a tumble of jagged boulders, my heart seems to liquefy. I slow into a brisk walk, the breath sawing out of me as I scan her body. She's whole, unharmed. Thank the Goddess. Thank Her spirits.

I meet the sea witch at the base of the rocks.

"Viola," I rasp as she finally hits the sand. "We need to talk."

I step forward, reaching for her.

Before I can even touch her, she raises her chin in defiance, locks her sunset eyes with mine, and slaps me across the face. As I stagger back, she raises the amulet between us, the chain wrapped around her hand and the vibrating pendant dangling beneath. "What is this, and why is a strand of my hair trapped inside of it?"

"You don't understand," I gasp. "Fluke gave that to me."

Her caustic laughter silences me. "Don't back down now, Aric. You were the one who brought it into the cave. Fluke doesn't even know the whirlpools exist, so you were his feet instead, his eyes and ears, weren't you? Is that what you were planning this whole time? You wanted to get my guard down and then leave me behind with this *thing*? Are you using it to weaken me somehow? Well, I'll tell you right now, I'm not afraid of this and I'm not afraid of you."

"Viola, how long has it been humming?"

"What does it matter?" she spits.

I step forward, too quickly for her to recoil, and rip the pendant out of her hand. Fuck... it's humming as violently as it had in the basement of the cathedral. She reaches out to take it back, and I place a hand on her chest to stop her.

"It matters because the louder it is, the closer he is."

Her eyes widen. "Who is *he*?"

Before she can argue with me, I turn and fling the pendant into the ocean. It's far too easy to do. Which means the magic connected it to me is weak, which means the priest is far too close. "We need to get you out of here." I grab her hand.

Confusion swirls in her purple eyes. She tries to wrench her hand away from me. "I'm not going anywhere with you."

I glance around, searching for any sign of dark robes. So far, the coast is clear, but it might not be for much longer. "I understand you don't trust me," I say. "You have every right to be angry with me, to want to kill me for the part I played in all this, but I *swear to you*, if you don't come with me now, you might never get a chance to hear the truth."

When I yank on her hand again, she lets me drag her up the beach. Only a few feet, and then she's fighting me again, hissing at my back.

I turn to scold her and freeze.

She wasn't fighting me at all.

A silver arrow protrudes from the center of Triton's mark. It penetrated through the very center of her hearts, nicking all three of them in one foul blow. Dark blue blood pours down the front of her. It seeps into her cotton dress like a pool of spilled ink. Her mouth gapes, her eyes fluttering as she looks down at the head of the arrow. I hold onto her hand, paralyzed, even as the strength leaves her fingers. Even as her knees buckle.

She collapses, and I lurch forward to catch her.

I see past her body then, to the rocky peak beyond. The priest found us. Beside him, kneeling amongst the jagged boulders with a crossbow braced on her shoulder, is Hazel.

Or at least, it's her body.

The princess's eyes are a dusty, clouded brown. More color than the nuns had back at the cathedral, but not by much. Her necklace gleams with a sinisterly familiar blue glow. That magic is mirrored by the glow emanating from a second pendant, hanging from the priest's neck. I'd bet anything that's another artifact.

That's how he controls them.

His hand grips Hazel's shoulder possessively as he smiles down at us.

The roar that tears out of me is part animal, part spirit, and wholly vicious. My magic radiates toward them, streaking through the air like several sharp spears. Such a dark purple, they're almost black. Hazel's mind appears blank when I slam into it, but as I unravel my rage inside her, it affects her just enough to make her lower the crossbow. The priest hears me loud and clear, and that forces his magic to halt as my vision takes root in them both.

The stone beneath them seems to crumble and they scramble back to avoid being swallowed by the earth.

They disappear between the boulders, likely returning to the city on whatever hidden path that led them here. As they leave, I end my song. My magic twirling up the rock face dissipates.

I lower myself and Viola to the ground.

"Viola," I whisper, looking again at the extent of the arrow's damage.

She starts coughing, blue blood speckling her chin. Her hands flail between us. She gestures at the arrow. "Get it out. Take it out." Her voice is weak, frantic.

I shake my head.

There's not a chance of her surviving if I take it out, not without some sort of healer present. Surely I can find one in the city? Humans have healers, don't they? Jussi would know where to go, but I don't even know if she'll survive the staircase. "If I pull on it now, you'll bleed out," I rasp, my throat swelling. "You need to shift or something, regenerate your hearts."

"That's not how it works," she growls. "Just rip this thing out of me and be done with it."

Those words burn into me, rending through my mind and soul. "I'm not ripping the arrow through your hearts, Viola. I'm not going to watch you die."

"Coward," she hisses. "I'll do it myself."

Her hand wraps around the stem just below the arrow head. I can hear and smell her skin sizzling in reaction to the silver. She's really going to do it—she's going to pull the arrow out of her own chest.

I grip her wrist. "Stop, don't do this to spite me. You can't die thinking I wanted this. I don't want this. I love you." I never dared to even think that before now, but I crumble under the truth of it.

She grits her teeth. "It's far too late for that, Prince."

At once, her body shifts. Her tentacles reach up, wrapping around my neck and arms. She pries me away from her just enough to grasp the arrow with both hands and tear it the rest of the way through her chest with a sickening cry.

Her body begins jerking, her tentacles losing their strength and falling away.

My fingers press against her chest, slipping into that wound as I try to staunch the heavy blue blood spurting everywhere and soaking the sand beneath us. But nothing can stop it. Every thump of her hearts hurtles her closer to death. She looks up at me, the tears in her eyes overflowing. The hatred in her eyes slowly fades, her *life* fades. And I clutch to her, screaming, wishing I had the power to save her.

But my wishes amount to nothing.

She dies in my arms.

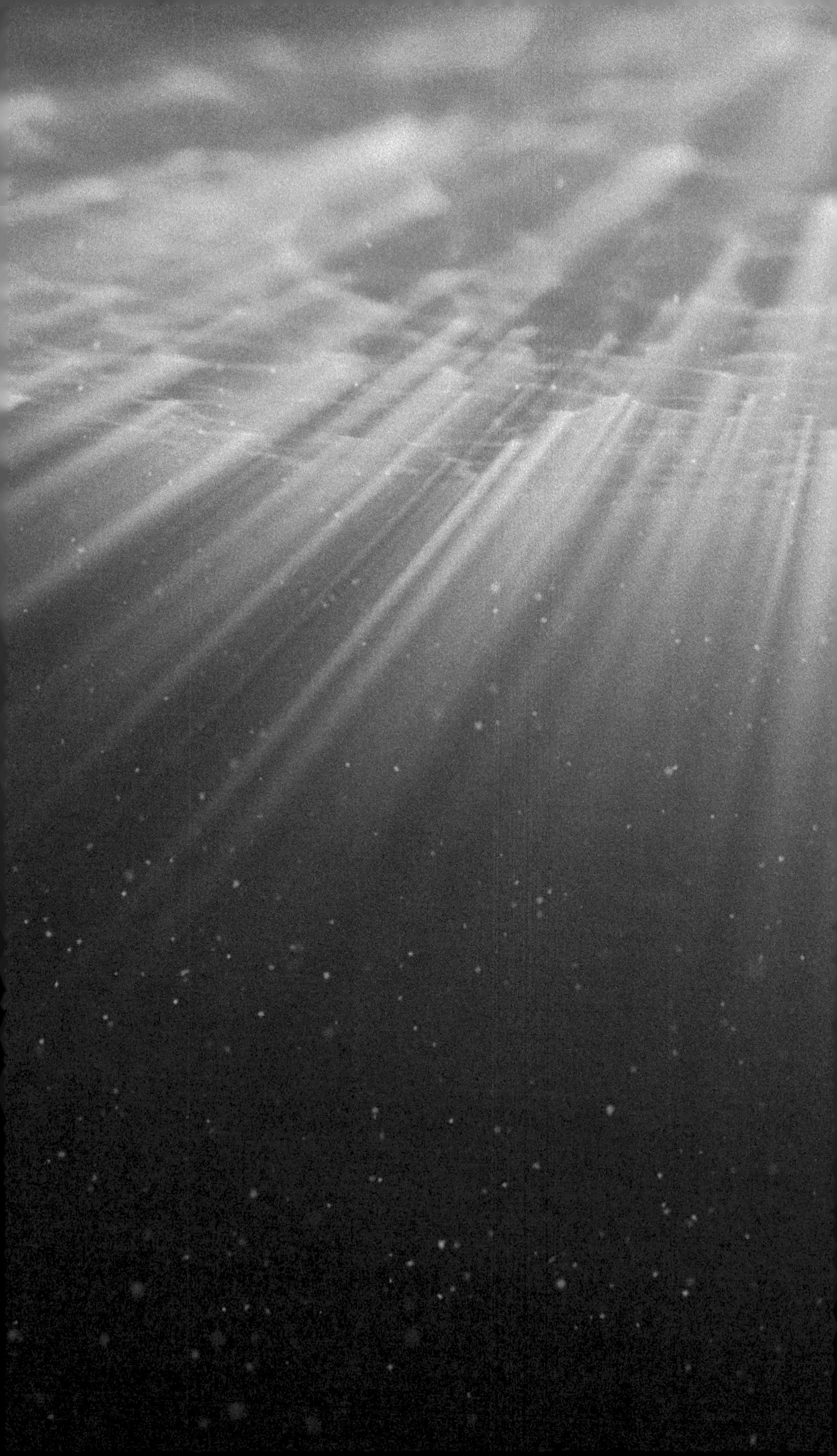

CHAPTER 35

ARIC

I have heard it whispered in Atlantis that when Triton murdered his father's court and rose to power, he briefly entered a killing calm. No emotion. No hesitation. The staff of the palace watched him execute hundreds that way.

I've always feared my father for those rumors.

But now, stalking through the city with my soul set on the cathedral, I understand it.

I grip the silver arrow in my hand, not registering the pain of the metal touching my bare skin. Pain is secondary. The false voices scream at me.

Sliding the silver arrow behind my earlobe, I carve them out of me. The falsities. I drop those bloody bits of starfish to the ground, crushing them under my feet. It's time for me to figure out what I am when the voices are silent.

There is no reality where Viola's death does not make me a worse version of the male I was.

She had been changing me, with everything she was and

everything I felt with her, and now I refuse to trust any voice in me that doesn't sound like hers.

The front doors of the cathedral are still shut when I reach them, though public hours for worship and prayer have already begun and the entrance *should* be propped open in invitation. I chant under my breath as I climb the staircase. Hazel and those other robed women may still be under his influence, but I'll *make* them hear me. I focus all of my power into the tendrils of swirling purple falling from my lips. They slip into the crack beneath the double doors.

As I wrench on the golden-brushed knob, the door creaks open. No longer locked.

They're expecting me.

I build my song into a billowing haze beyond the doors before walking in. In the cloud of magic, they can't see any part of me; they are my shadows. However, through the spinning purple threads, I can see enough to assess the room.

Robed women stand between the columns on either side of the room, their bows aimed at the haze.

Archibald stands at the front of the room.

On the floor beside him, Hazel lies unconscious, a hand limply clutching her necklace.

They can't see me, but they can hear me singing. They know I entered the room. A few arrows blindly slice through the air around me, and I sidestep them easily. With a wave of my hand, I send spears of magic hurtling toward the women as they draw new arrows.

They take aim again.

At my will, the robed women turn on one another. Now they see *me* in the place of their sisters. One by one, arrows and daggers fly as my song spreads through the room. I latch onto that layer of control the priest has over them, molding it, creating commands of my own.

Better that they die than live their lives in service to the priest. Better that they are free of this place, before their bones are buried in the walls and their souls are trapped forever.

As the mistress's pets drop around me, I let the haze clear. I let the priest see me coming.

He scrambles for the sword on the altar beside him. As he presents it between us, his arms shake from the effort of holding it up. It's too heavy for him. Funny, that a man as frail as him can do so much damage—that so many people *allowed* him to do that damage.

My chant turns a bit throaty as I close in on him, as I choke on a laugh.

He swings at me with that old blade, but I duck and keep on singing. I beckon to the spirits lying beneath our feet, the spirits who beat on my subconscious every time I step foot in this wretched place. I'm too close for him to parry again.

My hand closes around his wrist, and I crush the bones there. The sword clatters to the ground as I shove him back against the wooden statue in the center of the stage.

Those human spirits rise from the basement, tickling the back of my mind. They influence the song, turning it crimson around the edges as my magic invades every orifice of the priest's face.

I let the spirits take full control.

Red wraps around the priest, spinning in a tight vortex around his ankles. He's swept off his feet, and his back slams into the ground. The spirits grab him by his ankles, turning him upside down, lifting him higher and higher until he's being pressed against the statue. The red wisps grasp at the scarfs hung on the statue and wrap them around Archibald's legs and arms.

Then the spirits funnel themselves into his ears.

His eyes begin to bleed. The veins in his head bulge. He screams, fighting against the restraints, but it's no use.

I watch until the very end.

When I pull the vision back, I see the priest strapped to the statue exactly as he had been in the fantasy. Somehow, the spirits managed to breach the void between dream and reality.

There's so much I don't understand about my gift, even after the centuries I've had it, so I'm not as shocked as I probably should be. Spirits have always sung through me. Is it really so inconceivable to believe they could take that extra step into the physical realm if they were furious enough? Each mind is its own a world of thought, and the dead are little more than that. They exist because we remember them. Because we believe in them.

The priest is bleeding out, but he's still alive.

The spirits gave me the last word.

I step forward with the silver arrow. As I raise it to his face, I see that the silver has eaten its way all the way down to the bones in my hand—but I only grip the stem tighter and dig the tip into the priest's skin. I take my time. His organs are littering the ground at my feet when I finally step away. My hands are coated with his blood and guts.

There was no getting around it. I had to see his heart for myself. I had to know that he was human.

I rip the artifact of control off of his neck and turn to the form lying on the platform behind me. Hazel... I don't know what to do with her yet.

My feet slide with every blood-slick step I take toward her. Her eyes aren't open, but the rhythm of her breathing isn't quite right. She's awake. So I kneel in front of her and wait. And wait. *And wait.*

Eventually, she opens her eyes, and our gazes meet.

She doesn't make a sound, not a word. She's too scared. And I find I cannot kill her, just as I could not kill her that night when I was sitting beneath her balcony.

There are no voices to argue with this time. There is no guilt to collar me.

She's a princess who longed for freedom. Who has to fight for it at every turn. Perhaps that's the real reason I was drawn to her balcony, why I found myself returning to it time and again, the same way she kept calling for me. I recognized the similarities between us. She did not choose the beliefs hung around her neck. The weight. The crushing control.

I drop the blood-stained arrow and the artifact at her feet. "Take it for yourself," I rasp. "While you still have a chance." I see the look on her face, the moment she recognizes my voice.

But I don't linger long enough for her to ask questions.

Control. Power. I hope she uses that pendant to her advantage. I hope she meets the love of her life and has a beautiful life in a palace far, far away from here.

Whatever world she meets after this one, I hope it is her own.

✾

I sit at the worn dining table in Jussi and Guillermo's house, my hands dripping thickened blood onto their ivory tablecloth. It could be hours I sat there, or years. The house darkens around me.

My ears catch movement—the sound of a door opening and closing.

I blink, but I can't move beyond that.

I don't remember how I got here or what the world

looked like when I left the cathedral, but the sunlight peering through the windows is orange and dusky. It's been a few hours at the very least.

Suddenly, I'm being wrenched out of the chair and slammed into a wall.

Guillermo's anguished face appears before me, his eyes trailing down to mark the red and blue blood spattering my chest. His hands fist in my shirt; they shake me hard. I can barely register it. I'm nothing. Nothing without her.

"What did you do to her?" he demands.

"Guillermo," Jussi interjects. "Look at him."

Warmth is bursting behind my eyes. My vision blurs as that heat breaches the surface and trickles down my cheeks. It takes a moment for me to realize what's happening—that I'm *crying*. I open my mouth to reply, but only a strangled sob escapes. The pain overwhelms my senses and I crumble at the end of Guillermo's hands, becoming nothing more than this twisted, broken feeling in my heart.

"My darling," I hear Jussi whisper, his voice closer now than it was before. I can't see him. I can't see anything beyond my grief. "Let him go."

The anchor on my chest disappears and I collapse, sliding down the length of the wall.

I bow my head between my knees, my hands fisting in my hair as I try to understand this sensation. It feels as though my entire soul is pouring out of me.

This is love, isn't it?

Love is the cruelest mistress, a siren all its own.

"She's gone," I croak.

Jussi kneels before me, and I can only stare at his leather sandals, can only mark the way he threads his fingers together in front of his knees. "What happened?"

"She died. She was shot in the hearts by a silver arrow. I

should have protected her. I should have warned her." My voice cracks. "I'm a monster."

Guillermo scoffs, stalking to the kitchen and swiping a bottle of wine from the counter. A tear falls across his temple as he tips his head back for a deep sip. But somehow, he doesn't seem as devastated as I expected him to be. Angry, yes. Irritated and deeply upset, but not sad. Not mournful.

I should be dead right now. I should be dead, and she should be living.

"Aric," Jussi mutters, a demand for my undivided attention. When I look at him, he says, "Viola isn't dead. She *can't* die."

My heart skips. "What?"

He glances over his shoulder to Guillermo, who simply shakes his head. "When Triton cursed Viola, he bound her to the ocean. So long as the tides ebb and flow, she exists with it—he made it impossible for her to escape him, even through death."

"She's alive?"

He nods.

Oblivion... I left her behind on that beach. After the cathedral, I couldn't bear to return and look at her again, with blood pooling beneath her and emptiness in her eyes. If I had, would she have been awake and waiting for me? If she was alive, why wasn't she here?

I turn to that connection inside me and gasp when I discover it still there. As strong as ever.

"And may the spirits have mercy on whoever dared to betray her," Jussi adds, grimacing at the door to their home, as if expecting her to barge in at any moment.

Fluke will be at the top of her list.

Once she's done with him, she'll come for me, and I will happily rip my own heart out and lay it at her feet.

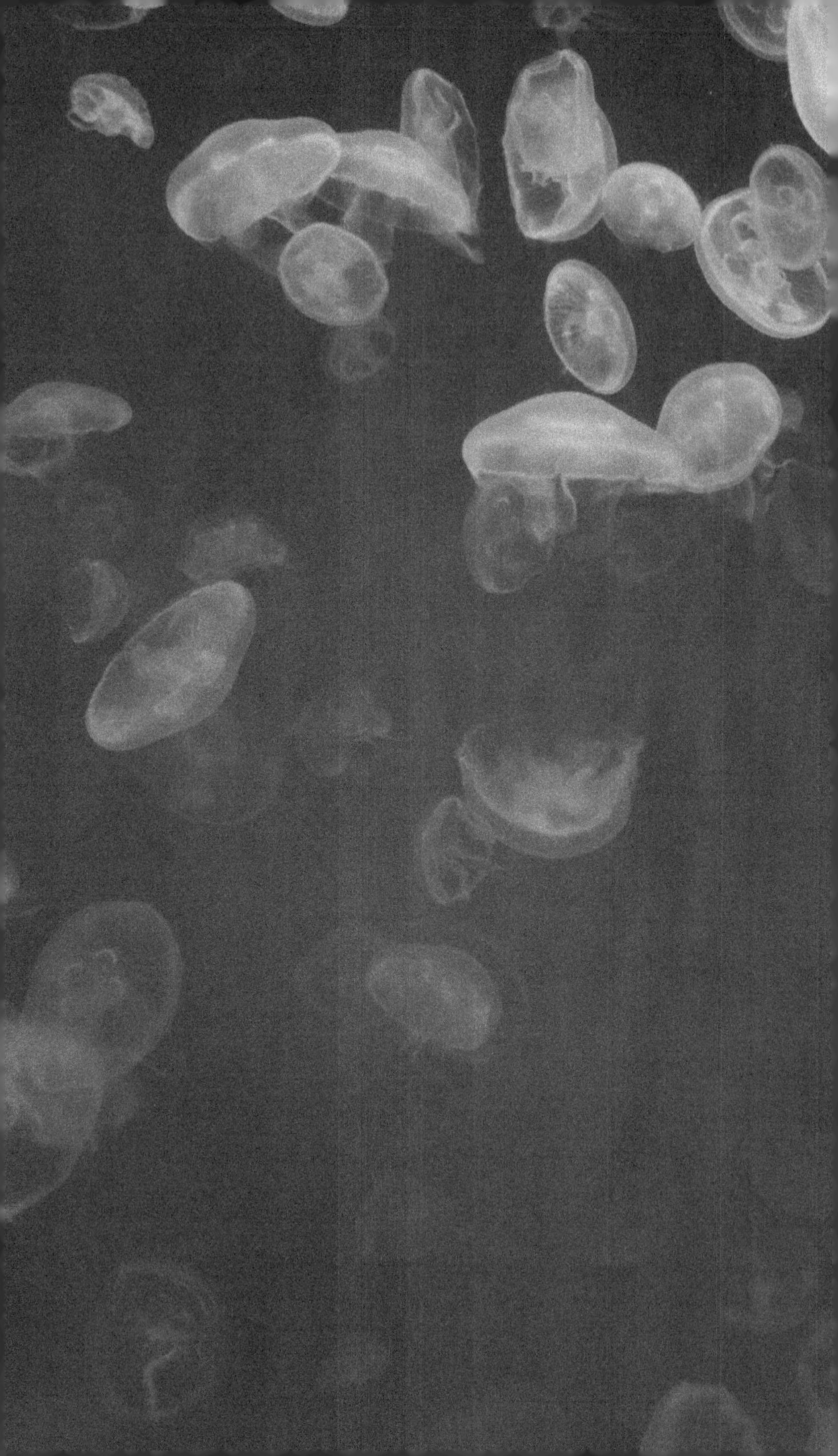

CHAPTER 36
VIOLA

The throne room is clouded with blood, and the bodies of Triton's court bob around me as I sit on his throne, as I wait.

I taste Fluke's blood between my teeth, like a layer of oil I can't get rid of. Several victims, and still I taste him. He was my first priority when I woke on that beach. I found him and my second soul-bound back at the shipwreck, terrorizing the females there like the disgusting, short-sighted fools they were. Perla had already killed Wiggles by the time I got there.

The memory of Fluke's face when I appeared in the Captain's quarters followed me all the way to Atlantis—his shock and terror. I gave him everything he deserved. And when I was done, I ripped out his heart.

My hunger has never felt so sated, my body so powerful, but I know this is temporary. I've fed on several mer in the last few hours. Soon, their hearts will begin to digest and their gifts will fade from my body. The enhanced hearing. Current manipulation. There had even been a hunter on

Triton's court too. The entire room pulses with blue and green heat, highlighting the thickest clouds of blood.

Right now, I'm strong enough to face him.

Aric and I planned to deal with Triton together, but there's not a chance of that anymore. There's no way to use the bones either; it's not as if I can pin Triton down, plunge them into his heart, and drag him into a sufficient prison on my own.

And besides, I refuse to carry anything that would weaken me into his palace. Into this throne room.

I ache under the weight of Aric's betrayal. I feel him, the heartstring, communicating his agony across all these miles apart. I hope he suffers my absence for the rest of his human life... because that's what he'll have.

Regardless of how things turn out here, I won't take Aric's legs.

That's what he wants, what he's *always* wanted. I also suspect, now that I can think about it without an arrow impaling my hearts, that he didn't really want me to die. He'd been telling the truth about that. But he didn't do anything to stop it, either. He didn't warn me. He didn't *protect* me.

He didn't mean all of those things he said to me in the cave. Love is the same to me as it's always been. *Untrue.*

I care too much for Aric. It's dangerous for me to be around him. Now that I no longer have my other soul-bound to mitigate my hunger when it returns, I can't be anywhere close to Aric *or* the surface. I can never be close to him again.

My enhanced senses mark Triton's approach, the slight rumble in the water outside the throne room before he appears in the archway.

He was away from the city when I came.

Him *and* his favorite son.

Triton's bright blue eyes scan the death around me, his hands fisting to either side of him. I clutch the armrests of his throne and utilize every gift surging through my veins, assessing the currents wrapped around both of us in case I need to use them. His body is outlined in the coolest green, with a burst of white hot life centered in his chest.

His gaze finally lands on me.

And he smiles.

"What games have you been playing on my throne, witchling?"

The implication in his voice sends my body into a fit, my tentacles spinning all around me. Triton only smiles wider.

"Let me go," I command. "This mark you've made, this curse you've created, I want you to get rid of it."

"And why would I do that?" As he swims closer, I use the currents to push him back. His chest only twitches at the harsh caress as he keeps coming, and his smile turning sickeningly smug.

I rise from his throne, trying to get some sense of advantage, ignoring the wickedness in his eyes. "I have already torn out the hearts of your court. I will feast on *everyone* that matters to you, if I must. I will take your children and your wife. I will take *everything*."

I never dared to stoop to this level before, to kill innocents in an effort to force his hand. I thought it was too cruel. But if I have to take a few dozen innocent souls down with Triton, maybe that's for the best. I just wish the threat landed even half as hard as I wanted it to.

Triton shrugs. "You can try to take them, my dear. But if anyone is weak enough to fall prey to you, then they deserve their fate, and you deserve the meal. This is the way of the ocean." He draws closer, his lightning slicing through a battling current I send his way.

"It does not matter what you do, I will *never* release you."

"Then I will fill your palace with blood again and again until you do," I snarl.

His expression turns predatory as lightning bursts around us. It scatters through the water in a small cage around the throne, trapping me in with him.

Triton lurches forward and I recoil, landing in the seat of the throne as his hands grips the rests to either side of me. He sneers, "You still don't get it, do you? I can establish a new court in a day, I can fix anything you break, but *you* will *always* starve. I have ensured you never know peace apart from me. Give in, Viola. Give in, and I will give you everything you want in return."

He leans in, and I freeze as his long, white hair brushes my shoulder. Too close to the memory for comfort. He whispers in my ear, "I'll even make it good for you, I promise."

Triton grabs my arm, and I try to jerk out of his hold.

"*Let go of me.*"

He doesn't let me go, and I can't break free. Not yet.

Lightning buzzes in my ears, the cage slowly shrinking around us. It popples over my skin. My skin breaks out in gooseflesh as I recoil even harder against his beautiful coral and pearl throne.

"You think I don't know why you've spent this time with Aric?" he continues. "Why you keep him? Tell me, witchling—how often do you look at him and think of me?"

I thrust my hands against his chest and shove him back. It's just enough to push his face away from my neck. "*Never.*"

It's true.

Even when I first met Aric, I could not see the resemblance, and I haven't searched for similarities since the day Aric told me to kneel in that abandoned library. I'm aware of how twisted it is. Knowing who he was and wanting him anyway, *needing* him.

But I didn't think of Triton at all in those moments. I never saw his face.

That, in and of itself, was a fucking miracle and I refused to waste it. I'm glad I didn't. I don't regret loving the siren, despite how much it hurts now. Despite how much it will ache in the future like some kind of eternal bruise.

There is not one inch of me that belongs to Triton, not now and not then.

I rip at Triton's fingers with my claws, crying out as my soul is ripped a little bit as a result. The claim he made on my soul demands that I stop, but I can't. *I can't.*

Triton's lightning creeps in to caress my tentacles. He grits his teeth as he grabs my other arm in a fierce grip and lifts me from the throne. He's massive, larger than life, and I am far too small in his hands. I shake the thought away.

I'm not a helpless little witchling. Not anymore.

He's battling that pull on his innards too, the consequence of causing me pain. The bond travels both ways. I can't hurt him and he can't hurt me, and beyond his broad shoulders, I see the shadows in the room swirl, drawn to our compromised bond. I hear them whispering—the deities of the ocean. I feel their fury.

Triton feels it as well and turns his head to mark the movement. He casts his lightning toward them.

I smile at his violence, at his unease.

A harsh laugh rasps out of me as I revel in their triumph. Someday, the veil between us and them is going to become thin enough that those deities can touch him, punish him, *teach him.* And despite how tired I am of this life, I hope I'm there to witness it.

In Triton's distraction, I stretch my tentacles out to press against his electric cage. I let his electricity sweep through my body, let it flow through me and build into a tidal wave before I send it back into him through his grip on my arms.

The electrical current sends his body hurtling through the water in an eruption of bubbles.

I launch toward an opening in the room.

His roar of failure follows me, and blinding spears of light explode in front of me to cut off my escape... but I never had any intention of letting him trap me here.

I continue through that window carved into the wall, ignoring the sharp pulse of electricity as I draw nearer to it. Then I shift. My limbs go a bit molten as they retract into my torso. My vision yellows, my line of vision shifting to either side of my face as I lengthen into an eel.

My veins pump with electrical currents as I pass through, but it doesn't stop me. It doesn't hurt.

As I emerge from Atlantis into the open waters of the ocean, I treasure that piece of Francis inside of me. That part of him I kept in a jar. My old friend.

He couldn't protect me back then, but *no one* could. And no one is going to protect me now. I'm the only one I can rely on, the only one who is willing to scheme and kill and steal in order to put a stop to my suffering. It was a mistake to believe anyone else might. I allowed Aric to slip beneath my skin, allowed him to touch me without flinching, and look at what came of it... I'm still alone and broken. Hurting more fiercely than ever before.

I have never met anyone who would willingly sacrifice a piece of themselves without expecting something more valuable in return.

We are all starving hearts.

Every one of us.

CHAPTER 37
ARIC

I sit on a boulder in front of the blue-stained stretch of beach where she died.

I've been here for what feels like eons, but the lapping tides haven't shifted to reveal her yet.

It couldn't have taken her this long to track Fluke down. Something's gone wrong. She's in trouble somehow. I leap off of the boulder and begin to pace at the foot of the rock tumble, my eyes trained on the horizon, my heart beating harder as my worries spiral.

Fog rolled in overnight, and as the sky lightens, the world turns a charcoal gray. The clouds cling heavily to the waves and the shore despite the impending dawn. The sky beyond that is stormy. The humidity of the ocean fills my lungs with every inhale, my breath puffing in the cool air.

I tug again on that connection between us. She's out there, somewhere.

The space between us thunders with pain. I can taste her unhappiness, bitter in my mouth and sour in my stomach. My hands tremble as I wring them. What if she never returns? What if this is my punishment—to never see her again, but feel her pull on the back of my heart for the rest of my life but never feel her with my hands?

That's a fate worse than death.

Abandoning the blood-soaked beach, I walk toward the city. There has to be a better solution than sitting and waiting. If she *is* in trouble, then I have to find her. I veer past the long staircase leading up to the city and scan the bay stretching up ahead, the boats bobbing in the bay. The fishermen must recognize the storm brewing because this stretch of beach is quiet and the bay is empty.

Except for a singular lantern swinging in the distance, illuminating a small patch of the fog.

That sliver of unease in my chest grows as I draw even closer. This is no coincidence. I see a small fisherman's boat being anchored down, and then I see who has been out on the sea. *Jussi.*

He's been to see *her*. I know it.

I stalk down the pier and jump up onto his small boat before he even realizes I'm approaching. It's a decently-sized boat—not a ship by any means, but spacious enough for one man. Spears and knives are attached to the inner ledge. Fishing tools.

Beneath them, on the seat in the center of the boat, his parchment and a small box of charcoal sit together.

Everything has a light dusting of water.

"Where is she?" I demand to his back.

Jussi startles, dropping a tangle of rope and netting. He kicks the bundle behind him as he turns to face me. He frowns as his eyes land on me. "Forget about her, Aric. She's not coming back."

Impossible. I could never forget her.

The skin around his eyes are puffy, and the whites of his eyes are red. He's been crying, I think.

That's when I notice the frayed end of the rope he'd been holding, the utter wetness of the deck and the seaweed caught up in the twine. "What is all of this? What have you done with her?"

"I have only done what she asked me to."

"What—what does that *mean*?" I take a step toward him.

"She's not coming back," he repeats coldly. "Not for a very long time. You should be thankful that she decided to spare you."

"I won't be thankful for her absence," I hiss. "Tell me where you've left her, or I'll—"

"And here come the threats," he interjects with a sigh, crossing his arms in front of his chest. "You know, she warned me about that. But she also warned me of how hollow they are. I won't tell you where she is. I swore to her I wouldn't, and besides, she's gone somewhere you cannot possibly follow."

I close the space between us, pulling the air deep into my lungs. It could have been ocean spray sliding down my throat. "There is no place I will not search for her, will not drown for her."

Jussi's eyes soften, but he quickly averts his eyes to the bay around us, to the baleful fog and choppy waters.

"That is precisely why she doesn't want you to know," he admits. When his eyes meet mine again, my stomach turns. "That is why I will never tell you."

It feels like I'm losing. Losing her. Losing everything.

She asked him not to tell me so she could protect me from whatever she's done. In my head, I know I should probably just respect her wishes and let her go. I know I have not earned her love. I have done nothing but hurt her.

But I can't let go.

No matter the distance or the mistakes that separate us, I will never stop caring for her. I won't stop until she's free.

I promised I would help her. I promised I would protect her. She may not want it anymore, but she's going to have it, even if she hates me for it. Even if she kills me for it.

"Fine," I say through gritted teeth.

Then, before Jussi can see what I'm planning, I punch him. My fist connects with his jaw, and he hits the ground unconscious.

"I'll find her myself."

I drag his body out of the boat, then carefully lay him on the pier before pulling the anchor out of the water and untying the boat. As I settle into the main seat, I grasp at that heartstring deep inside and search for direction.

Viola can't be far if Jussi was able to meet her in this boat. It's not built for the open ocean.

I focus on that tug on my heart, the tension of it growing stronger and more solid the more I turn inward. If she can find me, I can find her. We are equals in this bond, regardless of how much she has tried to convince me of the opposite.

Opening my eyes, I align myself with that luminous connection and drift out to sea.

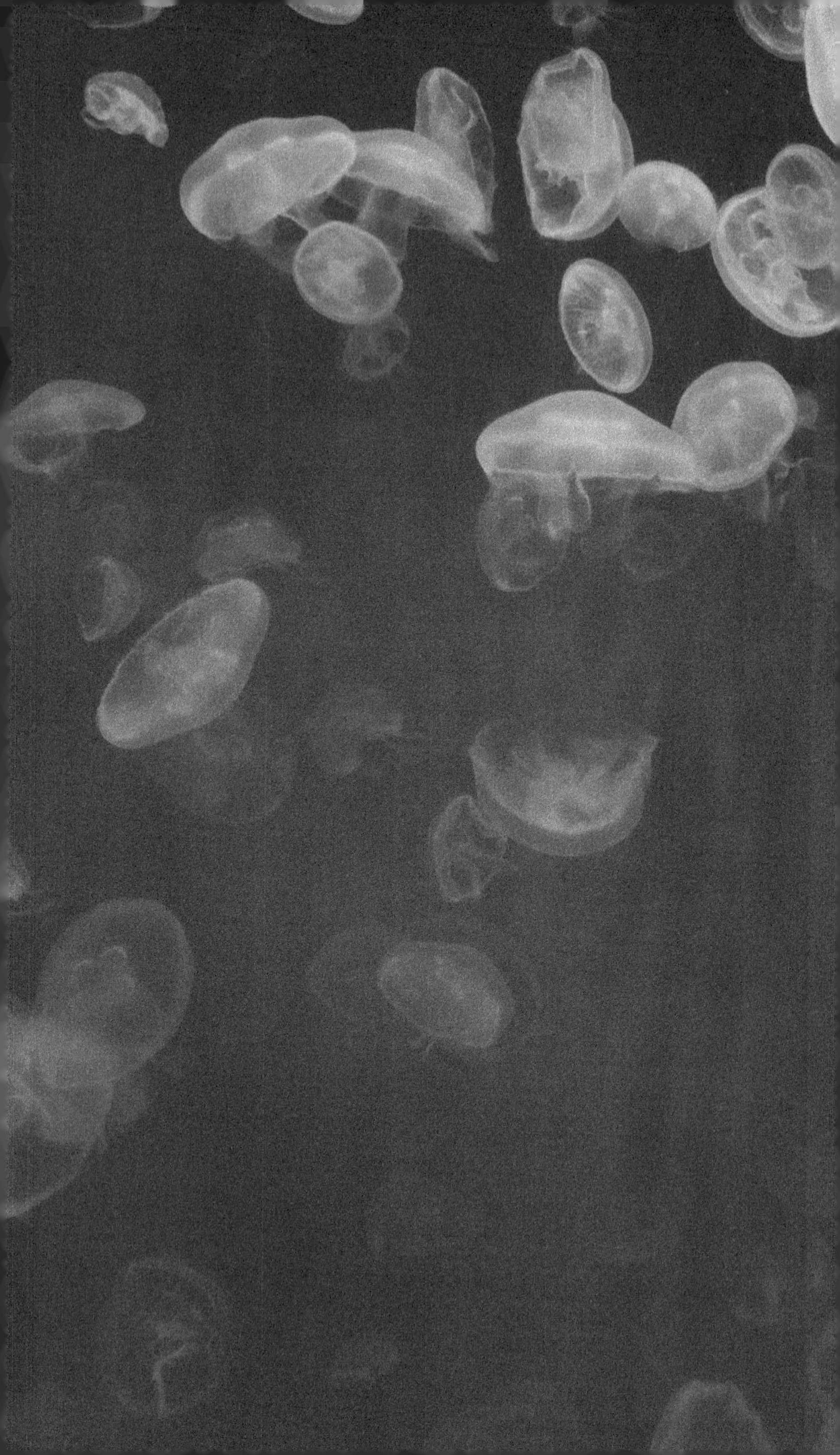

CHAPTER 38
VIOLA

The unearthed castle is exactly as I expected it to be. Dilapidated and blissfully secluded.

Hovering above the stone floor, I stare up through the water at a crumbling roof and the distant night sky beyond. I do my best to ignore the slicing throb in my back.

The castle was already filling back up by the time Jussi and I arrived here a few hours ago, and he had to wade through the waist-deep water to tie me down. It's nearly to the roof now. Soon, waves will cover this place completely.

I understand what Jussi meant about the pull—the water around me moves constantly, the current tugging me toward the far corner of the castle where a black chasm opens up. Another hour, and Jussi wouldn't have been able to get back out.

This is the best solution I could come up with to keep myself from pursuing Aric, to keep myself from reaping him once the power in my veins runs out. I don't trust myself. I feel too much for him, too deeply. Already, I feel my hunger rising again. I feel him now, tugging on my heart, seeming so close that I can almost hear his voice. I can almost hear the apology, the lovely lies and empty words.

I'm selfish for not severing that connection between us, but I would rather tether myself to an empty castle and wait for his human life to come to a natural end than let him go.

Selflessness has never come easily to me.

I've done *this* once or twice before, tied myself to the ocean floor or in the pit of a crater, back when I was new to my curse and feared it greatly enough that I tried to starve myself to death. I soon learned that even starvation could not kill me. Both attempts ended when something stumbled upon me and set me loose, and I can only imagine how much bloodshed and violence followed—truly, I cannot remember it. Starvation never allowed me much presence of mind. Hopefully, here, I might be kept secluded for a lifetime.

I shifted into my oldest form.

As I curl up on my side, waiting for sleep to take me, I watch the purple scales of my tail glisten. This is the first time I've returned to my natural-born state since I was gifted my hearts and tentacles. I never had a desire to return to it, but right now, I need a form that can't break free from these restraints.

This was the weakest version of myself I could think of. The orphan with pretty purple hair and no one to love her.

There is no rumble, no charge in the water or unease in my chest. There is *no warning*. For the first time ever, I *see* him before I *feel* him, thanks to the bones impaled in my back. Triton swims through the gaping hole that might have once been an archway, and my body freezes with terror.

His gaze consumes me.

I push myself up and away from the castle floor. I'm not sure how he knew I was here, but I immediately regret letting Jussi chain me. I regret letting him pierce the skin of my back with the ancient bones from the cathedral to prevent me from shifting. I regret ever coming back to the ocean in the first place.

I'm as helpless as the day I first entered Triton's home.

He smiles, and I know I'm doomed.

"Look at this." Triton beams. "You're bound up for me like a present."

"How?" I snarl.

He swims into the room. "How what? How did I know you were here?"

I don't respond because I know it's not a real question.

"Oh, dear witchling." He gives me a simpering look. "I've watched you your whole life. Do you think I would have taken my eyes off you for even a second of your banishment? You're the strongest witch Atlantis has ever seen. What kind of king would that make me?"

I frown, my limbs burning with the need to shift.

I'm only strong because he forced me to be. Maybe I am dangerous, a threat to Atlantis and everyone in it, but that's only because I was given no other choice. It has nothing to do with who I am or what I want.

What I wanted was a quiet life. Small happinesses.

He swims closer. "I see you everywhere, Viola. You are my destiny, my match in all the ways that matter. You are the only one worthy of me. I will make you see that."

My stomach churns, every remnant of blood and heart tissues from my last meal threatening to erupt from my throat. My skin prickles as he circles me, pausing at my back. He hums to himself.

"Ah, so that's what I've been feeling." His fingertips graze the bones pierced through my skin, and I shudder.

I strain against the cuffs to get space between us.

"How clever you are, witchling—where did you find such irksome magic?"

Victory burns through my chest. The ancient bones are working to weaken him. It's a relief to know they affect him at all.

"In the pits of hell," I growl, jerking again in an effort to jostle his touch from my skin. Then I sneer at him over my shoulder. "Oblivion is calling for you, you know. The deities scream your name. Exactly how long do you think you'll be able to fend them off?"

His face turns ashen as the ocean around us wavers. He has a weakness, and now he knows I see it. I see right through him.

He composes himself. Reaching across his torso, he withdraws a savagely long tooth from its holster. The sharp tip curves into a hook. This isn't a shark tooth. This kind of blade would have come from something far more ancient. Something from the deepest depths of the ocean.

Triton tsks quietly.

I lurch backward, but the restraints hold me in place, hold me hostage to his cruelty as he comes so close that I can feel the warmth of his desire and anger.

Triton lowers his tooth to my stomach.

Black spots crowd in on my vision as he drags that blade downward, opening my skin. I hiss, glaring up at him with all the hatred in my heart.

And that's when I realize the worst part of it.

He didn't feel the cut.

With the bones in my back, the bond between us is quiet. He can hurt me all he wants without the consequences to stop him, and I don't know how far Triton will take this.

He smiles and deftly slides the blade between two of the scales in my tail before I can stop him. And then I don't dare move. If I move, he'll cause far more damage. He slices into the tender skin between my scales, and I scream. I scream because I can do nothing else. He continues that cut across the entire width of my tail, maneuvering the rows of scales with precision.

I start sobbing, and his eyes begin to glow with delight.

"I think," he says sweetly, "a cut for every year you've defied me will be sufficient."

CHAPTER 39
ARIC

The fog is no better out on the water. I've narrowly avoided crashing into rocks twice now, and this area of the sea is strange, the floor appearing far closer to the surface than it should be.

Pillars pass by on either side of me, and I realize that there must be a ruined city under the boat.

I squint at the haze, my mind too preoccupied by the obstacles up ahead to notice the splashing behind me—not until it's right on top of me.

The boat halts unexpectedly, and I'm launched forward off the bench seat. I catch myself as the craft oscillates from side to side, too violently to be from a wave. By the time I glance back, I barely catch a flash of pale skin before it disappears beyond the side of the boat. The rope of the anchor unfurls rapidly before my eyes. Someone dropped it.

Then the boat lurches backward at the mercy of whatever's tugging on the anchor, and I nearly topple into the waves again.

Managing to stay upright, I brace myself against the

ledge of the boat and reach for the knife stored on the inner wall of the hull.

The anchor underwater is dragging me toward a cluster of pillars. Whoever this is, they plan to wreck me. Water spills into the boat from the tethered end. I grasp at the end of the taut rope and begin sawing through the twine.

Faster, I hurtle toward those pillars.

As I tear through the last strand of rope, the tension evaporates, but I continue to tear toward that gathering of marble.

I leap toward the section of boat about to collide and extend my legs over the edge to take the brunt of the collision. That last few yards closes in, and my feet hit stone. I kick off with all my strength. My knees pop, but I manage to turn the boat enough to avoid crashing.

As the hull spins, I return to the seat and grab the oar to bring the craft back under control.

But those pale hands reappear. Slender knuckles close over the edge of the boat, and as I turn to them with my blade in hand, a second set of hands wrench the oar out of my grasp. I'm crouching there, helpless, as five heads rise up to surround the boat.

My siblings look different above the surface. Less alive. Their hair clings to their scalps and necks, every angle of their faces dull in the gray light.

Simon is the one holding onto the boat. He sneers up at me as he folds his arms along the edge and rests his chin on his slick skin. "Where do you think you're going, Aric? You look out of place here, and with legs."

Viola has to be nearby, and in danger if my brothers are guarding her. Guarding *Triton*. My stomach rolls at the thought of him being alone with her.

My fingers tighten on my knife. "Get out of my way, Simon."

"We have our orders, brother."

That response comes from Warley. I pinpoint him on my other side.

He stares at me with something close to sadness. He's only following orders, the way we were all raised to. Father's command is law. But he has to be as unhappy with that as I used to be. I protected them when I could. I tried my very best to be a good brother. They have to remember that. They have to remember *me*. It can't be as simple as scratching my name out of Atlantis' walls.

"I have never asked anything of you," I rasp, meeting each of their gazes, "of *any of you*. I am begging you now. Allow me to pass."

Warley's nose flares.

I don't imagine he expected that. The truth. I never asked anything of him, not even company when I desperately wanted it, *needed* it. They formed bonds with one another, and I was left to freeze in the ocean alone. Whenever they came to me with a problem, I never hesitated to fix it. They never treated me as a brother, but that's all I've ever seen in them, all I've ever wanted: Family.

Simon scoffs. "Are you so hypnotized by The Violent Sea that you are now willing to face Father's wrath?"

I only say, "I will protect her with my life."

Simon's eyes blacken, and I know that's what he'd been waiting for. A reason to get rid of me for good. A vicious smile spreads across his face. "Then we will be forced to take care of you as Father takes care of *her*."

And maybe they will.

Maybe there's no chance for change here for them, for us.

If they attack, I won't go down without a fight. I'll kill some of them, and I'm certain they will eventually kill me. I accept that possibility as I look at them one last time. At Warley, who exchanges nervous looks with our siblings to either side of him. At Luca, holding my oar, his face impassible. At Benji, floating apart from the rest of them and looking as lost as I feel.

If I have to die, they deserve to know.

"Do what you feel you must, but know that Triton is *not* going to kill her," I say firmly. "He will stop at nothing until he *possesses* her. He tried to murder my mother in an effort to win Viola's love, and if it wasn't for the sea witch, he would have succeeded."

Warley drifts forward. "What are you talking about?"

"Don't listen to him," Simon hisses. "He's lying."

"I wouldn't lie about this. About Mother. I've seen the truth of it with my own eyes."

I let them see every ounce of my feeling, all that I've kept locked up tight my entire life. Tears track my cheeks, as raw and swift as the ocean. Now that I've started crying, I can't stop. How beautifully human.

Before I can say anything more, Simon starts dragging himself into the boat, and I fall against the opposite side to keep from capsizing. "You're a gullible fool," he growls, crawling toward me.

I'm not sure why Simon refuses to believe me. Maybe all his time with Father brainwashed him more than the rest of us—I know what it's like to strive for the approval, the love, that we often went without. I don't blame him. I pity him.

I wish, in that moment, I had been able to protect him too.

Guilt burrows a hole into my heart. Simon's denial weighs on my bones as he drags himself toward me, and I can't quite find it in me to use the blade in my hand. I scoot back, grappling with the spear at my back. Maybe I can fend him off. It's a foolish idea, but it's better than killing my own brother—the only brother I never did enough for.

Simon nods to something behind me, and suddenly a hand wraps around my arm.

My wrist smacks into the ledge of the boat, disarming me, and before I can turn to face whichever brother is assisting him, a knife appears at the base of my neck. My skin begins to sizzle, and I still entirely.

It's Benji.

Of course it is. I already knew she was under Simon's spell, enchanted by the promise of familial loyalty. The knife inches higher, scraping my skin in a slow, pointed threat. *Don't move.* One word, one noise that even resembles a song, and she'll slit my throat. I don't sense any opposition beyond the two of them—but I didn't expect my other brothers to intervene anyway.

Simon is next in line for the throne.

They will never openly challenge him if they wish to survive his ascension.

I lift my chin, my throat bobbing as I stare at Simon's brilliant blue eyes. He keeps his gaze averted from mine as he wrenches one of the other fishing knives from the side of the boat and rests the point in the center of my chest.

The tip of the knife presses past my shirt to pierce skin.

Simon leans in, speaking softly enough into my ear that I know no one beyond Benji and I will be able to hear him. "I always hoped I would be the one to end you."

Tears continue to course down my face.

They embody everything I ever suffered at the hands of my father. They bear witness to all that I have allowed in order to feel like I belong on the throne. Little did I know that I could never feel at home under the surface. I loved sunlight and stars too much. I longed for art and sweat-filled squares. I desired legs to dance with, kisses to drown in.

I tilt my head up even farther, seeking a different face than Simon's.

Benji meets my gaze without flinching, without hesitation. I planned on pulling her into a vision if I could, to give myself a fighting chance—but she makes her move faster than I can blink.

The hand in front of my neck whips out, and the silver blade slashes Simon's neck open.

All I can do is watch as Simon's eyes bulge in surprise, as a cascade of dark red blood pours from his throat. He reaches up, abandoning the knife in his hands to claw at the wound, trying to stop it. The blood slides across his chest and abdomen as he collapses backward.

I slowly sit up, shoving him off me.

My head finally registers what just happened, and I turn to look at my siblings in the water. They all stare at our sister with the same shock in their eyes.

Benji calmly dips her blade into the water, leans into the boat, and wipes the silver knife clean using the back of my shirt. She doesn't even look up to watch Simon take his last breath. Once her blade is holstered, she looks at me and says, "I got your message."

The message I sent to her from Viola's ship, detailing where she would find my stash of pearls and how she would be most likely to make it out of Atlantis undetected.

"I'm real fucking glad," I rasp.

It must have meant something to her, finding out that I had every intention of keeping my promise, because she smiles at me now. Only a brief flash of teeth before she turns to the others.

"Well, Warley?" Benji drawls. "Shall we let him go?"

Warley gaze slashes between the two of us. He hasn't quite gathered his thoughts yet, but after watching one sibling kill another, I suppose I can't fault him for needing a moment. My own thoughts are still spinning.

Simon's blood is spreading toward my feet.

"You're the one in charge now," Benji continues. "You're our crown prince. What's your decision?"

That's right...

Now that Simon is dead and I am the way that I am, the title *would* fall to Warley. Honestly, I can't think of a better outcome.

The way Benji rests a hand on her holster makes it clear that there's only one correct answer, the deadly little snake. Pride blooms in my chest. She's finding her way.

Warley's surprise fades as he realizes the same thing. "We'll let you go." He looks around at the others and they nod in agreement, slowly backtracking through the water to give the boat room to move.

I slide my arms under Simon and lift him, whispering a song of farewell as I toss his body over the edge.

Chances are, he won't get a memorial.

Luca swims up to the boat and hands me the oar, the faintest frown furrowing his brow. "I hope the sea witch is worth all of this, worth your life."

I return quietly, "She is worth more."

"Then make sure Triton winds up dead, or we all will be."

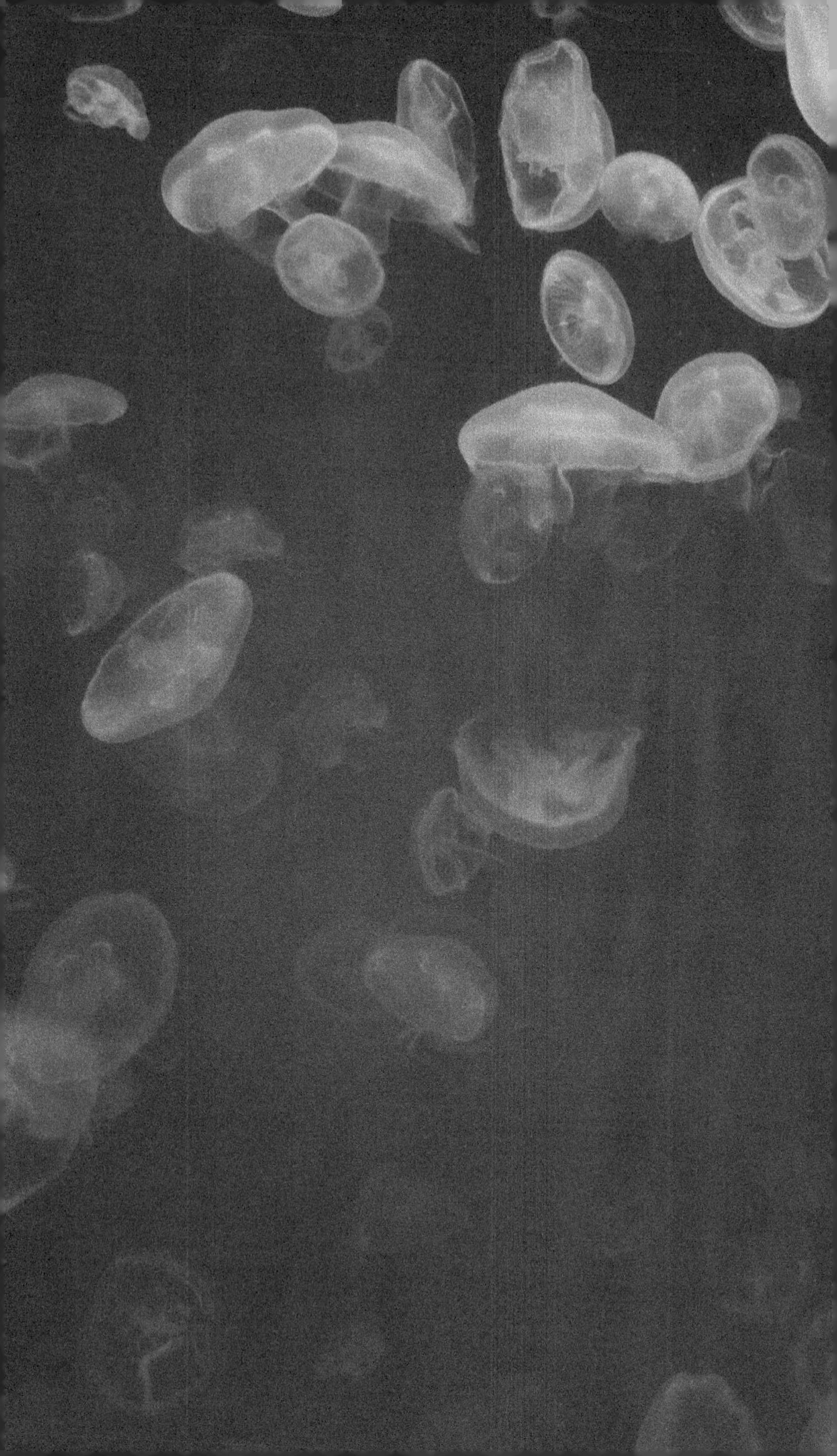

CHAPTER 40
VIOLA

I'm floating and it's not just because the ocean has risen enough to completely fill the castle. Colors and shapes blur in my vision.

I stare up at the only source of light: that crumbling roof.

I stopped feeling Triton's cuts a while ago, stopped fighting a little earlier than that. There was no getting away from him, no winning. He has me exactly how he wants me, and maybe I was lying to myself to ever think I could run from him, could deny him what he desires most.

Maybe it won't be so bad. I can't feel anything right now anyway. I try to open my mouth to surrender, but my body doesn't respond. Words muddle together in my head.

I continue staring at the gray light above me, evidence of a distant sky. Evidence of a world outside of this one. I wish I could reach it somehow, become a bird and learn to fly.

Triton's voice is a constant hum in the back of my mind.

He laughs now. His words are a garble I can't quite understand. Suddenly, my chin is pinned in between his fingers, and he wrenches my face toward his.

My brow furrows as he speaks again, my gaze training on his lips as I attempt to make sense of it.

I think he says, "Have I broken you at last, sweetling?"

I'm not sure what he means by that.

Something horrible, surely.

Broken. Am I broken? For a long time, I felt that way. But then something changed. The memories feel close enough that they could be condensation on the other side of a pane of glass. Something made me feel not so broken. I can't remember what.

Goddess Mora whispers in my ear. *Be strong, young one.*

How?

Hold on a little longer.

Why? What use is it to hold on when I want to let go?

Hope is always worth holding on for.

A shadow passes over us, sudden enough that it draws my gaze upward. The outline of a boat spins towards us. A silhouette peers over the edge, and then the ceiling erupts in a cascade of bubbles as something plunges through the opening.

What is that?

Hope, she whispers again.

Something darts through the water and pierces through Triton's shoulder, knocking him away from me.

The bubbles part, revealing Aric as he dives toward us.

Triton roars, grasping at the spear. By the time he rips the spear out of his shoulder, Aric has already reached me and starts sawing through the rope tied to my right wrist.

Aric barely gets through the first section of twine when Triton reappears and tears him away from me. The fishing knife that was in Aric's hand is lost to the current. Triton lifts Aric by his throat, blue lightning crackling down the length of Triton's arms.

My thoughts clear enough to register reality. He's really here. He came for me.

I lurch into motions, tugging hard on the rope around my tail, dragging that iron anchor inch by inch across the floor so that I might reach him.

"You never should have come back to my ocean, Aric," I hear Triton growl.

I glance up and watch as flickering blue bolts skitter from Triton's hand onto Aric's neck, down over his chest. He screams, the sound muffled and achingly mortal. The only air he brought down here with him escapes his lungs.

"*No*," I scream, fighting the restraints.

Sensation floods back in: fear and anger and pain, so much pain. I scream again as Triton drops him, the lightning still razing through his limbs. I fight against the rope, but the anchor isn't moving fast enough.

My soul calls for help from anything, anyone.

Triton leans over Aric's convulsing body, lowering the ancient blade to his neck. And that's when something invisible rips Triton backwards by his tail. He claws at the water as he's pulled away, his face twisting in terror. I blink through the spots in my vision and realize they aren't spots at all. They're flickering figures, dark enough that they blend seamlessly into the ocean.

As the gray light of day shines on them, I see what they are. The spirits of this sea. *Her* spirits. They rise out of the deep abyss in the corner of this room. The blue figures meld and spiral, forming a cyclone around Triton's tail, trying to drag him into the chasm.

They're giving us a chance to get away.

I turn to Aric, who's crawling across the floor to me. His limbs shake. When he finally comes close enough, I pull him in and scan his body.

This close, I can feel the damage. I see it. Triton's lightning struck him in the heart.

Fingers of dread rake down my back. The veins in Aric's body are vibrant green as his blood keeps trying to pump, but the lightning destroyed his most vital organ. The only organ that I can't fix.

Aric doesn't show any fear.

He embraces me and drops his hands to the bones in my back, ripping them from my flesh and tossing them into the furious current blasting past us.

Triton sends his lightning flying. Pushing back the figures rising out of the chasm. The room brightens and flashes like a stormy sky as he throws bolt after bolt. He's not as powerful as he usually is, because of the bones, but he's powerful enough.

Aric's eyes droop, his face paling.

I feel my magic return to me, measure by measure as the bones near that hole. It's not quite enough to shift, but it's close. I take Aric's face in my hands and press my mouth to his, transferring air into his lungs. It's not much. I'm just hoping it will be enough to keep him awake, to keep him alive. The only alternative is that he…

His body slumps against mine. I reach down and claw at the rope tied around my tail, trying desperately to shift my nails into something sharper.

As I glance up to track the bones, they finally breach the cavity and disappear.

Triton frees his tail from the ocean spirits. Then he backs away from the hole, continuing to send brilliant bolts into it. With each flash, I see more of that massive creature roiling beneath, stretching right at the mouth of the abyss.

Aric sees it too. He turns my face toward his with a single finger, and as our eyes meet, he captures me.

We stand on solid ground together, in a grove similar to the one his mother once lived in. Instead of olive trees, we're surrounded by grapevines. The sun burns on the horizon, just beginning to set as it casts a golden glow over us. I can almost feel the warmth of it.

Aric holds me tightly in his arms.

"I'm sorry," he murmurs. "That I didn't love you well enough, soon enough."

I try to remove myself from the vision, from him, but he keeps a fierce grip on me. He isn't letting me go.

"Stop this," I snarl. "Or you're going to drown."

He smiles. "I'm going to die anyway, Viola. I know it and you know it." With my magic returning in full, I sense the truth of that. This connection is weak.

Aric nods, seeing the anguish in my eyes. "Triton knows it, too, but we still have a trick or two left, don't we?"

I shake my head, not understanding, not *wanting* to understand. His hand skims to the nape of my neck and holds me there as he brings his lips to mine.

"You can protect yourself," he whispers. "You're strong."

Then Aric kisses me, and I start to understand.

A wave of power crashes over me. *His* power. He's using that heartstring to give himself over to me. I never realized it could work in the opposite direction. Against my will, he shoves his life force into me and my hunger latches onto it, gobbling up every bit of it even as he offers me too much.

That was his plan.

He wants me to reap him.

He wants to free me from my curse.

The vision flickers out, but his mouth remains on mine. I could attempt to push him back, could shift and make myself strong enough to end this. Maybe I should, but it's too late. My hunger is undeniable, and now that I've had a taste of my rapture, I can't pull away. He fills that deep ache inside of me, every pulsing crevice and starving scream in my head.

He gives me everything, and I feel myself start to give in, give *back*.

I wrap my arms around him, holding him closer, and as he gives himself over completely, offering what's left of his broken heart in order to mend mine, I stretch my magic over his body. He grows gills and fins and a tail in place of his scarred legs. He returns to his natural-born form. The form that belongs here, beneath the surface.

Aric goes limp in my arms, and I cherish the last few moments of our connection. Because I know, once I'm done, I won't be able to feel him anymore.

The heart in his chest slows, and mine begin to beat even harder in tandem. They pull on that last speck of life inside him, and the curse that has weighed on me for centuries starts to peel away from my soul. The skin of my chest prickles as the wound closes up.

Then the heartstring snaps in two, and I let Aric go.

CHAPTER 41
TRITON

He drives away the spirits, one after another after another, forcing them back into the depths they've churlishly risen from.

They form a great beast, their magic combining in the dark to create something... rather impressive. He hears their voices curl around his head in overlapping hisses. The sound of snapping teeth and trilling danger, echoing loudly, reminding him of the promise. Of the betrayal. He doesn't know why they chose now to come for him.

He's prepared for it, nonetheless.

Bolt after bolt flies from his hands into that great void. He'll burn them all to seafoam if he has to. Every spirit. Every deity. He builds a magnificent ball of light between his hands, bracing himself against the current to fling the energy at that beast—but suddenly, the chasm falls still. Silence spreads through the room, that eerie blanket that always precedes death.

He lets the electricity sputter to nothing between his fingers.

They *fled*.

He smiles. They knew they would not best him, could not claim him. He squints at the hole for another moment, waiting for any last hint of movement, and his smile broadens when he senses nothing. Well, of *course* not. He's the most powerful being in the entire ocean. They were unwise to challenge him in the first place, to try and overpower him.

Aren't the ocean's spirits meant to be clever, he muses. Isn't that why he once consulted them for their guidance, why his father and his father's father trusted their wisdom as well?

He always knew better.

Their children were useful in obtaining the blood for his crucible, but nothing more.

Triton turns, his eyes landing on Viola. Her mouth covers Aric's. The sight might have made him angrier, might have stirred that jealousy that's been building inside him for days now, if it wasn't apparent what she was doing.

She's reaping him.

His witchling even did Aric the mercy of returning him to his mer form to die. He doesn't much care what his son looks like in death, doesn't give him as much as a second glance as she releases him and lets him sink to the floor.

She looks similar to the way she did when they first met. Scales and hair the prettiest shade of purple. Her face pinched with a sadness beyond her years. His match, in power and beauty. Together, they will create a new Atlantis, a *better* one.

And their children... how very strong they will be.

Viola's gaze departs from Aric's body and slides across the room to Triton.

As he swims toward her, she doesn't recoil. He dares to believe, for the briefest moment, that she has seen reason. He dares to believe that her smile is one of love and devotion, the way it should be. The way he deserves.

If only he looked a little lower—to the healed skin of her breast—he would have known.

He opens his arms to embrace her, and she greets him with a savage thrust of her hand. Her claws drive into his stomach.

In that moment, hovering on the edge of death, he sees past the veil.

He sees the deity hovering behind Viola, clutching her shoulders, with eyes of vengeance and the claws of nightmares, with tendrils of blackest black spread all about her. A Goddess in the flesh. In her smile, he sees the fault of his father and his father's father. The faults of a hundred kings that all led back to one.

She has found the same fault in him.

Triton tears his eyes from the deity. Viola's face is a mirror of Her vicious hatred. Before he even realizes how it happened, he succumbs to her stolen song.

She sings him under.

The world becomes dark and cold, and the pain that invades his body is excruciating. Horrifically divine. *Endless.* Her claws rip into his heart and through his gut, her laugh slamming into his thoughts like teeth as she shreds him apart.

This isn't the way he wanted her.

He isn't sure how long she keeps him in that prison in his mind. He only knows that it feels like centuries, like an eternity, and his last thought is one of profound realization and infinite regret: that the spirits did not flee, and they were not afraid.

They only swam aside to make room for *her*.

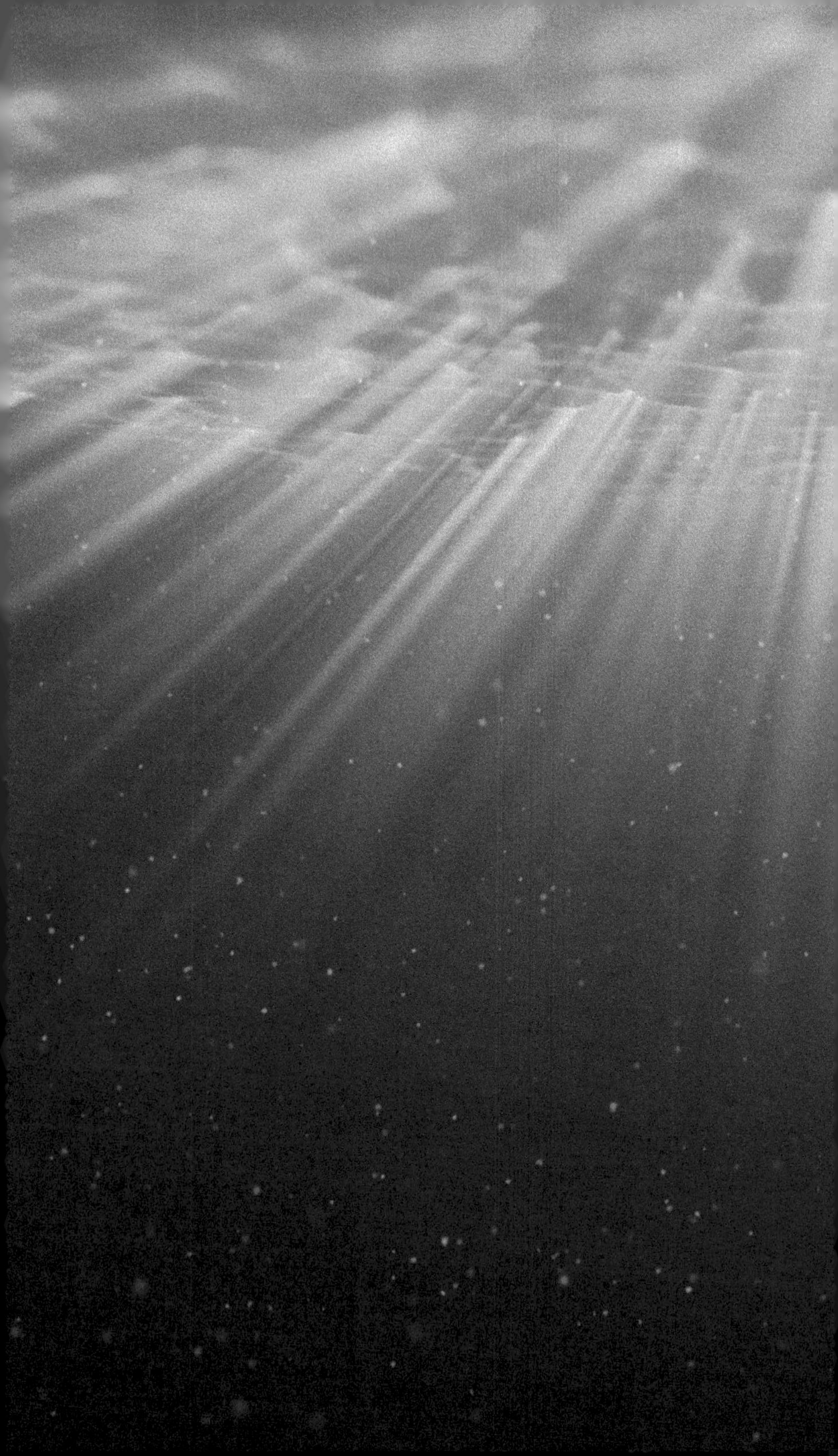

CHAPTER 42
ARIC

When I gave myself over to Viola, pushing myself into her heart and letting that hunger consume me, I assumed those were the last moments of my life. Apparently, I was wrong.

The first thing I see is the crumbling castle. My body aches. A rope is wrapped around me, keeping me from being pulled into the current and swallowed by the hole under the foundation.

I press a hand to my breast.

There it is.

A heart is beating, steady and strong, but its position is wrong. The pounding organ sits higher than it should, and I feel an empty heaviness where my damaged heart still remains. I have two hearts now, but the second isn't mine.

Or at least, it *wasn't*.

I suddenly remember what happened before the world went dark—the rising beast and how imminent Triton's wrath was. I scramble to disentangle myself from the rope as I frantically look around the room.

Triton is nowhere to be seen, and the void is still.

The only other person in the room is Viola, but she's unconscious, drifting in the current with her only anchor being a rope around her wrist.

I push off of the floor and swim to her, my hands finding her face. "Viola." I brush my thumbs across her round cheeks. "Viola, wake up."

She's shifted back into her witch form.

Her tentacles twitch, responding to the sound of my voice, twisting weakly in the water beneath her. Her eyebrows pull together. She moans softly, and although she doesn't open her eyes, I exhale in relief.

Whatever happened after I fell unconscious must have exhausted her.

I glance down at her chest. The skin there is fully healed, but I know if I could see past it, there would only be two hearts beating in her chest.

Warmth tickles my ribs as I shake my head in disbelief, laughter shaking my shoulders as I lean in and press a kiss to Viola's forehead. This wonderful witch. I turn my focus to the rope around her wrist and finish untying her before I gently gather her into my arms.

In sleep, her tentacles curl around me. They attach to my torso and neck, unconsciously binding herself closer. I grimace at the cuts still healing on her ivory skin.

If I wasn't so sure Viola already finished him off, I would track Triton down to kill him myself.

As I traverse the maze of stone halls back to the open ocean, I find myself glad it was her who finished him. After everything he did to her, she deserves that satisfaction. The victory is for her soul alone to consume.

We emerge from the castle ruins and I see my brothers waiting a distance away.

I turn without hesitation, paying them no mind, and begin to swim toward the shore. Warley and Luca break off from the others and rush to catch up with me. I don't slow down. My focus is on one thing and one thing alone, and that's making sure Viola is in a safe place when she wakes up. And that we're *alone*.

Warley reaches me first, his eyes flicking nervously between the two of us. "You really did it? He's gone?"

"*She* did it," I reply.

Luca appears on my other side, his piercings glinting in the light pouring in from above. The fog seems to have finally parted. "What does that mean?" he demands. "Does Atlantis belong to her, now?"

I pause.

That's tradition. Whoever kills for it, inherits the title.

Both of my brothers are uneasy about this idea. About *her*. Their fins vibrate, creating a hum in the water around us. I feel their animosity rise, their instinctual desire to hate and hurt. Father ingrained it in us so well. I don't think we'll ever be completely free of it. They do not know and love her as I do, and I could never expect them to. And I know, in my heart, that she would not be happy there.

"She doesn't want the throne," I say quietly. "She has *never* wanted the throne."

They don't say anything in response. They only exchange a bewildered look.

It must be confusing for them, to realize in mere hours what it took me days to come to terms with: that The Violent Sea desires her freedom, and nothing more.

I hold Viola a little tighter and her tentacles echo the squeeze. "I'm headed back to the surface," I declare, "and you need to return to Atlantis. There is a great deal for you to do."

Warley blinks, his face paling. "How can we return without you?"

"It's as Benji said, brother." I smirk at Warley, shaking my head. "You're next in line for Atlantis' throne."

"You were the one prepared for this day, not I." His hands raise between us in supplication, and I know he is searching for guidance. But I know now that the best, most authentic voice is the one deep inside us, urging us toward one another. We are stronger when we lean on those around us. When we value even those we cannot understand. Warley rakes a hand into his hair. "What am I supposed to do?"

"You must make our world a better one. For all of us."

Luca watches us carefully, a thousand thoughts swirling behind his eyes. For what may be the very first time, he looks at me, and I feel as though he sees me. The real me.

Warley nods slowly. "If you are sure."

I smile at them, then drop my stare to the slumbering witch. I thought she was the sunset of my life, but that isn't quite right. She's a transition into something far more beautiful. A new beginning. "I have never been more sure of anything."

Warley clears his throat.

I glance up at him, and he asks, "Were you telling the truth earlier, about our mother?"

"She's gone now," I say gently. "But she lived a long, human life."

His lips purse as he seems to search for the right words. "Do you think she was... happy?"

"I don't know," I reply honestly. "That's all we can hope for, isn't it?"

Luca averts his eyes, gazing off into the ocean—in the direction of Atlantis. In the direction of his mother. The damage Triton did to our family, our relationships with each other and the relationships we possess with ourselves, is something that might not ever be perfect. But I think we all want to try to fix what we can.

"Hope," Warley echoes, a small smile flitting across his face. "Yes. I hope for happiness for you, too."

"And I you, King Warley."

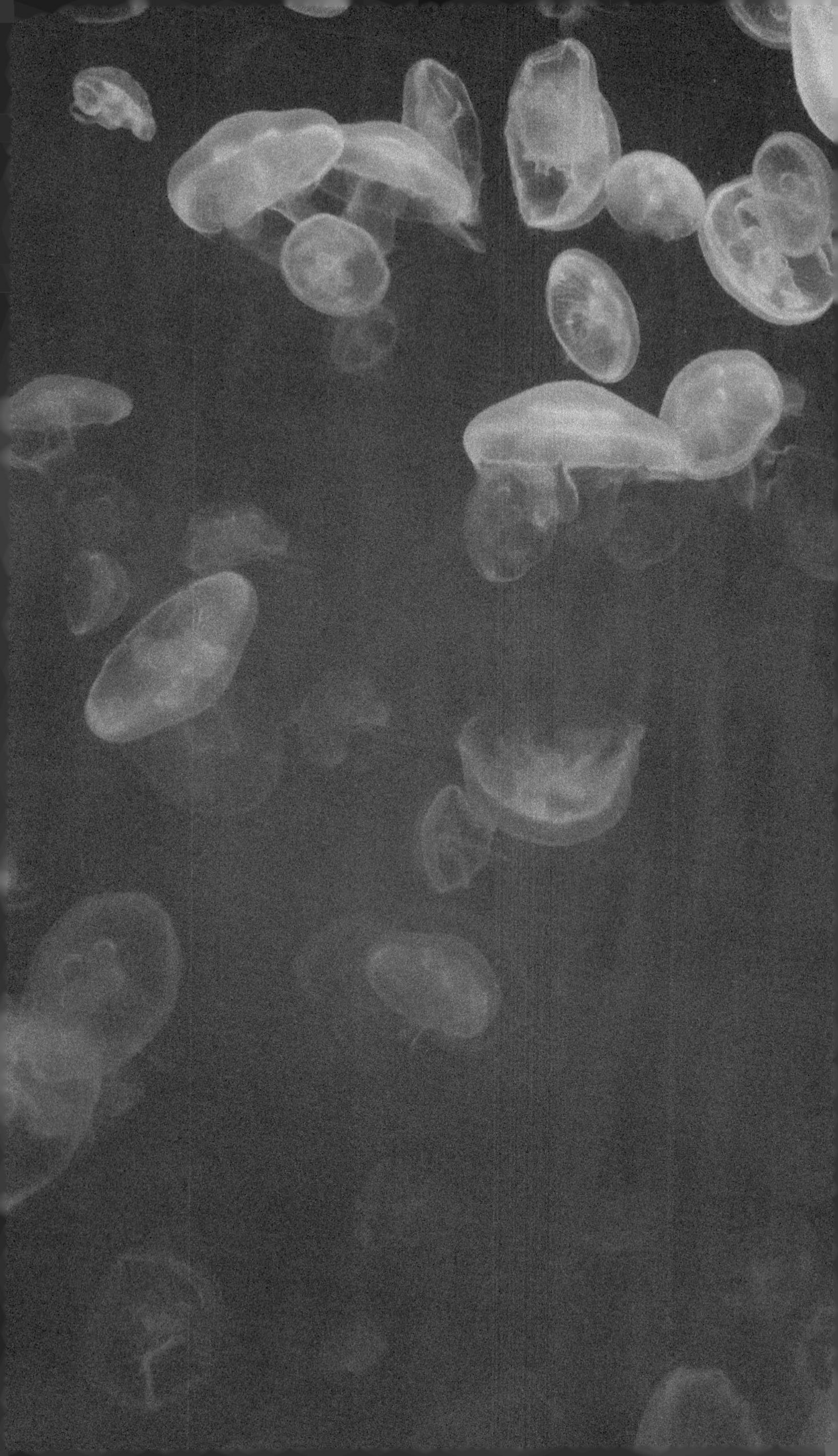

CHAPTER 43
VIOLA

S unlight infiltrates my sleep, drawing me out of the nothingness. The world on the other side of my closed eyes is brilliant red.

If it wasn't already apparent from the light levels, I can tell from the breeze caressing my skin that I'm above the surface. My head oscillates against wet sand, the particulate shifting noisily beneath my scalp.

I've been dragged back onto a shore.

The last thing I remember before I passed out in the ruins is sending Triton's lifeless body into the chasm and wrapping a length of rope around Aric's body to keep him from joining his father. I could barely keep stay awake long enough to do that.

Peeling one eye open, I find that I am indeed lying on a beach, the sun beating down and turning the distant waves into a glittering blanket of blue and white foam.

A cool darkness moves over me, blocking out the light.

Aric is leaning over me, his shoulders and face outlined

by a glorious orange sunset, his red hair darkened and dripping with saltwater. "You're finally awake."

I have to catch my breath at the sight of him. He's too beautiful to be real. Too beautiful to be mine. But then, he *isn't* mine. He never was.

His fingers argue with my treacherous thoughts as they brush over my brow, pushing back my hair and trailing down the column of my neck, *lingering*.

I slap his touch away and try to sit up, but his hands find my shoulders.

Aric presses me back into the sand. Gentle pressure, but a warning all the same. His eyes declare wicked intent and molten warmth curls in my core as he leans closer, his cool palms skimming down either side of my torso, exploring, worshiping every curve. "I've been going out of my mind waiting for you."

I bring my hands to his bare chest and shove him. I force myself to snarl, "*Stop touching me.*" My voice still manages to betray me. I don't want him to stop. Not really.

And he knows it.

He catches my wrists in the next breath to pin them above my head, stretching his body out on top of mine. There's no other choice, seeing as his legs are gone. "If you want me to stop, pretty witch," he growls. "You're going to have to *fucking make me.*"

I stiffen.

My thoughts return to the night we spent in the whirlpools. All the lovely lies he told while he carried that vile pendant with him. Whether he meant to betray me or not, he couldn't be honest with me then. How can I trust him now? Trust him ever?

He sacrificed himself for me twice now.

Does that make up for his betrayal?

I don't know...

Aric's tail tilts against my mating plane, pulling me from my concerns. His eyes scour my face for an answer to his earlier threat. *Am I going to stop him?* The warmth and hardness of his bulging pocket presses so close to the funnel on my underside—the apex between my tentacles—that I gasp.

I'm already seeping for him. My tentacles start to reciprocate his affection despite my hesitation, curling around his body to hold him closer to me.

He lowers his mouth to my ear, nips it, and I squirm.

I feel him smile against my neck.

When he nuzzles my ear, I shiver. "Oh, pretty witch, I desire you more than life itself. Punish me if that's what you need. Rip me open and make me bleed." He grazes his teeth across my neck to kiss the hollow between my collar bones.

"Just let me inside of you," he pleads in a rasp.

His words slice through my center. I arch into him, my tentacles writhing all over his flesh and scales. He tilts his head up to meet my gaze, as if to consider my choice—but I surge forward and claim his mouth with mine before he can change his mind.

The kiss is sunlight and golden sand, the luminous relief after centuries of torment dancing between our tongues.

With a soft moan, he releases my wrists and slides his hands under my back. This male is not what I thought I needed. He's more than safety. He's passion, the burning glow of stars rather than the calm cocoon of darkness. He's a flame born in the wild; both danger and natural restraint. And I want him as badly as he wants me.

I loosen my tentacles enough for me to break off the kiss and look into his eyes. I reach down for his pulsing pocket, licking my lips, but he catches my hand.

"No," he says hoarsely. "All I want right now is for you to

choke my cock with your sweet cunt and make me forget what we've just been through."

I don't know if I could deny him *anything* when he says it in a voice like that—dark and wanting, desperate. I nod eagerly, and he flips us over so that I'm sitting astride him. His hard pocket settles against my underside, and it takes everything in me not to let my eyes roll into the back of my head, not to completely lose my mind and start grinding against him without freeing him first.

Aric spreads a hand over my hip, tracing the purple flecks spattering my skin.

I brace my palms on his lower abdomen and lift myself off his lap enough to drag a hand to his pocket. His muscles are cut sharply; it's like brushing my fingertips over dimpled stone. His scales are slick as pearl, with varying shades of green and light blue under the fading sunlight.

Slipping my fingers into that hidden pocket on the front of his tail, I grasp his length and free it.

His cock gleams with sticky, male secretion. The skin is a dark blueish-green, a few shades darker than his tail.

I lower myself onto him, a trill tearing unbidden from my throat. We're both soaked for each other, but he's still large enough to stretch my clamping muscles, to fill me to the point of aching. His fingers tighten on my hips, and he pulls me the rest of the way down with a growl, eliciting another cry from deep in my chest.

I'm adjusting to the fullness of him, unable to open my eyes or close my mouth, when he starts bucking into me. My claws dig into his stomach, into those hard muscles. His hands control my hips, lifting me with ease and slamming me back down, his cock hitting that sharp, succulent place inside me. My cunt starts to soften around him, accepting him. Drawing him *deeper*.

All the veins in my body flush to near-bursting, heating my skin and echoing in my ears. My hearts beat hard enough that I wonder if they might tear a new hole through my chest, a mark just for him.

The skin over my hearts pulses with a reddish-gold glow. Pure *joy*.

I look down and see the heart I gave Aric, glowing like a sunburst in his chest. As I near that blissful peak, Aric takes one of my tentacles and rests it against his pounding heart.

"Do it again, witch," he whispers. "Make me yours."

I still, even as my cunt continues squeezing around him.

Tears well in my eyes, and a different sort of heat spreads through my chest. "What?" I breathe.

"This heart in my chest will always be yours," he replies softly. "It beats for you. Bind us together the way we should be."

My throat tightens, and I find I cannot respond to that confession. It is too great.

The air all around us starts to radiate a brilliant warmth. I feel Goddess Mora here, humming her approval; I can almost see her sharp fangs bared in a smile. Her voice is fainter now that I've given one of my hearts away. I wonder if that means Aric can hear her too.

"Do it," he repeats, his brow lowering over his brown eyes, "or I'll show you what it looks like when *I* beg."

My stomach takes a thrilling dip. Something tells me his *begging* is anything but. And maybe I'd like to push him to that point someday, but not right now.

I shift my tentacle over his chest, giving it a sharp edge.

Leaning down, I mold my mouth to his as I cut that precious rune into his skin. The Gift.

Everything that led me to him is the true gift.

No sooner have I sliced him open and the blood begins to

flow does Aric flip us over, thrusting into me harder than before. Harder and slower, as if communicating how much he feels for me with every thrust, as if asking me to give him everything I have in return—all the love I can spare. He doesn't realize it's already his.

I've been his for a long time.

His eyes anchor in mine, those thick lashes sweeping low. He takes my tentacle in hand. He carves the same rune over my heart and presses his wound to mine. His cock impales me at a new angle, driving all coherent thought from my head as our hearts twine together.

He doesn't kiss me again. He only looks deeply into my eyes as the air fills with a golden hue.

Aric smiles, a wondrous flash of teeth, and pleasure spears through my body in racking shudders. I surrender as that heartstring flutters back into place. I let go of the hurt, the uncertainty, even the anger I've been holding onto.

There's no room for it here, between us.

I am his, and he is mine. Two furious hearts with the souls and scars to match.

My cunt captures him, every bounce tugging roughly on that glorious spot inside of me. My breathing turns erratic as I hurtle to the tipping point, my core clenching as I finally tumble over it, and a ringing fills my ears as I lose myself in sensation. His arms pull me tighter against him. His thrusts turn brutal and unforgiving. His cock starts to engorge right at the tip before finally bursting, reigniting my ecstasy. And his cries—*great goddess and all her spirits*—his soft cries against the shell of my ear carries my pleasure on and on.

The world comes back into focus slowly.

The crash of a wave on my back. Aric's heaving chest expanding against mine where I collapsed on top of him.

His face nuzzles my hair. "You smell of the sweetest eternity," he murmurs.

I slide off of him, but he doesn't allow me to move far before his arm wraps around my waist and pulls me into his embrace.

His eyes are closed, his smile faint.

"How are you feeling?" I ask quietly, resting my head on his shoulder.

He blinks up at the dark blue sky as the marks carved over our hearts keep bleeding.

"I feel as though you've filled every cavernous pit in my body with daylight, or maybe something even brighter than that." He tucks me against his chest, his breath warming my hair as he continues, "I feel like I've been searching for this sort of clarity my entire life."

I nestle closer. "Good, because I want you to know…"

"What?" he mutters into my hair.

"That I love you, too."

A finger hooks under my chin. When our eyes meet, a thrill races up my spine. His gaze is dark, foreboding. "Try saying that to me without hiding from it."

Heat blooms in my cheeks, but I swallow my nerves. "I love you, Aric."

"Can you really mean that after what I've done?"

"In spite of what you've done," I reply tightly. "And because of who you are."

He sweeps his thumb over my cheek, shaking his head. A tear wells in the corner of his eye and slips over the bridge of his nose. "You are unbelievable," he says. "It is *I* who should be asking how *you* are feeling. After everything that transpired with—"

I press my fingers against Aric's mouth, silencing him.

"Don't say his name," I whisper. "He does not deserve to be remembered."

He nods in agreement and removes my hand from his mouth. "*Are* you all right?"

"I'm just relieved it's all over, and that his reign of terror came to an end by my hands. Goddess Mora will take care of what's left of him. I didn't leave much."

He nods again, listening, waiting for anything else I might need to say. But that's it. That's all that will ever be.

I nestle into his chest again. I'm happy here, in his arms, for however long it might last.

Aric looks down at our bodies. "This tail isn't convenient for holding you. I miss my legs."

I smile. "Is that so?"

He takes my hand and kisses it, his eyes simpering pools of earth. He kisses my wrist, then my forearm, moving steadily in a line up to my shoulder. He places my palm on his scales, over his pulsing pocket, and I laugh at him

By the time he's nibbling on my ear, I've already thrown my magic across us both.

Aric tangles his human legs with mine, holding me tightly. I roll my eyes as he reaches down to squeeze my rump and rumbles an appreciative noise.

After a long moment of silence, I venture, "So, when will you have to go?"

"What do you mean?"

"Atlantis." I swallow against the swelling of my throat.

He disorients me with a small smile and a shake of his head. "There's no home for me in Atlantis."

"But—"

"That will never be a safe place for you," he says firmly. "For *us*. I thought we might consider staying up here instead, together?"

My head spins at how sure he seems.

"I suppose," I reply through the pounding of my hearts, "we can always return to Jussi and Guillermo's until we figure it out."

"Oh." He grimaces.

"What?"

"That means I'm going to have to tell Jussi what happened with his boat, doesn't it?"

I pique an eyebrow at him. "You stole Jussi's boat?"

"That's the one I crashed into that sink hole. After I punched Jussi back on the pier."

My jaw drops.

"Don't look at me like that. I did it for *you*."

I shake my head in disbelief, trying extremely hard to keep the amusement from my voice. "You'll be lucky if Guillermo doesn't throw you out on your ass for the night."

Aric shrugs. "I'll just let him hit me back, and then we'll be even."

"You've never seen how worked up Jussi can get."

Aric only tugs me closer, kissing my brow. "I'll work hard to replace everything. I'm sure there's something up here for a washed-up siren to do for money. They can teach me... and you can teach me too, little wife."

My body tingles.

"Little wife?" I echo.

He grins. "Oh yes."

I wrinkle my nose at him, even though heat has started wrangling its way down my spine. My body likes those words more than my mind does. "If you think I'm going to wait on you hand and foot like some of these human women do for their husbands, you are sorely mistaken."

"Mmm," he hums, kissing the tip of my nose and then

the bow of my mouth. "I wouldn't dream of it. I plan on spoiling you rotten, my pretty bride."

I giggle, surrendering. "We'll see about that."

He cradles the back of my head and pulls back to look me in the eyes. "I love you more than you will ever know, Viola. Be whatever makes you happiest, and I will keep on loving you that way. I will follow you wherever, however."

Someday, I will tell him exactly how long I've loved him. How deeply. I'll tell him every detail of my feelings for him.

Today, though... I'll let us both feel like he loves me most.

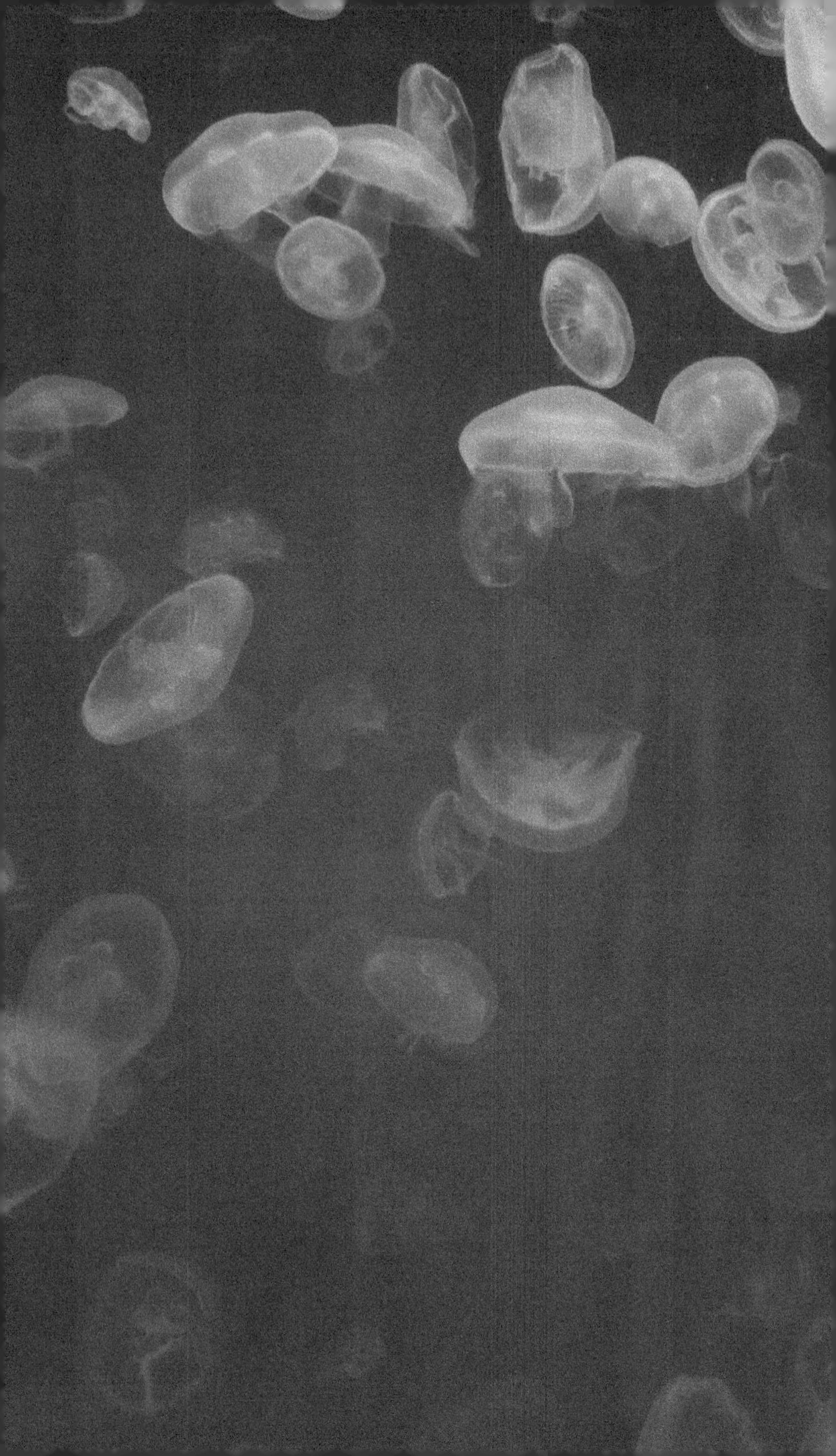

CHAPTER 44
VIOLA

The whirlpools froth in excitement.

Their anticipation is palpable, the blooms hanging from the walls opening a little wider in welcome. The spirits, greeting us. I smile at them, turning in a tight circle on the stone island to take it all in.

Aric carries Perla into the cave, kneeling on the walkway when they reach the main cavern to deposit the mermaid into its spinning waters.

Perla is eager to be out of his arms, dipping into the pool and emerging in the center of one of the cyclones. Her dark eyes scan the room as it pulls her around and around.

The sun is dawning, casting the room in orange and pink.

It's been a few weeks since that fateful day in the castle ruins. In that time, Warley ascended to the throne, and I've been receiving regular updates from Perla about the goings-on in Atlantis. Aric's brother is doing the impossible. He extended the protective bubble around the city to enclose the under-dwellings, and now he has sent word into every ocean, searching for witches who might help get rid of the inner gates. They hesitated, of course, considering his father's reputation.

But I have started to hope, to trust...

So here I am, in the whirlpools, preparing to make a new witch.

I sit on the edge of the island, dangling my human legs in the churning pool as I beckon Perla toward me. I haven't felt any temptation to return to the ocean. Not even a fleeting thought. And what a relief it's been, to sink into the sunlight and cherish rainstorms at Aric's side.

He asked me, when Perla first informed us of Warley's plans, if *I* wanted to be the one to assist Atlantis, to be the one to set things right—but I know that isn't my place anymore.

It's time to pass on my inheritance to another, and Perla, after everything she's been through and all the goodness she's shown me, deserves it the most.

Perla glides to me, her hands bracing the stone on either side of my knees. "What now?" she asks.

I offer another smile and pull the blade tucked into the waistband of my skirt. "We must create a bond. Come, sit beside me."

She hauls herself out of the water, glancing nervously at Aric, who has leaned back against the wall of the cave to watch us. His eyes glitter with interest, his hand stroking the red beard filling out across his jaw. I love that beard.

"Don't worry about Aric," I mutter, taking her hand in mine and wrapping her fingers around the hilt of the blade. "He's only curious. When was the last time *you* saw someone receive a gift straight from the gods?"

Her lips twitch. "Fair enough."

"Make a cut over your heart," I instruct.

Perla does as I ask, then hands me the knife as red blood trickles from her chest.

I unbutton the front of my blouse and slice into my own breast to let the blue run free, avoiding the scar already there—the mark of love Aric and I both carry. When I turn to face her more fully, I raise my hands between us in invitation. "The worst is over. You only need to embrace me and accept the gift."

She eyes my arms for a moment. "It won't... hurt?"

"Not at all," I tell her through a smile.

After another moment, she wraps her arms around my neck. She rests her breast against mine. My chest tingles as the heartstring wiggles its way through my tissues and into hers.

She gasps, but otherwise remains silent, the tightening of her embrace the only sign that she feels what's between us. The entire world brightens. The flowers and the pools begin to radiate a faint golden light.

A sign of Goddess Mora's approval.

Once the heartstring pulls taut between us, I do for her the same as I did for Aric in the ruins. The same my coven mother did for *me* when it was my time. I give her a heart. So that the Goddess may touch her and grant her the rest.

Magic ricochets through our connection.

The pressure battering my chest eases as it slips away on that thread. My power and my gift, everything that I have treasured as a beast of the deep.

One heart is all I need for Aric and our human life. Life itself is enough. The human heart is so often neglected, forgotten, with nothing but a flicker of magic trapped inside it as a reminder of where we have been. I feel it buried inside me still, softened under the layers of humanity. But it's *there*. Because what is existence, *survival*, if not magic?

I release Perla and grip her shoulders to look her over. Her eyes are filled with wonder, the same as mine. She's ready.

I shove her into the whirlpools.

The water captures her, stronger now that the Goddess has filled them with Her magic. Perla tumbles under the surface. Her black limbs tangle with the foam. Her scales shift and fade, and in their place, ebony tentacles appear, writhing and spinning in the cyclone alongside her dark hair.

The golden glow of the room flares a little brighter.

I stand up, a smile plastered across my mouth. I remember this moment so well, how *beautiful* it felt to come into my inheritance and feel the support of an entire ocean. To feel the acceptance of a family.

Glancing up, I see Aric standing on the edge of the walkway, his eyes trained on me. Every inch of his body is taut, as if he's trying with all his might not to jump into the waters himself to swim to me. Considering what's happening, I know he won't. This is the end of a journey apart from him.

Warmth spreads through my core, knowing he wants to be by my side, even now. That heartstring endures, thin and delicate between us. *Human mates.*

The glow of the room fades as Perla breaks the surface.

She looks down at herself, at her black tentacles spreading out around her. The skin over her hearts illuminates with the same golden glow I once held in my own.

I press a hand to the steady thump of my pulse, knowing that if I could shine with her, I would. I take one last look around the room, letting the details ingrain themselves in my memory. This is not my place anymore. It belongs to Perla and the coven she will recreate.

And me? I have a thousand new places to go.

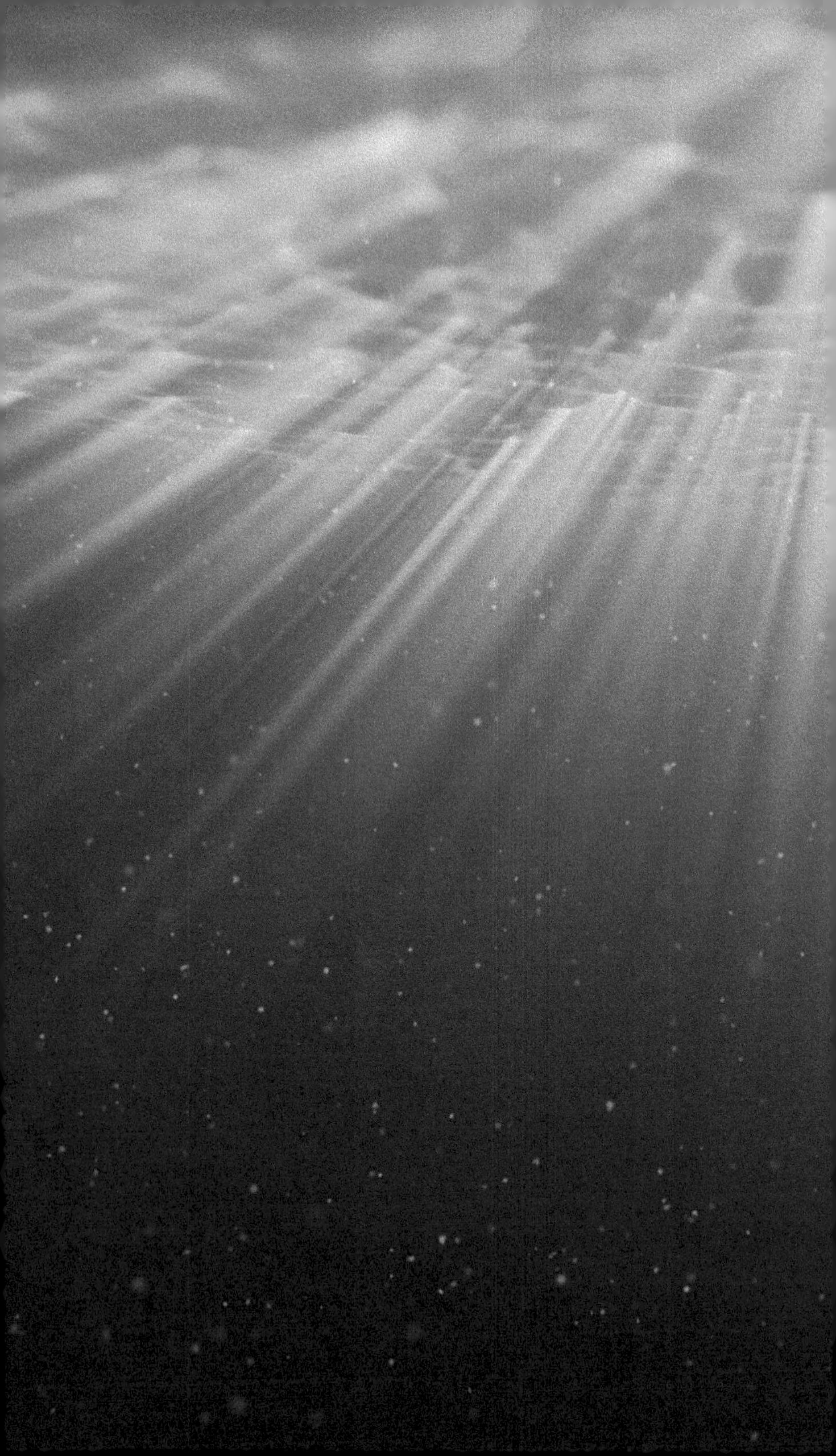

EPILOGUE

A sea of masks spreads out before me.

I push my way through the ivory porcelain faces and sloshing goblets, scanning the crowd. Somewhere close by... I can *feel* her. There's too much noise, too many voices and jostling bodies.

It's difficult to concentrate.

My heart skips when I catch sight of a colorful silk scarf up ahead. I lurch for the body and turn it around, choking on a gasp when a pair of hazel eyes glare up at me.

"Oh, terribly sorry, Miss. Excuse me."

Diving back into the crowd, I clench my fists. I don't know why I agreed to this. I should have known she only did it to win, to disorient and frustrate me. To show me once again how clever she is. Chewing on my cheek, I try to feel for that frail connection between us, stalking in a circle around the square for the hundredth time.

I close my eyes for a moment and feel that tug, faint as a feather.

Opening my eyes, I search the swarm of colors around

me. My brow furrows. I can't see a sign of her tell-tale purple hair anywhere.

Entering the dense throng of people, that tug grows stronger. I'm tossed between those engaged in dance and lively conversation, and then I see a flash of blue eyes, so deep and dark that they could be laced with violet. So lovely, they might have once belonged to a ghost patrolling these very canals. Her face is covered by a mask painted in the visage of a cat.

Fitting, truly.

I follow that dark head of hair, picking up my pace, slowly gaining on her as we make it to the other side of the crowded square. When I finally draw up behind her, I catch her around the waist and lift her into my arms. She kicks and scratches me, but I don't so much as flinch. Neither do any of the drunks around us. I drag her to a secluded little nook between shops and shove her into it, trailing after her with a dark laugh.

She quickly realizes that she's trapped and spins to face me. Her lips hook up into a violent, crimson smile, and my body reacts instantly. My stomach floods with flames.

I close in on her, and she backs away slowly, inching toward the dead end at the back of this little alley. "Where are you going with those pretty lips of yours? Sweet little tease."

Her smile broadens into a toothy grin, those blue eyes fluttering innocently.

I burst forward and she squeals, trying to curl into a defensive position. But I'm already on her. I lift her by the waist and pin her to the wall, my hips nestling against hers and my hands locking around her wrists. My teeth find her neck and she giggles, the sound nearly a trill as I torture that sensitive spot above her collar.

She immediately surrenders to my ministrations, rocking her sex against mine.

A thrill scores up my spine, and I release her wrists to brace myself against the wall, returning her lecherous movement with one of my own. She gasps, tugging on my hips to urge me on, but I pause to remove my mask, then push hers up onto the crown of her head.

Viola gazes at me, her eyes hooded with desire. "Why did you stop playing the game?"

I frown. "Your hair is making me uncomfortable."

"It's only powdered pigment," she laughs. "Jussi says it'll wash out."

"It better," I grumble.

I love her as she is, the sunset of my life.

She's changed a little in humanity. A few wrinkles have settled into her face now, and her nails sometimes break. There are sun spots on her skin from the time we spend outdoors, traveling together throughout this country and the worlds to either side of it. She can't change form anymore, but she still changes me. Day by day, we evolve, becoming more human. Her hair is one of the only things left to remind us of the creatures we used to be, the world we conquered, and I hope we get to keep it. At least until it turns gray.

She narrows her eyes at me. "I only did it to win. Though, if you keep talking to me like *that*, I'll be tempted to keep it this way forever."

"Yes, well, *I* won," I reply proudly.

Her eyes turn a bit liquid, my insolence already forgotten. "Then why aren't you collecting your prize?"

My heart jumps into my throat.

I lean in without another word and mold my lips to hers. Her hands thread into my hair, twisting in its loose curls and pulling me even closer. I hook a palm under one of her knees and hitch her leg over my hip. She tilts into me, and I grind against her softness. Our tongues writhe together in a messy dance, and what starts as a fit of passion—of lust and possession—turns into something far more tender.

It's no longer about the prize. This is no longer a game. Every undulation of our bodies is fueled with a heated sleepiness, our breathing synchronizing as our lips slip together and apart, meeting with eager sweetness.

It's almost enough to send my throbbing cock right over the edge.

In the back of my mind, I think of how shocking I would have found this a few years ago—that her mere presence could have such a powerful effect on me.

I pull back an inch, giving us a second to catch our breath. Not that I care much about breathing when she's in my arms. "I love kissing you," I whisper.

"I love *you*."

No matter how many times she says it, those three words never fail to fill me with unfettered, bubbling joy. Like ocean foam rising to the surface.

I nuzzle her nose with mine. "With all my heart."

"Do you want to return to the celebration?"

I nod, but lower my face to press a kiss to her shoulder. "In a moment. Let me hold you for a while first."

Her arms tighten around my neck, and we stand there a minute longer, embracing in the relative silence. We only part again when a lick of water begins to pebble our overheated skin.

I glance up at the weeping sky, then back at Viola.

She blinks into the drizzle as it beads on her face, smiling as water courses over her smeared red lips and into her hair, slowly stripping away the dark dye. Heavier and heavier, it falls. The revelry behind us erupts with hoots and hollering

SONG OF DARK TIDES

as the sprinkle becomes a cascade, and it reminds me of the first time we danced in it, Viola and I.

The day I realized that I love her.

Viola smiles at me, and I know she's remembering the same thing. She closes her eyes and extends her arms to either side of us as she tilts her head toward the sky, welcoming the storm and everything beyond it.

THE END

If you enjoyed this story, please consider leaving a review on Amazon and Goodreads.

ACKNOWLEDGMENTS

To my readers, thank you for making room for my stories in your heart. This one meant a lot to me.

To my husband, thank you for loving me deeply and unconditionally, and for being my support system. Thank you for being such a wonderful partner and father to our two beautiful children. You are my human mate. <3

To Shannon Bright, who has been a steadfast writing (and real life) friend to me, I don't know if you will ever know how much I cherish and admire you. You are a BRIGHT light in my life. Thank you for your valuable feedback, your encouragement, and your humor. (And thank you for writing magical rom coms that make me giggle and kick my feet—I will never get enough of them.) ILY.

To Erin and Ashley, my literary sisters, thank you for your enthusiastic beta feedback and encouragement. Writing to contract for the first time was a struggle, but you guys made the revisions *joyful*.

And to Lake Country Press, thank you for believing in my ability to tell this story, and for reviving my love of mermaids. *wink*

About the Author

Beka Westrup is a genre-hopping author of fantasy and romance. Song of Dark Tides is her third full-length novel. She lives in the PNW with her husband and two children, collecting more books than she'll ever be able to read and drinking copious amounts of iced coffee.

Stay in the know with Beka's Newsletter:
https://www.bekawestrup.com/coming-soon-03

facebook.com/bekawestrup
instagram.com/bekaboowrites

Milton Keynes UK
Ingram Content Group UK Ltd.
UKHW012005131223
434291UK00004B/310

9 798987 739198